THE WILDLANDS

ALSO BY ABBY GENI

The Lightkeepers
The Last Animal

THE
WILDLANDS

A NOVEL

ABBY GENI

COUNTERPOINT
BERKELEY, CALIFORNIA

THE WILDLANDS

Library of Congress Cataloging-in-Publication Data
Names: Geni, Abby, author.
Title: The wildlands : a novel / Abby Geni.
Description: First hardcover edition. | Berkeley, California :
Counterpoint, 2018.
Identifiers: LCCN 2018008262 | ISBN 9781619022348
Subjects: LCSH: Domestic fiction. | GSAFD: Suspense fiction.
Classification: LCC PS3607.E545 W55 2018 | DDC 813/.6—dc23
LC record available at https://lccn.loc.gov/2018008262

Jacket designed by Nicole Caputo
Book designed by Wah-Ming Chang

COUNTERPOINT
2560 Ninth Street, Suite 318
Berkeley, CA 94710
www.counterpointpress.com

Printed in the United States of America
Distributed by Publishers Group West

1 3 5 7 9 10 8 6 4 2

For my parents

THE WILDLANDS

PROLOGUE

I never heard the siren. I slept through the rising wind and the tree branches wrenching loose and colliding with the roof. I did not catch the sound of the cows lowing in the back field or the horses stamping anxiously. I was taking a nap. It was late afternoon on a Saturday in spring, so many years ago.

By the time my sister woke me, the sky had turned green. That was the first thing I noticed, blinking and yawning, still dewy with sleep. Darlene threw off my blankets. I was only six years old then, still young enough to be slung over my sister's shoulder and carried down the hallway at a trot. Bouncing on her back, I glanced out the window and saw the Oklahoma sky soaked with a new color. Damp jade. Split pea soup. Moss on stone.

Darlene set me down on the couch and dashed upstairs again.

I sat dazed for a moment. There was turmoil both inside the house and out. My whole family seemed to be in motion, a babel of footsteps and voices. All the lights were lit. It was raining, but not in any way I recognized. The drizzle came in lashing, inconsistent bursts, tonguing the window, splattering a door, then subsiding into an eerie silence. My father hurried past me at a breathless jog, his belly bouncing. He was holding a box that clanked with each step as he lumbered down the stairs into the basement.

I got to my feet and went to the window, pushing the curtains aside. The breeze was laden with flecks of white and brown—papers and leaves and trash. The wind seemed to be picking things up and putting them down again like a child selecting a toy to play with. I tried to gather my wits. From the upper floor, voices filtered down, high and shrill. Tucker and Jane were shouting. From what I could tell, they were agreeing with one another, albeit angrily.

A mosaic of raindrops dusted the glass. I saw the big oak tree bow as though in prayer. A bird whizzed past the window, flying backward. I nearly laughed at the sight—the beak pointed in the wrong direction, neck extended, every muscle straining. It could not make the slightest bit of headway; it could not even turn itself the right way around. Its feathers were rumpled, sticking up at sharp angles, its beak agape. The breeze swept it rearward, borne away on the current like a twig in rapids.

Daddy reemerged from the basement, his face waxen and speckled with sweat. He checked his watch and roared at the top of his lungs, "Two minutes! Not one second more!"

He pounded out the back door, slamming it hard enough to shake the house. Then there was stillness. For a moment, I could hear nothing but the wind.

I laid a hand on the glass. The sky was darkening as though someone had spilled ink into the clouds. Our lawn chairs were piled in an untidy heap by the fence. The yard did not look like the place where I had played yesterday. It was strewn with plastic bags and dirty papers, other people's refuse. Tree branches dotted the grass, and my toys were gone—no hula hoop, no Frisbee, no tennis racket. Shimmering veils of rain hid the barn and the cow paddock.

Our land sprawled across several acres. I squinted through the drizzle, trying to find order in a jumble of droplets and debris. The trees were no help, swaying ominously, blocking my view, their trunks groaning from the exertion. In the distance, the cows were lying down—silvery shapes in the wet grass. This was worrisome. I knew a lot about cows; I had walked among them, patting their meaty necks, listening to their chewing, their tails swishing the flies away, their eyes tracking my every move. I had offered them bunches of grass, keeping my palm flat to avoid their massive teeth. Their breath was always milky and hot, their tongues as rough as sandpaper. They spent their days pacing the field, communicating with one another in bellows. They lay down only when things were bad—not enough water, too much heat, a bewildering storm.

I could not see the rest of the animals. The horses were probably safe in the barn. We had three: an old gray stallion, a moody mare, and a pony with a bronze coat and a joyful temperament. Most afternoons the colt could be found cantering in the grass, kicking his legs high and twisting his thin torso into jaunty leaps, as though with a little effort he could undo the binds of gravity and gallop away on the wind. My brother was particularly good with the horses. Tucker had a way of whispering to them, coming close and stroking their flanks. They would grow still, ears cocked forward as though absorbing his words intently, nuzzling against him, their breath commingled with his.

At that moment, Darlene bounded downstairs. She was flushed, and her bangs were disheveled, rising off her forehead like steam. She darted around the living room, collecting the photographs of our mother. There were half a dozen displayed in nice frames. On the mantel, Mama stood backlit against the sun in a field of flowers. On the coffee table, Mama sat astride our gray stallion, pointing at the camera and laughing. On the end table, Mama posed in an unknown forest with an unknown black dog at her side. Darlene piled all the picture frames in her arms. I opened my mouth to ask her a question, but she was already gone, heading for the basement.

I turned back to the window. Thirty feet away, a lone calf darted into view, dashing out from behind a tree and disappearing into a clot of bushes. There were a few new calves among the herd; I wondered which one this might be. I wondered how the chickens were faring in their cramped coop. I wondered where our little goat—shy, skittish, with fur like pulled cotton—had found shelter.

A hand fell on my nape. My brother was standing beside me.

"The sky is green," I said.

"I know."

"The cows are acting worried."

Tucker knelt down, his eyes level with mine. He was seventeen, wiry and muscular, every movement lush with intention and grace. His curly hair was tugged back in a ponytail. He put one hand on each of my shoulders.

"Do you understand what's happening?" he said.

"No."

"Remember the tornado shelter in the basement?"

"Yes."

"We're going there now," he said.

Then I heard a scream—panicked and unearthly, carried on the breeze. Tucker and I both checked, staring outside. The wail went on and on, fretful, wrenching. I tilted my head, trying to locate the source of the sound.

"It's the horses," Tucker said.

"What?"

"They're in the barn. I put them there—" He broke off, frowning. "It was only supposed to be a thunderstorm. There wasn't anything on the news about a tornado until a couple minutes ago. I told Daddy—"

He trailed off again. His face was pale except for a bright triangle of pink on each cheek.

In the distance, the horses were still screaming. There was an anonymous quality, I realized, to the sound of a frightened animal. The intensity of the cry washed out all the usual characteristics of species, size, and kind. It might have been women sobbing, or birds squawking, or coyotes baying.

There was a scuffle behind us, and Jane appeared. She came down the stairs with a bulging bag slung over her shoulder. Jane was tall for her eleven years, a stocky athlete with a river of blond braid. Usually she was steady and composed, but today her forehead was furrowed, her arms shaking visibly beneath the weight of her burden. Even her hair seemed upset, flicking around her face in golden shards.

"Get over here," she spat out. "Help me!"

Tucker jumped to obey. Jane lost her footing, almost falling down the remaining stairs, but he caught her elbow in time. Working together, they hefted her bag into an awkward position, balanced between the two of them, and began to waddle toward the basement. I heard a door open, and their voices dwindled away.

I leaned closer to the window. The sun umbrella stood on the deck, rocking. In bad weather, my father usually folded and tied it shut. On balmy days, it would flare open, a faded tent of red and yellow, its rod weathered by the years into an indifferent black. Daddy had forgotten to furl it today. Perhaps there had not been enough warning. Before my eyes, the umbrella started to turn, pivoting on the spot, the panels of color flashing. The stand bounced, clanging against the deck. It jumped once, twice, then floated straight into the sky, rising like a UFO. I watched it go, my mouth pooling open, hands tangled together as I tried to understand.

I knew what a tornado was, of course. I lived in Oklahoma; I had heard the warnings all my life. Our small town, Mercy, sat smack in the middle of Tornado Alley. I had helped my father stock the bunker in our basement with canned goods and batteries. I had listened to his lectures about what made a strong, sturdy shelter—completely underground, the walls solid concrete, at least one foot thick. I had taken part in tornado drills at school, crouching against the wall with a line of other children, all of us hot, squirmy, and bored, waiting for the teacher to blow her whistle and tell us it was over, that the imaginary threat was gone.

But none of these experiences had prepared me for what was happening now. The roar picked up. A blur of fabric whizzed past the window—a shirt, maybe, torn from someone's clothesline. The air was a quilt of flying detritus. The horses had stopped screaming, or else their voices were lost in the wind.

Out in the back field, the cows began climbing to their feet. As I watched, the herd orbited the paddock in a bewildered shuffle, the calves trailing at the rear. In the manner of their kind, they operated as a single organism; none was in charge, all fired by a shared idea, prey animals overcome by the instinct to flee. They jogged in unison, bulky bodies skimming against one another, shoulders working, moving faster with each revolution until they were pelting flat out. There was nowhere for them to go, but they ran anyway.

The cloud layer began to change shape. I saw movement, a wriggle, one tuft curling away from the rest. A smoky finger arched and distended downward. There was a flash of something bright in the corner of the sky. I wondered if it was our sun umbrella, miles up, waving goodbye. A bird soared past the window, this one upside-down. Near the horizon, a hole had opened up in the silken pouch of the clouds. Ash poured toward the ground. A gray pillar. Almost dancing.

It seemed like a magic trick—the tornado willing itself into being out of empty air. The wind took on a new noise, a kind of pattern, regular in its pulsing, loud enough to sting my ears. The funnel cloud flowed downward with the certainty of water. It appeared to be finding its way through a riverbed in the air, a pathway imperceptible to the human eye, swaying, trickling in a new direction, unhurried and inexorable in its progress. Just above the horizon, it paused, hovering.

I never saw it touch down. At that instant, rough hands yanked me away. Tucker carried me like a football. I cried out, but he did not notice, running toward the basement stairs.

The others were there too, my whole family moving in formation.

Cradled against Tucker's shoulder, I saw Darlene behind me, eyes wide, mouth open in what looked like a silent yell. Jane jogged with a soldierly determination. She was dressed strangely—an old pair of jeans with paint on the knee, her shirt on backward, only one sock. I noticed that her hair was wet. Maybe she had been in the shower when the cry had gone up and she had thrown on whatever was closest to hand.

We wheeled downstairs like birds on the wing. I tried to resettle myself in Tucker's arms, but his biceps and wrists made a fierce vise. I could not shift position; I could not make a sound. The basement was dark and mildewed, hung with spiderwebs. There were storage bins, an old refrigerator that did not work, and Mama's bicycle, dusty with disuse, both wheels deflated. Daddy's workbench took up half of the space: his toolbox, hacksaw, and the woodworking projects he loved so dearly, though they rarely came to anything. A board leaned against the wall, bejeweled with bent nails. A half-completed dollhouse for Jane had stood on the countertop for as long as I could remember, its rooms mismatched in size, the whole structure leaning ominously to one side. Jane had outgrown playing with dolls in the time our father had been assembling that thing.

Tucker reached the shelter first, with Darlene a step behind. My brother pushed me inside. Something struck my temple, and a firework exploded behind my eyes. I found myself on a bench in the dark, my head ringing. I appeared to have whacked my skull on a shelf of canned goods. Everyone was yelling. Darlene was doing a head count, saying our names over and over like a nursery rhyme: "Tucker, Jane, and Cora. Tucker, Jane, and Cora." My brother was trying to find the light switch, narrating his progress aloud: "To the left—hang on—" Jane's cold hands wrapped around me as though I were a security blanket.

The light came on. Dingy walls. Low ceiling. Rows of boxes and bottles of water. Tucker shut the door, and the world went quiet. The space was small and cluttered, the shelves casting deep shadows. In the center of the room, Darlene spread her arms, reaching for all of us as though it was not enough to see us with her own eyes; she needed the verification of physical contact.

My father was not there.

It took us all a moment to realize it. I was still getting the lay of the land: Jane's duffel bag crammed in a corner, framed photos of Mama stacked on the floor, Tucker's cell phone and charger on the bench beside me. I could smell sweat and perfume and the peculiar, coppery musk of the storm.

"Where is he?" Darlene said.

"I'll go," Tucker said.

He began to fumble with the knob. Darlene reacted so fast that I almost couldn't follow it. In a heartbeat, she had batted my brother's hand away and planted herself with her back against the door, her arms braced outward.

"Nobody leaves," she said.

"For god's sake," Tucker said. "Daddy could be—"

"No," Darlene cried. "He'll be here in a second. Any second."

"What if he—"

"There's nothing we can do," she said.

Her lips were drawn back in a snarl, catlike and feral. Tucker took a step toward her. In response, she flattened her body against the door. Her feet were dug in, her neck taut, her hands splayed like suction cups.

"Daddy could be hurt," Tucker said softly. "He could need help."

"I know that," she said.

"Please."

She ground her palm into the corner of one eye, but she stayed where she was. The bare bulb flickered overhead. Jane was holding me so tightly that she had pulled me halfway onto her lap. In the middle of the room, Tucker hovered uncertainly. His expression was defiant, but his posture suggested that he had given up the fight. Darlene was the oldest, after all. My brother kicked aimlessly at the floor, then slung himself onto a bench with an adolescent flounce.

I tried to picture where my father might be. At the barn, maybe.

Soothing the horses. Making sure the chickens were latched securely in their coop. Trying to stop the cows from running themselves into exhaustion, as they had done once before when a coyote broke into their paddock. I was waiting for Daddy's knock. If I shut my eyes tight, he would knock. If I held my breath. Any second now.

Something wrenched loose above us. It sounded like wood breaking. I wondered if my father was up there rearranging the furniture. Something skidded and slid, a gritty, painful scraping. I had the confusing sensation of being near a train track, listening to the rhythmic rattle of the wheels.

Only a few minutes had gone by before I heard the rain. It was a gentle tapping right above us. For a moment, I was soothed by the sound.

This is my first memory. This day, this storm, the calamity that set everything in motion, all the strange and terrible things to come. Huddled in the bunker. Jane's hands in mine. Photos of my mother in the corner, the frames now cracked. My father's absence. I was picturing him with all my might, as though somehow I could conjure him into being—his paunch, his crooked smile, his wide shoulders. Above my head, the drizzle picked up. I did not understand what it meant. I did not know why Tucker buried his head in his hands and Darlene went boneless, slumping to the floor. It did not occur to me that I should not have been able to hear rainfall in the basement. I leaned against Jane and listened to the soft pattering. Six years old, still filled with hope, not realizing that my father and the house above us, the farm and all our animals, were gone.

MAY

1

This is the story of the summer I disappeared. It all began on a warm spring evening. At the time, I was nine years old. I lay in bed, unable to sleep, as Jane snored against my shoulder, her breath tickling my skin.

It was three years after the tornado—almost to the day. The window was open, letting in a faint breeze. The moon was high. With care, I extricated myself from the blankets and grabbed my flashlight. I shone the beam around the room—shabby curtains, empty hamper, clothes on the floor. There was a desk smothered in papers and a plate dotted with sandwich crusts. In the mess, my stuffed animals lurked like woodland creatures in the underbrush.

I crept into the living room, where the shifting flashlight beam made the couch and TV look different—two-dimensional and lifeless, more like an artist's rendering than actual furniture. Darlene was asleep on the sofa, a murky shadow, a huddle of blankets. I held still, listening hard, until she let out a whispery snore.

The trailer had only one bedroom, which Jane and I shared. The rest of the space was open—part kitchen, part den, always immaculate and gleaming, the air rarified by cleaning solvents. This was Darlene's doing. She had no room of her own, no door to close, no privacy. The couch was her bed, but there was never any sign of her presence there during the day. Each morning, she folded up her blankets and tucked away her pillow as though her sleeping habits were a guilty secret.

Stepping outside into the night air, I inhaled a sweet rush of pollen. The sky was a chalkboard slate, the moon not quite full, a circle scribbled imperfectly and smudged. It was May, on the cusp of summer, the wind parched and slow. I turned off the flashlight to let my eyes adjust to the darkness. The trailer park was a medley of gray. As I moved down the path, I heard the skitter of crickets in the grass, roused into motion by my presence.

Darlene liked to say that we lived in a *permanent mobile home*, despite the obvious oxymoron. She thought it sounded classier than *trailer*. From the outside, our unit looked like a house in a board game: precisely rectangular and made of flimsy materials. It was ringed by a fence that came up to my waist. All the trailers in our row were more or less identical, though many residents had added a few individual touches—a fire pit, wind chimes, a dog chained to a spike in the ground, a NO TRESPASSING sign.

We lived in No. 43, which sat beside a ravine that dropped into a dry riverbed and a tangle of brambles. This had been our home since the tornado left us dispossessed and broke. Our trailer was distinguished from the others by a certain quality of neglect. Some of our neighbors liked to grow vegetables in clay pots, but we didn't have the time. Some of our neighbors liked to cook a hearty meal each night, filling the air with spices, but we didn't have the energy. No. 43 bore the unmistakable signs of subsistence.

Somewhere in the distance, a coyote howled—a mournful, throaty cry. I was not supposed to be out at night. Darlene was a routinized and rule-bound person, both in her own behavior and her governance of Jane and me. The trailer was covered with handwritten notes taped up over the sink, by the door, in the bathroom. *Wipe your feet. Hold down the toilet handle for fifteen seconds. Jane, stay out of my makeup.* The coyote bayed again, hoping for an answer from one of its kind. Its hoarse melancholy hung in the air like mist. There was no reply. Darlene would have pitched a fit if she knew where I was, and Jane would have swatted my behind. I did not care. It wasn't the first time I had gone out looking for adventure at night, and it wouldn't be the last.

Tucker would have understood. For a moment, I held still in the darkness, missing my brother. The sensation was as familiar as breath. For more than two years, I had lived in a world of women. I had learned the hard way that men were inconstant. Daddy died in the tornado. A few months afterward, Tucker ran away. My father had left us through no fault of his own, whereas my brother packed a bag of his own free will. But the result was the same.

I did not remember much about my father, but I remembered Tucker. I remembered the physicality of him—all tumble and roll, tackling me onto the couch in a joyful greeting. I remembered him imitating the tornado that destroyed our home, whirling around the living room of No. 43 with his arms outstretched. I remembered him kissing my forehead when I awoke from a nightmare. My brave, ecstatic, beautiful brother. There was nothing to do for that kind of loss—no solution to it, no medicine for it. You just coped as best you could. The ache was dull but profound, like the unanswered call of a lonely coyote. Most of the time I could handle it, but whenever it grew too great, I would grab my flashlight and head out into the darkness.

The moon and wind were a kind of salve. I strolled down the path, keeping the flashlight off. I could see well enough now, the ground painted with a dusty glimmer of moonlight. Each step was accompanied by rustling. Grasshoppers and beetles scuttled to make room for me, their metallic bodies clattering like applause. An owl screamed somewhere. A hunting cry. I passed No. 42 and No. 41. The trailer park was called Shady Acres, which was a misnomer. There were a few trees around, but their leaves were withered. The grass, too, was yellow and wilted. Greenery did not thrive in the arid Oklahoma climate. Even now, on an evening in May, the air held the incipient warmth of a teapot beginning to simmer.

I tipped my head back, the wind swirling around me and touching my long hair. I always felt closer to Tucker outdoors. I could imagine that he was somewhere nearby, still here with me, momentarily out of sight. Behind that tree, maybe. Hiding in the ravine. Chuckling to himself. Before he had abandoned us, he took me on more than a few night walks. Darlene knew nothing of this; Jane had never been invited. It was a special connection that only Tucker and I shared.

The first time it happened, we had just moved into No. 43. Four orphans. Disoriented and stunned. Heartsick and homesick. One night, Tucker and I snuck outside together while our sisters slumbered. I remembered tiptoeing at his side, holding his hand, giddy from the thrill of our transgression, awake and alive. I remembered Tucker murmuring in my ear, telling me facts about the bats fluttering overhead, their use of sonar, their curious bone structure, the elongated digits on their hands that comprised their wings. I remembered sitting with my brother at the base of a tree and leaning against his shoulder, his profile printed crisp against the moon. The only man left in our world.

Now a sound beside me made me pivot. I tugged the flashlight from my pocket and spun the beam around. There was a flicker of motion. A scorpion was caught in the curl of a dead leaf, rocking and scrabbling. It freed itself and slithered toward me. I darted a few steps back, and the creature crawled past me, its tail raised aggressively. I kept it pinned in the light. I thought about trying to catch it; I could bring it to school in a jar for show-and-tell. But Jane had once been stung on the arch of her foot, and I remembered her lolling miserably on the couch, her entire leg swollen, vomiting into a bucket until the venom left her system. The scorpion scrambled away, its shell glistening in the glow from my flashlight. I tracked it until it was out of sight.

Then I was alone again.

I walked along the rim of the ravine, following the owl's call. There was something breathtaking in my solitude—surrounded by lightless rooms and unconscious sleepers. I raised the beam of my flashlight to the nearest mobile home, No. 24, which had a skull and crossbones spray-painted on the side. The place belonged to the Grangers, a young couple Darlene could not stand—the man tattooed and toothless, the woman pigtailed and drug addled. My sister seemed to take their behavior as a personal affront, fulfilling every stereotype of trailer trash. I switched off my flashlight. For a moment I could see nothing at all; I might have turned off the whole world.

Tucker was still on my mind. On our second night walk, we had traveled farther. He led me miles down the road to see the horses on a farm. The moon was a sliver that night, a fishhook lodged among the tree branches. Tucker and I had raced each other out of Shady Acres. I remembered the eerie weightlessness of his figure in flight, the way his feet scarcely seemed to skim the ground. Once we reached the main road, he guided me through the brambles and bladed grasses. There was not much traffic, just the occasional truck lumbering along, splitting the night open with its noise and headlights. Tucker and I held hands as we walked, partly for company and partly to keep our footing on the inky, uneven ground.

He told me stories about our family's animals—the ones that had died in the tornado. Nine cows. A stallion, a mare, and a pony. Six chickens. The goat named Sweetie. My brother had loved them all, so I did too. He told me about grooming the horses, brushing their coats and watching the tiny earthquakes of pleasure that shuddered across their flesh. He told me about visiting the cows, who followed him wherever he went, drifting behind him through the prairie, trusting him to lead them. He told me about the floury smell of the chickens, the spill of their feathers, their beady, intelligent eyes. He told me that the loss of the farm was tearing him in half. A house was not a home without animals.

We heard the horses before we saw them. They seemed to be playing in the darkness, snorting, their hoofbeats echoing. At my side, Tucker froze as though hearing music. Then he laughed. I loved his laugh. We approached the fence and he lifted me over, helping me into the paddock before climbing in himself. The horses were shadows against shadows—maybe three, maybe four, all with dark coats, all in motion. They darted away from us, melting into the landscape of gray and prancing closer again, tossing their heads, a flash of teeth in the moonlight, a nervous whinny. Their curiosity gradually overwhelmed their unease. They spiraled around us, filling the air with an earthy musk. A tail brushed my shoulder. Tucker was no longer laughing; instead he seemed to be vibrating with ferocious joy. He held still, letting the horses grow accustomed to our presence. He gripped my hand so tight it hurt.

We stayed there a long time. The horses investigated me, one shoving a bristled snout into the hollow of my throat, another poring through my hair with a spongy tongue. They backed away and strutted forward again like dancers in a tango. One by one, they fell in love with Tucker, surrounding him, four black heads competing for his touch. He stroked their manes, murmured in their ears. In the darkness, the horses seemed too big to be real—mountains on the hoof, volcanic breath. Tucker said he would steal them. He said he would free them. He promised them, and he promised me.

I did not remember coming home that night. I had grown drowsy after a while, sinking into the grass beneath a bush where the horses could not trample me. I watched them shift and stamp in the breeze, and then I watched the constellations burn, and then Tucker was carrying me, my head on his shoulder, the rhythm of his stride lulling me into a dream.

2

I woke to the sound of banging on the door. For a moment, I was disoriented, unable to place myself. Sunlight tangled in the curtains. Drool on my cheek. I did not remember making my way back to No. 43 the night before.

"Y'all are going to be late," Darlene called.

It took force to extricate my arm from beneath Jane's torso. She went on sleeping as I sat up. Somewhere in the distance, a lawn mower buzzed. I could smell cut grass and cigarettes.

Today was the three-year anniversary of the tornado. As I remembered this fact, I groaned aloud. I knew what to expect: a memorial service at school, a forced mournfulness that bore no relationship to my private, genuine sorrow. I climbed out of bed and fished through the pile of clothes on the floor, looking for something relatively clean. I tugged on a T-shirt, realized it was Jane's, and removed it. Outside, the lawn mower sputtered and stalled. The next-door neighbors were arguing in their way, cawing back and forth like crows. I caught the faraway squeal of a baby crying. You could hear everything that happened in the trailer park if you just took the time to listen. I knew more than I was supposed to know.

In the kitchen, the smell of coffee was overpowering. I sat at the table, and Darlene handed me a bowl of cereal. Sometimes I liked to pretend that No. 43 was a train car. Same shape, same size. It wasn't hard to imagine that any moment now a whistle might blow, wheels might turn beneath us, and we might be carried away to somewhere else—somewhere better.

Darlene sipped her coffee. Her hair was swept up in a severe ponytail. She was dressed for her job at the supermarket, her beige uniform freshly laundered but still smelling vaguely of onions, adorned by her name tag and a broach that had belonged to our mother. Her face was angular and unbeautiful. Boxy glasses offset the jut of her cheekbones.

"We're going to the cemetery this afternoon," she said.
"I know."
"I'll pick you up at four. Right at four. No dawdling."
I knew better than to argue. I nodded.

AT TWO O'CLOCK, ALL OF Mercy Elementary School poured into the gym. The windows were smeary with sunlight, the stink of sweat singeing my lungs, too many bodies crammed into the space. The fluorescent lights blanched us all with a porcelain glow. My class sat at the back of the gym beneath the basketball hoop. Ms. Watson stepped cautiously over our legs and backpacks, reminding us to be quiet, to sit still. She was a big woman with a sweet, generous face.

She sought me out, as I had expected she would. Of all the families affected by the tornado, mine was in a category by itself, and everyone in Mercy knew it. Ms. Watson was discreet about her sympathy, touching my head gently in passing.

Third grade had been kind to me. The school year would end in a few weeks, and I was expecting to miss Ms. Watson over the summer. As she shuffled away, I closed my eyes, imagining that I was back in her classroom now—the walls painted friendly colors, a mobile of the solar system swinging from the ceiling, a feeling of safety and ease—rather than here, preparing once again to remember our loss.

A hush fell over the gym. The principal stood up, holding a stack of notecards. His tie was crooked, his voice hoarse, not quite carrying. I did not mind. I had no interest in hearing his platitudes. I had heard them all before.

"Welcome," he said. "This is a sad day for us all."

The word *sad* was a kind of trigger. Several heads turned in my direction, teachers scanning my face, kids nudging each other. Even the principal shot a glance my way before continuing his speech. I felt myself blush. I was used to pity, but that did not make it any easier to take.

The tornado that struck the town of Mercy had been Category Five. Technically it was Category EF5: *E* for "Enhanced" and *F* for "Fujita," the scale on which all tornadoes were measured. Mercy had become infamous overnight. Everyone in Oklahoma—maybe the whole country—was aware of the extent of our town's tragedy. There was a national obsession with what Darlene called *weather porn*: the sensual, exhaustive analysis of a natural disaster, complete with lurid photographs. Three years ago, Mercy fell into its spotlight.

At two and a half miles across, the tornado crashed into my old neighborhood like a baseball bat into a wasp's nest. It reduced our house to kindling. It flung my family's belongings across the landscape. Only remnants had ever been recovered—Darlene's bike jammed beneath a mailbox, our stove smashed in a swimming pool, Daddy's hammer embedded six inches into an oak tree. My brother's gym bag had been found twenty miles away. The tornado flattened buildings and crumpled cars like soda cans. It peeled asphalt from the sidewalks and yanked plumbing out of the ground. It killed twelve people in all, including my father.

"Now we'll sing," the principal said. He lifted his chin, and in a surprisingly deep bass, he began the first verse of "Amazing Grace." All around me, the other students joined in, crooning the words in the cautious mumble of children singing out of obligation. Ms. Watson dabbed at her eyes with a handkerchief.

I wanted to raise my hand and complain. It made no sense for me to attend a memorial service, since I could not remember anything. The tornado was the starting point of my conscious life. Everything before it was an empty space. I knew the numbers that belonged to the storm: wind speeds of three hundred and twenty miles per hour, forty people injured, twelve dead. Houses picked up and dropped. Trees debarked. Cars thrown. The technical phrase was *incredible intensity*.

For me, however, the tornado had been something else. Something personal, internal. My first recollection of my father was also my last. Big belly. A worried expression. Strong, calloused hands. I remembered him carrying a box that clanked. I remembered him shouting for us all to hurry. I remembered his absence in the shelter, his absence when the storm subsided, his absence every day that followed. I could not mourn him—not really. Even in death, he was a mystery. His body was never found; he was one of several to perish that day without a trace, sucked up into the sky. Presumed dead. Nothing to bury.

All that was left of him were pictures, anecdotes, and secondhand information. I gathered what knowledge I could. I had asked Darlene and Jane for stories—and Tucker, before he ran away. I had looked through the photograph albums Darlene saved. Flipping through the pages, I hoped to spark some latent memory, but the images—my parents at their wedding, my sisters in their infancy, a group of blurred figures on a picnic—seemed like illustrations from somebody else's past. To me, they were empty of meaning, but

Darlene and Jane treasured them. Along with the framed snapshots of our mother, Darlene had preserved these albums from the storm at the expense of her laptop, her jewelry box, and her nice leather jacket. (She had told me this many times. In the moments after the siren sounded, she made her choice. Only a couple of minutes. Only so much she could carry.) After transporting the family photos to No. 43, she even spent precious money to replace Mama's cracked frames with new ones—a devotion I did not understand.

For me, the tornado had been something beyond a force of nature. The havoc it wreaked on the physical landscape was echoed by an equal measure of devastation in my mind and memory. As far as I was concerned, we had always lived in No. 43. As far as I was concerned, we had always been poor. Darlene was always hard, Jane always vague. And I never knew my father.

AT FOUR O'CLOCK, DARLENE PULLED up in front of Mercy Elementary School. The playground was a madhouse. Small bodies ran every which way, backpacks bouncing on their shoulders. The monkey bars were so crowded that children kept colliding and dropping to the ground. A few girls kicked on the swings, rising higher and higher, finally leaping from the apex of the arc, their silhouettes printed on the sky for a long moment as though they might float down as gently as leaves.

Darlene waved. She looked incongruous behind the wheel of the pickup truck that once belonged to our father. It was corroded around the hood and pocked by dents, prone to coughing smoke from its exhaust pipe. It did not suit Darlene's inherent tidiness. I climbed inside, inhaling the tang of leather, gasoline, and a musky cologne that must have been Daddy's brand. My father was a mechanic, fixing other people's cars for a living, but his own vehicle had been a wreck of rust and nostalgia. The shoemaker's children were never shod. In fact, the pickup survived the tornado simply because it was in such bad shape. When the storm hit, the truck was parked across town, awaiting repairs in the garage where Daddy had worked. An accidental legacy.

"Buckle your seat belt," Darlene said.

She threw the car into gear, and we pulled away from the curb with a squeal of tires. She looked anxious. There was a suggestion of blue beneath each eye, the stamp of fatigue, underlined by the frame of her glasses. After a moment, she switched on the radio.

"—the likes of which our small town had never seen before," the announcer said. "This kind of tornado is called 'the finger of God,' and for good reason. I'm sure none of our listeners have forgotten where they were on the day when—"

Darlene smacked the button again.

"Jesus Christ on a crutch," she said. "Enough already."

I glanced into the side mirror, watching my school recede into the distance. It would take us over an hour to reach the cemetery. My parents shared a headstone in the family plot, thirty miles outside of town. Though only Mama was actually buried there, Darlene insisted on a pilgrimage every year on the anniversary of the tornado. I did not know why, since she was not sentimental or religious, and these trips seemed to offer more heartache than comfort. Still, I knew better than to question her. Darlene's will was an irresistible force, in this and everything else. When she wanted something to happen, there was nothing to be gained by objecting. Opposition would only lead to friction and bad feeling, and in the end, Darlene would get her way.

I sighed. To make matters worse, Jane would not be joining us at the cemetery this year. She was the family's athlete, an exalted position that afforded her certain luxuries. She got trips to the doctor for her shin splints and ingrown toenails, whereas Darlene made do with home remedies for her periodic migraines. Jane got shiny uniforms, whereas I made do with hand-me-downs that were always too big or too small; I had never in my life walked into a store and purchased an item of clothing new. Jane had an important game today—important enough that Darlene gave her permission to skip the annual ritual.

She would be on the field now, surrounded by other eighth graders in blue uniforms. She would be running hard in the heat, fearless in cleats and shin guards.

We drove past a group of oil derricks. They were working, always working, bobbing like drinking birds, their gears squeaking. Long ago, in another life, my brother explained their function to me, how they drew the oil out of the ground. We passed a field of wheat, a ramshackle farmhouse, and a rusted water tower.

Twenty miles outside of town lay the cosmetics factory, a vast gray building with small windows. There was something impersonal, even forbidding, about its aspect. Jolly Cosmetics was part makeup laboratory, part production hub. I imagined it filled with vats of mascara bubbling like cauldrons in a witch's cave. I pictured towers of lipstick, solid and maroon, flanked by workers who whittled away at the sides, carving out tiny scrolls to place inside the kind of tubes Darlene carried in her purse. A few of our neighbors worked at Jolly Cosmetics. Everyone in Mercy lived close to the bone, and good jobs were hard to come by.

At the gravesite, no wind stirred the branches of the trees. The clouds looked as solid as though they had been baked in a kiln. Among the grass and nettles, crickets moved ceaselessly. Their bodies were deceptive. Black, shiny, and fat, they looked as though they would be slimy to the touch, but I knew they were as dry and light as paper cranes.

Darlene did not cry. She did not speak to the dead. She had not even brought our parents flowers, though fresh bouquets were laid out on many of the other headstones. My sister stood ramrod straight, her expression steely, every particle of her being telegraphing her discomfort. It was as if she were counting down the minimum number of seconds for a proper show of grief, even though no one was keeping track.

Our parents' headstone was marble, etched with scrolling cursive. *Dear Wife and Mother. Beloved Husband and Father.* Mama had died in childbirth, and Daddy had perished when I was six; I had been an orphan for as long as I could remember. I had been raised by Darlene, and, for a brief but glorious time, Tucker. *Mama* and *Daddy* were words I never used, unlike my friends at school—normal kids.

I shook myself. As a rule, I tried to avoid self-pity. The pity of the whole town was bad enough without adding my own to the mix. Besides, if I ever started feeling sorry for myself, all I had to do was look over at Darlene, who had it much worse.

When the tornado struck, Darlene was eighteen years old. A senior in high school. Filled with enthusiasm and anticipation. She had just been accepted to Oklahoma University. She pinned a map of the OU campus to her bedroom wall, using thumbtacks to mark the places she wanted to visit. She often chanted the OU fight song: *I'm a Sooner born and Sooner bred, and when I die, I'll be Sooner dead.* She was on the cusp of achieving escape velocity from Mercy, something she had longed for all her life.

I did not remember any of this, of course. I had heard about it from Jane, who retained vivid memories of what Darlene was like back then, bubbly and wide-eyed. I knew about the college jacket Darlene planned to buy, the sorority she hoped to pledge. I knew that she had been preparing for a career in medicine. She planned on becoming a nurse in the trauma ward of an important hospital, combining her pragmatic mind, natural calm, and the extensive medical training she would acquire at OU to do great things.

Now, however, she was twenty-two and stuck in Mercy. The sole provider for Jane and me. Carrying our world on her shoulders. She ferried us around and helped us with our homework. She kept the trailer spotless and left polite comments on the social media posts of her friends off at college, people with lives not ruined by the tornado. She worked at the grocery store—a job that was beneath her in every way.

I bent over my parents' headstone. A tracery of grit patterned its surface, and I used my palm to wipe the marble clean. Then, in the distance, a hint of movement caught my eye. A man was standing amid the trees at the edge of the cemetery.

I straightened up, staring. Something about his posture intrigued me. He was all on his own, separate from the other mourners, furtive and slim. He reminded me of Tucker—but then, so many things reminded me of Tucker.

"Look," I said, pointing.

Darlene did not hear me. She checked her watch.

"That's long enough," she said.

We made our way to the pickup truck. I threw a glance back at the woods, but the figure was no longer visible. A trick of the light. A glitch. A ghost.

THAT NIGHT, I COULD NOT sleep. Once more, a wild, reckless mood came over me, and I let myself out of the trailer alone. I crept past Darlene's shape on the couch. I slipped on my flip-flops and tucked my flashlight into my pocket. The night was filled with insects and a hesitant breeze that seemed to change direction with each gust.

As I stepped onto the path, I heard a noise. A clatter like beads in a rain stick—I knew that sound. Everyone in the Southwest knew that sound. I sucked in a breath but did not release it. Slowly, cautiously, I swung the glow of the flashlight, scanning the ground until I located the rattlesnake.

It was coiled beneath a bush, too far away to strike. I watched as the creature lifted its head, its tongue dancing, sniffing the air. Its eyes were as glassy and unblinking as buttons. The sinewy neck was tattooed with whorls, the flesh rippling and swaying hypnotically. The knobs of its tail shimmered.

I felt a strange surge of pride. Everything native to Oklahoma was tough and warlike. Only the strong survived here. Our snakes came with venom and a warning signal. Our insects were armored against predators and dehydration. Our birds possessed talons, telescopic vision, and hollow bones. These animals were designed for hardship. All weakness and softness had been beaten out of their genetic lineage by the dust storms, the droughts, and the tornadoes. Disaster was as much a part of life in Oklahoma as the weather-worn sky. The crayfish were plated with complex carapaces. The coyotes were shy and clever, as elusive as dreams. The groundhogs dug deep burrows, safe from heat and wind. The turtles and frogs lived a halfway existence, dipping between tepid water and balmy air. The porcupines carried weaponry on their backs. The mule deer had lightning reflexes. The alligators were stupid but heavily armed. I was jealous of them all—their savage strength and vivid senses, their power and tenaciousness. The way they were born was the best way to be.

Even the tornado had not fazed them. The day after the finger of God scored a path through Mercy, the wild animals resumed their lives as they had always done—hunting, feeding, and mating, untouched by sorrow and shock. Only the humans had suffered—and our livestock, of course. The lazy, docile creatures confined to barns and cages. They never stood a chance. Like my father, our cows and horses had vanished into the blue.

Now, as I watched, the rattlesnake wheeled and slithered away through the grass. I was tempted to follow it, to see where it made its home. Once more, I thought of Tucker. I remembered him telling me that rattlesnakes evolved over millions of years to say only one thing: *Leave me alone.*

That was the moment it happened. I was standing in the dirt lane when I felt the ground shiver beneath my feet. A shock wave pulsed through the earth. The trailer doors creaked on their hinges and the trees rustled their desiccated leaves. It was as though the town of Mercy had taken a deep, shuddering breath.

A tremble. A tremor. I had never felt anything like it before. Oklahoma was not a place of earthquakes. For a moment, I thought the rattlesnake had done it—shaking its tail hard enough to move the whole world. I did not know what to make of it, and there was no one around to ask. No one in Shady Acres was awake except for me. I stood still, waiting to see if the ground would shudder again.

3

The next morning, the TV was on when I emerged from my bedroom. It was Saturday. Jane was in the shower singing off-key, her rough alto reverberating around the trailer. The light through the window was muffled by heavy clouds. Darlene wandered like a hummingbird in a garden, pausing at the coffeepot, the sink, and the fridge, at once busy and desultory, moving just to be moving. I did not think she was even aware of her restlessness; this was just how she watched TV, orbiting the living room, constrained by the small space. The entire trailer measured around three hundred square feet.

I climbed into my chair and reached for the box of cereal. On the screen, a male announcer was framed in front of a familiar backdrop. I recognized the flat gray exterior of Jolly Cosmetics, twenty miles outside Mercy. The newscaster stood in front of the building, speaking in solemn tones, his auburn hair ruffled by the wind. The volume was louder than I would have liked, clashing against the birdsong outside.

"I can't believe this," Darlene said.

She pointed at the screen, where BREAKING NEWS flashed in a red banner. I tried to follow what the announcer was saying. I was still weary from the previous day—the cemetery and my late-night wandering—and the man kept interspersing his monologue with words I did not recognize. *Willful damage of property. Manufacturing, possessing, and transporting a destructive device.*

"What happened?" I said.

Darlene folded her hand into a fist. "Boom."

Jane emerged from the bathroom on a wash of steam, her hair turbaned in a pink towel. She paused at the table, grabbing a piece of toast from Darlene's plate.

"Somebody let out all the animals," Darlene said. "I didn't even know they kept animals at the factory. I guess the scientists were doing tests on them."

The image on the screen melted into a series of photographs. An open cage. A group of white rats. Broken glass. The hind end of a beagle escaping around a corner. A wire cage was deformed into a shape that was almost artistic, the metal charred and glittering.

"There was an explosion," Darlene said.

"*Our* factory?" Jane said. "You mean Jolly?"

"Yeah. It happened last night. Some nutcase waited until all the workers were gone. There was just the janitor and a security guard. This guy—this *suspect*—chased out all the animals and set off some kind of explosive device."

I remembered the tremor in the darkness the night before, the ground shimmying beneath my feet. Was it possible that I had felt the blast? The announcer reappeared on the screen, his expression serious. The factory was in bad shape, it seemed.

Then the TV showed a pool of red. There were droplets on the tile, a shard of glass with crimson smeared on the point. I felt my gorge rise. The announcer began to speculate about how the blood came to be there. None of the workers had been hurt. Perhaps an animal had been caught in the blast. Perhaps the bomber himself was injured.

"All this at Jolly Cosmetics," Jane said. "That ain't right."

I SPENT THE NEXT FEW hours in transit. This was typical for a Saturday. Jane had soccer practice, and Darlene never got the weekend off. As a rule, she took every shift she could. As we drove out of Shady Acres, I sat in the truck bed. Jane had seniority, claiming the passenger's seat. Darlene, behind the wheel, was quiet. I could see nothing but her ponytail and the occasional flash of her eyes in the rearview mirror. Jane lounged with her feet on the dash, her thumbs dancing over her phone, while I lurched and jolted over every pothole and rock. There were no seat belts back there, just the side to clutch and the curve of the wheel well to jam my body against. The radio played a country song, though I could make out only the tune, not the words, over the rumble of the tires. The truck hit a bump, and my teeth jangled. We drove past the gas station and the town's only motel.

Mercy was a model of efficiency. It contained exactly what was needed for life in Oklahoma, no more, no less. There was a supermarket. There was one school for each age group—elementary, middle, high—and they all shared the same principal. There was a police station, a fire department with one weathered truck, and a movie theater that showed one film per week, usually several months after its initial release. The main drag offered two restaurants and a hardware store. Some of the neighborhoods were paved, while others had dirt roads and wild lawns, the houses hidden behind brambles. On the outskirts of town, there were swaths of farmland: bristling corn and luscious soybeans, some pastures lying fallow and others given over to grazing. Shady Acres lurked to the west, tucked off to the side like an embarrassment.

The flower shop had a sign in the window, reminding everyone that Mother's Day was coming up. I experienced a familiar surge of discomfort. At school, my class had been making cards loaded with glitter and stickers. I planned to throw mine away when Ms. Watson wasn't looking.

My mother had exited the world an hour after I was born. Placental abruption. No symptoms. Her pregnancy had been fine; the labor and delivery were normal. My father was holding me, a sticky, squalling starfish, as the obstetrician bent over my mother, palpating her abdomen. Then a geyser of blood erupted between Mama's legs. She perished within minutes—hemorrhagic shock, an unusual blood type, not enough stock for a transfusion. The first photographs taken of me as a newborn showed my father blank with horror, Jane with red, swollen eyes, and Tucker as pale as ash.

Darlene, who was not squeamish, had told me the details of Mama's death more than once, always in matter-of-fact tones. Every now and then, I would ask to hear the story again—hoping, perhaps, that this time my sister might tell a different tale, one in which I had not, however unintentionally, been the cause of Mama's demise. Darlene seemed to understand. Her voice would soften a little, and she always ended by saying, "And none of what happened was your fault."

I did not know much else about my mother. The clear, cold facts of her death were something I could ask for and receive, but the ethereal mishmash of her life was harder to define. According to her photographs, she was a woman of generous curves and timid pastels. She had given her eyebrows to Darlene, her mouth to Tucker. Her figure offered a reasonable approximation of what Jane's sturdy frame might blossom into when she reached adulthood.

I was not sure what Mama had passed down to me.

I did know that she began our family's acquisition of animals. When Darlene was little, Mama purchased a used chicken coop and filled it with happy, dust-colored hens, who provided warm brown eggs every morning. When Mama was pregnant with Tucker, she hired a neighborhood boy to build a fence for a cow she had her eye

THE WILDLANDS / 35

on. One became two, and then four, and then an amiable herd. Every few years, a new animal would appear in the back field. The paddocks were arranged in no particular order, their layout haphazard, their fencing mismatched. There was a benevolent chaos to the place. Just after Jane came along, Mama rescued a fat gray stallion from a breeder who was about to sell him to a slaughterhouse. She named him Mojo and visited him every day, teaching Darlene and Tucker how to brush his coat and tend to his hooves.

As it turned out, the horse outlived her. Mojo mourned when she died, recovering only when Daddy bought a mare to keep him company.

DARLENE AND I DROPPED JANE at the soccer field and watched her melt into a cluster of girls in identical uniforms. We went to the drugstore. We stopped by the library. At last, my sister pulled into her usual spot in the supermarket parking lot and sat for a moment with her head bowed. I did not disturb her. I waited until she sighed and climbed out of the car. Then I swung my backpack onto my shoulder and followed her.

Over the past two and a half years, Darlene had risen through the ranks of the grocery store. She recently attained the status of assistant manager, which came with a tiny raise. She could climb no higher; the manager was the owner's son, and he had an office with a desk and a window, even though Darlene more or less ran the place. She could recite the cash register codes for every product. She could assume any task on the floor, sweeping, pricing items on the shelves, or bagging people's groceries. Today she had been asked to spend a few hours in the stockroom taking inventory. My job was to wait and wait. I brought a stack of library books in crackling plastic covers. I sat against a wall and read about dinosaurs, listening to the cash register.

At the end of her shift, Darlene called me over to a table at the back of the store. She had a standing arrangement with her boss; any food that was destined for the garbage bin was hers for the taking.

Together we pored through gallons of milk that were past their sell-by date, expired cans, and all the fruits and vegetables that were too withered for the customers. There was a carton of eggs, a few broken and leaking. There were apples with wormholes and potatoes sprouting green shoots. Darlene and I filled several bags. The bulk of my diet was made up of food other people would have thrown away.

On our way back to the car, we were intercepted by Mr. Carter, an elderly man with a cane and a frizzled mop of white hair that seemed to possess its own agency, coiling around his skull like the tentacles of an anemone. I knew all about him, of course. Mercy was a small town; everyone knew all about everyone else. Mr. Carter had run the pharmacy until his retirement a few years back.

"Why, it's Darlene McCloud!" he boomed. "My goodness, you've gotten tall."

My sister flashed a flinty smile and allowed him a brief hug, during which she did not set down her grocery bags, probably so she would not have to actively reciprocate. Darlene hated to be touched.

"How are you, sir?" she asked, stepping away quickly.

"Can't complain. And who's this?" He squinted at me, then pretended to stagger backward, clutching his heart in feigned astonishment. "It can't be little Cora! Last time I saw you, you were knee-high to a grasshopper!"

"Yeah," I said awkwardly.

"You look like your mother," he said. "I remember her very well, you know. Such a shame! You've got her curls, don't you?"

"Yes, sir," I whispered.

He lunged toward Darlene, prodding her with his forefinger. His mouth pooled open, revealing the plate of his dentures.

"I don't blame you," he said. "I want you to know that."

"Excuse me?" she said.

"I know what people say," he said. "But you did what you had to do. As far as I'm concerned, you can hold your head up as high as anyone."

Darlene ushered me into the pickup truck. She eluded Mr. Carter's attempt at a second hug with a sidestep and a wave.

"Old coot," she said, once we were on the road.

I laid my forehead against the window, watching a row of white stucco houses spooling past, the landscape blanched by the sun into a palette of ochre and cream.

IN THE EVENING, WE SPRAWLED on the couch like a litter of puppies. The night was windless. The news was full of the bombing at Jolly Cosmetics, but Darlene insisted that we watch something else; the explosion had nothing to do with our lives and she didn't want us to have nightmares. Eventually we settled on a reality show. Our tiny washer/dryer unit—a cube the color of hoarfrost—sat in the corner of the living room. There was some misalignment inside that made it rattle at the peak of each cycle, loud enough to drown out the TV, sometimes hard enough to shake the whole trailer. We could not afford a new one, and Darlene lived in fear of the day it died and left us with no recourse but the laundromat.

Eventually Jane went to bed. Darlene was sound asleep now, her hands interlinked across her belly, her breathing deep and regular. She had removed her glasses, and her face looked younger without them.

I stayed where I was, thinking about Mr. Carter again. *I don't blame you*, he had said. I knew what he was referring to.

After the tornado, film crews and journalists had descended on Mercy like a plague of locusts, snapping photos of ruined houses and questioning hollow-eyed refugees. By and large, the town responded to the media assault with chilly politeness—a brief soundbite here, a reluctant portrait there, nothing too intimate. People then closed ranks and looked after their own.

All except Darlene. I did not know exactly how it all came about—I was only six years old then, and shell-shocked besides—but I knew that our family had gone on the record when nobody else would. I remembered being in front of a camera. Wearing my best dress. Sitting on a couch with my sisters. Taking turns speaking into a microphone. Tucker wasn't with us—I was not sure why at the time. Someone handed me a photograph of my father and told me to hold it up and look at the camera. A strange woman with a fierce expression put makeup on my face for the first time. The lights were hot, my hands were shaking, and I was glad when it was over.

That was not our only interview. We had done quite a few. I could not recall the sequence, whether the newspaper articles came first, or the TV spot, or our photograph on the cover of a magazine. We had captured the public's imagination: four orphans, homeless and destitute, perfectly pathetic. The requests came pouring in, and Darlene said yes to all of them, as long as there was money involved.

For a brief moment, the McCloud family became the face of the tragedy. I remembered sitting in Darlene's lap as a cameraman told me not to smile. I remembered one headline in particular: THE SADDEST FAMILY IN MERCY. These words ran over a photograph of Darlene, Jane, and me, looking as lost and forlorn as stray cats.

Something about all this had been shameful. After the TV crews left town and the reporters stopped calling, it became clear that the people of Mercy did not approve. I was used to the way they looked at me, even now. A cloying pity. A hint of disgust. They patted my hand. They stepped up at the dollar store to pay for my school supplies. They greeted Darlene formally, as though she were a stranger. We had all gone through the tornado together, but my family now stood apart from everyone else. Darlene had sold our story; she had sold all of us. The stigma of that lingered to this day.

At the time, Tucker was angry. I remembered him turning away when the reporters approached. He would not pose for pictures. I wished now that I could ask him why—I wanted to ask him so many things—but of course I couldn't. He had abandoned us not long after. I wanted to ask him how we could stop being the saddest family in Mercy. The words had proved as indelible as a brand.

4

On Monday, I went to Mercy Elementary School for the last time. I did not know this, of course. I did not know I was about to disappear.

The morning was unpleasant. The neighbor's dog woke me before dawn. Beau was a friendly hound, never leashed, wandering around the trailer park at will, sleeping under cars and begging for scraps. I often fed him on the sly myself. Now I was dragged out of sleep by a howl—Beau barking in an irregular rhythm.

I sat up. Jane was still slumbering; that girl could sleep through anything. I pushed the curtain aside, noting that the sun had not yet risen. Beau was a shadow against a smoky landscape, the white patches on his back aglow. He was standing at the edge of the ravine and barking into the gulch.

Darlene's voice rose from the other side of the wall. "Goddamn that dog to the pit of hell!"

I slid out of bed. In the living room, my sister was stumbling through the darkness, tugging on a sweatshirt and her rain boots, the closest footwear to hand. She stormed to the front door, too angry to notice me.

The dewy grass felt good on my bare feet. The air was filled with the chorus of the first cicadas of summer. I squinted up at the sky, struck by the seamless gradations of blue that transitioned from an electric glow in the east to solid black in the west. A few stars still glimmered. Darlene was ahead of me, moving at a quick clip. She swept down on Beau, who continued to howl, his whole body rigid, his tail at an anxious half-mast.

"We get it," Darlene shouted. "You heard something in the ravine. There's an animal down there. Shut up! I'm taking you home."

She grabbed him by the collar. Beau scrabbled at the dirt, trying to find purchase. I watched the two of them move down the road, their silhouettes straining in opposite directions.

I approached the edge of the ravine. The ground dropped away sharply, and the bushes and brambles made a spiderweb of branches that trapped the darkness in velvety pockets. I was not an animal; I could not hear what Beau heard, smell what he smelled. I wondered what might be hiding in that gully of shadows.

Over breakfast, I found myself out of sorts. Darlene was in the shower. The TV was on. There was a rainbow glint on the wall. Jane had hung crystals in a few of the windows. She thought them pretty, but I found them disconcerting, casting random flares of light around the place.

With a grunt, Jane slid into a chair beside me. She had her cell phone out, and the look on her face suggested she was texting boys. I observed her thoughtfully. None of the women in our family were beautiful. We all shared a rawboned angularity—strong foreheads, wide shoulders, stubborn chins—that had been carried down the genetic slipstream from our mother, based on what I had seen of her in photographs. I was a stick-skinny child, marked all over by the stigmata of growing up in rural Oklahoma: scraped shins, chigger bites, and scars from falling out of trees. I could not even boast a style of my own, since all my clothes were hand-me-downs. Jane had prominent front teeth and an oversized nose, yet she possessed a quality of loveliness that had nothing to do with her features. She was steady and still, her gaze perpetually unfocused. She always seemed to be thinking about something faraway. I envied her ability to escape the present, keeping her mind elsewhere.

Now she turned the TV volume up. A newscaster appeared, a woman with perfectly coiffed blond hair and a gash of lipstick. She gestured while she spoke, her nails glittering. Behind her, a diagram blossomed onto the screen. A sketch of a pipe bomb. From what I could tell, this appeared to be exactly what it sounded like: a length of plumbing filled with explosives and armed with a fuse.

It seemed that the police had run some tests. The blood from the crime scene was human rather than animal. To no one's surprise, the chromosomes indicated a male suspect. It was a rare blood type and did not match any of Jolly's employees. Therefore, it must belong to the perpetrator. The police were not sure how badly he was injured— he could be on the run, desperate for help. They would circulate a description shortly. They were testing his DNA.

The bomber had evidently crafted his weapon out of common household items. He took known elements—plumbing and gunpowder and thread—and transmuted them into something wicked. I was glad, at least, that no innocents had been injured. None of the animals had died in the blast, though they were lost in the wild now, unable to care for themselves. Seven beagles, thirteen rabbits, thirty-two white rats, and a chimpanzee were the victims of unwanted freedom. The public was cautioned to keep an eye out for them. They could not survive on their own.

DARLENE DROPPED ME OFF AT school a few minutes late. I trudged up the wide flagstone steps and pushed through the front doors to find the hallway packed with unsmiling faces. Kids jostled one another on the way to class. One girl stood at her locker without moving, her hand frozen in midair as though she had begun reaching for something on the top shelf, then lost the will to continue. All of Mercy Elementary School was in a bad mood.

I knew why. The tornado was often called "an act of God"—but to my mind, it was the opposite. My family were not churchgoers, but I had gleaned enough from the pervasive stew of religion in the Oklahoma air—as omnipresent as summer heat—to grasp the basics. I understood that God was order, safety, and the clear duality of heaven and hell. But the tornado had been none of these things. It struck without warning, logic, or pattern. A tornado did not smite the wicked and spare the virtuous. A tornado was just wind and air, and it took everything.

Even now, the neighborhood where the funnel cloud had touched down remained as a vivid, dreadful monument. There had been a cleanup effort: bulldozers packed the rubble into heaps and cleared the roads. But then the first barrel was found. A fifty-five-gallon drum. Jet-black. Stamped with the logo of Jolly Cosmetics. The steel was torn and leaking. The ground beneath was wet and rank with noxious waste.

The cleanup crew promptly stopped its work. The storm had done something miraculous and terrible: the funnel cloud had bypassed Jolly Cosmetics, roaring instead through the far parking lot to the east of the factory, where the barrels of hazardous chemicals were kept, awaiting removal and reclamation. The tornado carried and flung more than a dozen five-hundred-pound drums, hurling them like bullets across the miles into my family's neighborhood. Smashed in ditches. Broken in riverbeds. Poisoning the groundwater. Killing the plants. Filling the air with acrid fumes.

It was the end of that place. These days, the region was no longer unsafe to pass through on your way to other parts of town. But our house and barn would never be rebuilt. The residents had salvaged what they could and fled. The local government was lodged in a quagmire of environmental regulations and lack of funds; there were town hall meetings on the subject every so often, but they never came to anything. In the meantime, the old neighborhood—unkempt and uninhabitable—lurked like the collective unconscious of the people of Mercy. We all knew it was there, but we did not travel through it unless we had to. We avoided it as best we could.

I did not blame Jolly Cosmetics for the fact that its chemicals tainted our town. Nobody did. The company had stored its hazardous waste by the book; then the tornado plowed through to make a mess of things. Human action caused the situation, but human intention did not. There was no fault, no guilt, only misfortune.

Now, however, some idiot had set off a bomb. Another disaster, but an avoidable one. It was too much. It was too much for everybody. My mind was slow to grapple with the idea of deliberate harm. A tornado was one thing, but calculated violence was something else entirely. Someone had willfully targeted our weary little town. Even before the storm, Mercy had not been a wealthy place. Now, three years later, the community was limping along on food stamps, welfare checks, and grit. There was only so much that one town could take. I remembered Tucker telling me that luck was no lady; luck was a mean drunk who didn't know when to stop punching.

As the hours passed, there were more than a few meltdowns. One boy began sobbing in the middle of a lesson on cloud formation because his father worked at the cosmetics factory and could have been killed. Several children went to the nurse with stomachaches. People whispered about unemployment, back pay. Jolly Cosmetics was going to be shut down for a long while. Such a thing had never happened before. The place had been open for business the day after the tornado. The storm never touched it, carting off its waste while leaving the factory unharmed. Jolly Cosmetics escaped the maelstrom only to be assailed three years later by human hands.

At lunch, there was a fight in the cafeteria. I was eating around the mold on my sandwich when a soda can whizzed over my head. Kids began to vault out of their seats, a slow-motion explosion of bodies. At the epicenter, two boys wrestled furiously. The lunch ladies trundled out from behind the counter and separated them.

Later, I heard that an older girl—a fifth grader, no less—had been carried down to the nurse's station by her teacher, screaming all the way that the town of Mercy was cursed. My classmates whispered about it, passing notes back and forth. Seated at my desk, I considered the matter. It made a certain kind of sense. I spent my final hour of class wondering what kind of black magic had been cast on our poor, dried-up town.

The sunlight sliced between the blinds, striping the room with slats of golden gleam. The teacher's voice droned over the scratch of pencils and the tick of the clock. I was not listening. Tucker was on my mind again. I could not seem to shake him.

I remembered the musty odor of the tornado shelter in the basement, the patter of rain. I remembered Tucker and Darlene working together to open the door. Furniture and chunks of masonry had lodged outside, making our exit difficult. I remembered Jane squeezing my hand as we stepped into what had been our basement and looking up at what had been our house. I remembered blinking in shock, dazzled by the unaccustomed sky.

For a little while, it stayed like that—the four of us against the world. Together, we met with a social worker. We always kept within sight of one another, never straying too far apart, often making physical contact, Darlene looping her finger through the tag on the back of my shirt, Tucker leaning his head on her shoulder. When one of us needed to use the bathroom, we all went along, Tucker lingering on the other side of the door. Everything seemed to be at a remove— vague and slightly unreal. A veil had fallen around us, blurring and distancing the rest of the world. Only my siblings remained unchanged. I sometimes felt as though I could sense them with more than my eyes—as though I had developed infrared vision like a snake. Against a drab, bleak landscape, only they burned bright.

For two weeks, we were nomads. We moved from building to building—the post office, the town hall, a stranger's living room. We slept on the floor, surrounded by people who had been our neighbors, chilly, pillowless, and wrapped in sleeping bags that were not ours. There was never enough food, so we subsisted on vending machine snacks and juice boxes. There were no showers. I did not exactly mind the chaos—it seemed similar to what sleepaway camp might be like—but I minded the waiting. I minded that there was nothing to do. I minded that my siblings were behaving like survivors in a zombie movie. Jane was sleeping constantly. Darlene looked like she had just been slapped hard.

In retrospect, Tucker was no better off. The stress manifested differently in him—he was a ball of fire. He paced. He teased me to get me to chase him and then he ran with abandon. He snuck outside to smoke cigarettes away from Darlene's disapproving gaze. He did not sleep. I remembered waking once in an unfamiliar lobby where we were spending the night with a few other refugees of the tornado. The air was dark, filled with whispery exhalations. Darlene was pressed up against me, Jane on the other side, the room illuminated by the red glow of an exit sign. I saw my brother standing against the wall. His back was erect, his hands tangled in his hair, his expression somewhere between awe and horror. He did not move, struck in a posture of sudden insight.

Yet most of the time he seemed fine. It was Tucker who ushered me across the threshold of No. 43 for the first time. It was Tucker who salvaged a mattress from an alley and dragged it home—the same mattress where Jane and I still slept. It was Tucker who christened our new oven by heating up a frozen pizza. It was Tucker who sang me to sleep every evening, playing an accompaniment of air guitar. It was Tucker who did magic tricks to cheer me up, pretending to bend spoons and pull coins from my ear. It was Tucker who stole me away at night to visit somebody else's horses in a faraway field.

I did not recall much about the evening he ran away. It began with an argument between my brother and Darlene. I was in bed, lying beside Jane, who, of course, slept through the whole thing. Through the wall, I caught the sound of an open hand smacking against the table. I could hear most of what they shouted, but none of it made sense to me; I could not figure out why they were fighting, only anger and mysterious accusations and long words and sudden changes of subject and the intensity of their overlapping voices. They might as well have been speaking some other language. I held my breath in the darkness, twisting the sheet in my fingers. I prayed for Darlene to get control of her temper, for Tucker to back down, for the argument to fade away.

Instead, a door slammed. On the other side of the wall, Darlene let out a choked sob. There were footsteps on the gravel path outside.

And just like that, Tucker was gone.

5

The heat baked the air into paste, and the row of trailers cast little shade. A pair of turkey vultures floated high in the blue. I was looking forward to having No. 43 to myself for a few hours. Jane had study group and soccer practice; she and Darlene would not be home until late. Jewel-bright grasshoppers buzzed around me, their wings aglitter. Each day, the grass was a little higher and the insects a little larger.

Outside No. 43, I stopped. Something was not right. The door stood ajar, and there was a smudge on the metal. I stared in bewilderment, trying to figure out what I was seeing. Paint, maybe. A splotch of crimson. Looking closer, I could make out a slippery bracelet of red encircling the doorknob.

For a while I stood there, the straps of my backpack digging into my shoulders. The sun was a blazing pinwheel. My plan for the afternoon was still bright in my mind: a snack of peanut butter and pickles, an hour or two of solitude, some cartoons.

Through the door gap, I glimpsed the familiar linoleum, a slice of couch. I took a step back, trying to think. There was something I was supposed to do now. I was nine years old, a latchkey kid, capable, not easily frightened. Most afternoons I rode the school bus home and let myself in. I knew what to do if a stranger knocked on the door. I knew what to do if the toilet backed up, if the power went out. I knew where the fire extinguisher was.

But I had never anticipated this particular situation. My brain was boiled, limp, useless. A crow gave a jagged cry. I set my backpack down and shaded my eyes with a hand, gazing up and down the indifferent row of trailers. Not a soul in sight.

I leaned close, sniffing the blood.

"Hello?" I called.

No answer. I pushed the door open, careful not to touch the red smudge. There was a bang from inside, followed by a splash. Water began to run in the bathroom, making the pipes knock. The toilet flushed like a lion's roar.

There was blood on the linoleum—a shoe print with a geometric tread. A track led through the trailer. Just one foot. The blood was fresh, still wet enough to glisten. There were not many places where a human being could be concealed in here. No. 43 was a crisp rectangle with the kitchen on one end and the bedroom I shared with Jane on the other. The bathroom sat in the middle, with a tiny hallway—as narrow as a burrow—passing by it. The living room was dim, the air filled with dust motes.

The bathroom door crashed open. A man strode toward me.

He was holding one hand aloft in an awkward way. His fingers were bent at wrong angles, the palm a mangled pulp. I was too startled to make a sound. Blood streamed down the man's wrist. The fabric of his shirt was marred by irregular blotches of mottled crimson.

On the left side, his pant leg was torn. Beneath it, the flesh was torn too. The wound was so terrible that for a moment my mind grew quiet. I could not take in what I was seeing, and the sense of unreality made me feel calm. His calf had been gouged as though a bear clawed him. The skin hung in strips—deep, symmetrical scratches. A pool on the floor. A bloody sock. A red shoe.

"Thank God," he said. "Please help me."

I screamed. The sound rose out of me like an ambulance's wail. It seemed bigger than my body, shrill and high.

"You get out," I shouted. "This is my house. You get out!"

"Calm down," he said.

"Look at this mess. Blood all over Darlene's floors!"

He stepped back, holding up his intact hand in a placating gesture. I stepped back too, doubling the space between us. I inhaled the tang of the air freshener, my fists clenched at my sides. For the first time, I noticed that the man had a messy brown ponytail and a thick golden beard.

"I don't know how bad I'm hurt," he said. "I might be dying."

I stared at him.

"I'm so glad it's you," he said. "I wanted it to be you."

Confused, I let my gaze roam across him again. He was tall, lanky, and angular. One hand was broken, maybe beyond repair. He did not seem to have the right number of digits, and the ones that remained were no longer uniform in length. The pinkie and ring finger had been reduced to sodden stumps. His jeans were not blue anymore, soaked with mud and blood. His weight was planted on the right side, the left knee bent, his foot just skimming the ground. His shirt was inked with red—squiggles and smears like an alien alphabet—but I could not see a wound there. He was both dark and pale, with a broad jaw and straight nose. At last, I met his eyes.

He swayed and stretched out a hand, groping for the wall to steady himself. With a wail of elation, I ran to my brother.

6

Tucker told me to feed him, so I made him a sandwich. He asked for water, so I fetched him a glass, which he drank in frantic assault, spilling it down his chin. I fixed him another sandwich. I refilled his glass again and again. He ate and drank as though he had not seen food or water in weeks. In his haste, he smeared blood on the bread and ate it anyway.

He told me to help him out of his clothes. The smell coming off him was intense—mud, sweat, a tang of sewage, and some kind of curdled sourness that reminded me of the dead mice I occasionally found in Darlene's traps in the kitchen. Tucker's clothes were stiff with blood, which presented a problem. The fabric would not fold. Several buttons were pasted shut. His wounds were too severe to allow for contact, and I could not figure out how to pull his cuff over his mangled hand or tug his pants down without brushing against his injured skin. Eventually I took a pair of scissors and cut the cloth away, as I had seen doctors do on TV. I was no longer nauseous or shaky. The urgency of the situation elevated me into a pragmatic state of mind.

Tucker told me to clean his wounds. He told me I would have to be brave and persist, even if it made him scream. I guided him toward the bathroom ahead of me; the hallway was too narrow to accommodate both of us at once. We did not have a bathtub in the trailer, only a shower stall. With my help, Tucker climbed in, naked now except for his underwear, and slumped down onto the tile. From this angle, I could see the full extent of his thinness—the definition of his ribs, the knobs of his spine. He laid his cheek against the wall and closed his eyes.

I knew how to care for cuts and bruises, but this was new territory. After a moment's consideration, I grabbed Darlene's soap, which was unscented and hypoallergenic. Perhaps it would be easier on my brother's injuries than Jane's floral body washes. I poured a dollop into my palm, then hesitated, reluctant to touch him. It seemed that he might have dozed off, lolling on the tile.

"Do it," he said without opening his eyes.

When I turned on the shower, Tucker flinched away from the sprinkle of water. I lathered up my hands and leaned down, preparing myself. Everything in the bathroom was an unpleasant sea-foam hue, against which the droplets of blood stood out like neon. Gingerly, I took hold of Tucker's damaged fingers. His left pinkie now ended at the second knuckle, his ring finger at the third. The tip of each wound was blackened. There was not much blood, as though the burn had sealed all the fluids in.

His other fingers were scraped and discolored, but intact. I pushed back a few flaps of loose flesh to lather the crevices beneath. Tucker growled. The skin on his palm did not seem like skin anymore—it was too sticky, too raw. Crouching awkwardly beside the toilet, I plucked pebbles from the exposed ribbons of his muscle. I rubbed soap into every orifice I could see. Froth and blood swirled down the drain. The door to the shower stall was open, wetting the bathroom floor, the toilet, and me.

Eventually I turned my attention to Tucker's calf. On closer inspection, the gashes in his leg did not seem as dire. They were long but not terribly deep. I washed them out as best I could, guiding the water through a riverbed of corrugated muscle, the liquid clouded with grit and soap. Tucker did not wince or protest as I finished my work. He was now ominously silent.

"Get up," I said.

He did not move. I tapped his shoulder.

"Get *up*."

He stirred, blinking at me.

Slowly, slowly, I helped him back into the living room. He leaned on me so heavily that I thought I might crumple beneath his weight. As I laid him down on the couch, he seemed to be drifting in and out of consciousness. He would lie quiet for a moment, breathing in the deep, rhythmic manner of someone asleep, and his muscles would go slack as though he had slipped beyond me. Then he would twitch and grimace. He would open his eyes and give me instructions. I got gauze and medical tape from the first aid kit. I smeared disinfectant—a few years out of date—onto his lacerations. I patched him up as best I could. He looked like a mummy when I was through, his hand and calf swaddled in clumsy loops of white.

As Tucker lay with his eyes closed, I realized that he was still dressed in only his underwear, nearly naked. I was confronted with the undeniable maleness of him—narrow hips, his chest a flat plane, his nipples embedded in a tussock of fur like strawberries in a garden, his legs devoid of excess fat, a man made of corners and lines. His white briefs were soaked, which meant that I could see the dark mat of his pubic hair through the fabric. I could make out the outline of his genitalia, a limp, coiled snake. I had lived in a landscape of women for most of my life. I had seen Darlene and Jane in every state of undress, but Tucker was a different animal altogether. His masculinity was astonishing.

"Does Darlene have any drugs?" he said.

"What?" I said, recalling myself to the moment.

"The prescription kind."

"I don't think so. Just stuff for headaches and cramps."

He shrugged. "Give me what you've got."

I found a few bottles of painkillers in the medicine cabinet. Normally I was not supposed to touch them. Tucker shook a handful from each container into his palm, not bothering to count the pills.

"I'm cold," he said.

Before my eyes, his flesh became textured with goosebumps. I hurried to the closet and dug through Darlene's things. There was an old pair of sweatpants, a stretched, faded T-shirt, and some wool socks. I was not sure what to do for shoes—Tucker's were too bloodstained to be salvaged, and his feet were too big to cram into Darlene's sneakers.

Back in the living room, I helped my brother dress. He was shivering so badly that I had to be firm with him, guiding his movements like a parent with a newborn. Blood had already started to soak through the gauze on his hand.

"I'm really here, aren't I?" he said.

"Yes," I said.

When he was clothed, I sat beside him on the couch, not touching him. For the first time, I could smell Tucker himself—not his wounds, not his filth, not the blood. There was a ripe adolescent tang that was all his own.

"Did it work?" he said.

I did not know what he was talking about, but it seemed best to placate him.

"Yes," I said.

"It went okay? I thought I planned for everything."

"You did great."

I glanced around the trailer. Tucker's clothes were piled by the wall, stained and sliced into swatches. His bloody foot had left a track across the floor. The bathroom was damp and scarlet splattered. Even the front door was streaked with red.

"What time is it?" Tucker said.

I looked at the clock on the microwave.

"Seven," I said in surprise. Only a few hours had gone by. It seemed like much longer. The sky was hazy through the window, the sun hovering above the horizon, filling the trailer with a thick, other-worldly light.

"Time keeps *passing*," Tucker said in frustration. "Listen, you've got to clean up now. Clean up everything, okay? Get rid of the whole mess. Make it look like it did before."

I was not expecting this. I anticipated praise for my heroism, rather than a list of new tasks, but it did not occur to me to disobey my brother. While he rested, I scrubbed down the surfaces in the bathroom and shoved the towels into the washing machine, making sure to use cold water that would rinse the blood out rather than hot that would bake it in. I mopped. As I wiped the front door, spray bottle in one hand, roll of paper towels in the other, I felt halfway between worlds. Behind me the sun was setting, the flat Southwestern sky dotted with oval clouds. Inside the trailer, my absent, present brother lay on the couch. With each blink, I was surprised again to find him there—as large as life, at once mysterious and solid, unknown and familiar.

"Get rid of my clothes," he said.

"Okay."

He propped himself up on his elbows, grimacing with pain.

"You've got to destroy them," he said. "Maybe bury them or . . . Can you burn them? That would be best."

I was not supposed to play with fire, but I sometimes did anyway. I knew how to light a match, how long I could hold my finger over the flame before it began to hurt. The neighbors kept a metal trash can outside their back door. Mr. Avila once told me that he burned his old documents since it was "better than a shredder when the government came knocking." He and his wife were not particularly friendly, but I was used to their cantankerous ways and felt comfortable trespassing on their property in an emergency.

I collected Tucker's clothes—what was left of them—and slipped outside again. Evening had fallen, enriching the air and lengthening the shadows. The wind carried the drone of cicadas. There was no one in sight. The Avilas would be at work until late; she was a waitress, he a bartender, always on the graveyard shift, furious whenever Jane woke them on weekend mornings kicking her soccer ball against our wall. Now I stuffed Tucker's clothes into the trash can and fetched Mr. Avila's bottle of kerosene from its hiding place. I lit a match, and the evidence went up with a whoosh of heat and light.

For a moment, I stood in the gloaming, savoring the hum of the insects, the faint glimmer of stars. The wind was cool. Summer was coming, and summer in Oklahoma was no joke, but for now the breeze lifted the tumble of curls away from my shoulders.

I was waiting for Darlene. I had been waiting for her since Tucker's arrival. With part of my mind, I had been listening for the crackle of car wheels in the gravel, the slam of a door. She would bring Jane with her, but Jane was not important to me now. Darlene would know what to do. When she arrived, the burden of Tucker's dreadful injuries would be lifted out of my hands. I would be free to celebrate the fact that he had returned to us.

As I entered the trailer, my brother rose to his feet, limping toward me. He looked strange in his too-small outfit, his ankles and a swath of belly exposed, as though he had been stretched like a rubber doll.

"What are you doing?" I said. "Don't get up."

"I have to," he said.

"Darlene will be home soon. She'll take care of you."

"No," he said savagely. "No Darlene. Nobody else."

He reached the front door and slumped against the jamb, breathing hard. He towered over me, his face contorted with pain.

"Help me down to the ravine," he said. "I can sleep there for a while."

"In the *ravine*?"

"I've been there for the past two nights. It's fine, Cora. Come on."

I opened my arms in an instinctive gesture, barring his exit. For the first time, I felt a surge of panic.

"I don't understand what's happening," I said. "You just got back. I missed you so much. Darlene has to see you. She'll take care of everything, I promise. You're hurt so bad, Tucker. You can't leave. You can't leave us again."

My brother reached out and cupped my chin in his palm. The touch sent out waves of familiarity strong enough to make me shiver. This was a customary gesture of his, reassuring and gentle. I remembered it at a level beneath consciousness. He had done it since I was little.

"I only want you," he said. "Not the others."

"But—"

"I'm not going far. You'll know where I am."

"I don't know," I said dubiously.

"We'll work everything out. Just you and me." He smiled. "Say it."

"You and me," I echoed.

"Good girl. Now help me outside."

I nestled against him, his uninjured arm digging into my shoulder. We stumbled together into the soup of evening. The sun had set, the high clouds painted with watercolor hues. We were operating as two halves of a single entity, albeit a lopsided and ungainly one. My brother grunted and swore, his heart thumping in my ear. The ravine looked ominous at this time of day, an absence, a hole in the world. Tucker and I made our way there at a snail's pace. I could feel the expansion and contraction of his ribs against my cheek. In the twilight, Shady Acres lived up to its name, a patchwork of silk and slate.

At the edge of the gully, Tucker sat down. It was more like collapsing, his legs folding, a gasp escaping him. The short walk from the trailer had cost him everything. I perched beside him, knotting my hands together anxiously.

"I want you to stay home from school tomorrow," Tucker said. "Can you swing that?"

"I guess so," I said.

"Tell Darlene you're sick. She'll leave you here alone, right?"

"Yeah."

"Good. We'll have the whole day together. We can figure out everything then."

His face was infused with affection. His eyes were the same brown as mine.

"You're my favorite," he said.

I did not want him to go. As he began his descent into the ravine, sliding down the slope on his backside, controlling his speed with his good hand, his ponytail swinging, his feet skidding, I felt a cry rise in my throat. Tucker did not hear me. He dipped into the pool of shadows, melting away.

7

My sisters came home a few minutes later. I was seated at the table when I heard car wheels in the driveway. I ran outside and plowed into Darlene, my face in her belly, my arms around her hips. She gave a dry cackle.

"What the heck?" she said. "You never hug me."

"I like you," I said.

She rumpled my hair. "I like you too, wild thing."

I pulled away and looked up at her. At once, I could tell that she was suffering from one of her migraines. I knew the signs—unnatural pallor, a tautness around the eyes, her shoulders rounded. My heart sank. I should, perhaps, have expected this. Darlene was getting her period, which often triggered a migraine. She and Jane were synced up; one week of every month was always fraught. My sisters' moods would clash in midair like the shifting winds and static electricity of a thunderstorm. Sometimes there were quarrels, sometimes shared crying jags about puppies on TV. This was what I had to look forward to. In a few years, I would join the coven.

Jane was already crashing into the house. Darlene followed sluggishly. She kicked off her shoes and set her bag down on the table.

"Y'all can get your own dinner, right?" she said.

"Does popcorn count?" I said.

"Tonight? Sure."

She peeled off her pantyhose and tugged her skirt down, showing none of her customary modesty, too tired to bother with her robe. She shook her hair out of its ponytail. There was a dent in the dark mane where the rubber band had been. Jane flopped onto the couch, still dressed in her smelly shin guards. I hovered in the middle of the room, feeling as though wings were beating in my chest.

Darlene removed her glasses and rubbed her temples. "I'm going to go sleep in y'all's bed for a while," she said. "Get me up when you're ready to hit the hay."

"All right," Jane said, her gaze on her phone.

I watched Darlene disappear into the bedroom. She flicked off the light and shut the door.

Even then, I understood on some level that my fate had just been sealed. If Darlene had been herself that night—alert and wary—she would have noticed that something was amiss. She would have turned her attention to me, her gaze as bright and unsparing as a bare bulb in a police interrogation room. She would have wormed the truth out of me—about Tucker, about everything. She would have stopped what I could already feel was coming.

Instead, I spent the evening on the couch with Jane, sharing a bowl of popcorn. As I got myself a soda, as I changed into my rocket ship pajamas, as I leaned against my sister's shoulder, I felt as twitchy as a fawn in the forest. I had a secret. I had never had a secret before. It was on the tip of my tongue, taking up all the room in my brain, cupped in both my empty hands. My voice sounded odd to my own ears. Beyond the window, my fire was still burning in the Avilas' garbage can, pale smoke trickling upward.

I glanced around the trailer. There were no photographs of Tucker here. Every snapshot of him was hidden away. Mama and Daddy were framed on the kitchen counter, smiling in their wedding outfits. My sisters and I were displayed on the fridge—grinning in school pictures or posing with our arms looped awkwardly around one another—but Tucker was entirely absent. If you walked into No. 43 unawares, you wouldn't know that we ever had a brother.

Jane changed the channel to a cop show. She glanced up from the little screen in her hands to the big one across the room every time there was gunfire. She announced that the show was too violent for me but did not turn it off. In the distance, the cicadas sang with renewed intensity, a nerve-jangling, rhythmic screeching. The moon wrapped itself in the curtains. Somewhere far off, a coyote howled, a guttural cry, pleading but unanswered.

As the night wore on, I found myself transported by recollections. Contact with Tucker had dredged hidden things to the surface. These memories were powerful, displacing what I was actually seeing, shoving Jane and her cell phone into the periphery. I remembered dancing with Tucker, standing on his feet as he pivoted and twirled, the music loud. This was an encounter from three years ago—post-tornado, pre-abandonment. I had been small enough then that my head did not reach his waist. His hands guided me as confidently and irresistibly as a puppeteer.

I remembered sitting with Tucker in a lobby. We were waiting for Darlene to finish an interview. He was spinning a story about the two of us on a journey in an enchanted kingdom. Though he was plainly making it up as he went along—every now and then pausing for inspiration or correcting himself, "No, we didn't go that way after all . . ."—he spoke with such assurance that even now, I still remembered his tale. Surrounded by the buzz of fluorescent lights and the stale taste of uncirculated air, Tucker and I were gone—climbing a mountain, fording a river, charming a dragon, mapping a deep forest, and finding a happy ending, relying only on our wits and each other. I had been young enough then to step inside a game of make-believe and shut the door behind me. Tucker transported me from our world to another, better place.

Perhaps I was still young enough. Perhaps I was being transported now.

The news came on. A female announcer appeared, standing in front of the familiar sight of the cosmetics factory. She had skin like amber and a braid made up of tinier braids.

"Breaking news," she said.

Jane set her phone aside, gazing at the TV with curiosity. The announcer touched her ear, then nodded and spoke to the camera. Her languid drawl suggested she was from somewhere farther south than Mercy. Louisiana, maybe.

"The police have enhanced the surveillance video," she said. "They now have a workable sketch to share with the public. Please be on the lookout for this man. He may be armed and should be considered extremely dangerous. If you see him, do not engage with him. Dial the hotline shown here and wait for assistance."

A drawing flashed on the screen. Even before I registered what I was seeing, I felt a frisson of fear. I might have moaned aloud, but Jane did not notice. She was frowning at the TV, one hand twirling a lock of her hair.

The man in the picture was Tucker. Of course it was Tucker. His prominent brow. His broad jaw with the dimple at the front. His ponytail of lazy curls. It was a pen-and-ink sketch, skillfully rendered, showing my brother's face tilted at a three-quarter angle, his mouth in a determined jut, his expression defiant.

If I had been older, I would have figured out the truth much earlier. But I was only nine. I had not yet asked myself how and why Tucker had been so badly injured. In the manner of a child, I was still busy with the essential revelation that he was home. I certainly had not made a connection between the recent news story and Tucker, between an injured man on the loose and my injured brother, between the blood found at Jolly Cosmetics and the blood in our bathroom.

My breath turned fast and shallow. To my eyes, it was obviously a sketch of Tucker, but I was not sure whether the resemblance would have occurred to me if I had not seen him just a few hours earlier. Some of the details were off. In the drawing, the man's neck was slender, whereas Tucker's was muscular. The man's eyes were scrunched and aggressive, whereas Tucker's were wide and watchful. The man's eyebrows were atilt, whereas Tucker's were straight across. Still, the artist had captured the gist of him.

A band seemed to constrict around my chest. Jane gazed at me in consternation as a wheeze escaped me.

"For heaven's sake!" she said. "What's wrong with you?"

I did not break down. I did not cry. I did not tell her anything. I waited for the agitation to pass through me like an earthquake, the vibration dancing across the length of my small body. Jane turned off the TV. There was no other light in the room. Shadows pooled around us. The moon was hidden, the cicadas finally silent for the night. We had outlasted them.

"Enough TV for you, young lady," Jane said.

Through tacit agreement, we decided not to wake Darlene and kick her out of our bed. Jane tunneled beneath the covers, and I folded my body against her. Darlene rolled closer to the wall to make room for us. That night—my last night at home—my sisters and I slept crushed together, not an inch of space between us.

8

When I reached the ravine, I heard a rustle at the bottom. My brother climbed out of the thicket, grinning up at me with twigs in his hair.

Tucker was not dead. I had been afraid of this—awful injuries, no medical attention, a night spent in a ditch. I had imagined insects crawling on him, making nests in his hair.

"Took you long enough," he said.

He scrabbled toward me, wincing but climbing fast, a hint of his previous athleticism visible in his movements. The gulch was filled with brambles and vines, scratching him with thorns and stuccoing his clothes with nettles. The sun was low in the sky, hidden behind a swatch of filmy cloud. The cicadas were just waking up, chiming here and there. Their discordant song was not yet at full throttle.

"Where's my breakfast?" Tucker said.

In the trailer, he consumed a box of frozen waffles. He emptied the syrup and finished the butter. He scrambled a dozen eggs and ate them all. He complained that there was no bacon. He told me to do the dishes, and then he told me not to bother. He turned on the TV, switched it off, and reached for the radio. When a country song came on, he flipped the dial all the way to the right and sang along in a voice as rough and sweet as brown sugar. He mimed a two-step dance move on his good foot. He was not yet at full strength; pain flickered across his face. But he was well enough to take a shower without my assistance, cursing beneath the hiss of water. He was well enough to change his own bandages, though I helped him tape up his hand. He was well enough to root through Darlene's closet for a better outfit, standing with a towel around his waist, his long hair dripping down his bare back. It was delicious to look at him, and a little painful, like eating too much birthday cake. Finally he unearthed a novelty shirt from the state fair large enough to fit him. He found a pair of plastic flip-flops that could accommodate his feet.

At last, he led me to the couch, sitting down with a lurch and a grimace. His injured hand was curled in his lap, blood mottling the gauze.

"I saw you on the news," I said.

The words came out in a rush. I found that I could not look directly at him.

"Yeah?" he said.

"You blew up the cosmetics factory."

I was not sure how he would respond. On some level, I was hoping he would deny everything.

Instead, Tucker laughed. With his good hand, he reached out and squeezed my fingers.

"Awesome," he said. "I was on the *news*. Man, I wish I could've seen it. My fifteen minutes of fame, and I spent the whole thing in a ditch."

"I don't understand . . ." I could not find the right words. Perhaps there were no right words for this situation.

"You can ask me anything," Tucker said. "No secrets here."

"Did you really make a pipe bomb?"

"Yes. Actually, I made three."

I kept my gaze locked on our intertwined fingers. The pressure of his grip increased, crushing my hand like a flower in a press.

"I cut the pipe myself," he said. "Then I went to a shooting range and gathered up some of the gunpowder off the floor. That's the best method. It's not specific to a particular brand. It doesn't leave clues."

At last, I managed to meet his eyes. There was no shame or regret in his expression.

"Did you feel the explosion?" he said.

"Yeah," I said. "The ground shook."

"I thought I had the timing of the fuses figured out," he said. "Three simultaneous blasts." He let go of me, stroking his bandages. "One of them went off early. That's how I got hurt. I'll get it right next time."

"Next time?"

"Sure. My work isn't done. Not by a long shot."

The light in the room changed. Clouds were scudding across the sky, creating rhythms of gloom and glow. The sun threaded bright ribbons through Tucker's hair. For a moment I experienced an eerie illusion of mirroring. From this angle, with that gleam on his cheek, there was a powerful resemblance between us.

"Three years after the tornado," he said. "Three years to the day. It was perfect, don't you think?"

I did not answer. I was experiencing a collision of irreconcilable emotions, horror and gut-wrenching love and slow anger splashing and caroming off one another.

"But the bomb wasn't the important part, Cora," he said. "I freed all the animals. Every bunny and dog. You heard about that, right? It was on the news too?"

"Yes."

"Good," he said. "I looked into Jolly Cosmetics after they poisoned our whole neighborhood. That place is evil. So many rats. You should have seen the state they were in. A few had been intentionally blinded. Some had their fur shaved off, and the bare skin was covered in hives and boils. The scientists were using beagles for their experiments, too. Do you know why?" He did not pause for a response. "Beagles are so sweet tempered that you can do pretty much anything to them and they won't turn on you. Shoot them full of poison or amputate a limb. They never get mean, even when they're dying. They'll still wag their tails when they see you coming. It makes it easier on the researchers, you see."

His voice was hard. He was glaring into the middle distance as though seeing something I could not. The sunlight shifted again, bisecting his face, illuminating his cheekbone. Now he resembled Darlene.

"I learned that a while ago," he said. "Jolly Cosmetics had a whole wing filled with hound dogs. It haunted me."

"Oh."

"There was a chimpanzee," he said. "Can you imagine? I didn't know that beforehand. Those animals are sentient. No one to help her."

Tucker glanced around the room as though he had forgotten where he was. He rolled both shoulders backward, working out the kinks in his muscles.

"One day I'll explain everything," he said.

"Okay," I said.

"Do you have a suitcase?"

"What?" I said, thrown by the change of subject.

"A duffel bag or something. To pack your stuff."

I frowned, trying to gather my wits. I was unsuccessful.

"I don't understand," I said.

"Oh," he said, a slow sigh.

The sun winked out, leaving a cold, sleepy pall. Tucker fingered his hair, which was loose, drying in untidy ringlets.

"I haven't told you the plan yet, have I?" he said.

"No."

"How old are you?"

"Nine," I said. "You?"

"Twenty."

In one smooth movement, he tugged his hair into a topknot at the back of his head. I waited for him to secure it with a rubber band, but he didn't. His mahogany mane was thick and curly enough to cling to itself like velcro.

"There's a connection between us, isn't there?" he said. "Always has been."

I nodded.

"You remember the night we snuck out and went to find the horses?"

"I think about it all the time," I said shyly.

"Me too. Remember how the horses came right up to us like they knew us? Remember how I carried you all the way home?"

"I remember," I said.

He was watching me steadily, a grin hovering around his mouth. A single brown curl detached from his bun and twisted across his cheek.

"I want you to come with me," he said.

"Where?"

"Everywhere."

He swept a hand toward the wall, an expansive gesture. Then he laughed, a brash, bright sound. In that moment, I had a sense of wild motion, as though I were caught up in another tornado, a current of air too powerful to resist.

"I've got plans," he said. "I've taken the first step. I freed the animals and I blew the place up. I marked the day."

"Yeah."

"I broke the law," he said. "I broke all kinds of laws. You get that, right?"

"I sure do," I said fervently.

"Now it's time to go on the run." His grin broadened. "The cops are going to be coming for me."

He was looking at me without blinking, his eyes as warm and inviting as a swimming hole in summer. I felt myself smiling in an involuntary echo.

"You trust me, don't you?" he said.

"Yes."

"It's time for magic, Cora," he said. "Let's leave this place behind."

He brushed the hair out of my face. He tapped my nose.

"But . . ." I began hesitantly. "What about Darlene and Jane?"

His countenance darkened. Every new emotion seemed to consume him entirely, remaking his posture, requiring its own facial expression and set of gestures.

"No," he said. "Darlene can't see the big picture. She's caught up in the machine. She's lost." He paused, frowning, then said, "I never wanted to leave y'all. You know that, right?"

"You didn't?"

"You're my family, Cora," he said. "I love you more than life."

"You do?"

"This isn't real." He thumped his good hand on the arm of the couch, maybe indicating the trailer, maybe the whole of Mercy. "Not the real world. This is mundane human nonsense. I can't stay here. I can't exist in this place."

He reached toward me, cupping my chin once more.

"It's time to get to work," he said. "There's so much to do. Let's go right now. You and me together."

I experienced a shiver of déjà vu. It seemed that I had dreamed this or heard about it once in a story—Tucker's hopeful face, his question hanging in the air between us, the stillness of the room, the possibility of transformation. I felt as though I already knew my answer, as though I had made up my mind a long time ago.

9

Tucker found an old blue knapsack of Darlene's, bigger than my school bag. Together we filled it with my teddy bear, my lucky red shirt, my favorite picture book, my rocket ship pajamas, the locket Darlene had given me, and my toothbrush. On Tucker's recommendation, I detached a few snapshots of Darlene and Jane from the fridge and tucked them in the front pocket.

"You don't want to forget what they look like," he said sagely.

For his part, he grabbed a framed photo of Mama off the countertop—Mama astride a horse, laughing at the camera. Tucker gazed at the picture with a mournful smile, then shoved it into the backpack too and told me to get the lead out. I did as he instructed, gathering up pants and shorts, folding my tank tops and sweatshirts, and locating my heaviest coat. I stuffed a pair of rain boots into a side pocket. I rolled my socks into tight balls to cram them into the leftover spaces. I brought as many pairs of panties as I could fit.

"Good thing your clothes are tiny," Tucker said.

When I was done, the backpack was too heavy for me to lift, but my brother swung it onto his shoulder with ease. He was using a branch as a makeshift cane, which allowed him to move more comfortably. It freed me up, too, from having to serve as his default limb. At the front door, I paused to take one last look around No. 43. Tucker was already outside, whistling between his teeth. I stared in turn at the kitchen table, the TV, and the couch. I tried to sear every particle of the place into my memory.

I did not have a clear sense of what was going to happen next. In a way, I did not care. In that moment, I trusted Tucker the way a child trusts a parent—absolutely, unquestioningly, joyfully. His time away from home had not broken my faith in him. If anything, I felt as though our connection was stronger than ever. I had never bothered to consider the way I loved my sisters; our mutual affection was as unremarked as oxygen. But Tucker was something else. His love for me, and mine for him, was intoxicating, sweetening the very air I breathed.

There was relief, too, in my submission to his will. Darlene had raised me, but she never pretended to guide me with the confidence of a mother, as much as I sometimes wanted her to. She was just doing the best she could in tough circumstances, trying to get Jane and me through high school, looking after us in her exhausted, well-intentioned way. For years, I had yearned for the safety that other children seemed to feel around their parents. They were tended like flowers in a garden, watered, weeded, and protected from harm. I had longed for that sense of security all my life and had never once experienced it. Other children always seemed weightless to me. The burden of their lives was borne in somebody else's hands.

But Tucker was here to change all that. He had a plan. No one ever had a plan for me before. He wanted to lead as much as I wanted to be led.

"The car is this way," he said, pointing down the lane.

The afternoon was uncommonly cool. Heavy clouds roiled along the horizon, promising rain. The air was murky enough that Tucker and I cast no shadows. Even with the aid of his walking stick, he had to stride with care. He was able to put his weight only on the toes of his injured leg, not the heel. The backpack on his shoulder threw off his center of gravity. With each step, his bandaged hand swiveled awkwardly in space.

The more we walked, the more he bled. Movement reopened all his cuts. His pant leg was soon stained maroon. His flip-flops slapped and squished beneath him, one dry, the other slick. In a perfect world, his gashes ought to have been sewn shut by a surgeon in a hospital. Instead, he would have to make do with the contents of a first aid kit. He was expecting to have scars.

"I had to park pretty far away," he said. "I couldn't leave the car in Shady Acres. Somebody would've noticed it."

In the distance, there was a rumble of thunder. I could smell rain, though the sky above us was still a clean, cottony white. The storm lurked near the horizon, where they always did.

At the main road, we turned west, staying on the shoulder, watching semis and pickup trucks pass, blinded by the explosion of dust cast off from each vehicle, sharing sips of water, Tucker in front, me behind. The temperature dropped with each gust of wind. The thunder came with increasing frequency, making the tree branches judder overhead. Shards of lightning illuminated inconsistencies in the thickness of the cloud layer. The storm was not yet close enough to reveal the causality between the flash and the sound; the lightning pulsed and the thunder moaned, but they did not relate to one another in any perceptible pattern. The clouds darkened like wet charcoal. An occasional droplet marked the pavement. Tucker was no longer bleeding quite as freely. His injured leg was a brown, sticky column now, the pant leg attached to his skin by lashes of dried blood, his flip-flop glued to his foot.

At last, we reached the dirt lane. I knew the place by sight, though

I had never actually turned and followed the narrow path among the trees. The forest was an old one, the trunks wide and swaddled with vines. A single house stood off to the side, ramshackle and unclean. The lawn was decorated by rusted cars in various stages of disuse. Grass grew inside one engine block. The building had window screens so thick with dirt that you could not see through them. Perhaps this was just as well.

Tucker limped onward, now gasping with each step, and I trotted beside him. Rain began to fall. The canopy of branches rustled and shook overhead, the leaves dancing. The drizzle was chilly on my skin, blackening the ground. Tucker tipped his head back to feel the rain on his face.

The car was well hidden—a tawny station wagon camouflaged against the tawny underbrush. I could easily have walked past the spot without noticing anything. As I pushed through the branches to the passenger's side, twigs snagged in my hair and scraped my skin. Tucker collapsed into the driver's seat, pale and clammy. For a while we sat like that, rain falling on the roof. The windshield was a mosaic of water and light, dead bugs and bird droppings. I glanced around the interior of the car and saw evidence that my brother had been living there. A tumble of dirty clothes was stuffed beneath the back windshield. There was a grocery bag filled with granola bars and potato chips. There was a pillow on the backseat.

Tucker groaned. He stuck the key in the ignition.

"Are you sure—" I began.

"Don't worry."

"Maybe you should wait until you catch your breath."

"I'm fine," he said, starting the engine.

"Where are we going?" I asked. This question had been ricocheting around my brain for a while. It felt good to let it out.

"A safe place," Tucker said.

"Okay," I said.

He backed the car out of the thicket with a screech of twigs on metal. I flinched at the sound. He swung the wheel, steered up the bumpy lane, and flipped on the windshield wipers, which functioned imperfectly, smearing and blurring more than they cleaned. Tucker hit the gas. The station wagon was old enough that it whistled and roared at high speeds, the wind wailing through chinks in the casing.

"Where are we going?" I asked again.

"Home," Tucker said.

We drove toward downtown Mercy. I saw Shady Acres, smaller at this distance, gone in the blink of an eye. We passed the movie theater, the high school, and the public library. The clouds hung low, shimmering with lightning. Tucker switched on the radio and smiled at the pop song that played.

There was a crash of thunder, the sky shattering right above our heads. All along the block, the lights went out. The warm glow of the restaurant on the corner vanished. The streetlamps, which had come on automatically in response to the darkness of the storm, fizzled into gray. Power outages were common in bad weather, but just now it seemed like a sign, though I wasn't sure what it might mean.

We left the grid of central Mercy behind and entered the winding roads and spacious sprawl of the outskirts. There was no one in sight; the rain had forced everyone indoors. With each mile, the neighborhood grew shabbier. The houses were farther apart and seemed less and less cared for. Acres of grass relinquished to weeds. Wooden fences with gaps like missing teeth. The street a quarry of potholes.

I knew where we were going now. I had not been there in a long time—three years, to be precise. I saw broken windows that had been replaced by cardboard and porch steps crumbling into mossy ruin. Even if the power had not gone out across Mercy, I doubted whether the electricity worked in this neighborhood anymore.

Then we turned a corner, and the last vestiges of civilization fell away. I could see the path the finger of God had gouged across the world. The trees were splintered into forked fragments. Telephone poles lay down instead of standing up. The houses were not houses anymore. Some had holes ripped in their walls, showing empty rooms where vines had begun to grow. Others had been wrenched sideways on their frames, leaning perilously, tethered to the earth by struts of wood, wire, and plumbing. And a few were gone altogether. Only the concrete shapes of their foundations remained.

I realized that the chaos was somewhat contained. It did not look the way I remembered it—right after the tornado. The cleanup crews had done what they could, bulldozing everything into piles, clearing the street, and heaping fallen trees into bristling forts, now probably inhabited by animals. Here and there in the unkempt prairie were scars of bare dirt. Presumably these were the places where the pools of toxic waste from Jolly Cosmetics had rendered the earth barren. Not even our hardy Oklahoma grass could overcome the noxious sting of those chemicals. A few chain-link fences still marked the delineation between acres of property that no one owned anymore.

It made me think of Jane and her Legos. She had been obsessed with them once; she would build elaborate castles that no one was ever allowed to touch. Her work would stand on the kitchen table for days like a sculpture on display at a museum. Then she would destroy the structure as meticulously as she had crafted it, separating each tiny block from every other, reducing it to the smallest possible parts.

The tornado had done something similar here. The houses had been deconstructed into bricks and wood and dented appliances and unattached doors and fat, candy-colored wads of insulation. Then the jumbled contents were heaped into hillocks and towers. It was no longer a residential area—it was the plastic tub where Jane kept her Legos piled carelessly when they were not in use.

Home, Tucker had said.

He swung the wheel, and the station wagon skidded off the road into the grass, the axels screeching in protest. I climbed out of the car, looking up at the hazy sky, inhaling the smell of mud. The rain had all but stopped.

Tucker spent a few minutes hiding the vehicle from sight, pausing every few seconds to breathe deeply and glower with his eyes shut. I stood out of harm's way as he dragged a section of roofing tar paper from a nearby heap and laid it over the engine block. He leaned a square of plywood against the side window, then limped out into the empty street to examine his work, verifying that the car would not be noticeable from this vantage point.

"Good enough," he said, and led me into the wreckage.

We passed a smashed dishwasher and a pile, taller than I was, of what appeared to be crushed furniture. We stepped into the yard that once belonged to our family. I could see what was left of the barn—a single wall, sagging to the side and tinged with a mottled blush, the weather-beaten remains of the cheerful red paint I remembered. I could see a few shards of fencing still standing sadly where the cows lived long ago. There was a gleam of black in the grass, maybe the husk of a fifty-five-gallon drum.

"Is this safe?" I asked. "With the . . . the toxins?"

"Come on," Tucker said.

A staircase led down into a basement that was filled with scrap and chaff, coils of wire and masonry, muddy at the bottom, carpeted by dead leaves. I picked my way down the steps. The boards were spongy beneath my weight. The basement floor was uneven, glistening with puddles. I thought I heard the scurry of a mouse, or maybe a scorpion. Amid the fallen beams and chunks of concrete, it took me a moment to locate the door of the tornado shelter.

"The police are looking for us," Tucker said. "They'll expect us to run, but we won't. We'll wait it out right here. Do you see?"

I bit my lip.

"This is no-man's-land," he said. "The perfect hideout. We'll drink bottled water, okay? It won't kill us to live here for just a little while."

The rain had dwindled into mist, floating on the air, collecting against my skin like cheesecloth. I was damp, glimmering, breathless. Tucker reached the bunker door and laid his injured palm reverently against it.

"They'll drop a net over the whole state," he said. "Roadblocks and checkpoints, a full-on manhunt. But we'll be hiding right under their noses. Eventually they'll have to take their focus off Mercy and look elsewhere. Then we can make our move."

He tugged the door open with a groan of hinges. The shelter was cramped and dim, smaller than I remembered. The shelves were stocked with the same canned goods, gallon jugs of water, and batteries our father prepared so many years ago. Nothing had been used or touched or taken. My family abandoned the bunker as soon as the storm passed, and no one had set foot inside since. Tucker lifted a pack of matches from a shelf and lit a candle, shielding the flame inside the bandaged curl of his palm. I stepped deeper into the musty cave. He shut the door, sealing out the light.

And just like that, I was gone.

JUNE

10

The thunderstorm began in the afternoon, not long after the animals entered the supermarket. Darlene was working the cash register. Everything was grating on her nerves: the fluorescent lights, the saccharine pop music on the overhead speakers, even the smell of rain gusting through the open door. Her migraine was duller now, diminished but not gone. She rubbed her aching temples.

There was only one customer in the store. Old Mrs. Rodriguez had been wandering the aisles for at least an hour, shuffling behind a shopping cart with a squeaky wheel. Every so often she would consult a list in her pocket with an expression of profound confusion. She stared for so long at the selection of peanut butter jars that Darlene wondered whether the old woman might be suffering a stroke. Even by the standards of a small town, it was a quiet day. Darlene sanitized the conveyer belt. She sorted and resorted the cash in the register. She was considering whether she ought to call Cora at home and check in when a scream rang out.

Baylor crashed out of the storeroom, pale beneath his red hair. He nearly collided with Mrs. Rodriguez as he dashed down the aisle. Baylor was the stock boy. An adult man with the mental range of a schoolchild, he was well into his forties but had always been the stock boy.

"Something got in," he hollered.

"Beg pardon?" Darlene said, startled.

He pelted up to her, out of breath. "I was taking out the trash, and there was an animal in the alley. I don't know what kind. It ran inside. Right by me."

There were three white rats among the shelves. The storeroom was small but contained plenty of places for a rodent to hide—boxes that had not yet been unloaded, stacks of unused grocery bags, shadows in corners. Darlene alternated between chasing the rats with a broom, assuring Mrs. Rodriguez that this was an anomaly rather than an infestation, and calming Baylor down. He was no help. The rats were no help either. Stupefied by panic, they seemed unable to find the back door, though Darlene propped it open and kept shooing them in that direction. They squealed desperately. They dashed the wrong way every time.

The rats were, at least, incapable of camouflage: snow colored and pink eyed. They had clearly been the subject of some kind of experimentation. Each was shaved in a different configuration—one with bare back legs, another with a raw, scarred belly, the third scraped and stubbled all down its spine.

Darlene wondered whether there was someone in particular she ought to call. The rats were obviously runaways from the cosmetics plant. The news had said to keep an eye out for them, but no one had specified what to do next. Jolly Cosmetics was still shut down. She couldn't dial 911 about a few rodents.

At quarter to four, the manager ambled in, late for his shift as usual. Fred was damp around the shoulders from the rain. Darlene had the rats pinned against the wall and was easing them toward the door with her broom. Baylor stood in the corner, pointing and shouting, "They're over there! Right there!"

Fred took in the scene with raised eyebrows.

"What's all this?" he said.

Darlene swung her broom, and the rats poured through the back door in tandem, their snaky tails whipping around the jamb, gone into the drizzle. Baylor whooped. She wiped the sweat from her brow.

"What happened?" Fred said.

At that instant, there was a crackling sound. The fluorescent lights flickered and dimmed. Everyone looked up in alarm. And then the power went out.

The tinny beat of the music stilled, along with the persistent rumble of machinery from the freezers. It took Darlene a moment to realize what had happened. The wet, gray glow through the back door was now the only light in the storeroom. Baylor remained fearfully in the corner, staring around as though concerned that the blackout might be the second wave of the rats' assault.

The patter of the rain filled the silence. Darlene shot a glance toward the back wall, lined with refrigerators. The glass doors displayed the milk and cartons of eggs within, the panes fogged by condensation. Each unit was now a sleepy, shadowed mystery. The contents would begin to thaw in a matter of hours. Any delay in repairs could cost the supermarket hundreds of dollars in spoiled stock.

Fred gazed at her with an expression of fishlike amazement.

"What on earth is happening?" he cried.

Darlene glanced at her watch.

"Sorry, boss," she said. "It's after four. I'm off the clock."

THE PICKUP TRUCK WAS CANTANKEROUS, as it always was in wet weather. The street was the same smoky hue as the sky. Darlene passed a tawny station wagon going the other way, its windshield too smeared with filth and rain for her to see who might be inside. Long ago, in another life, she might have stayed to help Fred with the situation. It would have been a kindly thing to do, but these days she was "plumb wore out," as Daddy would have said. She had called the electric company's hotline, learning from the mechanical voice on the other end that it could be hours before the power came back on. She discovered that the outage was limited to central Mercy; the farms on the outskirts still had electricity, along with Shady Acres and poor Cora, home sick. She clocked out and departed with a wave, feeling nothing but relief. It was rare and lovely to encounter a problem that did not fall squarely on her shoulders.

Now she switched on the radio, humming along to a country song about heartbreak. She pictured Cora's ashen face and glazed eyes. Her sister had not looked well that morning—distracted, feverish, unlike her usual self.

On the radio, the announcer began to talk about the Oklahoma City bombing. Darlene knew the story, though the tragedy had happened back in 1995, before she was born. At the time, it was the worst terror attack the United States had ever experienced. Darlene had seen pictures of the Murrah Building after the explosion, one whole side calved away like an iceberg tumbling into the sea. Dozens of people died and hundreds of buildings in the downtown area were harmed or destroyed.

By comparison, the bombing at Jolly Cosmetics had not been that bad. Darlene tried to find solace in this. She switched off the radio, listening to the swish and click of the windshield wipers instead. She drove past the church, its steeple black against the haze of rain. Once upon a time, the McClouds were regular visitors there, shepherded by Mama, dressed in their Sunday best. But Daddy was never a religious man, and his lack of faith was cemented by the untimely death of his wife. Darlene had not darkened the church door in years. Cora had never attended services at all.

When Darlene pulled up in front of No. 43, the rain had blown over, leaving a pleasant chill in the air. Moving quietly, she let herself inside. She expected to find the TV on, but the trailer was silent. Cora's bedroom door was shut. Darlene assumed that her sister was napping, which was all to the good. Cora could use the rest, and Darlene never got the place to herself, something like privacy. She changed out of her beige uniform, observing that the pant leg was now stained from an olive oil spill earlier in the day. She sighed. A greasy smudge like that would never completely wash out.

In an ideal world, she would now take a long bubble bath, perhaps with a glass of wine. That was what weary women did on TV. But those women did not live in a single-wide trailer with only a shower stall in the bathroom. Darlene spared a moment's thought for her beloved tub from childhood—antique, claw-footed, mottled from years of use. The basin was big enough to hold both her and Tucker, back when they were still young enough to bathe together.

She closed her eyes. Not a day passed that she did not think of the old house. The curlicued staircase. The lemon-scented kitchen. The leafy sprawl of the oak tree. After Mama's death—a gut punch— Darlene had found reassurance in the house itself. The high rafters. The sun in the curtains. The solidity and constancy of a place that did not change. The seasons that followed were not easy, with newborn Cora squalling in her crib, and Daddy dazed and out of focus, and the long trek to and from school, and diapers to be changed, and Tucker failing out of math, and one of the cows falling ill, and everyone still in mourning. Yet Darlene always felt that the house held her, supported her. Sometimes her lost home seemed more real to her than No. 43.

She wandered the trailer, picking things up and putting them down again. It was difficult for her to relax; she was out of practice. She felt a vague desire to clean. The place was tidy, but there was something a little off, as though someone else had been scrubbing the floors when she wasn't looking. Darlene put on her favorite sweatpants, the ones with OKLAHOMA SOONERS written in glittery letters across the fanny. She poured herself a cup of sweet tea. Her migraine was gone. The rain seemed to have washed it away, rinsing the pain out of her sinuses. Now there was just the concurrent nausea to contend with. Every migraine came with aftershocks: upset stomach, sensitivity to light, fatigue.

Still, she could rest now. Jane would not be home at all; she was having a sleepover with another girl from the soccer team, a halfback with freckles and her own bedroom. Darlene threw a fond glance at Cora's door. They would have a peaceful evening together. They would microwave something nice for supper. Pot roast, maybe.

Darlene gathered up the mail, carrying a stack of glossy catalogues over to the sofa. She never ordered anything from them, but they came anyway. She flipped through the pages, trying to focus her attention on a paragraph about summer pastels.

"Don't worry," she murmured aloud. "Don't worry."

Yet she was worried. Something was not right. She could not focus on the images in front of her. She could not put her finger on what was amiss. Perhaps it was the lab rats in the grocery store. Perhaps it was the bizarre series of recent events in general. She'd been keeping an eye on the story of Jolly Cosmetics in an idle way, too busy to pay much attention. Perhaps it was Cora, who was never sick; Darlene could not remember the last time her sister even had a cold. Perhaps it was the anniversary of the tornado. Darlene hated the annual visit to her parents' grave. It accomplished nothing—no connection, no catharsis—only serving to remind her of everything she had lost. Still, she could not bear to skip it either, to act as though the date meant nothing.

Once, long ago, she looked up the history of the graveyard. She wanted to know why it lay at such a distance from Mercy. To her surprise, she had learned that the cemetery predated the town by half a century. It was older than Jolly Cosmetics, older than the state of Oklahoma itself; the first people to be buried there had been casualties of the land rush. The dead had resided in this place longer than the living, and their home was convenient to nobody but themselves.

There was something important in this idea—Darlene was almost sure—unless it was the kind of half-formed, ethereal insight that sometimes came on the verge of dreaming. She nestled into the warm embrace of the couch and closed her eyes.

11

Darlene woke to the sound of the doorbell. It took her a moment to remember where she was. On the sofa. In the dark. Catalogue splayed open on her lap. Her arm was slung above her head, the fingers numb and tingly.

The doorbell rang again, an insistent clang. With a groan, Darlene got to her feet and flipped on the lights. She observed with some surprise that Cora's door was still shut, then shuffled to the front door and threw it open.

A man stood on the stoop. Darlene did not have her glasses on, so he swam in and out of focus. He appeared to be handsome, with a strong jaw and confident smile. Then she realized that he was a policeman. He wore a bulky uniform that both obscured and highlighted his strong shoulders. He was not alone, either. A female cop stood behind him, smaller and slimmer, milk pale in the porch light, her blue cap nestled on a thatch of flaxen hair.

Darlene fished in her pocket for her glasses. Once she was able to see, she recognized them both. This was the way of things in Mercy; no one was a stranger. She could not quite remember the man's name. They knew each other from high school. A music class, maybe. The woman was Kendra Drake, an old classmate. She flashed a false smile, and Darlene returned the expression like a mirror. Kendra had been both pretty and popular as a girl, wielding her good looks like a blade. It did not surprise Darlene to see that she had grown up to become a cop.

"Roy Rush," the man said, extending an arm.

"Darlene McCloud," she said. "I guess y'all already knew that."

"Band, right?"

"What?" she said, shaking his hand automatically. Then she remembered. She played trombone during her freshman year, before it became clear that she did not have the right kind of fingers. Roy was the drummer. A senior. She had a flash of memory: Roy at the back of the music room, a pleasant combination of muscle and paunch, his hands deft, his skin a rich brown with hints of copper that caught the light.

"We'd like to come in," he said. "Do you have a minute?"

"Sure. I guess."

A wind blew in through the open door. Darlene realized that she was wearing sweatpants and a tank top with no bra. Her nipples stood up in the chill. She folded her arms across her chest. She was still waking up. Awareness swirled through her body like sugar dropped in tea, only gradually absorbed.

Roy and Kendra made a great deal of noise as they strode into the living room, their uniforms rustling, holsters squeaking. Darlene perched on the arm of the couch and motioned for them to take the cushions. Roy smelled like cigarettes. Kendra's beauty had curdled over the years. Her scowl no longer had the seductive quality that Darlene remembered.

"We need to ask you a few questions," Roy said.

She nodded. "What's wrong? Did something happen?"

"Three people live in this house, is that right?" he said. "You and two sisters?"

"That's right."

Her heart seemed to be beating off-rhythm, giving strange little spasms that sent crackles of electricity through her body. On TV shows, the arrival of police officers at an odd hour always presaged a terrible injury, even a death.

"Was there an accident?" she asked. "Is Jane okay?"

"Jane?" Roy said. "That's your middle sister, right?"

"Oh, God. Is she all right?"

"Everybody's fine," he said. "Let me start over."

He was too tall for the low sofa, his body bent at an awkward angle, his knees poking up like spider legs. At his side, Kendra retrieved a notepad and pen from her pocket and began to jot something down.

"We're here about Tucker," Roy said.

At the sound of her brother's name, Darlene got to her feet. She circled the coffee table and caught a glimpse of herself in the little mirror above the television—her hair matted from sleep, her cheeks flushed. She ended up in the kitchen. There was no true separation between this area and the living room; the boundary was marked by a change in the linoleum, without walls or door. She was only a few feet from the cops on the couch, but somehow it felt good to inhabit a different space.

"Can I get you some water?" she said. "Or some sweet tea?"

"No," Roy said. "We have a few questions about your brother."

"I don't have a brother." She had not meant to say this. The words sounded absurd in her own ears. "I mean, Tucker's gone. He ran away."

She broke off, unable to continue her thought. Glancing down, she noticed that there was a pan in the sink. Evidently Cora had been cooking while she was home sick. There was a plate too, smeared with syrup and butter.

"When was the last time you talked to Tucker?" Roy said.

"It's been years," Darlene said.

"He hasn't called here recently?"

"No."

"Has he come by the house in the past few days?"

As Roy spoke, there was an accompanying scratch of pen on paper. Kendra was taking notes.

"I said no," Darlene said. "Absolutely not."

"You're sure you haven't seen him?"

"I'm sure," she snapped. "You can ask me the same thing a hundred different ways, but the answer isn't going to change."

The fact of the dirty dishes was suddenly untenable. She turned on the faucet, then pulled on her rubber gloves and poured a dollop of soap onto the sponge.

"Would you mind if we took a look around?" Roy said. He pitched his voice higher to compete with the hiss of the water. Darlene did not answer, scrubbing the saucepan. Cora appeared to have scrambled some eggs without cooking spray. It would take elbow grease to get rid of the residue.

Roy approached her, hovering in her peripheral vision.

"Did you hear me?" he said. "We'd like to take a look around."

"No." Darlene switched off the water with a savage movement. "My little sister is sick. She's asleep in her room. I can't believe the doorbell didn't wake her. All this noise!"

Roy was standing very close, his eyebrows cocked at a watchful angle. Darlene could smell his cologne, a combination of fruit and spices. The odor mingled in an oddly harmonious way with the residue of cigarettes on his breath.

"I don't like to talk about Tucker," she said. "It's upsetting. You're upsetting me." She could hear her own voice rising. She flung out a hand, pointing into the sink. "I'm very busy right now, as you can see. I have to wash these dishes."

Roy took off his policeman's cap, revealing a close-cropped mat of black curls. A few gray threads glistened around his temples.

"This is important," he said.

Now she had the impression that she was not thinking clearly. There was something she ought to ask—something she had forgotten. The whole interaction was a mess: a blur of migraine fog and postnap muddle.

"Tucker is a missing person," Darlene said slowly. "He's a runaway. He was seventeen years old when he left. I filed a police report back then. You should know that. Y'all probably know more about him than I do."

Finally, a question bloomed in her mind, clear and true.

"Why are you looking for him?" she said.

Roy turned away, his face closing like a door.

"I can't answer that," he said. "Police procedure. I can't comment on an ongoing investigation."

The darkness in the trailer seemed to intensify, the corners of the kitchen swallowed up by shadows.

"Tell me what you want with Tucker," Darlene said.

Roy reached into his pocket and unfolded a sheet of paper. He smoothed out the creases with his hands and passed it to her. It was a photocopy of an artist's sketch. A man's face. Bulging forehead. Vicious little eyes. Dangerous mien. The image seemed vaguely familiar, as though she had seen it recently in passing.

"Do you know this man?" Roy asked.

"No," Darlene said.

"Could that be Tucker?"

She folded the paper and handed it back.

"No," she said. "It doesn't look a thing like him."

From the couch, Kendra's voice caught Darlene off guard, as high and sweet as a flute.

"We need to know where Tucker McCloud is," she said. "It's urgent. We were hoping you'd let us look around the house, Darlene. It's more friendly that way. But we'll get a warrant to search the premises if we need to."

Kendra tucked her notebook into her pocket and came to stand beside Roy, elbow to elbow, a solid wall of officialdom. Darlene shook her head, trying to clear it. She lifted her hands, tangling them in her hair.

"I have to think," she said.

Kendra clucked her tongue. "Not much space, is there? If you were going to peddle your sob story on TV, I reckon you should have asked for more money."

Her voice was as soft as silk, but its menace was unmistakable. Roy glanced back and forth between the two women, not quite sure what was happening.

Darlene weighed her options. She'd been here before. She had endured some version of this conversation with nearly everyone in Mercy. They all had an opinion about her actions. Some people felt that she had done wrong by her siblings (*Those poor little girls, too young to have a say in any of it*). Some resented her for taking the easy way out (*All of us were hit hard by the tornado, but nobody else tried to turn a profit*). Some felt sorry for her (*Everything you said on TV was the God's honest truth. Nobody around here suffered more than y'all did*). And some felt indignation on her behalf (*You took care of your family. Don't you listen to those gossips*). Over the years, Darlene had encountered every possible viewpoint.

The expression on Kendra's face was familiar: narrowed eyes, flared nostrils. Roy frowned in confusion, chewing on his thumbnail. Darlene took a calming breath, then drew herself up to her full height.

"I want y'all to leave," she said, summoning the tone she used when she wanted her sisters to obey her instantly, without question.

12

The last time Darlene had seen Tucker was in the kitchen of No. 43 on a moonless evening. She remembered that night often, against her will. Sometimes it cropped up in her dreams: Tucker's stentorian voice, his face burning with anger, his torso as slender and erect as a sapling.

The fight had not started as a fight. Darlene had been at the kitchen table when Tucker came home from a friend's house. Cora and Jane were asleep in their shared bedroom. The clock ticked languidly. When the front door opened, Darlene did not look up. She did not know Tucker was in a bad mood until he hurled a handful of mail onto the floor beside her.

"Look," he said. "More blood money."

He was glaring at her, his hair disheveled from the wind.

After a moment, Darlene stood up from the table. She bent over and gathered up her brother's mess.

"Two checks for you today," he said. "Quite a haul."

She took her time responding. Among the catalogues and bills, there were, indeed, two envelopes that appeared to be payment for interviews—one from a magazine, one from a TV station. Darlene knew better than to open them with Tucker glowering over her shoulder.

"Two checks for *us*," she said. "All of us. So we can eat."

He disapproved. She was well aware of this. For the past month, ever since she had made the difficult decision to allow the media into their lives, Tucker had been mulish and withdrawn. He refused to participate in a single interview, even though his presence would have allowed Darlene to negotiate for more money. He dropped snide comments and gave her the cold shoulder. (He did not, however, seem to blame Jane and Cora one bit. Darlene was both grateful and irritated about this.) Whenever the McCloud family was featured in the pages of a magazine, an advance copy would be mailed to them. Darlene learned to hide these from Tucker, who would throw them away if he got to them first. He bluntly refused to watch his sisters on TV or listen to their voices on the radio. He would leave the house instead.

Darlene had indulged him the way she always indulged his tantrums—quietly, gracefully, holding the image of their mother in her mind. She knew she was in the right; the moral high ground offered her a lofty perspective. Daddy never invested in life insurance and amassed little in the way of savings. On her own, Darlene had scraped together enough to buy the trailer. After the family's most recent interview, people from all over the country sent donations. Some items were helpful: nonperishable foods, a set of new dishes, and hand-me-downs for the girls. A few generous souls sent money. Darlene also received things she could not use, either because their condition was too poor (cracked glassware, broken toys, and what appeared to be bloodstained sheets) or because they were too nice for her current life (a brand-new espresso machine that she immediately sold online). Little by little, she was rebuilding their lives out of nothing.

The situation would have been easier, she knew, if she and her family were still church members. The religious community looked after its own. But Daddy had cleaved away years ago, and Darlene was a loyal daughter.

Right after the tornado, the pastor had been a constant presence. He asked Darlene to join his prayer circles, asked if she would be there for Wednesday-night Bible study or the Sunday service. He sent his bright-eyed volunteers to offer her pamphlets of scripture that she might find helpful in this trying time. *The church brigade*, Daddy would have called them. Darlene was wise enough not to let her true feelings show. Like her father, she always paid lip service to the received wisdom: *Thank God. Bless you. I'll pray for y'all too.* But in her heart of hearts, she did not believe in the existence of a soul or the afterlife. There was no all-knowing, omnipotent deity watching over Mercy, and Darlene did not appreciate the pastor's sanctimonious brand of goodwill.

Once the McClouds were featured in the media, of course, the church brigade withdrew. Along with everyone else in Mercy, the pastor now kept his distance.

"Are you hungry?" Darlene said, tucking the envelopes into her purse. "There's some mac and cheese in the fridge. Jane made it, so it might be a little soggy."

Darlene moved toward the table, but her brother blocked her path. The expression on his face brought her up short. This was not just snippiness, after all. Tucker appeared to be furious.

"You're not even sorry, are you?" he said.

"Sorry for what?"

"For the *money*," he said. "For what you've done to us."

Gently but firmly, she took hold of his shoulders and shifted him out of her way. She sat down, showing with her averted gaze that she was busy, that she did not want to have this conversation now. But Tucker did not budge. He loomed over her, waiting.

It was only a few months after their father's death. His loss had left a wound in Darlene's chest that felt physical, a perpetual ache. She did not know how he died, where his body ended up, and in the absence of certain knowledge she often found herself speculating. The tornado offered plenty of clues about how Daddy might have perished—broken trees, overturned cars, and a teapot that had been flung so hard into a brick wall that it mushroomed into a deformed gong and embedded itself inextricably in the stone. Despite herself, Darlene had considered all the possibilities. Her father might have been decapitated by flying debris. He might have been picked up and spun so fast that he suffocated, unable to inhale against the terrible wind. His body might have been hurled into the canopy of a forest or deposited in a riverbed. He might have been carried high into the icy wasteland of the stratosphere, crystallizing like a snowflake among the clouds. He might still be up there.

There had been no funeral. Loved ones were supposed to leave remains—ashes in an urn, a body in the ground, something to hold, visit, mourn over. The funeral director tried to talk Darlene into buying and burying an empty coffin "to give y'all a chance to say goodbye," but she refused. She did not want to put her siblings through such an eerie pantomime. She could not afford it anyway.

For the past three months, Darlene had waited for the fact of her father's death to reach every corner of her mind. She had been through this process when Mama died; she knew how it would unfold. Right now, each morning was its own little funeral. She would wake up and listen for Daddy's footsteps, sniff the air for his pipe smoke, open her eyes, and remember. Every morning she lost him, and the house, and her college education all over again. Every morning she expected to be back in her own bed, beneath the comforter that was precisely the violet of the sky at sunset, looking up at the ceiling decorated with glow-in-the-dark stars. She was not quite sure who she was without a closet full of her clothes, her books on the shelves, her posters on the walls, all the physical manifestations of her former identity.

She had lost, too, the little farm she adored. The old gray stallion was her friend for a decade. She whispered her secrets to Mojo. She checked his hooves and brushed his flanks. She smiled at his foibles—his inability to recognize her when she wore a cowboy hat, his tendency to startle at a particular fence post that stood at a slight angle, and the feisty mood that sometimes induced him to run flat out in a whinnying frenzy. He would lead the mare and colt behind him, both caught helplessly in his wake, neighing too without knowing why, three horses pelting madly for no reason at all. It used to make Darlene laugh.

More than this, Mojo had known her mother, which was a source of comfort. Darlene would sometimes talk to him about Mama, which she could never do with Daddy, who would begin to dab at his eyes, or Tucker, who would cut the conversation short. Mojo never got teary or impatient. He just listened, letting Darlene lean against his warm throat, murmuring memories in his ear. She lost the hens she had fed as a young girl at her mother's side. She lost the herd of cows she had known for years, strolling among them whenever she felt anxious, letting their mild blankness wash over her. Their easy, empty minds infused her own like a kind of meditation.

Darlene knew the whole family was in shock. It affected everyone differently. Jane was operating in a stupor. Cora, too young to really understand, was more or less herself, albeit bored and cranky, as if she had only woken up to the world once the tornado arrived, as if that day in the shelter was her first memory.

But it was Tucker who worried Darlene the most. Something was happening to him—something she could not identify. He was speeding up, growing more intense by the day. Their great loss had created a mechanism inside his person—buried in his chest or the core of his brain—and it was always humming. She could practically see the vibration of the engine beneath his skin.

Darlene was doing her best to be patient. As usual, she could grasp the big picture and he could not. She had lost as much as her brother, as much as anyone in Mercy. But someone needed to keep the family together. Someone needed to lead them to another life, and it had fallen to her to do so. Tucker could frown and snipe all he liked, but it would not put food on the table.

Now Darlene picked up her pen. With a flourish, she started making a list of errands. Then she glanced up at Tucker, who seemed unaware of the tacit messages she was sending.

"I was just at Louie's house," he said in an accusatory tone.

"Uh-huh."

"His mom made us dinner, and then she stared at me during the entire meal. Like she was about to start crying. Like I was the most miserable thing she ever saw. She kept saying she would pray for me."

Darlene pursed her lips.

"The way people look at us," Tucker said, with a wrench in his voice. "I can't hold my head up out in the street."

She glanced at the bedroom door. She hoped the girls were sleeping soundly. She did not want them to see Tucker like this.

"'The saddest family in Mercy,'" he quoted in acid tones. "You agreed to that. You let them print that about us. Literally anything else would have been better. We could've been the toughest family. Or the smartest. The strangest, maybe."

"I didn't write that headline," she said. "I don't have control over everything."

"You let those reporters into our life. You let Cora go on the air."

"I had to."

"You didn't—"

"I did!" The words came out louder than she intended. She took a breath, lowered her voice. "There was no money. Do you understand that? There was *nothing*."

The fridge kicked into gear, a shuddering groan. The sound made both of them pause, glancing toward the appliance as though awaiting its commentary.

"I'm not sorry," Darlene said. "Not for any of it."

Tucker blinked at her.

"I didn't do anything wrong," she said.

"Seriously?"

She waved a hand around the interior of No. 43. "We have a roof over our heads. We have a TV. We have silverware. How do you think I paid for all that?"

"Blood money," he said.

She snorted. She could not help it.

"Don't be so dramatic," she said. "Whose blood? What does that even mean?"

"It's the principle of the thing. You have no principles at all, do you?"

Darlene closed her eyes, once again picturing her mother's face. She heard the wind in the trees, the chug of the fridge, the knocking in the pipes as the toilet refilled. All the sounds of the trailer park were still foreign to her, each one new enough to catch her attention.

It was just her and Tucker now—the elders of the family. She felt as though they were playing house. Any minute now, their father might interrupt their game, calling them away, returning order to the universe.

"You know what?" she said. "I was supposed to leave for college yesterday."

Darlene stood up from the table. She and Tucker were the same height, their eyes lining up precisely.

"It's orientation week at OU," she said. "Daddy was going to drive me down. I was supposed to be settling into my dorm right now."

"Damn."

"It was still on my calendar. I never erased it."

"Poor Darlene," Tucker said softly.

There was a tightness in her chest. She kept her eyes averted. If she saw any sympathy in her brother's face, she knew she would cry.

"Even now, we're not out of the woods," she said. "All that 'blood money' just barely got us on our feet. You need to get a job. Part-time for the moment. You'll work on the weekends and after school. You have to graduate, and I have to figure out how we're going to pay the utility bills this month. We've got to feed the girls. That's all that matters. Just surviving."

There was a long, crystalline silence. Tucker shifted his weight, bouncing on the balls of his feet.

"This can't be what happens to us," he said. His tone was almost pleading. "This can't be it."

Darlene wanted her father. Not for the first time, she wished for Daddy with all her might. He would have been able to settle them both down. Daddy had been a silent man by nature, but he exuded an intense calm. His mere presence would have helped. Without him, the chemical mixture of the family was unbalanced. Daddy's placidity was necessary to douse Tucker's spark and soothe Darlene's restlessness. She did not know what to do without her father. She was not sure how to go on living in the world without him.

"Do you believe that everything happens for a reason?" Tucker said.

"No," she said, with some force.

"Well, I do," he said. "I've been doing a lot of reading lately. Trying to keep my brain busy. Have you ever heard of the Anthropocene Mass Extinction?"

"Excuse me?"

"There have been five mass extinctions in the history of life on earth. Each time, the planet has been stripped of almost all its living things. Thousands of species dead. Did you know that?"

"No."

"And it's happening again, right now. This time, though, it's not a natural disaster. It's us. That's what *Anthropocene* means: the Age of Humans."

Darlene stared at him. "What are you talking about?"

"I'm talking about having a purpose. Finding meaning."

He made a strange gesture, spreading his arms wide, the fingers vibrating.

"Maybe we can't understand what a disaster is," he said. "Not really. Not until we actually experience one. It's about perception,

I guess. What happened to us—the tornado—it was some kind of alarm bell. There has to be meaning in it."

His tone was musing and sad. For a moment, Darlene thought the argument was over. That they had made it through to the other side. She yawned surreptitiously behind her hand. The sofa was already made up, and her pillow beckoned. Her brother's sleeping bag was unfurled on the floor. They had agreed to take turns on the couch. Jane and Cora—growing girls—would need the only bed. Darlene was about to suggest that they turn in when Tucker spoke.

"Daddy would never have let you do what you've done," he said, his voice icy. "He would have found some other way."

Darlene took an involuntary step backward.

"What did you just say to me?" she whispered.

"If he were here, he would have stopped you. He'd be ashamed of you."

"Tucker," she said, and faltered.

"But Daddy isn't here, is he? Do you know why?"

She felt a sob erupt from her chest. Hot tears singed her cheeks, and she dashed them away with the back of her wrist.

"The tornado," she said. "A force of nature."

"It wasn't nature," Tucker said. "It was you."

The words landed like a blow, making her gasp.

"It's your fault," he said. "You kept me in the shelter that day. You stood in front of the door. I wanted to find Daddy. I *begged* you to let me go."

"My fault," she repeated, a blank echo.

"There was still enough time," Tucker said, his voice rising. "I could have saved him. You were the one who said no. You let him die."

For an instant, Darlene was back in the shelter. The smell of rain and lightning. The commotion of wind. The rough pressure of the door against her spine. She remembered staring around the cramped space at her siblings as Tucker hovered wild-eyed in the middle of the room.

It had been one of the proudest moments of her life. She blocked the exit with her body. She did what Daddy would have wanted her to do. There was no doubt in her mind about that.

Now she snatched up her to-do list from the table, crumpled it into a ball, and flung it into Tucker's face. It bounced off his temple. He flinched away a second too late, then lifted a hand to his head in surprise.

"I saved your life," she cried.

"You think so?" His mouth twisted into a sneer. "Is that what you tell yourself so you can sleep at night?"

"We got to the shelter maybe two minutes before the tornado. Do the math. You're only here now because of me. Is that what you blame me for? Keeping you alive? Keeping all of us alive?"

"Daddy was alone," Tucker roared. "That's how he died—scared out of his wits, thinking we abandoned him. Two minutes? Two minutes would have been plenty of time for me to save him. You're goddamn right I blame you."

Things happened quickly after that. The argument flared from a lit match into a forest fire. Now, looking back, Darlene remembered screaming as she had never screamed before. The anger building since her father's death came out in an uncontrolled tide. She remembered every word she and Tucker threw at one another. The walls seemed to shake with them. She remembered stamping her foot. Slamming her palm on the tabletop. Throwing a pen at his chest. They fought as only siblings could fight—with the brutality of familiarity. They knew each other's weak spots. Soon both of them were crying, yelling through the sobs.

"I'll never forgive you," he shouted at last. "You always think you know best, Darlene. That's what killed Daddy."

She punched him. She didn't plan to; the action seemed to happen without her volition. Her hand clenched and she struck her brother. A glancing blow on his chest. A shocked exhalation. A quick exchange of stunned eye contact.

Then he punched her back.

She saw a blur in her peripheral vision, and his fist connected with her eye socket. There was an explosion of red. The floor seemed to tip beneath her feet, sending her stumbling backward. For a moment, she could not see.

She heard motion, muttering. Gradually she realized she was now sitting on the couch. One eye was functioning, but the other saw only shadows tinged with pink. Tucker was darting around the room, picking things up and shoving them into a backpack. Darlene blinked, which was painful. Gingerly, she touched her face, caressing the spot where his fist had landed. The flesh was already swollen. Her fingers came away stained.

The door slammed behind him.

She had not seen Tucker since. Two and a half years gone. He survived the tornado, but, in the end, it took him too.

13

Through the window, Darlene watched the squad car glide away, its taillights shimmering in the gloom. She pulled the curtains closed and took a moment to relish the quiet. Then she began to move, walking widdershins around the couch. She murmured to herself, a comforting habit in times of turmoil. Speaking her thoughts aloud gave her clarity.

She picked up the phone to call Jane, then decided against it. Her sister would be asleep now, and the truth was that Darlene had nothing to report. The police were looking for Tucker, but she did not know why, and Jane wouldn't either. Darlene knocked on the door to Cora's room and peered inside. In the darkness, there was a lump in the bed. She resisted the urge to peel back the covers. It would be better if both her sisters slept until morning. She needed time to think.

It was strange to have a clue, at last, to what had happened to her brother. Over the years, there had been little to go on. Tucker simply disappeared. He tumbled into the blue like a pebble dropped into a pond—out of sight, the ripples stilling, the surface of the water growing opaque.

The week after he ran away had been the worst of Darlene's life—even worse than losing her mother or the tornado itself. She had curled up in her brother's sleeping bag every night, inhaling the smell of him. She sobbed until her chest was sore. She tried to cover her black eye with makeup, but the bruise darkened and spread, her cheekbone purple, the white of her eye blotched with crimson. There was no hiding it. She woke at odd hours, going to the window and staring out at the moonlit expanse of Shady Acres, waiting. The days were dimmed by a pervasive sense of failure. She had been the head of the family for only a few months, and already she had failed in every possible way. She and her sisters were now the poster children of the tragedy. Tucker was gone.

She had never been struck by a man before. The force of it had been remarkable and horrific—the jolt in her vertebrae, a supernova bursting in her optic nerve. She spent a lot of time looking in the mirror. Her black eye continued to flower, a ring of green blooming around her orbital crest. Even her upper lip swelled. She did not know how to categorize this new iteration of her brother's capacity for violence.

The days ran together, filled with her sisters' anxious faces, their hands on her body, so many questions. Jane seemed to understand on some level what had transpired between her older siblings; she fetched Darlene packages of frozen peas to bring down the swelling in her cheek, and she did not ask when Tucker would be home. Cora, however, was only six. She asked about Tucker constantly.

Darlene did not know how to answer. At first, she still hoped he might come back. Surely he would not desert his family in this way. She called and called, but his phone went straight to voicemail, and then his mailbox was full, and then his number had been disconnected. Darlene filed a missing persons report with the police. They offered her little, however, in the way of reassurance. Tucker was just a few months shy of his eighteenth birthday. Runaways that age often weren't found—unless they wanted to be.

So she waited. Eventually her brother would cool down and come to his senses. After he spent a little while off the grid, maybe panhandling for his supper, maybe working odd jobs, maybe sleeping in homeless shelters or fields, he would appreciate the modest comforts of No. 43. He would remember that his sisters needed him.

During that time, Darlene kept busy, which was not difficult. There was always something to be done: a toilet cleaned, a meal cooked, her phone ringing. She needed to go to work and feign something like normalcy. She needed to move the laundry from the washer to the dryer so her sisters' clothes would not grow mildew. She needed to brush out Cora's curls so they wouldn't knot. Her face healed until she looked like her old self again. She kept the TV on constantly—a kind of medicinal noise, blunting the sharp edges of the day, keeping her sisters distracted, their worried eyes fixed on something else for once. Darlene wondered if a person could die from heartbreak.

Finally she understood that this was their new reality. Tucker wasn't coming back. The knowledge settled over her like cold rain in autumn, gradual but inexorable, darkening the landscape. She threw away all of his things—his clothes, his shoes, everything he had not been able to take in his backpack the night he left. She gathered up all the photos of him and shoved them in the garbage. Everything went in the trash, nothing donated or sold. Darlene did not want her brother's belongings out in the world being used by strangers.

She had not cried since. As the months slipped by, she underwent a transformation, a hardening of the spirit. She felt it happening but could do nothing to stop it. Over time, her voice grew softer and more precise. Her eyes in the mirror were sadder.

Occasionally her phone would ring, *Caller Unknown*, and no one would speak, the line clouded by static. Darlene wondered if this was Tucker checking in. Sometimes she would see a man in the distance with her brother's gait, and she would find herself recalling the details about Tucker that she still possessed—the jut of his wrists, the slimness of his waist, his pigeon-toed stance. It was both pleasant and awful to think about him, each recollection from childhood followed by the sting of his desertion, each moment of joy infused with the essence of its opposite. She was used to the sensation by now.

I'll never forgive you, Tucker once told her. But Darlene knew now that nothing she had done was unforgivable. It was her brother who broke the bonds of their family. His cruel words, the punch— she could have accepted all of that, given time. Only his abandonment was unjustifiable. *I'll never forgive you*, she would throw back at him one day. If she ever saw him again.

NEAR MIDNIGHT, DARLENE STOOD ON the front stoop of No. 43, inhaling the musk of the recent rain. The storm had traveled west toward the mountains. The sky was a cloudless, tinny expanse, pocked by stars like dents in metal.

At last, she went to Cora's room and hesitated outside the door. Darlene knew she should go in and check on her sister, but she could not do it. She was exhausted, overwhelmed, and frightened. She laid her forehead against the wood of the door. She turned away.

That night, Darlene tossed and turned, pummeling her pillow and adjusting her hips to avoid an errant spring in the couch cushions. The light in her mind would not switch off. She felt that she ought to be vigilant for some reason. Jane was not there to fill the air with her usual raspy snores. On the other side of the wall, Cora was silent; she seemed to have slipped into the profound state of rest specific to young childhood.

Darlene gave up on sleep when the birds began to sing. The sun had not yet risen, but the robins caroled louder than any alarm clock. As the coffee percolated, the sky outside altered by degrees, blueing and glimmering. The high clouds caught the light first, outlined in copper.

She prepared Cora's favorite breakfast, plain toast with butter and jam. It was her hope that her sister had slept away the worst of her illness. If she was well enough to go to school today, that would be a weight off Darlene's mind—one weight among many.

At seven o'clock, she opened the bedroom door.

"Rise and shine," she said.

The heap of blankets in the middle of the mattress didn't answer. On closer inspection, there was something odd about its appearance—a little too immobile, no suggestion of breath. Darlene came closer. She lifted the edge of the coverlet. Then she snatched up the whole mess of bedclothes and shook each layer loose, the billowing sail of the sheet, the lumpy quilt, a pillow falling with a thud, nothing but a lone feather twirling in the sunlight.

14

The police station was quiet, every surface bathed in a harsh, fluorescent glare. Roy sat behind a desk cluttered with knickknacks. Occasionally a phone rang somewhere, a strident shout. The Mercy police station was small, as befitted a small town—one story, an open workspace with three desks, and a single lavatory that smelled strongly of bleach.

"Let's go over it again," Roy said. "Did you see your sister yesterday?"

Darlene recalled herself to the moment.

"Yes," she said. "Only in the morning, though."

"Cora was too sick to go to school?"

She felt a lump in her throat. "That's what she told me."

"And when you got home—"

"The bedroom door was shut, and I thought she was asleep. Then y'all came by to talk about Tucker. Then I poked my head in and saw the sheets in a pile—I thought it was Cora—I should have—I never—"

She broke off, her mouth opening and closing. Roy leaned across the desk and patted her forearm. She noticed that he had dirt under his fingernails.

"Do you have a recent picture of Cora?" he said gently.

Darlene fumbled in her jeans pocket and retrieved her cell phone. She flicked through the images stored there—a sunset, a flower she had noticed growing between the cracks in the sidewalk, a snapshot of Jane giving the camera the finger. There was a photo of Darlene's bare feet with a new nail polish. There was a selfie that Jane had taken without Darlene's knowledge, a close-up of her sunburned visage, the eyes and mouth comically wide.

She settled on a picture of Cora at Christmas. The light was natural, no filter. Her sister knelt beneath the family's artificial tree, a blow-up replica as slick and green as algae. She wore a sweater with a reindeer on it. She was holding a wrapped present in her hands. Something about the photograph captured her entirely—little face, delicate bones, a cascade of dark curls.

As Darlene passed her phone across the desk, she realized that her fingers were trembling. Roy examined the picture and smiled.

"She's a doll," he said. "I'll email this to myself, okay? That'll get the ball rolling."

"Fine."

"Can I get you some coffee?"

Darlene blinked at him.

"Something to drink?" he said. "Did you have breakfast?"

"I don't remember."

The past few hours had swirled away from her like water down a drain. It took her a while to figure out that Cora was actually missing—not in the bathroom, not outside, not anywhere. Darlene had upended the contents of every closet in the trailer and shouted into the crawlspace. She knocked on her neighbors' doors, receiving ire, then confusion, then sympathy. She walked the edge of the ravine, peering into the brambly gloom, a gully formed by the action of water decades ago, now parched and filled with wiry bushes.

Without warning, Roy loomed over her and pushed a paper plate into her hands. A Danish, a bruised apple, and a mug of black coffee.

"Thanks," she said.

"Eat. It'll help."

She obeyed. The frosting crumbled into the crevices between her teeth, the dough as spongy as cardboard. The coffee cup was ceramic, with *World's Greatest Mom* written on the side in bubble letters.

"I'll be right back," Roy said.

He hurried down the hall, striding with an eager bounce. Darlene took a bite of her apple and spat it out, unable to tolerate its mealiness. In a corner of the room, a TV blared the morning news.

Sometime soon, the screen would change. Maybe in an hour, maybe this evening, a picture of Cora would appear. A laughing child. A reindeer sweater. A missing minor. Another tragedy to befall the saddest family in Mercy. Darlene was trying to prepare herself. She was failing to prepare herself.

There was a clatter in the street outside, and she gazed hopefully at the front door. Kendra had headed off in a squad car to pick Jane up from school. It was strange to see people on the sidewalk, going about their ordinary lives, untouched by the possibility of tragedy. Darlene watched the town librarian walk by with her spaniel. The florist was cleaning her shop window with a bucket and squeegee. The cup of coffee tilted in Darlene's fingers, splashing down her thigh. She groped for a napkin and dabbed at her jeans.

The bell over the front door jangled, and Jane was there, moving fast with her arms outstretched. She careened into Darlene at full speed, enveloping her in an embrace.

"Good lord in heaven," Jane said. "What is happening to us?"

"I don't know."

"Where is she?"

"I don't know," Darlene repeated.

They stood that way for a while, intertwined like a pair of trees planted too close together, their trunks overlapping into a single broad base. Jane pulled away first. She wore a hot-pink T-shirt with *Sassy* written on it. Her hair was sleek beneath a polka-dot headband. Her entire outfit, upbeat and colorful, clashed with the shipwrecked expression on her face.

Kendra hovered off to one side, arms folded. Roy reappeared, hurrying toward them down the hallway. Darlene watched as the two officers put their heads together, murmuring in low voices. They glanced in her direction. Roy shook his head, a rosy blush of emotion blooming beneath the umber of his cheeks. Kendra poked his chest with her forefinger.

"What's going on?" Darlene said.

"Y'all should sit," Kendra said, with something like kindness in her voice.

"Is there news?"

"Yes and no. Please sit."

Darlene reached for Jane's hand, and they each took a chair. Kendra settled on the edge of the desk, fidgeting with her cuffs. Darlene realized that the woman was nervous. Her own anxiety spiked in kind.

"We have reason to believe that your brother's in town," Roy said. He was still standing, towering over them all, his tone formal.

"Excuse me?" Darlene said.

He cleared his throat. "We have evidence to suggest that Tucker has been in Mercy."

"I don't understand," Darlene said. "What kind of evidence?"

"We don't think Cora ran away," Roy said. "We think your brother took her."

Jane let out a moan. Kendra fiddled more urgently with her cuffs. Darlene sat frozen for a moment, gripping her sister's hand like a lifeline.

Then her cell phone buzzed. She tugged it from her pocket, an automatic reflex.

A new text message. It was marked by a triangle with an exclamation point inside; it seemed to be similar in kind to the emergency warnings she sometimes received before a bad storm. With some dim, distant part of her mind, Darlene realized that she had last seen that little symbol on the day of the tornado. She read:

AMBER ALERT. Mercy, OK. CHILD: Cora McCloud 9YO W/F Hair: BLK. SUSPECT: Tucker McCloud 20YO W/M Hair: BR.

15

The interrogation room was not as intimidating as Darlene expected. On a TV show, it would have been a steel box with a one-way mirror on the wall. Instead, there was a turquoise sofa, a painting of horses in a field, and a row of file cabinets. Roy bustled around the room, tucking a manila folder under his arm and turning on the box fan in the window. Darlene was on her fourth cup of coffee now. She and Jane sat together on the couch, the cushions slippery and thin.

Roy took a seat on the other side of the table: an oaken expanse, maybe an antique. He was explaining what would happen next. His voice was ripe and mellifluous, which had the unfortunate byproduct of lulling Darlene into a daydream, listening to the sound of his words rather than the sense of them. She had not slept much, and her worry about Cora seemed to be manifesting as a kind of sensory overload—every lamp too bright, every smell an assault. It was difficult to focus on any one thing. At her side, Jane was in her usual process of devolution. She began most days looking fairly put together, but the entropy of her nature could not be denied. Already she had twirled her blond mane into tangles and smudged her cheek with ink. Her shoes were untied.

"Normally my sergeant would be the one talking to y'all," Roy said. "But Charlie had a heart attack a few weeks ago. Maybe y'all heard?"

"Oh no," Darlene said. "Please tell him we're thinking of him."

"He'll appreciate that."

"He was a family friend when I was little. Daddy used to talk about him."

"Yeah," Jane added.

Roy nodded. A small pause blossomed in the room—the usual beat of respectful silence to honor someone who had died in the tornado. Both girls knew it well.

Then Roy pushed a few forms across the table and handed Darlene a pen. She signed them all without reading a word. He was saying something about wiretaps. Something about searching for bodily fluids. She was distracted by the feel of the pen in her hands—unusually heavy, made of fancy metal, not plastic.

Roy explained that the FBI would be involved soon; the Mercy police simply weren't equipped to handle a case like this. He said these things without resentment. The FBI had a crime lab, he said. Their equipment was state of the art.

"Y'all will still liaise with me though," he said. "I'd like to stay involved. Do y'all have any idea where Tucker might go? A familiar place. Somewhere he would feel safe."

For a moment, an image of their old house shone in Darlene's mind. She saw Tucker jumping down the stairs two at a time, slipping through the back door with a grin, and strolling away through the long grass toward the farm. Then she shook herself. That place—their entire street—had been reduced to rubble and tainted by toxins.

"We have an APB out," Roy said. "We're still in the first forty-eight hours, so that's good. Do you have extended family anywhere? Are y'all aware of any friends Tucker might get in touch with?"

"We don't have any family left," Darlene said. "The tornado took everything."

Roy made a note on his pad. His face was illuminated from beneath by a small desk lamp. Darlene could see a swatch of stubble beneath his ear, a place he had missed while shaving. There was a clock on the wall, loud and insistent. Jane kept jiggling her feet. Her restlessness shook the sofa.

"Evidence," Darlene said at last. Her voice came out higher than normal.

"Excuse me?" Roy said.

"You said that y'all have evidence. Why do y'all think Tucker is involved in any of this?"

He set down his pen with deliberate slowness.

"Right," he said. "So."

"What's going on?" Darlene said.

"The bombing," he said.

"At Jolly?"

Roy nodded, his expression grave. "Blood was found at the scene. We sent the DNA to a lab in Oklahoma City. We got the results back yesterday. Your brother was already in the system, and they were able to match—"

"No," Jane said. Her voice was firm but flat, as though she were answering a question posed by a teacher in class.

"I'm afraid there's no doubt," Roy said. "Tucker set off the explosion. That's why Kendra and I came by yesterday. We needed to know if y'all had been in touch with your brother. We thought he might be hiding out with y'all. Taking shelter."

Darlene closed her eyes. The sensation was novel. It was equal parts comprehension and distress—two things she had always thought of as unrelated, now mingled into a single, painful surge. Without meaning to, without being aware of it, she had been gathering information about Tucker for days. From stories on the news, from gossip at the grocery store, even from the police officers during their visit to No. 43—despite their reticence—Darlene had gleaned enough. All the unrelated scraps and shards were merging into a story.

"What about Cora?" she said.

"I don't believe in coincidences," Roy said. "We know Tucker's in town. Now Cora's missing. It makes sense, doesn't it?"

"I don't know," Darlene said helplessly. "None of this makes sense."

Roy passed a manila folder across the table. She saw *Tucker McCloud* written on top in large, angry print. There was a picture of her brother paper-clipped to the front. Darlene snatched at the file. Looking closer, she realized the photograph was a mug shot. Tucker wore an orange jumpsuit and held a black sign with white letters on it: a date, a location, and a long string of numbers. The name of the county was one she recognized, farther east, near Tulsa.

"Let me tell y'all about your brother," Roy said.

Darlene breathed.

As she opened the file, he began to speak. He talked as though he knew Tucker well—not as a person but a case study, a composite of various traits and actions. Leafing through the pages, Darlene was listening with half her mind, reading with the other. Roy did not know everything, of course—only what ended up in the official report. A second mug shot showed Tucker with a blond beard. In a third, he stood framed in profile. A pixelated image of Tucker at a rally looked as though it had been printed out from somebody's social media feed.

"He's a criminal?" Darlene said, gesturing to the thick file. "I mean, he was *already* a criminal?"

"Yes," Roy said.

For so long, questions about Tucker had droned in her mind like bees in a hive, a hum that lasted for the past few years. On good days,

Darlene pictured her brother working in a coffee shop, living in a big city, sharing a rundown apartment with roommates. On bad days, her imagination took her to darker places. Perhaps Tucker was sleeping in the street, begging for spare change. Perhaps he had become addicted to drugs. Every so often, she would be jolted by a surge of despair, wondering whether he was dead. An anonymous corpse found in an alley. A plain pine coffin. A headstone reading *John Doe.* Maybe he never came home, not because he was heartless but because he was six feet under. Maybe she had been furious at him all this while for something he could not help.

Now, without warning, she was being offered all the information she could ever ask for—all of it terrible, surprising, and strange.

"His first arrest was a month after his eighteenth birthday," Roy said. "He wasn't a minor, so I reckon that's why nobody contacted y'all at the time. There was an illegal protest at a zoo in Pawnee. I believe Tucker was kept in jail overnight and released with a warning. There should be a note in there—"

Darlene flipped through the file. Roy was saying something about jurisdictional regulations. It seemed Tucker had joined up with an animal rights group called the Environmental Conservatory Organization. ("ECO for short," Roy said. "It's clever, I guess.") Six months after his first offense, Tucker was arrested in Muskogee. Along with two other members of ECO, he attempted to sabotage a lumber crew in an old-growth forest, the habitat of a rare breed of owl. Since it was Tucker's second offense, he was fined and given probation, his DNA entered into the system. His codefendants had longer rap sheets, and their punishments were more severe. Tucker was warned to stay away from ECO, to make regular contact with a probation officer, to find a job, to forget about saving the animals and worry about saving himself.

He did not listen. He violated his probation immediately, falling off the radar for the entirety of that long, gray winter.

As Darlene leafed through the folder, her heart quickened its pace. *Criminal mischief. Vandalism. Possession of a deadly weapon.* There was a photograph of Tucker standing beside a young woman with tattoos up and down her arms, her breastbone emblazoned with a phoenix in jewel tones. Tucker was grinning, but the young woman was stone-faced and held one arm in the air, flashing the sign for peace, or possibly victory. Both of them were lanky and underfed, dressed in ragged ensembles and visibly unwashed.

Dimly, Darlene heard an echo of her brother's voice ringing in her mind: *Do you believe that everything happens for a reason?* During their fight, he had mentioned natural disasters and alarm bells. He talked about finding meaning and needing a purpose. At the time, Darlene did not put much credence in any of this—the misguided ramblings of a grief-stricken boy—but maybe she had been wrong. Perhaps ECO gave him the meaning he sought. With these people, he might have found some kind of purpose. Darlene did not entirely understand it, but a pattern was forming in her mind.

Roy was still talking; from a police standpoint, Tucker's behavior had been erratic. He was a person of interest in a bomb threat at a puppy mill. In a town called Sulphur, he chained himself to the door of a CEO's office to protest the company's policy of animal testing. A month later, he was picked up for vagrancy, sleeping on the streets of Oklahoma City and panhandling. His fingerprints were found in Lawton at the scene of a failed arson attempt on a chicken farm. According to Roy, activists often displayed this kind of chaotic decision-making. Groups like ECO were disorganized by their very nature, a loose cadre of like-minded radicals who did not act in lockstep, who all had different passions and levels of commitment. Some hoped to save the dolphins. Others were frantic about invasive species. Some could only talk about melting ice caps and rising sea levels. Others insisted that the biggest threat to life on earth was deforestation. Some wanted to engage in nonviolent protests: sit-ins, hunger strikes, and letter-writing campaigns. Others—like Tucker—were out for something more.

"So he's serious about all this," Darlene said. "It's not just some hobby."

"Serious as a heart attack," Roy said. "The boy's on a mission."

"An activist," she murmured, trying out the term.

Beyond the window, a siren sounded. Darlene glanced up in surprise. She heard an engine turn over as a squad car pulled away. She had forgotten that the whole police station was not involved in her personal disaster. The sun poured through the window, coating the table with luminescent fractals. She listened to the wail of the siren, mournful and robotic, until it faded from earshot.

Near the back of the file was another photograph, the most recent image of Tucker that the police seemed to have. Darlene leaned forward and peered at the stranger captured there, dressed in a T-shirt with the sleeves ripped off, his chin lifted. He was barefoot and tan. She wondered when the snapshot was taken, who took it—who her brother was smiling at with such affection and brio—and how it found its way into a police file. Squinting, she caught the hint of an outline on Tucker's shirt. A faded white shape. A polar bear.

With a jolt, Darlene recognized the T-shirt. She had given it to him for his birthday many years ago. (Her brother always loved polar bears. He saw them as an emblem of the wild—powerful, beautiful, untamable, and endangered.) Tucker must have packed the T-shirt specially when he left No. 43. He carried it with him on the road all this time. He tore the sleeves off, but he kept it. Somewhere inside this lean, angry man was her brother. If only she could chip away the hard surface and unveil the lost, familiar boy within.

"A year ago, Tucker's behavior escalated," Roy said.

Darlene glanced up. "How so?"

"There was an act of sabotage at a factory in Noble County. Not long after, there was a case of arson in Tulsa. Your brother has a few open warrants in his name. He's left fingerprints and DNA all over Oklahoma."

"My lord," Jane breathed.

Roy paused, frowning. Darlene watched him apprehensively. The sunlight touched his jaw and throat as he shifted in his seat.

"Tucker's first bombing was in Ponca City," he said. "Six months ago."

"His *first*?" Darlene said.

"I reckon he didn't like the look of a slaughterhouse. The blast—let me see—" Roy recited from one of the reports in his hand. "It shattered the pneumonic killing box and the quarter-carcass lifting machine. A thousand head of cattle got loose that day."

Jane leaned forward and spoke, her voice higher than normal.

"Tucker blew up a slaughterhouse?" she said.

"Yes," Roy said. "Him and a few other ECO members. They used homemade pipe bombs, similar to the ones we believe were used at Jolly Cosmetics."

Jane slumped back in her seat, looking horrified. She had obviously reached her quota for terrible news.

"And his second bombing was just a few days ago," Roy said. "Right here in Mercy."

"So there's no doubt . . ." Darlene began, then trailed off.

"None. Perfect DNA match."

Jane covered her eyes with a hand.

"Tucker lost quite a bit of blood at Jolly Cosmetics," Roy said. "Not enough to be fatal, but still, pretty bad. Enough to slow him down. I'm thinking that's why he wanted Cora with him. Maybe he'll let her go once he's healed up."

Darlene swallowed hard.

"This is a trying time for both of y'all," Roy said. "I appreciate your cooperation."

"Of course," she whispered.

"Moving forward, things are going to happen pretty fast. To start with, we'll get the ball rolling on those wiretaps, and hopefully—"

He went on, speaking with circular gestures as though painting an imaginary mural in midair. Darlene closed her ears. On the final page of her brother's file was a police sketch, taken from the security footage at Jolly Cosmetics. She had seen it before; Roy had shown it to her in her living room. *It doesn't look a thing like him*, she said then. And yet, this was her brother—she knew that now.

Malicious little eyes. A sharp beak of a nose. A smug smirk

hovering around a narrow mouth. The criminal depicted in this sketch had built pipe bombs with his own two hands. He had returned to Mercy on the anniversary of the tornado to cause more harm. He had taken Cora—maybe by force, maybe through coaxing and coercion.

Darlene could not recognize her brother in any of those actions. She could not find his face in the drawing. She slammed the file shut and pushed it away.

16

They spent the next few nights in a motel. The trailer was now a crime scene, wreathed in yellow plastic tape and besieged by reporters. The Amber Alert summoned them to Mercy from all across the country. Darlene was reminded of birds of prey circling in the desert. In the past, she had sometimes seen a throng of hawks, falcons, and turkey vultures wheeling on a distant updraft. This could only mean one thing: an animal was wounded or dying out there. The predators came in anticipation of blood.

The reporters converged on Shady Acres to take pictures of No. 43, even though it stood empty. Nothing this salacious had happened in years. Three years, to be precise. The saddest family in Mercy was once again front and center—even sadder than before. Not just orphans. Not just victims. Now there was a bomber and a stolen child in the mix.

Jane did not go to school; the reporters were there too, lurking in the parking lot, waiting. Darlene called in sick from work, dipping into her meager savings. Over the past few years, she managed to put away a tiny amount in case of disaster. Every week, rain or shine, she would add a few dollars to the stockpile, even if it meant skipping a meal or letting the pickup truck go too long without an oil change. Experience had taught her that there was always another disaster coming. She needed to be prepared.

Their motel room, at least, was free. Given the family's history, the owner proffered their accommodations. The reporters were here too—it was not hard for them to suss out that the McCloud sisters had taken refuge in the only hotel in Mercy—but they got no farther than the lobby. The clerk at the front desk was a model of Southwestern reticence, implacable beneath his cowboy hat. He kept a shotgun in easy reach, leaning against the wall nearby, clearly visible to all. He would not give the reporters the gift of eye contact, much less Darlene and Jane's room number. Stymied, they lingered outside the front door.

Time moved strangely. Sometimes it lunged ahead, a few hours gone in the blink of an eye, and other times it dripped like honey from a spoon. The motel room was small and brown, the carpet uneven, the wallpaper too faded to tell what the pattern had once been. Each morning, Darlene hung the DO NOT DISTURB sign on the door to keep the maid away. The hallway smelled of boiled cabbage. The pipes knocked whenever someone flushed a toilet.

The motel did, at least, have an indoor pool. Darlene and Jane had not thought to bring bathing suits, but they didn't mind swimming in T-shirts and panties. It was a pleasant enough way to pass the time. Most days, they had the water to themselves. Sounds echoed against the tiled walls. A bank of windows let in the sun, muted through condensation and steam. The pool was a shade of blue that did not occur in nature. The water was so rank with chlorine that just walk-ing into the room made their eyes sting. Jane and Darlene cut slow strokes. They practiced the dead man's float, Jane lying on her back, blond locks flaring around her head as Darlene stood beside her, one hand delicately brushing the small of her sister's back. The bottom of the pool was coated with a stubbly stucco that marked their feet with something like razor burn. Jane's hair took on a greenish hue.

They did not watch the news, only the movie channel, mostly classics and musicals, nothing contemporary. Once Darlene turned on the TV and saw live footage of the motel's dreary exterior, the camera panning across the windows. If she had gone over and opened the blinds, she would have been on national TV right then and there. Quickly she changed the channel.

This time, she had decided that there would be no interviews. She kept her cell phone off, in a drawer, out of sight. She did not check email or social media. She knew exactly what the reporters would say if they could reach her—at once shameless and sympathetic, prom-ising money and a spotlight and "a chance to tell your side of the story." Darlene did not care if she went bankrupt. She had learned her lesson: she would never again make the mistake of crossing over to the other side of the TV screen.

One evening she went for a walk to clear her head, leaving Jane on her twin bed inside a nest of fast food wrappers and dirty napkins. Darlene used the fire exit at the back of the motel. The clerk informed her that the alarm on the door was broken, and he stepped outside first, scoping out the sidewalk to make sure no one else was there. The wind was as warm as bathwater. Fireflies pulsed above the prairie as the sun dipped beneath the horizon. It was June, and the air smelled of summer—pollen and fertilizer and sweet pesticides.

Darlene strolled down the lane toward the convenience store, rev-eling in her solitude. The landscape was distinctly unlovely. The motel stood near the highway, built for travelers who had nowhere better to stop for the night on their way to someplace more interesting. A patchwork of fields stretched to the horizon—one glistening with knee-high soybeans, one bald and brown, one so thick with dande-lions that there seemed to be more yellow than green. A few oil der-ricks were working in the distance. Now, in the evening, they became almost beautiful, silhouetted against a multicolored sky, architectural in their design, at once bulky and insubstantial, dancing and dancing.

At the shop, Darlene bought bread and peanut butter and jelly, a few cheese sticks, and a tub of ice cream. There was no fridge in the motel room, but Jane would finish everything before it turned. The clerk wore a scarlet uniform that brought out the pimples on his cheeks. He was chewing tobacco, spitting periodically into a cup. Darlene slid her money across the counter, but he pushed it back and shook his head.

"On me," he said.

Above his head, a TV was bolted to the wall. Against her will, Darlene glanced up. She saw her sister's photograph on the screen. Little Cora. Lost Cora.

"I hope they find her soon," the clerk said.

She hurried outside. The wind blew gritty and dry, trying to tug the bags from her hands. The trees swayed overhead like kelp in a current, stars flickering in the gloaming. The night was awash with the screech of cicadas. These insects had reached the molting stage of their annual transformation. They first emerged in May as sluggish, flightless, dun-colored beetles, but after enough exposure to heat and sunlight, they would undergo an unpleasant metamor-phosis. First they would find a tree or a house or a telephone pole and start to climb—slowly, clumsily, driven by mindless instinct—until they reached a particular height known only to themselves. They would cling tight, hold still, and gradually become translu-cent. Their outer skin would slough away. They would burst out through the napes of their former shells and rise into the sky as steel-spun creatures with wings as loud as joy buzzers. They left their spent husks everywhere.

Once, long ago, Cora took it upon herself to collect cicada skins. She hid them in a drawer in No. 43 until she amassed twenty or so,

at which point Darlene stumbled upon them, unnerved by these grotesque symbols of change.

For a moment, her mind was filled with Cora. Images of her little
sister flashed behind her eyes like the whirling frames in a slide carou-
sel projected on a screen. She saw Cora shuffling resignedly up the front
steps of Mercy Elementary School. She saw Cora climbing the highest
tree in Shady Acres, mounting into the branches without hesitation
or fear. She saw Cora lying on her belly in the dirt, her skin painted
gold in the afternoon sunlight, her gaze intense and focused, holding
a spider in the hollow of her palms. She saw Cora making her favorite
snack of peanut butter and pickles. She saw Cora running across the
playground. Her sister was athletic, even graceful, yet unaware of it.

In some ways, Cora was a mysterious child. She had a group of
friends at school but never formed the kind of passionate attachments
that Darlene remembered from her own youth. (She wondered if this
was her fault too—after all, the McClouds had not yet been "the saddest family in Mercy" back when she was young.) In truth, Cora never
seemed to mind being on her own. Unlike most kids her age, she said
nothing without forethought, never giving too much of herself away.
She kept her exterior as placid as a pond, and as reflective too, mirroring back whatever people expected to see. You might assume she was
happy unless you noticed her slumped posture. You might forget she
was in the room until you caught the gleam of her watchful eyes. Darlene was aware that she had often taken her sister for granted. Life was
hard enough without plumbing the depths of a quiet child. It was simpler to take Cora's calm, impassive exterior as a sign of contentment.
It was easier to assume that all was well, to focus on other things.

BY THE TIME DARLENE RETURNED to the motel, the parking lot contained only her pickup truck, no more news vans. Night had fallen,
and the reporters returned to their roosting places like falcons after
a hard day on the hunt.

When Darlene reached her room, Roy was there. She was pleased to see him. Over the past few days, he had transformed from a threat to a neutral party to a touchstone of sanity in a bizarre, sideways world. His square, honest face and coffee-colored eyes were a relief to the senses. Darlene set her groceries on the floor. Roy was sitting on the edge of the bed, playing a card game with Jane.

"Any news?" Darlene said.

"No," he said. "But the crime scene guys are hard at work. We've got wiretaps on all your phones. It's only a matter of time. Hey now!" This last part was directed at Jane, who had just smacked his hand, evidently as part of the game.

"I win!" she cried.

"Winner cleans up," he said, rising to his feet.

Obediently, Jane gathered the cards into a pile. Her hair was still tinged with green from the pool. She had not been to soccer practice in several days. Darlene knew that the lack of physical activity was starting to wear on her sister.

It was understood within the family that soccer would be Jane's ticket out of Mercy. She was a strong player, religious about her participation and compliant to her coach's wishes, neither a grandstander nor a sore loser. She would be a perfect candidate for a scholarship. Darlene had gone over the cost/benefit ratio many times as she paid for new cleats or shin guards or yet another uniform. It would all be worth it the day she saw her sister boarding a bus for college.

Roy stepped close. "Take a walk with me."

"All right," Darlene said. "Jane, eat. Before it melts."

Her sister nodded, grabbing the carton of ice cream and the remote control.

Darlene and Roy stepped together into the hallway, which was both dingy and dark. She could never decide whether its shabbiness came from accumulated filth or insufficient lighting. Roy led the way toward the exit sign. They passed through the lobby, where the clerk was nodding off behind the desk, his cowboy hat tipped forward over his eyes, his shotgun leaning against the wall. Roy waited until they were outside to speak.

"We're past the forty-eight-hour mark," he said.

"What does that mean?"

"Nothing good."

There was a bench beside a bush. Roy took a seat, and Darlene followed suit. He was wearing khakis and a button-down shirt, the collar open to reveal a swatch of fur. As always, he smelled like a tea shop, spicy and sweet. There was a gap between his front teeth. He tugged a pack of cigarettes from his pocket.

"Do you mind?" he said.

"No," she said, though she did.

He lit up and took a long drag. He was polite in his exhalations, blowing the stream away from her. Darlene saw something twitching on the bench beside her. A cicada had left its skin there, still latched to the wood and shifting in the breeze. With a grimace, she flicked it into the bushes.

"The crime techs found blood at your place," Roy said.

"What?"

"They found it—well—everywhere. All over the bathroom. All over the kitchen floor."

"Oh my God."

"It's Tucker's," he said hastily. "None of it seems to be Cora's. It didn't show up, you understand, until they used a chemical spray and a special lens. You wouldn't have seen it with the naked eye."

Darlene did not reply, struck dumb by the image of No. 43 awash with blood.

"We knew Tucker was injured in the bombing," Roy said. "So it's not really a surprise. It wasn't a life-threatening amount, but he did make one hell of a mess."

"He does that," Darlene said wearily. "My Category Five brother."

Roy took a final, contemplative drag on his cigarette, then ground it out on the bench.

"Listen," he said. "I have to ask this."

Darlene frowned. She thought she knew where he was going.

"In most kidnapping cases, it's a custody thing," he said. "One parent will snatch a kid from the other when they have the chance. But this . . ." He broke off. "An older brother taking his younger sister . . ." He paused again.

"Tucker isn't like that," Darlene said.

Roy let out a quick breath. "You're sure? One in five little girls—"

"Not Tucker," she said.

"It's often a family member who—"

"Trust me on this one. Tucker might be a lot of bad things, but he isn't that."

She met his gaze steadily. She did not blink. Roy stared at her as though trying to see through her to the wall behind. Then he nodded, satisfied. He leaned back, running his hands across the crown of his head.

"So what's your take?" he said. "What's Tucker going to do?"

Darlene shrugged.

"All right, he stops by the old homestead," Roy went on. "He finds Cora there. She helps him patch up his wounds. But why would he take her with him? Why bring her on the run?"

"You said it yourself—he was still in bad shape. He needed help. He's always been good at getting other people to take care of him."

"Right," he said. "But there are police checkpoints all around Mercy. They won't get to the next town without being stopped. Cora's picture is on every TV screen in Oklahoma. What's Tucker's plan?"

Darlene laughed without warmth. "What makes you think he has a plan? I reckon he'll keep Cora with him as long as he needs her. Then he'll dump her somewhere and move on. He's never had much use for family."

Roy glanced at her, his face filled with compassion.

"I just hope . . ." she began, then sighed. "He'd never hurt Cora on purpose. She was always his favorite. But he's reckless. So careless. I just hope he remembers to feed her. Make sure she wears a seat belt. Brushes her teeth."

"Yeah."

"God, poor Cora. She must be so confused." Darlene shook her head. "I don't know what Tucker told her to make her run off with him. Some guilt trip. His life in her hands. I'm sure she didn't think she had any choice."

She wrung her fingers in the fabric of her shirt. The wind swirled around her, carrying the floral scent of the prairie.

"He's the most selfish person alive," she said. "Whenever I think he can't do anything worse, he tops himself."

"I get that."

"Just pray that he has enough sense to find a safe place for her when he leaves her behind. That's all we can hope for."

For a moment, Darlene was too angry to breathe. For years, she had considered her brother with a mixture of heartache and jealousy. This cocktail of emotion was so much a part of her makeup now that she could not remember who she was without it. Rage burned in her chest like the flame of a lantern. She had nourished it tenderly since Tucker's departure, sheltering it from the wind, keeping it alight.

Darlene found herself thinking about Mrs. Hamilton, a social worker from long ago. She had not seen the woman in years, but she still remembered the flounce of her ponytail and the rainbow of bracelets she wore, jangling with every gesture. A week after the tornado, Mrs. Hamilton brought all four of the McCloud orphans to her office. In a chaotic time when everything ran together like blurred ink, her face stood out clearly in Darlene's memory.

Mrs. Hamilton had asked questions, her voice deceptively kind, her eyes bird bright. She missed nothing. Darlene recalled the smell of the woman's lavender perfume, the feeling of being given an exam she had not studied for. She and her siblings sat in a row of plastic chairs, unsettled and fidgety. Tucker was playing cat's cradle with a rubber band. Jane was picking her cuticles. Cora was staring out the window, looking for shapes in the clouds.

Mrs. Hamilton was the one who had laid out their options. There was no extended family to take them in. They could stay together, but that would mean Tucker and Darlene "stepping up in a big way." The two of them would have to provide for their sisters. They would have to help the girls with their homework, make sure they got enough food and sleep, attend parent-teacher conferences, and look after their emotional needs, too. Darlene and Tucker would have to become grown-ups overnight—not just adults, but guardians.

As Mrs. Hamilton spoke, Darlene glanced at her brother. They locked eyes over the top of Jane's head. Tucker nodded solemnly. He reached across the space between them and squeezed Darlene's shoulder—a gesture as reassuring as a promise.

Then Mrs. Hamilton talked about foster care. She did not mince words as she described "the system." Darlene, at nineteen, was exempt, but her siblings would be carted away from her, carrying their worldly goods in garbage bags. They would be placed in a group home at first. Tucker, a few months shy of the age of majority, would probably never find a foster family. Teenagers were always a tough sell. He would live in the group home until he turned eighteen, at which point he would be spat out into the world on his own. Cora and Jane were more likely to be fostered, but even if they found a family of strangers to take them in, they would almost certainly be separated from each other. They would not be able to remain in Mercy, maybe not in Oklahoma. It might be years before the four of them saw one another again.

"Together, together, we'll stay together"—they answered in one voice. No hesitation. Nodding desperately. Reaching for one another's hands.

Later, Mrs. Hamilton asked to speak to Darlene on her own, so Tucker took Jane and Cora to get some lunch. Alone in the social worker's office, Darlene tried to sit up straight, to look mature and responsible. Mrs. Hamilton came around the desk and leaned in close, her broad face caked with sedimentary layers of makeup.

"Are you sure about this, Darlene?" she said. "Tucker can help, but it all falls on you. I need you to really consider what your life will look like."

"I am."

"Nobody will think less of you if you say no. Foster care isn't so bad. There might be a rough few years, but y'all will get through it. Your siblings will be fine in the end, no matter what you decide."

Absently, Darlene touched the place on her shoulder where Tucker had laid his hand. In that moment, she felt certain. Her parents would have wanted them to stay together. The future would be difficult—she knew it would be difficult—but at least she would not be alone.

"We can do it," she said. "Tucker and I can do it."

Now, remembering, she closed her eyes tight. She heard the echo of her own words again. Back then, she was so young. She trusted her brother implicitly. It was painful to look back on how innocent she had been. Though she had already suffered a great deal—death and accidents and tornadoes—she had only encountered tragedy, never human cruelty. She had not yet seen the depths of what one person could do to another.

Three months after that conversation, Tucker ran away.

With a weighty sigh, Darlene wondered how she would have answered Mrs. Hamilton's questions if she had known then what was coming. She wondered if the social worker had seen something in her brother that she herself had not. A restlessness. A fickle streak. A capacity for savagery.

17

June now moved like a freight train. Soon enough, Darlene was back in the trailer, back at work. The summer wind was hot and dry, flash-frying the grass and filling the air with iridescent mirages of buttery light. She spent her days ringing up other people's groceries and dodging the reporters in the parking lot. She spent her nights pacing the trailer in the darkness. There was an empty chair at the kitchen table. Over pizza one evening, Jane smirked and said, "And then there were two." A moment later, her face fell, and she and Darlene both looked away. One by one, the McClouds were vanishing.

Darlene avoided the news. She and Jane stuck to their guns, refusing to give even a single interview, but their reticence did not make much difference. The full story paraded across the TV and the internet in exhaustive detail. Darlene tried to shield Jane—and herself—from it. She did not want to hear the newscasters interviewing psychologists, lawyers, or environmental activists. She did not want to hear speculation about what her brother's motives might be. She did not want to hear Tucker referred to as a sociopath or a terrorist. Most of all, she did not want to hear about Cora. The announcers invariably described her in angelic terms—"a heart of gold," "popular with her classmates," "loved by all." This kind of talk was unbearable. It was a preemptive nostalgia, a retroactive remembering, a halo bestowed on a child who everyone seemed to believe was as good as dead. Darlene did not want to hear any of it, but she caught hints against her will as she changed the channel or walked past a radio blaring in the storeroom. The story was in the very air she breathed.

Every few days, Roy would call to check in, his voice a little darker each time. No news, no word. The cops were still on the case, the FBI would keep up their wiretaps as long as possible, and he personally remained hopeful. But the focus of the law was no longer trained on Tucker and Cora. The FBI dismantled the checkpoints around Mercy. Tucker's name was one on a long list of similar criminals, just as Cora's was one on a long list of similar victims.

Still, Darlene jumped every time her phone rang. She would stare at the little screen, and invariably her heart would sink. It might be Jane needing a ride home. It might be Fred calling from the supermarket. Every now and then, she could hear a soft click on the line that told her the FBI was listening too.

A week passed, then two. At last, the reporters moved on. They followed the scent of decay to fresher kills. Darlene noted their absence with pleasure and regret—she was glad to see them go, but their departure meant nothing good for Cora.

Before leaving No. 43 each morning, Darlene would stare into the bathroom mirror and steel her features into a polite mask. She would practice a few noncommittal responses: *No word yet. Thanks for your concern. I'm afraid I can't talk now.* She would armor herself against the inevitable onslaught of the day. The reporters might be gone, but the people of Mercy were nearly as relentless. They all seemed to address Darlene in exactly the same way, their voices lilting, their heads cocked at a sympathetic angle. There was something robotic about the precise repetition of it, so many different people behaving identically. They were particularly irrepressible when she was at work, behind the cash register, unable to flee, required to be civil. They would ask her how she was doing and whether there was any news about Cora. Then they would grin solicitously and falsely. It grated on her nerves.

In the past, Darlene had often heard talk about the Oklahoma Standard. After the bombing at the Murrah Building, there was an outpouring of support for the victims. Strangers became a community overnight. People used their own cars as ambulances and emptied their wallets. They gave their time, their blood, the clothes off their backs, the shoes off their feet. Darlene had heard the tales all her life. She had observed her neighbors' vicarious pride, even the ones who were not in Oklahoma City at the time, who were not yet born.

Now, in the wake of her own tragedy—yet another in a long line— she wondered. Perhaps the Oklahoma Standard would have applied to her life if the circumstances were different. Perhaps the people of Mercy wanted to be considerate and helpful, rather than curious and stilted. But there was no script for this. If Cora had returned home safe and sound, everyone would know what to do: calling with congratulations, cheering in the streets, bringing food. If Cora had died, everyone would know what to do: calling with condolences, sending flowers, bringing food. But as things stood, Cora was a question without an answer.

Darlene grew increasingly thankful for Roy's presence. With him, at least, there was no pretense. He knew what she had suffered—what she was continuing to suffer—and she did not have to feign normalcy or change the subject to something less upsetting. He never told her to smile, to trust in God, that he was praying for her.

She missed Cora more than she thought possible. She had always loved the feel of her baby sister climbing into her lap. Wishbone torso and knobby knees. Sometimes Cora would nap there, her brow nestled against Darlene's throat. These moments were rare. Her sister was never one for embraces or kisses, and Darlene was wired the same way. Nowadays, as much as she tried, she could not remember the last time they had touched. It seemed important somehow. That was the thing about hindsight; only in retrospect did the significance and prescience of little moments spring into being. The last hug. The last goodbye.

Over time, Darlene became more and more aware of the irrepressible systems of human life. Both great and small, both interior and exterior, these unstoppable mechanisms maintained and supported her existence. Without her will or consent, her body continued to function, her heart pumping blood, neurons firing in her brain. Without her will or consent, the town of Mercy continued to function too. Electricity flowed through the wires overhead. The supermarket opened every day at 8 a.m. sharp. Garbage trucks collected the refuse and carted it away to the dump. The hardware store held a summer sale.

Down the highway, beyond the horizon, on the other side of the TV screen, the indomitable infrastructure of civilization prevailed. Cell towers operated. Airplanes took flight. The internet continued its mysterious existence. There was news from Chicago, something about a riot after a baseball game. There was news from Europe, something about a controversial statement from the pope. There was news from outer space, something about a meteorite that might be heading toward the earth in a thousand years.

The deeper, older rhythms of the world flourished too. Days grew longer, nights shorter. The moon waxed and waned. The summer constellations rose higher and burned with greater intensity. Watermelons overran the supermarket, and tiny biting ladybugs overran the parking lot. There was a rainstorm that flooded the streets for a few hours, the ground too parched to absorb the overspill. There was a tornado warning in Dover that turned out to be nothing. One morning, there was a double rainbow.

•

WHEN SCHOOL LET OUT FOR the summer, Jane took over the trailer. She was constantly underfoot, sprawled across the couch, her cleats on the welcome mat, her shin guards in the living room, clumps of dirt and grass everywhere.

Darlene tried to make allowances. Jane was under strain too, though she could not express it directly. She never talked about Cora. She did her best to pretend that everything was fine, though she always seemed to be on the verge of tears.

Darlene often found herself thinking of Tucker—remembering him the way he used to be. Her best memories of her brother were her earliest ones. Tucker laughing at her with a toothless mouth through the bars of his crib. Tucker in diapers, his bare belly taut and golden. She remembered teaching him how to braid Mama's hair. She remembered pushing him in the stroller at her mother's side. She and Tucker were less than two years apart, and for a long time they had been the only children in the house. Babies together. Toddlers together. They shared their toys, their books, the sandbox in the backyard, their evening bath, their mother's lullabies, and their father's lap.

As a boy, Tucker was fearless. He once slid into third base so ferociously that he broke his arm in two places. He was a child composed of scrapes and bruises. Riding his bike with no hands. Clambering onto the roof on a dare. Hammering nails into the back fence just for the noise of it. Starting fights with his favorite challenge: "Your ass is grass and I'm a lawnmower!" Darlene would often find her brother at the very top of a tree, higher than anybody else dared to go, swaying with the movement of the trunk, his gaze on the horizon as though he half expected to take flight. For a while, he believed that the phrase *tuckered out* was about him personally. At the end of a long day, he would nuzzle close to Darlene and whisper, "I tuckered you out."

He loved animals, even then. He became a vegetarian at an early age, announcing that meat was murder and reminding everyone over dinner exactly what their meal would have looked like when it was still alive. This was not really acceptable for a young boy in a small Oklahoma town, but Tucker pulled it off with a combination of humor and charisma. He laughed away the backhanded comments, and soon enough, people stopped commenting.

The family farm had been his home and heart. He and Mama were both designed like that. At any hour of the day, Tucker could be found in the cow paddock, Mama sitting by the henhouse. Darlene liked the animals too, but they did not draw her the way they drew her mother and brother, who treated the shabby shed and mildewed barn as portals to wonder. Mama was never so quick to smile as she was with Mojo. She spent hours with the stallion, not riding him, not feeding him, just communing with him in his own language of touch and gesture. Tucker had a similar bond with the cows, more profound than the inherent divide between species. The herd would look for him every afternoon, their heavy heads turned toward the house, swishing their tails. They would wait for him to come home from school, and when they saw him strolling toward the paddock, they would call to him, long necks extended, mouths wide, the same cry they gave to greet their own kind.

After Mama died, Tucker redoubled his devotion to the animals. Sometimes Darlene thought there was no other outlet for the love he had lavished on their mother—a rushing river with no path—so he redirected it all toward the farm. He brought treats to the shy goat, despite its disdain for humanity. He took over Mama's relationship with Mojo. When the stallion fell ill, Tucker tended him with affection and grace. He intuited that Mojo was grieving for Mama too and organized the purchase of a mare and pony. He spent weeks helping them acclimate to their new home.

He did not neglect the cows, either. Darlene remembered a rainy week one August, perhaps a year after their mother's death: the sky papered over, the trees fat and dark, the air in the house so humid she could almost swim in it. Glancing out her bedroom window, she noticed the cattle lying down, as they always did in wet weather. There was a lean shape among them. Looking closer, she saw Tucker lounging between two females in the grass, letting the rain soak him to the bone.

After the tornado, none of the farm animals were ever found. The horses, the cows, the goat, the brood of hens—they were erased as completely as the house, the barn, and, of course, Daddy. All of it blown away. Darlene knew better than to hope that any of their animals had fled to safety. There were a thousand ways to die in a tornado. She only hoped it had been quick.

A week after the storm, she and Tucker snuck back to the old house to pick through the wreckage for anything they could salvage. They crept between fallen trees and chunks of drywall, looking for clothes, pots, or toys. They wriggled under pieces of plumbing and climbed over splintered boards. Most of what they uncovered was useless: a single shoe, a picture book torn into fragments, a pillow in a puddle of mud and sewage, half a guitar.

Darlene saw the object first, though she did not recognize it. A silvery shape. Soft and furred. Bedewed with red droplets. It took her a moment to register that it was the severed foot of a horse.

The leg had been sliced clean through, leaving just a hoof, a boxy joint, and a gleam of sleek gray coat. The wound was surprisingly clean, as though it had been cauterized. Darlene reached for the dreadful thing, hoping that her senses were deceiving her, hoping to touch plastic or wood.

The flesh was cold. The hoof and hair felt exactly the same in death as they had in life. The blood had dried into paste. She could smell the onset of decomposition now—rotten, curdled, and earthy.

Then a shadow fell over her, and she glanced up to find Tucker standing there. His expression was one she had not seen before or since. So much pain that she had to look away. He took a handkerchief from his pocket, spat into it, and knelt down to wipe the patina of dried blood from her fingers.

18

On a dry, balmy afternoon, Darlene was sweeping the sidewalk in front of the supermarket when she heard a screech of tires. She turned to see a squad car braking wildly. Roy climbed out of the driver's seat, waving to her. Darlene shaded her eyes with a hand, taking in his determined expression, his movements brisk with purpose.

"They found a girl," he shouted. "At the Texas border."

Darlene let go of the broom, which landed with a clatter.

"Is it Cora?" she cried.

Roy hurried around the hood of the car. "No identification yet. I just got the call ten minutes ago. A couple fishermen saw something floating in the Red River. They dragged her out and took her straight to the ER."

He handed his phone to Darlene. There was an image on the

screen, slightly out of focus, as though the photographer had been in motion. She saw a gleam of ruddy water. She had never been to the Red River, but she knew that its banks formed the rumpled border between Oklahoma and Texas. The snapshot was framed by trees and a thicket of wet grasses. She looked closer.

A child lay in the mud. Two adult figures were bending over her. Her posture suggested that she was unconscious. Her clothes were soaked, her skin dappled with patterns of rust-colored silt, hair plastered across her cheek. Darlene used her fingers to enlarge the image, but the girl only dissolved into pixels.

"I can't tell," she said. "Do you think it's Cora?"

"She'll be in the ER for a few hours at least. With a little luck, we can be there when she wakes up."

Darlene squinted at the picture again. An anonymous child. No distinguishing features. In the background, the river was the color of blood.

THEY TOOK ROUTE 81 SOUTH across Oklahoma. The sun hung unmoving in Darlene's window, cooking her skin. The squad car was clean but shabby. Roy drove well above the speed limit—the policeman's prerogative—while Darlene read an article on her phone about the Red River. She had never thought much about it before, its biblical hue. According to the internet, the river was usually a nondescript mud brown, but during flood periods it became saturated with crimson soil.

Darlene could not seem to find a comfortable position in the passenger's seat. An air freshener in the shape of a sunflower hung from the rearview mirror, filling the small space with an artificial approximation of perfume. Roy did not attempt small talk. He turned on the radio, but they were far enough into the countryside now that each station was awash with static.

Outside the town of Chickasha, Roy stopped to refill the gas tank, grab some bottled water, and smoke three cigarettes in a row, pacing around a barren field of dirt behind the parking lot, far from the pumps and fumes. Darlene considered texting Jane about what was happening, but restrained herself. Her sister was spending the day with friends, probably flirting with boys at the dollar store or trying to sneak into the R-rated movie at the cinema. Darlene would wait until she had actual news to share.

Out in the field, Roy took a call on his phone. She was too far away to hear what he was saying, though she watched him avidly as he gestured with his cigarette. She gnawed her thumbnail until it bled.

"Anything?" Darlene asked as he approached.

"Not yet," he said.

They drove on. Roy's clothes were now drenched with the smell of smoke, which mingled discordantly with the stench of his air freshener. The sun was lower in the sky, boiling the clouds into vapor.

Darlene suddenly found the silence untenable.

"You weren't here, were you?" she blurted out.

"Beg pardon?"

"When the tornado hit. You weren't living in Mercy then."

"That's right."

She nodded. "I thought I remembered that. You were away for a while."

"College," he said. "Police academy."

"Where?"

"Oklahoma City." He thumped his chest with a fist. "Sooner born, sooner bred."

Darlene debated whether she ought to tell him that she had once planned to go to OU, to be the first member of her family to get a degree. A thousand years ago.

"What brought you back to Mercy?" she asked.

Roy rubbed his chin. "Well, my mother got sick."

"I'm sorry."

"Thanks. Cancer took her quick. Just a couple of months." He sighed. "After she passed, I realized I wanted to stay. No place like home, right?"

Darlene did not answer. She laid a hand over her heart.

"There," Roy said. He pointed at a road sign, but it was gone before she could read it.

"Are we close?" she asked.

"Half an hour."

It occurred to Darlene that there was a lightness about Roy—a quality she herself did not possess. His default state seemed to be optimism. She wondered what had made him this way, armored against sorrow. Perhaps his temperament was an inherent trait, woven into his DNA, present from birth.

Roy had never treated her the way other people in Mercy did. He was not formal or distant. Maybe it was because he had been away when the tornado struck. He either missed the subsequent media coverage entirely or was kindhearted enough to leave it in the past, where it belonged.

THE VAST WASTELAND OF TEXAS glimmered along the horizon. The hospital stood at the edge of a small town, overlooking a steep slope studded with bushes and boulders. As Roy pulled into the parking lot, Darlene could see the faraway gleam of the Red River. From this angle, touched by the sunset, the water shone like neon.

She wished she believed in God. She wished she could pray.

Before the car reached a complete stop, Darlene was out on the pavement, pelting toward the hospital doors. Roy yelled something behind her, but she did not look back. As she skidded into the lobby, the man at the front desk glanced up in alarm.

"Where's the girl?" Darlene cried.

"What?"

"The Red River. The girl!"

The man scooted his chair back, wide-eyed, then reached toward the phone on his desk.

"Let me just call security," he said.

"That won't be necessary," Roy said, appearing at Darlene's shoulder, a little breathless. He held out his badge.

A nurse in pink scrubs led them down the hallway. She moved with a languid Southern slowness, and Darlene had to resist the urge to shove her out of the way. The hospital was tiny, the walls a distractingly bright blue.

"Here we are," the nurse said, gesturing to a door. "She's sedated. You won't be able to talk to her."

There was a small figure in a white bed, tucked beneath a blanket. The girl was hooked up to an IV and a monitor that displayed her pulse and respiration. The beeping of the machinery was both reassuring and irksome.

Darlene moved closer. She touched the rough weave of the hospital blanket. Then, without warning, her knees buckled. Roy leapt forward and caught her. He pulled her back up to her feet.

The girl in the bed was unlike Cora in every way. She was not the right size, the right age, the right ethnicity. A plump little thing. Maybe five years old. Her hair was sleek and straight, without the slightest wave, let alone tumbling ringlets. Her skin was russet-colored, as warm as sunrise against the white coverlet.

Someone else's child. Someone else's sister.

Darlene staggered backward, her body colliding with Roy's. He stayed close, supporting her, his hands tight on her shoulders.

The heart monitor beeped. The IV bag glowed. The girl in the bed breathed, her arms folded limply over her belly.

"Take me home," Darlene whispered, turning away.

THE HIGHWAY WAS DESERTED. NIGHT had fallen, absent of moon. Roy drove as Darlene leaned her temple against the window, rocking with the movement of the car. A few lonely stars glinted above the horizon. A truck lumbered past in the opposite direction, nothing but headlights and wind. Darlene texted Jane, explaining that there had been a false alarm and she would be home late. She did not feel sad; she did not feel anything. She seemed to have moved into a quiet state beyond human emotion.

Cora was not the only missing child in the Southwest. Of course she wasn't.

Roy fumbled in his pocket, then passed Darlene a handkerchief. She turned it over in her hands. The fabric was crumpled, smelling strongly of nicotine.

"I'm not crying," she said.

"Just in case."

Then his phone rang. He answered without taking his eyes off the road. The conversation was short. "Uh-huh," he said. "Yep. Got it."

Roy hung up and cleared his throat.

"The girl," he said. "Her parents just turned up at the hospital."

Darlene closed her eyes, balling the handkerchief up in her palm.

19

Darlene woke to the sound of her phone. It took her a while to wrestle out of the tangle of covers. She groped across the coffee table, attempting to unplug her phone from its charger.

"Hello?"

There was a crackle of static on the other end. Darlene sat up, pushing her hair out of her face. She squinted at the clock on the microwave.

"Jesus Christ, it's four in the morning," she said. "Who is this?"

A laugh floated down the line. It was high-pitched, as sugary as cotton candy. A child's giggle.

All at once, Darlene was completely awake, as alert as she had ever been. She rose to her feet, clutching the phone with both hands.

"Is that you?" she whispered.

"It's me," Cora said.

"Oh God. Thank heavens."

She switched on the lamp. Her glasses were on the coffee table, lenses winking at her. When she put them on, the world came into focus. She reached for her shoes.

"Where are you?" she said. "Are you okay? Are you hurt?"

"I'm fine. Tucker was hurt bad . . ." A wave of static swelled, and Cora's voice slipped away into a sea of gray rustling.

"Are you there?" Darlene cried.

"Better now," Cora said at the same time. "He's better."

The connection between them faded in and out, tenuous and rough. Cora's breathing seemed to stretch along the line. Darlene tucked the phone between her chin and shoulder and dug through her purse, trying to find her car keys. She pictured her sister's face— feathery eyebrows, button nose, butterfly mouth. She knew every inch of Cora's body. She had wiped her sister's behind, bathed her, bandaged her scrapes and bruises. She imagined the knobs of Cora's spine, the scar on her left knee, and her nubbly belly button, not an innie or an outie but something in between.

"Tell me where you are," she said. "I'll come get you."

"What?" Cora said. The word caught and repeated in space, bouncing and reverberating: *What? What?* The pitch rose and fell, now deeper, now shriller, as though a chorus of other children had joined in too.

Darlene tried to stand still, hoping the reception would improve.

"I'll be there as soon as I can," she said. "God, I've missed you. Just tell me where you are."

"No," Cora said.

The throng of other voices dropped away. Suddenly the line was perfectly clear. Darlene stood frozen in the middle of the living room.

"What do you mean?" she said.

"No," Cora repeated. "I'm staying here. With Tucker."

She spoke without hesitation or sorrow. She was not asking for permission; she was stating a fact.

For a moment, Darlene wondered if she was still dreaming. The conversation had all the surreal hallmarks of a nightmare. The static on the line had lifted, but the conversation still did not make sense. The clarity of their phone connection seemed to operate in inverse proportion to the clarity of Darlene's brain: the crisper her contact with Cora, the more confused she became.

"With Tucker," she said. "You're with him right now?"

"Of course." Cora laughed, a note like a struck gong. "I'm always with him."

"But . . ." Darlene began, then faltered. "It's time for me to bring you home."

The line shivered with shadows again. There was a clatter, and Darlene heard her own voice resounding in her ear, thin and altered, faintly repeating her final word: *home, home.*

"Home," Cora said.

Or maybe she had not spoken at all. Darlene could not be sure if it was only an echo, her own voice distorted into her sister's.

"That's right," she said. "Time to come home."

"No, I'm not going back there," Cora said. "I just thought I should call to tell you I'm okay."

Darlene dropped her purse with a thunk. Her keys skittered across the linoleum.

There was a flurry of muted rustling on the line, as though her sister had covered the receiver with her palm. Darlene plugged her free ear with a finger, focusing all her attention on the noises inside the speaker.

A second voice. Low and gravelly. For an instant, Darlene could not tell whether it was real or not.

Tucker. His growl, his cadence. Tucker and Cora were talking back and forth. Darlene could not catch any words, just the interplay of soprano and baritone.

Then Cora said, "Tucker says the cops are probably trying to trace this call right now. You can tell them not to bother. This is a burning phone."

In the background, Darlene heard her brother laugh. A ripe, hearty chuckle, as vivid as though he were in the living room with her.

"A burner phone," Cora said, correcting herself. "It's a *burner* phone. That means it's disposable and nobody can trace it. Not for a few minutes, anyway. All right, Tucker. You don't have to be such a show-off all the time."

"I don't understand what's happening," Darlene said.

"It's the SIM cards too," Cora said. "Tucker switched them . . . What?" She broke off, listening to something Darlene did not catch. A moment later, she exhaled a sticky breath and said, "Oh yeah. I'm not supposed to tell you about that, Darlene."

The moon dipped behind a skein of cloud, darkening the world. Darlene felt a swoop in her gut, the first cold wave of terror. She was astonished by the intimacy that seemed to exist between her brother and sister. It had never crossed her mind that she would end up feeling like a third wheel, listening as her siblings communed on the other end of the line.

"Where are you?" she repeated helplessly.

"I'm on an adventure," Cora said. "Tucker has a plan."

"What kind of plan?"

"Have you ever heard of the Anthropocene Mass Extinction?" Cora spoke the words with great care, enunciating each syllable.

Darlene reacted without thought. She flung her phone away, tossing it onto the floor as though it had stung her. Her fingertips were burning. The phone rolled, bumped against the couch, and stopped. Darlene whimpered a little, shaking the feeling back into her hands.

Then she lunged for the phone and brought it to her ear again.

"What did you say?" she said. "I don't think I heard you right."

"The Age of Humans," Cora said. "It's happening right now. There've been five mass extinctions on our planet so far. A meteor, a volcano, and some other things, I forget what. This one is number six."

Darlene began to cry. The tears came suddenly and oddly, striping her cheeks, cool and quiet. A wellspring bubbling up from some interior cavern.

"You sound like Tucker," she said. "Just like him."

"Yeah. We're the same now."

In the distance, Tucker piped up again. Every time he spoke, Cora immediately fell silent. His words apparently took priority over hers. It was as though some part of her was always waiting for his voice, ready to give it her full attention.

Darlene dried her eyes with her sleeve, but the tears continued to pour. For weeks, she had been waiting for this call. She had run scripts in her head. She had practiced with Roy, then on her own, rehearsing in the bathroom mirror. She thought she was ready for any possible contingency. But she wasn't prepared for this. She could not have imagined this strange child—the one imitating her sister, mimicking her voice, unrecognizable and eerie.

"What happened to you?" Darlene whispered.

"Nothing," Cora said. "I'm great."

The line flooded momentarily with a harsh electric sizzling. Darlene wiped her eyes and tried to gather her wits.

"Does Tucker have any idea what he's done?" she said. "Does he realize how much trouble he's in? Bombing and kidnapping and God knows what else."

"Kidnapping?" Cora said. "How could he kidnap me? He's my *brother*."

Darlene pressed her fist against her brow. She reminded herself that she was speaking to a child, and she made her tone gentle.

"Honey, it's gonna be okay. The police are looking for you. They're looking for you right now."

Cora laughed. "They won't find us."

That laugh. So confident. The girl sounded giddy, almost drugged.

"Tucker doesn't have the right," Darlene said. "He doesn't have custody of you, and he knows it. He cannot just force you to go away with him—"

"He didn't," Cora said, her voice higher now. A small child. A child on a field trip. "I wanted to come. He asked, and I said yes."

"No, you didn't," Darlene snapped. "That's not what happened."

She did not mean to say this. She was still trying to have the conversation she had rehearsed, one in which the world possessed order and balance. But the world no longer possessed order and balance. Darlene caught a glimpse of herself in the mirror over the TV. She looked wild, her hair disheveled, her eyes pink and brimming.

"Listen to me," she said. "Please. I know you love Tucker. I know you've missed him. But . . ." She trailed off. "Something happened to his mind. It's not his fault. Tell Tucker I said that, okay? It was the tornado's fault. I don't blame him. But you both have to come home now."

There was stillness on the line, pristine and profound. Darlene thought for an awful instant that the call had been disconnected. But it was only a respite from the static. When Cora spoke, her voice was dreamy but bell clear.

"The tornado was a gift," she said.

"What?"

"A gift. Tucker told me so. It opened his eyes. It showed him reality. Most people go their whole lives without that. They're too sheltered. But Tucker and me—we see it now."

Darlene began to pace around the living room, skirting the coffee table. A wind buffeted the trailer, and the front door squeaked on its hinges. She wanted to throw her phone again, hard enough this time to shatter the screen. She wanted to make a mess—fling plates at the wall, kick over the TV. She wanted to rip the door down, she wanted to punch through the walls. In that moment, she could have pulled No. 43 apart with her bare hands.

"Everything happens for a reason," Cora said. "Animals lose their homes and their families all the time. Human beings come in and take everything from them. That's what a mass extinction is. And that's what happened to us. The tornado took everything. Do you see? We *lived* it, Darlene. Now we know."

Darlene moved faster. Her breath was tight in her chest, her gait brisk enough to jingle the cutlery. The tiny, shabby trailer was no match for her anger. On the other end of the line, Tucker's voice rumbled like faraway thunder.

"I have to go," Cora said. "That's long enough."

"Where are you? Tell me right now."

"Oh, Darlene." It was an indulgent sigh.

"You have no idea what I've gone through. I've been sick with worry. Sick and frantic."

"I'm fine." Cora sounded tinny, a little hollow.

"Tucker's dangerous. Did you know he has a police file? He's a criminal. Please listen to me. You have to come home, you have to. I miss my little sister."

"Oh," Cora said, a long, slow exhalation that looped around Darlene's neck like a rope. "She's already gone."

A flurry of other voices rang out in a sudden, blistering chorus, loud enough that Darlene jerked the phone away from her ear. She heard what sounded like a woman shouting—a man complaining— not Tucker—not Cora—only strangers. Too many sounds to name, at once human and mechanical, a soup of words and crackles and electric chiming. They were not talking to one another, and they were not talking to Darlene. All across Oklahoma, these unknown souls were having individual conversations, chatting on the phone about the weather, spilling secrets, sharing gossip, unaware that their voices had been gathered up and mixed into a cacophony, deafening and indecipherable, without meaning.

Then there was silence.

"Are you there?" Darlene shouted. "Cora? Cora, where are you?"

She looked at the screen in her hand and saw the truth—dark, blank, the call terminated. She looked around No. 43 and saw it for what it was—a beat-up thirdhand trailer on its last legs, the door ill hung, the furniture salvaged from alleys, the window screens patched, the washer/dryer unit listing to one side, the paint peeling, the plumbing rusted, not a scrap of comfort to be found, bleak and grim and hopeless. Something within Darlene splintered. She held the phone as if it were her sister's hand and broke down, her body wrenched with sobs as she slumped onto the couch. She had never been more alone.

And just like that, Cora was gone.

JULY

20

The room was so dark that I might as well have left my eyes closed. Groggy and disoriented, I waved my fingers in front of my face. I could not see my own hand, not even a flutter of motion against the black.

Tucker's gush of breath at my side was the only verification that I was awake—that the physical world still existed at all.

"Tucker," I whispered.

The rhythm of his snoring did not change. I sat up and groped across the uneven floor for the flashlight. My brother and I usually slept with it between our bodies, but now I could not find it. My hand bumped the base of the bucket we used as a toilet, sloshing the urine inside.

"Tucker," I said, louder this time.

No response. I felt a surge of claustrophobia. I remembered now that I had been dreaming about being buried alive—thinning air, the mass of earth pressing down above me, dying by slow degrees in a sealed coffin, never to be rescued.

Maybe I was still dreaming. After all, I was with my missing brother in a ruined tornado shelter, beneath the absence of our former home, amid the wreckage of our former neighborhood. I did not know what time it was, what day it was. The air was scented by a foul combination of mildew and sweat. There was no electricity and no running water. The background thrum of human life was absent here—no appliances, no plumbing, none of the mechanical purr that had once been so omnipresent. The bunker was small enough that I did not want to get to my feet without first locating the flashlight; I might brain myself on the shelves.

I whimpered a little as I searched the floor. At last, I touched the solid fact of my brother's hand—his skin warmed by fever, burning like an ember in mine—and shook it.

"Wake up," I said.

He grunted. "Gimme a minute."

I stayed where I was, clutching his hand. It always took him a while to untangle his mind from sleep—especially now, when he was still healing.

For the past few weeks, Tucker and I had lived underground. The hours passed with excruciating slowness. In the morning, the space would be tolerably cool, but it was no match for the Oklahoma sun, and by the afternoon the bunker would become a black oven that trapped and intensified the heat. The stench was a hand pressed over my mouth—our urine evaporating and condensing in the pail, the rotting residue inside the cans of food we had all but emptied, the mud and rodent droppings. Tucker's sweat and mine were each different enough to stand out from the other. The top note of the whole mess was the clotting of his injuries. I did my best to change his dressings and spread disinfectant on his wounds, but his recovery was sluggish and ripe.

He spent most of his time asleep, weak from blood loss and shock. So I napped too, sprawled on the floor beside him. There was nothing else to do. I was not allowed to go outside in daylight. Tucker did not have a real cell phone with apps and games, just a plastic bag of disposable devices that were to be used once and thrown away. I had never gone so long without looking at a screen. I missed the TV with a visceral ache, almost the same way I missed Darlene and Jane. I would count breaths until I lost track. I would try to decide whether I could detect a whiff of hazardous waste in the grotesque miasma (even though Tucker kept telling me not to worry about it). I would replay my favorite movies in my mind, attempting to remember every scene in the right sequence. Sleep was a welcome respite from the darkness, the silence, and the unrelenting odor.

The only thing that kept me sane was Tucker's voice. Whenever he was awake, he would lecture me. At first these conversations had been few and far between—but as he began to heal, he was alert more and more. He would tell me what he learned during his time away, and I would hang on his every word. His voice was true and certain. Everything else was unreal and dreadful: absenting myself from home and school, unwashed and greasy haired, sleeping on cement, buzzing with pent-up energy. It was a strange kind of torture. There was deprivation (no light, no clock, no Darlene, nothing familiar) and constant, terrible stimulation (the stench, the heat). All I had to cling to were Tucker's lessons.

He often spoke about how life on earth was in free fall. Half the primates on the planet were at risk for extinction. *No more monkeys and lemurs*, he had whispered. *No more gorillas.* Half of all invertebrates were endangered too. *Insects, mollusks, and octopuses—bye-bye, guys.* A third of all vertebrates were at risk. Forty percent of fish. *Hundreds of bird species are already toast. The amphibians are hanging on by a thread.*

Tucker said that insects were dying out in droves. Bees were in trouble. A third of all the butterflies were already gone. *Almost all the species of Orthoptera have kicked the bucket. That's crickets and katydids.* He explained that when the pollinators died out, so did the plants. The forests of our world—all the prairies and orchards, each green and growing thing—would wither. *And whose fault is it? Who's polluting the air and water?*

Humans, I would answer.

Who's chopping down the rain forests?

Humans.

Who's bringing in invasive species?

Humans.

There was often a call-and-response aspect to these lectures. I could not just listen passively. Tucker required me to be intent and engaged.

Half the animal kingdom would be gone in a few decades. There was no question about these facts, no debate in the scientific community. The pattern was clear. The usual extinction rate for a stable ecosystem was one to five species each year. Animals were now dying out at a thousand times the rate they should be. Dozens of species went extinct every single day.

Who's destroying their habitats?

Humans.

Who's killing them for sport?

Humans.

What does Anthropocene mean?

The Age of Humans.

Now I felt my brother shift in the darkness beside me. He sighed, exhaling, letting go of my hand. A moment later, the flashlight clicked on. The bulb was dim and sputtering, but my eyes still took a moment to adjust. I flinched as Tucker swiveled the beam, illuminating each corner of the little space in turn.

He sniffed the air. "You stink," he said.

"*You* stink."

"Truth," he said. "Let's see what time it is."

He pushed himself upright, grimacing in pain, his wounded arm curled protectively against his belly. His hand was a sight to see:

mangled and mottled, two fingers reduced to stumps. The scabs had peeled and fallen off, revealing new, intact skin that was mauve and tender to the touch.

His leg was in a similar condition. The deep gouges had narrowed, sealing themselves shut. They looked like tattoos now, red lines inked across muscle. His calf was bumpy and uneven, the limb weary and sore. He still needed a great deal of rest. He was better but not well.

I watched as he shuffled to the door of the bunker. Cautiously he tugged it open. A cool breeze spiraled inside, and both of us inhaled gratefully.

"It's dark out," he said. "Near midnight, I'd say."

I sprang to my feet and pushed past him. I lived for the nights. As I mounted the basement steps, I felt the wind pick up, kissing away my sweat. I knew that it was warm summer air, but it felt like an arctic gust after the stuffy tomb behind me. I stared around at the ravaged neighborhood. Nothing looked man-made now that the darkness had washed away the colors. The heaps of rubble might have been hillocks. The defunct appliances might have been boulders. The splintered remnants of the telephone poles might have been trees. I heard cicadas chiming, the hoot of an owl, and the flutter of bats overhead.

The tornado was a gift, Tucker often said. *It opened my eyes.*

Over the past few weeks, he had explained this to me. Most people, he said, were not capable of understanding the plight of the animals. They were too sheltered to comprehend it. Too safe. Even if they knew the facts and figures, they could not imagine the full measure of that kind of devastation.

That's how I used to be too, Tucker said. *The tornado changed me.*

It had stripped away the facade of human civilization. It reminded him that he was an animal too. The scientific terms—*loss of habitat, dead zone, on the brink*—were not just words anymore. He knew what it felt like from the inside now.

It's the end of the world, he proclaimed more than once.

Now, standing in the inky wreckage of our former home, surrounded by broken shapes and silence, it was easy for me to believe him.

"Hey," Tucker hissed behind me. "Come on back."

I crept down the moldering stairs into the crater of the basement
again. My brother moved the beam of the flashlight step by step,
lighting my way.

"I've got some good news," he said.

"What is it?"

He tipped the flashlight up, highlighting his face from beneath.
His upper lip and the underside of his nose flared gold.

"It's time to leave," he said.

I gasped. "Really?"

"Really and truly."

He smiled, his face still lit from below, eerie but cheerful. I dashed
toward him, plowing into him, hugging him with all my strength.

"Thank you, thank you," I murmured into his belly.

He laughed, patting my shoulder.

"Get your stuff," he said.

I moved fast. I did not want to give him a chance to change his
mind. During our time in the shelter, Tucker offered no indication
of how long we would have to stay. For me, our departure had shimmered like the light at the end of a tunnel, but I was never sure how
far away it might be. Every time I asked, Tucker would pause as
though checking some interior chronometer and say, "Not yet." From
the start, he made it clear that he was the gatekeeper of all knowledge,
both the wide world and our small part in it.

I scrambled around the shelter, snatching up a grimy T-shirt, my
teddy bear, and a pair of jeans crumpled in a corner. I began to pack
the remaining cans and bottles of water, too, but Tucker told me to
leave them. We would get fresh provisions once we were on the road.

When I was done, I shut the door with a bold flourish. There
was a wonderful finality to it. The car was where we had left it, half
hidden in the rubble. I had checked on it every so often, verifying
that our avenue of escape was still available.

Lugging my backpack, I moved toward the stairs.

"Wait," Tucker said.

Something flashed in the gloom. A silver shape. A pair of scissors. He must have found them on Daddy's workbench—what was left of it.

"Come here," he said.

My heart sank. Slowly I set my backpack down.

"Are you sure?" I said.

"Yes."

The first cut was the hardest. Tucker gathered my hair up into a ponytail. He nudged my head this way and that, examining my skull. The blades were not sharp enough to sever the ponytail cleanly; he had to hack and grind, yanking hard enough to bring tears to my eyes.

Then I heard the scissors close. My locks swung forward again, falling only to my chin now. He had removed a solid foot of ringlets.

I moaned. Nine years old. Rigid and openmouthed.

Tucker tossed my former mane to one side in a clump. It landed with a thud, a dead thing, bloodless and filthy. Years of my life were caught up in those curls. My father probably tousled them long ago. Jane often French-braided my long hair. Darlene spent hours combing out the tangles.

Tucker slid the scissors past my cheek. His expression was absent of pity. I felt no pain as he kept cutting, which made the loss worse somehow. More unsettling. I wanted there to be throbbing or blood, something to signify the profundity of what was happening to me.

The process took a long time. I closed my eyes, unable to watch. My brother did not speak, but his voice rang in my head anyway. His lectures swirled through my brain as his hands worked and the scissors danced.

Let me tell you about the Classification of Wildness. This is important. I expect you to remember it.

A blade slid against my throat. Tucker hummed in concentration.

Level One is Wild. It refers to the animals that are born in nature and die that way. They live their whole lives untouched by humans.

His hands fluttered over my forehead. He chopped an uneven shelf of bangs, and then he sheared them off entirely.

Level Two is Feral. These animals start out with humans—domesticated or caged—but they get free. They go back to nature and live a sort of halfway life. Neither one thing nor the other. There's only so much rewilding they can do.

He began cutting close to my skull, slicing away what remained. Shorter and shorter. Still no pain—nothing physical, anyway.

Level Three is Tame. It's the most dangerous kind. Wild animals that become accustomed to humans. They stop being afraid. If you feed the birds in your neighborhood, they'll start to rely on you, and if you quit for any reason, they'll starve to death. If you feed a deer one time, it'll go off and approach some hunter hoping for a handout and get itself shot. If you feed a bear, it'll turn into a menace. It'll break into somebody's house to get at the fridge or rip a tent apart to reach the cooler. Eventually it'll have to be put down. When you tame a wild animal, you're killing it.

Tucker was working slower now, trimming the crown of my head. The scissors seemed to move at the midpoint between my mind and body. He was severing both my hair and something more, something interior, snipping away at the membrane of my thoughts, vivisecting my identity.

Level Four is Domesticated. Dogs and horses and cows. These animals have lived with people for so many generations that it's changed them permanently. Their brains have evolved to become dependent on us. If you let them loose in the wild, they won't know what to do.

Behind me, Tucker grunted. I felt a stabbing pain at the top of my ear. Something wet began to dribble down the side of my neck.

And Level Five is Human. There's nothing else like us in the whole animal kingdom. We change everything we touch. We destroy most of it.

The crest of my ear was throbbing. I lifted a hand and gingerly palpated the place. Tucker had sliced away a tiny wedge of my flesh, and in the manner of all head wounds it was bleeding profusely.

I sighed in relief. Pain at last. This was just what I needed: an objective, physical indication of trauma and transformation.

"Hold still," Tucker said.

He tugged off his T-shirt and balled it up in his hands. Bare chested, he leaned toward me, mopping the blood off my throat. He applied pressure to the wound, which made me grimace. Then he circled me, examining his work.

"Done," he said.

He handed me a broken wedge of mirror and arranged the flashlight so I could see my reflection. The change was remarkable. I gaped at the stranger staring back at me. I looked like a younger version of Tucker. The child he had been, perhaps, before I was born.

The world around me was different, too. My vision was wider, unimpeded by the frame of my curls. The air was too close now, touching secret places on my body, the breeze kissing behind my ear and stroking my bare nape, an intimate caress I did not welcome. The sky was too broad. Every gesture felt alien. There was a weightlessness about my skull, and when I moved I no longer felt the comforting swish of my hair against my shoulders.

My mind felt lighter too—and not in a pleasant way. Something was missing, organs of the psyche, invisible but essential.

I was only nine. I did not yet have the language to name what had been taken from me.

But Tucker seemed to read my thoughts, as he so often did. He cupped my chin gently in his fingers.

"Abracadabra," he said. "Reborn."

21

We drove for miles. We drove for days. First it was back to the tawny station wagon, timeworn and unkempt, with a dent in the side that had obviously been made by somebody's foot. Next it was a pickup truck, brown with rust and grime, the license plate so filthy and faded that I couldn't make out the numbers. Then it was a green sedan with a fluffy pair of dice hanging from the rearview mirror, as well as a crucifix on a beaded chain. The upholstery smelled like cigarettes. The engine stalled below ten miles an hour and overheated above fifty.

I named each vehicle—Slowpoke, Dirt Face, Stinker—even though Tucker had warned me that none of them belonged to us. Whenever a new car presented itself, we would discard the old one like a snake shedding its skin. We left Slowpoke after a week. Tucker parked it behind a convenience store in a town so small that there was only one streetlight, blinking yellow. We left Dirt Face by a tumbledown farm. I was not sure whether Tucker had learned to hot-wire an engine in our father's garage or during his time away from us. He told me that we needed a quick and continual turnover. He did not want us to be linked to a particular car for too long.

It was July, and we were always on the move. Tucker had a plan, but he had not told me much about it yet. *We're going to make a difference,* he said. *We're going to change the world.* Sometimes he would dig a map out of his backpack and unfurl it across the hood. In the blazing sun, he would stand sweating beneath his baseball cap, staring at the image spread out before him as though it contained a prophecy. Hovering at his side, I would try to see what he did in the network of colors and symbols, the paper rumpled from incorrect folding. Tucker had circled a town to the west of us: *Amarillo, Texas.*

But he did not seem impatient to get there. There was time to wander, to get lost along the way. We stayed on the back roads. Tucker said that we needed to avoid the highway. There would be traffic cameras, speed traps, too many witnesses. So we drove through cornfields, down dirt roads, the undercarriage pinging with pebbles, the axels groaning at each pothole. The air was torrid and dry. Bugs struck the windshield and splattered into blots as we maneuvered down muddy side lanes.

For my part, I was just glad to be out of the tornado shelter. I did not care where we were going as long as it involved being out of doors and above ground. We drove with all the windows down. We turned the radio up, singing at the top of our lungs. None of the cars we stole had working air-conditioners, but I did not mind. Across the scrubbed golden fields, I could see forever. The sun began each day in the rearview mirror and ended in the front windshield. The sky was silky and pale, pinned to the horizon like a blouse to a clothesline. Patterns of light pulsed across the wheat. Dragonflies tumbled in the windy shock of our wake. Turkey vultures circled overhead, their wings spread but unmoving, riding the currents of air.

Tucker's wounds were still healing. He steered with his injured hand in his lap, only his healthy one on the wheel. The exact progression of his suffering was scored into his flesh like the paragraphs of a story. I could see everything that happened to him written there: the shrapnel imbedded in the muscle, a fingernail torn off, the satin ribbons where he had been burned.

Yet his mood was good. He relished being on the road. He laughed at my jokes. He offered to let me steer while he worked the pedals. He asked me about my life. I was unaccustomed to being the center of attention this way. At home, Darlene and Jane were always tired, dispirited, or on their phones. I was used to a certain degree of benign neglect, but being with Tucker was something else. His attention was as intense as a spotlight. I found myself preening in the warm glow.

Eventually we began to encounter hills. This was a phenomenon I did not have much experience with. Mercy was a flat town on a flat plain, a coin on a tabletop. I enjoyed the drop in my stomach as we plummeted downward, the swivel of the road bucking over peaks and dipping into dales. I loved the hollows of shade that came with this terrain—pockets of cold shadows between bluffs where the sunlight never fell. Crossing the hills of the Oklahoma panhandle gave me a renewed sense of momentum. When the ground was flat, even when we were barreling along at sixty miles per hour, I often experienced the illusion of stillness. All the landmarks were too far away to move as we did. The distant barns, a thicket of trees by the horizon, a miniaturized silo—they stayed where they were, as fixed and remote as stars. Only when we reached the hills could I perceive in a measurable way that we were getting somewhere. Up one slope and down another. Traveling west.

Sometimes I would glance in the side mirror and fail to recognize myself. My face looked different without the frame of my long hair—somehow naked, a little vulnerable, younger than before. My ears were always visible now. The architecture of my skull was visible too. I was a shorn sheep, a field in spring just beginning to bloom.

Tucker had sacrificed his curly mane as well. After cutting my hair, he had sliced off his own ponytail, then handed the scissors to me. The physical similarities between us were more pronounced now—boxy brows, delicate ears, crooked grins. This was all part of Tucker's plan. The police would be on the lookout for an adult man (with a ponytail) and his little sister (with long dark hair), so we had altered our appearances like spies in enemy territory.

I was now a boy.

In public, Tucker called me *Corey*, which was close enough to my own name that I would respond automatically. He did not allow me to wear my rainbow headband or my socks with whales on them. My glittery gel flip-flops and the heart locket from Darlene remained at the bottom of my bag. Instead, I dressed in denim shorts and tank tops. I wore my overalls, sometimes without a shirt underneath, my nipples discreetly visible. (I did not have boys' underwear, of course. My panties were purple or polka dotted or decorated with flowers, which brought me comfort, a private talisman of my former identity.) Tucker said I was young enough that my face was not yet recognizably gendered. I spent a lot of time looking in the side mirror of whatever vehicle we were using, wondering whether this was true. I examined my sturdy forehead, my frank brown eyes, my nubble of a chin. I practiced walking like a boy. I practiced spitting. I practiced sitting like Tucker in the car, my arm slung carelessly on the window frame, legs splayed, jaw lifted.

He was cautious about stopping for food and gas. No big towns. Even in rural areas, he would case each grocery store or pharmacy before going in, checking the vicinity for surveillance cameras or police vehicles. While shopping, he wore a baseball cap to obscure his face. We never went to restaurants. Tucker did not want to spend that long in a crowd, imprinting our presence on the waitress's memory. Instead, we kept a cooler on the back seat stocked with cheese sticks and Coke. We lived on peanut butter and jelly. (Tucker was a vegetarian, and by default, I was now a vegetarian too.) Whenever we stopped for gas, he would let me stretch my legs, moseying into the grass to pick dandelions and chase butterflies. He kept his chitchat with the clerk to a minimum. He paid cash for everything. When he was done, he would shout: "Corey, get your butt back here!" I would turn at the first syllable of my new name and startle at the second. I would jog to him, running like a boy. We would pull away in the sweltering July breeze, never to be seen again. Tucker told me that we needed to vanish. We were vanishing all the time.

Now and then, I wondered whether I was disappearing in a different way too. When I looked in the mirror, I saw a boy, tanned beneath a cowboy hat, dressed in overalls, dirty around the neck, barefoot, smelling of sweat and travel. When Tucker and I walked into a convenience store, the clerk saw two brothers on the road together, both watchful and lanky, communicating in grunts and nods, similar in gait and bone structure, sharing an unmistakable ease. Cora had become an unspoken name, a girl hidden in plain sight, a memory.

At night, Tucker and I slept in the car. We slept on the ground. We slept in a moldy tent we found, the nylon patterned with lacy mosaics of water damage. Night by night, we slept wherever the mood struck us. We did not have blankets or pillows, and we did not need them—July was warm enough. I dozed sitting up in the passenger's seat with Tucker behind the wheel, our car parked in the hollow of a cornfield. I napped on the forest floor with Tucker right next to me, the wind brushing my cheek, my ears ringing with bird calls. I loved the fact that the whole world was our bed.

In the manner of the very young, I was already adapting to my new life. There is something refractive about how children perceive time. A few weeks with Tucker felt like years. I could scarcely remember what things had been like before he had uprooted me from No. 43. Once upon a time, I lived in a house with my father and three siblings. Until recently, I lived in a trailer with my sisters. For a brief, dreadful interval, I stayed in a tornado shelter. Now I lived in a series of stolen cars with my brother. I ate from a cooler and slept in fields. I spent my days on the road, my nights in the open. That was the way things were.

I did not give much consideration to the future, though I knew that in the glove compartment there was a map with a target on it: *Amarillo, Texas.* I knew that in my brother's pocket, there was a folded sheet of paper with instructions for building a pipe bomb. I also knew that under the driver's seat, there was a gun.

22

We crossed into Texas in the middle of July. At the time, we were traveling on a dirt lane so small and out of the way that there was no sign posted at the state line. We were surrounded only by desert and dry grasses. I would not realize for several hours that for the first time, I had left Oklahoma.

Our passage kicked up clouds of dust that lingered in our wake. Tucker navigated down a road that was pocked with boulders, eroded into runnels and ruts. The wheels jolted. There were no radio stations this far out in the country, just a hiss of static, interrupted every now and then by ghostly voices reciting Bible verses. I sat with one arm slung out the window of our new car—another pickup truck, this one black. The sun was high, the air reverberating with the screech of crickets. The earth was so dehydrated that it had cracked into a network of fissures. The clumps of grass were uneven in hue, some vibrant green, some sickly yellow, some dead looking, rattling in the wind. I could discern no pattern to determine which plants thrived and which did not.

Tucker parked by a lone, spindly fir and got out to pee. I climbed out of the car too and stood in the shade, inhaling the nectar of the tree. It had been a day or two since I had seen anyone except my brother. There were no signs of human life out here. I could not smell anything artificial, only sun-splashed grass and the musk of the desiccated earth. There weren't any buildings in view, a total dearth of houses and farms, no telephone poles, no tractors, no wires overhead, not even an airplane in the distance. Tucker and I might have been the only survivors of an alien invasion or a nuclear war. The last humans on the planet.

He topped up the gas tank from a canister in the truck bed. He took a swig from a bottle of water and insisted that I finish the rest. He sniffed his own armpit, removed his tank top, and applied a layer of deodorant. Bare to the waist, he stretched and ran a hand over his cropped brown mane.

"Want to do some shooting?" he said.

He took his gun from the gap beneath the driver's seat and a box of bullets from the glove compartment. I watched him load the weapon, the fingers on his intact hand flicking deftly. I was not sure what kind of gun it was—only that it was heavy and shiny, with a recoil strong enough to nearly sprain my wrist.

I had been around guns all my life, but only at a distance. I had seen revolvers on dashboards and holsters on belts. Whenever I passed the Mercy shooting range, a series of tinny explosions echoed on the air. Each different brand and caliber seemed to have its own pitch, some high and crystalline, some low and guttural. Many of our neighbors in the trailer park owned a pistol or two—it was Oklahoma, after all—but Darlene was not crazy about guns, so I had never held one in my hands until recently. She steered me away from playmates whose parents appeared on social media holding hunting rifles. She refused to let me visit a gun show outside Mercy. She always said that guns had only one purpose, and it was not a purpose she cared for.

Tucker, however, did not share this opinion. He had named his weapon Mama Bear and handled it with poise and affection. Now he squinted along the barrel and nodded, satisfied. He was barefoot in the grass, and I was too.

"Want to go first?" he said.

"No thanks. My wrist is still sore from last time."

"Okay. Watch my technique. Remember—exhale when you squeeze the trigger."

His posture was relaxed but steady. He took aim at an upper branch of the pine tree. Even though I was prepared for the report, the sound still made me jump. A twig splintered. A clot of leaves fell. Tucker whooped with pride. The fir shook from the impact, and a cloud of sparrows took flight. I had not known they were there, dark shapes nestled among the dark branches, until they broke away, rising toward the sky in a spiral of wild cries.

ON THE ROAD, WE TALKED. We did not have individual chats so much as one long discussion that never really ended and contained all the subjects in the world. Tucker and I spoke about life and death and snacks and road games and movies and the history of our family and the future of the human race. Conversation ebbed and flowed between us like a dream-state, sometimes intense and focused, sometimes shallow and desultory, interrupted by long periods of companionable silence. I might catnap for a few miles in the passenger's seat. Tucker might sing along with the radio. Then one of us would speak up as though no pause had occurred, picking up the thread from before or answering a question broached hours ago.

On a cloudless afternoon, we came upon a tiny town—not even a stoplight, just four or five houses and a gas station. Tucker replenished the pickup's tank, as well as the spare canister he kept in the truck bed. He took a roll of bills from the glove compartment, banded by a scrunchy. (This was our bank. Tucker had not yet told me how he came by so much cash.) He peeled off a few bills and went to pay the clerk. I watched through the window, remaining out of view. He returned with a root beer for me and a bag of corn nuts for himself. We pulled away with a squeal of tires.

"Do you have a best friend?" I asked.

Tucker considered the matter for a mile or two. Then he said, "I used to."

"What happened?"

"His name was Mike," he said. "He's dead to me now."

"He died?"

"No. Dead to *me*." Tucker frowned. "I met Mike a few years back. I was spending a lot of time with this group called ECO."

I nodded.

"Mike brought me in," he said. "We had the same goals, or I thought we did. He was the one who taught me how to handle explosives. He showed me all the different kinds. Land mines. Pipe bombs. How to use fertilizer. That's tricky, by the way. If you get the mixture even a little bit wrong, you've got a big old dud. Mike taught me a lot of things."

He paused, chewing on his tongue. Then he turned to me. "What about you? Do you have a best friend?"

"I don't know," I said.

I thought he might make a joke at my expense, but instead he nodded.

"Friendship is a tough one," he said. "It takes some of us a while to figure out how to connect."

The next hour slipped by in a balmy wash. We passed windmills and silos. We passed fields being watered by metallic, insectoid sprinklers at least half a mile in length, silver and stark, rotating and filling the breeze with gusts of spray. We passed wide pastures strewn with sheep. We passed barns too decrepit to ever be repaired, their roofs caving in, sunk under curtains of ivy.

"Tell me about Daddy," I said. "What was he like?"

Tucker drummed contemplatively on the steering wheel.

"Let me think on that," he said. "It's hard to sum up a whole person. I'll get back to you later."

"Okay."

The radio gave a screech of high-pitched static. I hadn't realized it was still on and smacked the button to shut it off. A brown, stubbled field sprawled across the landscape. In the distance a tractor plowed doggedly along, carrying a comet's tail of dust.

"Once upon a time," Tucker said, and I smiled.

He began to tell me a story—the same story he had been telling me since our first day outside the bunker. It started as a road game, a way to pass the time, but it was blossoming into something more. He was spinning the tale of us on our adventure. He always referred to us in the third person—*Corey and Tucker*—as though we were well-known characters like Hansel and Gretel or Cinderella.

"Corey and Tucker were driving west," he said. "It had been a long day and they were both tired, starting to think about where they might sleep that night. They had to find the right place. Somewhere safe and good."

I nestled deeper into my seat.

"They saw a little forest," he went on. "Tucker thought it would be fine. He thought they should stop and spend the night there. But Corey knew better. The trees didn't look right somehow. Corey wondered whether the place might be under a spell."

I glanced eagerly through the windshield. A straggly copse stood to the side of the road. The branches seemed weary, the leaves withered and beige. A moment earlier, I would have thought the trees were just thirsty, but now they appeared eerie, even malevolent. Their trunks were crooked and swollen with burls.

"Then, in the distance, they saw a farm," Tucker said. "The barn was red. Corey noticed it first. He always had the sharpest eyes of anyone."

I sat up straighter.

"Maybe they could sleep in the barn that night," Tucker said. "They were so tired, after all. But as they drew closer, they saw that the farm was no good either." His voice dropped to a whisper. "There was a man walking in the pasture. A tractor working in the field. Too many humans. Corey and Tucker might be captured and thrown in jail if they stopped there."

I clung to the strap of my seat belt. I held my breath until the drab little barn was safely in the rearview mirror, shrinking into shadows.

"That was close," Tucker murmured.

I nodded.

"Corey and Tucker traveled on," he said. "Together and alone."

His stories were the best part of any day. He did not make things up—not exactly. Corey and Tucker never battled an ogre or visited a castle in the clouds or came upon a magic lamp that granted wishes. Instead, my brother would describe what we were doing now or what we had done earlier. Sometimes he broke his narration to announce, *This is all true, you know. This really happened.* He dropped a lens over the world that made the wind willful, every animal sentient, each object rife with possibility. Anything could happen.

"About Daddy," he said.

He had shaken off his storytelling voice now; we were back to conversation. I slung my feet on the dashboard and turned to look at him.

"I guess the best way to tell you about him is this," Tucker said. "All us kids have pieces of him. I got his hands. His way of working with them. He could fix anything with a motor in it, and I reckon I inherited that from him."

"Oh," I said.

"Darlene got his common sense," he went on. "That girl is nothing if not practical. She doesn't give a hoot about ideas or philosophy or the big picture, but she gets shit done. Daddy was always good in a crisis. Darlene is too."

I looked down at my lap.

"Jane got his laugh," Tucker said. "The way she throws her head back and guffaws all the way down to her belly. It's Daddy, note for note."

"Really?"

"Yeah."

Tucker wore a wistful expression. I had seen it many times before; this look crossed his face whenever he mentioned our parents.

"What about me?" I said.

"Heart," he said, without pause. "You love like Daddy did."

I considered this, my imagination tangled up with the rattle of the engine, the roar of the wind, and the irregular jolt of rocks under the wheels. The sun slipped below the horizon. The sky was gauzy and gray. A mesh of fireflies flickered in the fields. Occasionally one of them would smash against the windshield, and the pulp it left behind would continue to fluoresce for a little while after it was already dead. The air cooled with each passing mile.

I was not thinking about Darlene and Jane. This was an active process, rather than an unconscious forgetting. It took work not to consider them. Whenever their names came into my mind, I would pretend to shatter the words with a hammer. On some level, I was aware that if I stopped to consider what I had done—what I was doing—I would not be able to bear it, so I kept my attention fixed on the present. I stayed as close to Corey's perspective as I could, pushing Cora into the background.

Corey was unencumbered by memory. Corey had been around for only a few weeks, and his mind was filled with immediate things: food and shelter and the heightened state of his senses. The roar of the wind. The sting of root beer on his tongue. The scent of cow manure and hay.

And the stories Tucker told. Corey believed every word. Whenever Tucker spun his marvelous tales, Corey became both the audience and the protagonist. Listening, he was captivated by his own heroics, a glorious feedback loop of action and mythology, the epic journey of two boys on the run, alive with adventure and purpose, skirting danger and magic at every turn, united and sanctified by their fraternal bond.

"Once upon a time," Tucker said.

I turned toward him, eyes wide, waiting.

23

In the morning, I awoke to something kissing my cheek—a damp, fluttering pressure. I opened my eyes to see a monarch butterfly perched at the corner of my mouth. When I blinked, it took flight. I watched it dart away, its trajectory erratic, finally alighting on a clot of nettles.

The grass beneath me was wet with dew, and my clothes were sodden in the creases, clinging at the seams. My mouth tasted sour. Tucker was still sleeping, splayed on his back with every limb extended. It looked as though he had fallen from a great height, plummeting into slumber. Something was tickling my elbow. I plucked a large millipede off my skin, hurling it into the bracken.

It was just after dawn. We were parked in the shelter of a line of trees planted along the road to block the wind. The branches shifted in the raw light. The tallest leaves flared gold, high enough to catch the new sun's rays, but the lower boughs were still in shadow. I climbed into the bed of the pickup truck, where there were bottles of water and stale sandwiches. In the distance, a church bell clanged. I counted seven tones. It occurred to me that I did not know what day of the week it was. I was only vaguely aware that we were somewhere in July.

I breakfasted sitting on the plating of the truck bed, my bare feet swinging beside the bumper in the open air. My shins were decorated with mosquito bites. The light moved down the trees as the sun rose, the hot glow glazing each twig in sequence, painting each leaf a vibrant hue. A warm wind caressed my face and throat. I was still not used to the breeze touching my scalp so thoroughly, without my curtain of long hair to muffle the sensation.

Once again, I reminded myself that I was a boy.

I had never thought about gender before. I was a few years shy of puberty, young enough that I played with the boys at recess and thought nothing of it. While the girls sat in the shade, making friendship bracelets or playing clapping games—hands flashing, voices chanting—the boys ran for all they were worth across the field. I preferred their company, the full-body physicality of their games. Boys seemed simpler than girls—not dumber, not exactly, but less intricately calibrated. Unlike my sisters, unlike my girlfriends, the boys I knew seemed to have only one feeling at a time, a single strong emotion vibrating like the note of a tuning fork.

I had not yet reached the age of crushes. In some ways, I was a little behind the curve. I watched as the other girls scribbled *Mrs. Scott Westerman* in the pages of their notebooks or passed sweaty, folded notes down the row of desks to ask, *Do you like me Y/N?* I did not understand the adoration that gripped them, lingering in their blood for a few heady days before fading without a trace.

In truth, I often felt out of my depth among them. Some of this arose from my family's circumstances. Nobody ever wanted to come over to No. 43—the home of the saddest family in Mercy. I could not afford to join the Girl Scouts, though the uniform might have masked some of my otherness. I did not go to Sunday school or take part in services, which might have allied me with the children of the church brigade (Darlene's term, always spoken with an eye roll). I could not afford to attend sleepaway camp, a faraway environment where my family's stigma might have faded. The other girls weren't cruel to me, but I was never invited to birthday parties or playdates; the hothouse intimacy of one-on-one time was beyond my reach. That was where friendships were smelted from unrefined ore into pure metal: two girls staying up past their bedtime, painting one another's nails, trying on one another's clothes, wondering about ghosts, confiding secrets, swapping tokens of undying affection, hours of whispering in the darkness.

Still, I had rarely felt lonely. I found the other girls amiable enough in general, but their problems always seemed empty to me. Bursting into tears over a bad grade or a weekend being grounded. I would often fail to react to the climax of this kind of story, expecting that there had to be more to come. My experience of childhood was different than most—different in ways that were impossible for a nine-year-old to articulate. My friends from school still had living parents, houses with backyards, and their own bedrooms, or at least their own beds. Maybe they weren't rich, but they always had enough—enough food on the table, enough money to pay the bills, enough free time to grow bored, enough affection at home that they sometimes felt stifled. They could complain about a parent who insisted on helping them with their homework every night. They could grouse about an older sibling who went away to college and became a show-off. They never seemed to realize that their problems were actually gifts.

Now I glanced down at my body: my masculine pose, my cargo shorts, my dirty feet, my bare torso. I no longer felt uncomfortable wandering around without a shirt, even in public. It made the heat more bearable. Besides, nobody ever gave my exposed skin a second glance, not even the time Tucker and I washed our hair and armpits at the faucet behind a gas station.

I jumped down from the truck bed. A cardboard box of bullets was nestled beside my brother's roll of cash in the glove compartment.

I groped under the driver's seat, removed the gun, and loaded it as Tucker taught me. It was heavy in my hands and warm from the morning heat. The gun was not inanimate and inert in the way of most objects. It had the latent potentiality of an unhatched egg: not quite alive but suffused with possibility and power.

I took aim at a knothole in a nearby tree. Tucker had showed me what to do: cradle the gun in both hands, splay my feet for balance, hold my breath for a moment, and press the trigger gently rather than squeezing it hard.

The recoil and the report were terrifying. My ears rang and my fingers ached, but I did not flinch or stumble this time. I lowered the weapon calmly to my side and waited for the wave of disorientation to pass.

My aim was improving. As I stepped forward to examine my handiwork, I saw that I had missed the knothole but struck the right tree, which was progress. Splintered bark and oozing sap. A fresh, reddish scar.

AN HOUR LATER, WE WERE driving down a lonely road when my brother let out a noise. To the left of the car was a prairie vibrating with cricket song. To the right, a row of oaks shone in the sun. The tidiness of their organization suggested human intervention—planted in a row to block the wind—but it was obvious that nobody had tended to them in a long time. Many had succumbed to thirst, their greenery giving way to parched, denuded branches. A hawk perched high on a bare, ashy limb.

Beyond the trees was a paddock. In the paddock were horses, four or five of them grazing serenely. They were all but camouflaged against the golden grass. Their coats were mocha colored, their manes as white and frothy as whipped cream. They shared enough physical similarities with one another that I suspected they were all related: blunted ears, long noses, and spindly limbs.

Tucker threw the pickup into park right there in the middle of the dirt lane. He climbed out with a grin. There was no need to pull over to the side; we had not seen another car all morning.

I followed my brother between the trees. He was striding so fast that I had to jog to keep up. As we crashed through the underbrush, the hawk took flight overhead, slashing the sunlit grass with its shadow.

The horses lifted their heads at the sound. They gazed in our direction. I wondered who owned them. There was no house nearby, no barn. At the very edge of my vision stood a silo—a smudge the size of a postage stamp against the horizon—the only hint of civilization.

The horses began to drift our way. The largest of the group, a stallion, paused every few feet to graze. Two mares trailed behind him, shaking their tails to chase away the flies. A pair of colts followed at a distance, skittish and timid. Tucker and I helped one another through the fence, each taking a turn holding up the lowest skein of barbed wire so the other could wriggle through the gap beneath.

I felt a shimmer of déjà vu. So many years before, my brother and I had done the inverse of this—a night walk, black horses, over the fence into an inky field. Now the morning was lush with heat, the grass broiled blond, and we were scrambling under the fence to greet tallow-colored beasts. The stallion approached first. Tucker held out a clump of grass as a peace offering. He still possessed the animal magic I remembered. Within minutes, all five horses surrounded him in a ring, snorting against his shoulders, stamping their feet in anticipation of his touch, their flesh quivering beneath his hands.

"Open the gate," he said. "Over there."

He pointed to a gleam of metal down the road.

My heart began to pound. "Are you sure about this?"

"Hell yeah," he said.

I jogged away through the long grass, passing our pickup truck, heading for the gate. Weeds caught around my ankles. My progress launched scores of crickets into flight. I wiped the sweat from my neck.

The gate was fastened by a length of chain looped around a post.

No lock. The metal scalded my palms as I pushed it open with a screech of hinges.

The horses marched behind my brother in single file, as though they had known him all their lives. Tucker seemed too happy to smile, his expression solemn and prayerful. He walked with his arms wide, sunlight cupped in his palms.

One by one, the animals followed him through the gate. Their milky tails swished away the flies. Up close, I could see that their coats were patchy and dull, their ribs outlined by shadows. All of them were a little too thin. The colts were nervous about my presence, whinnying and tossing their heads as they passed. But once they were in the road, their attention was captured by the novelty of shade. The trees dappled them, cooled them. The colts began to dance. The mares watched, standing with their hips touching companionably. The stallion nickered, still hovering beside Tucker, his chin resting on my brother's shoulder, his murky eyes half shut.

"Come on," Tucker said.

He motioned me toward the pickup truck. I did not want to go, but it did not occur to me to argue with him. My brother stuck the key in the ignition. He paused, gazing down the lane for a long moment at the horses as though imprinting the image on his memory.

Then he slammed his palm against the horn.

The stallion reared up, doubling his height, his lips pulled back in a snarl, hooves flashing against the sky. The mares were instantly in motion, pelting toward the horizon, kicking up a wake of dust, both colts in hot pursuit. Their speed was astonishing. They dashed away with the intensity and purpose of wild animals, rather than domesticated beasts jogging for pleasure behind the safety of a fence. Perhaps they had never moved like that before, pushing their bodies to the limit. In flight, their equine legginess became grace, a kind of bony perfection. Within minutes, they were out of sight.

"That's right," Tucker said, smiling. "Run away."

24

The story quickly became a legend. Over and over again, my brother told me about the time Tucker and Corey freed the horses in a lonely field. I could not get enough of it, and the tale grew taller with each telling. Soon a cruel farmer who did not love his animals came into play. There were beatings and threats of slaughter, a lack of water and food. By the fourth incarnation, Tucker and Corey had rescued the horses from a life of vicious brutality.

"This is all true, you know," he said each time. "This really happened."

We spent the rest of the day on the road. Tucker steered with his good hand, gesturing with his damaged one. The stumps of his pinkie and ring finger moved in unison with his intact digits, a ghostly reminder of the bones and flesh he once possessed. This part of Texas was not exactly hilly, not exactly flat. The topography was composed of slow, gradual inclines that made everything feel slightly askew. The barns in the distance were sitting at an angle. The horizon never seemed quite straight. Occasionally we would see a weather-beaten sign with AMARILLO on it. Tucker would point and read the name aloud.

"Almost there," he said.

I did not ask what he intended to do when we arrived. I was not sure I wanted to know. Instead, we talked about the turkey vultures circling in the distance, spiraling like the ornaments in a child's mobile. We talked about the different kinds of crops. We talked some more about Daddy—his love of a good pipe in the evening, his hatred of the Arkansas Razorbacks. The sun poured through the back windshield, turning the dashboard into a slab of fiery bronze.

"What's the meaning of life?" Tucker said.

I stared at him. "You tell me."

"It's a stupid question," he said. "That's what it is. A *human* question. Animals don't worry about the meaning of life. They don't get bored. They don't sit around pondering their purpose."

"Huh," I said, considering this.

"The meaning of life is to live. You eat and drink and find shelter and have babies and keep your species going. That's it. That's all."

I trickled my fingers through the sunlight. The shadow of my hand was printed on the dashboard.

"Humans have forgotten so much," Tucker said. "It's so easy for us to live now that our lives have no meaning. So we start looking for something else, something more. Money. A bigger house. A hobby. Church."

My perceptions seemed slightly altered. There was a hierarchy to my senses: Tucker's voice, his smell, his physical presence took precedence over everything else. He was bigger than the sun and louder than the wind.

"The tornado was a gift," he said. "My life has meaning. Yours too, Corey."

"Yeah," I said. I was so used to my brother's brand of rhetoric that I found it soothing, like a familiar nursery rhyme.

"There's a tension to being human," he said. "People are the only animals that die in childbirth. Did you know that?"

I began to reply, but he interrupted me: "The only ones that die on a regular basis, I mean. It's really common for our species. Even now, with all our modern medicine, it happens all the time."

I said nothing. I bit my lip.

"It's because of our brains." Tucker reached across the gap between our seats and knocked on my skull with his knuckles. "It makes you what you are, but it doesn't fit easily through a tiny birth canal."

I averted my gaze, experiencing the elixir of sorrow and regret that Mama's death always evoked in me. Tucker seemed to understand. He gripped my shoulder and gave me a bracing shake—a boyish reassurance, brother to brother.

"It wasn't your fault," he said. "It's a flaw in the human design. We evolved to stand on two legs, which means we need a narrow pelvic girdle. We evolved to be smart, which means we need an enormous brain. That's bad math. You can't put those two things together and expect it to work right every time."

He clucked his tongue disapprovingly. I kept my gaze on the window.

"Tell me about Mama," I said.

There was a long, ruminative pause. I could almost feel the memories shifting inside Tucker's mind.

"The Wildlands," he said finally.

"What?"

"It's something Mama used to say to me. When I was in the cow paddock and suppertime rolled around, she'd holler out the back door, 'Tucker, come back from the Wildlands.' I'd hear her on the phone with her friends: 'That boy of mine has been in the Wildlands all day long.'"

His voice changed as he mimicked her cadence, high and sweet. It was the most gentleness I'd ever heard from my brother.

"When I was little, I didn't know what the word meant," he said. "Our farm, I figured. Or just outside anywhere."

He wiped roughly at his cheek as though palming away a tear. He did not seem to be crying, though. I wondered if the gesture was for my benefit, an attempt to illustrate the depth of his grief.

"When I got older," he said, "I decided that Oklahoma was the Wildlands. Mama's nickname for the whole state."

He wiped his eyes again, a little ostentatiously.

"After Mama died, things were awful," he said. "I missed her so much. One day I came across her old dictionary on the shelf. She had marked a few words. Notes in the margins. *Wildland* was underlined, and she wrote *Tucker* right next to it. Can you believe that?" He paused, pressing his knuckles to his mouth. "*Wildland* means 'land that is uncultivated or unfit for cultivation.' I memorized it."

I was holding my breath, hoping for more. I had never heard anything like this about my mother. Darlene had told me the basic facts of her existence—her place of birth, her lack of siblings, how she met Daddy, and how she died—but intimate, everyday details about her life were rare and precious.

"I can't remember the color of her eyes anymore," Tucker said. "I'm not sure how tall she was. She seemed so big and strong to me back then."

His eyes were red, maybe from tears, maybe from contact with his hands.

"Sometimes I wonder," he said. "I wonder what Mama was really saying about me. The Wildlands. Uncultivated land. Cultivation— that's what humans do."

I wrapped my arms around myself for comfort. Maybe Mama would have come up with a term to describe my temperament too. Something just for the two of us. If only had she lived long enough to do that for me.

"When he died, Daddy went to the Wildlands for sure," Tucker said. "He rode a tornado to get there."

•

THE NEXT DAY, THE HEAT became unbearable, the air so dry I had to concentrate on breathing. The gush of the breeze through the car window was the only thing keeping me cool enough to survive. In a red, austere desert, we drove past a wiry bush denuded of both leaves and bark, a sculpture of smooth silver limbs. The plant had perished long ago, probably of dehydration, but its skeleton remained erect, stained by bird droppings. A meeting place for crows, I guessed.

No one in my life had ever talked to me the way my brother did. He treated me as an equal, as if my ideas mattered, as though I possessed as much wisdom as he did. I was used to adults who spoke down to me. Teachers asked questions with specific answers in mind, and it was my job to guess right. Darlene asked questions that were secretly commands: *Could you get me some water?* or *What exactly do you think you're doing?*

Tucker, on the other hand, held nothing back. I used to think of adulthood as a hallway lined with doors, each marked by a different milestone: *Sex, Money, Marriage, Parenthood, Death.* As people entered puberty, they moved along the corridor, opening the rooms one by one, gaining access at last to the mysteries within. To children, however, the doors were locked. I knew the terms of adulthood—the words written outside—and that was all. Most grown-ups were willing to offer only a hint, a glance through the keyhole.

But Tucker did not have any closed doors. Mile by mile, he told me about his time as a runaway. He told me about loneliness. He told me about hitchhiking and panhandling, squatting in abandoned buildings and sleeping beneath overpasses, stealing wallets and eating from garbage bins behind restaurants. He told me about bathing in creeks and rainstorms. He told me about walking so far that his shoes fell to pieces. He told me about heartbreak as sharp as a splinter.

"Did you miss us?" I said.

"Just you," he said.

"I missed you too," I said. "Every day."

A mesa loomed up, spare and craggy. It was striped with horizontal layers: a vein of crimson, a seam of granite, a stratum of chalk. I could not gauge how tall it was or how far away. It might have been my height or the size of a skyscraper. There was nothing to use for scale. The mesa was the only object standing erect against the plane of the rust-colored desert.

"That summer, I met Mike," Tucker said. "A few months after I left home. I'd never known anyone like him before. So confident."

I remembered the name. A former friend. *Dead to me now.*

My brother told me about their bond—brief but swell, lightning in a bottle. The two of them organized a boycott of a pet store in Oklahoma City that was known to harm its animals. They spearheaded a letter-writing campaign to tackle invasive species in Lake Tenkiller. They headed out to Shamrock with seven other ECO members to test soil samples after hearing reports of illegal dumping in a nature preserve. As the months passed, Tucker and his new friends traveled across the Southwest. He had never felt so useful, so determined.

He and Mike quickly became the leaders of ECO's more radical wing. They donned guerrilla masks and used homemade smoke bombs to break up a dogfighting ring in Kingfisher. They sabotaged the engine of a city van bringing strays to a high-kill shelter near Dover, then released its cargo into the prairie.

As we drove, a bug struck the windshield and burst into green gel. Tucker switched on the wipers, which squeaked and groaned, dragging themselves painfully across the glass. We were out of washer fluid again.

"I did good work with ECO," he said.

"Why did it end?" I asked tentatively.

"Me and Mike had a fight."

"Like you and Darlene?"

Some powerful emotion flickered across Tucker's face, gone too quickly for me to identify what it was. His hand tightened on the wheel.

"Yeah," he said. "Just like that."

Another mesa appeared at the edge of my vision, far enough away that the heat in the air obscured its shape. It shimmered in and out of being like a mirage.

"I did some stuff on my own," Tucker said, "but it felt empty. Being alone didn't suit me. I missed being a part of *something*. I kept thinking about y'all. Especially you. Always you."

"Really?"

"Really and truly," he said.

I grinned into my palm.

"Sometimes I couldn't sleep," he said. "I'd be thinking about Mercy and everything I left behind. I would worry about you. Then I'd remember our horses and all the poor cows. That dumb little goat. And that would get me started on the cosmetics plant. Those barrels of hazardous waste. Animal testing. There were living creatures being tortured and killed right in my own backyard. It all got"—he churned a hand through the air—"tangled up in my mind. The third anniversary of the tornado was coming up. Eventually I figured out what I had to do."

He took his foot off the gas, and the car slowed to a lazy glide. Pebbles clanged against the undercarriage. He glanced at me, smiling.

"I came home," he said. "To you."

25

That afternoon we reached a small town, an oasis of struggling greenery in the desert. We drove past an elementary school—the playground empty, the windows shuttered—and a row of dingy houses. There were saguaros everywhere. I had never seen these cacti in such numbers: lurking next to a mailbox, bristling behind a parked car, darkening the street with their shadows. Their flesh varied in color from tropical green to gunmetal. The churchyard was full of massive plants standing sentinel. Each cactus had a different number of limbs, ranging from a single erect arm to a crown of fat, prickly oblongs. A few saguaros were taller than the telephone poles. Their omnipresence was disconcerting. The streets were empty of people—the heat had forced them all indoors—but the cacti appeared to have taken their place. A slow, stealthy invasion by enormous, well-armed vegetation.

Tucker stopped to refill the gas tank. He parked the pickup in the shade of a burger joint beside a thicket of nettles. We sat side by side in the truck bed, sharing sips from a water bottle.

"What are the rules of our trip?" he asked.

I sighed. We had gone over this before, but Tucker was fond of pop quizzes.

"Always pay cash," I said. "Speak only when spoken to."

"What else?"

"Stay under the speed limit. Don't shoplift. No littering."

"That's right. Obey all the little rules so you can break the big ones. People only get caught if they slip up." He nudged me with his elbow. "I read about a guy—an arsonist, I think—who'd been on the lam for almost two years. Then he stole a candy bar from a convenience store. There was a security camera, and that's how the police finally got him. Can you imagine? After all that time, a goddamn candy bar."

I nodded, wiping my mouth with the back of my hand.

"Holy shit," Tucker said.

I glanced at him in surprise.

"Look there," he said, pointing across the road.

A row of small shops languished in the midday glare. On the parkway there was a fire hydrant, a skinny three-armed saguaro, and a hound with mottled fur flopped on its side in the dirt, panting heavily.

"The dog?" I said.

"Behind the dog," he said.

I shaded my eyes with my fingers. It was hard to make out the words of the sign in the shop window against the flare of reflected sunlight.

"It's time for a project," Tucker said.

WE SPENT THE REST OF the day in the pickup truck, parked in an alley between two dumpsters. My brother kept an eye on the shop in the rearview mirror. He would not let me get out to stretch my legs. I did not know what we were waiting for—what was supposed to happen—and Tucker refused to explain. There was a six-foot saguaro beside one of the dumpsters. It was too young to sprout arms, an undifferentiated oval of green flesh. It reminded me of a hardboiled egg, dyed for Easter and balanced on its end. I kept catching it in my peripheral vision, worried that it had started to roll my way.

Then Tucker began to lecture me. This was soothing for both of us. I settled more comfortably in my seat, letting his voice flow around me.

The Great Dying occurred 250 million years ago, he said. The worst mass extinction in history. Over hundreds of thousands of years, the levels of carbon dioxide and methane in the atmosphere had become toxic. Tucker recited all this from memory, without pause. He possessed that sort of mind, retaining both the grand ideas and the factoids. He told me that 96 percent of the species on the planet had perished. All life today was descended from the 4 percent of flora and fauna that had survived.

"That happened over millennia," he said. "Guess how long it took humans to cause the Anthropocene Mass Extinction? One hundred years flat."

The saguaro by the dumpster caught my attention again—a bald dome, at once prickly and smooth, roughly human sized. Its bulbous trunk was corrugated lengthwise and garnished by starry clusters of spikes.

Tucker told me that sea levels were rising faster than scientists thought they would. The character of the saltwater, too, had begun to change—the acidity and chemical makeup of whole oceans. Snails in California were dissolving in the shallows; the same environment that was once their natural habitat now melted them like candles. The seabed was pocked with hypoxic dead zones. No algae, no krill, nothing.

"Let me tell you about the animal kingdom," Tucker said.

"Okay," I murmured. I was beginning to feel sleepy. The warmth of the day pressed on my chest and made my breath shallow.

At the bottom of the food chain, Tucker said, were plants. They produced the food that everything else depended on. Then came the herbivores, who ate exclusively vegetation. Above that were the omnivores, who consumed both plants and smaller animals. Then the carnivores, who ate only meat. At the pinnacle were the apex predators. They preyed on everything else, and nothing else preyed on them.

"Humans aren't at the top," Tucker said. "We like to think we're the peak of evolution. Right up there with polar bears and orcas and eagles. But when you take away all our technology and guns, we end up somewhere in the middle of the pyramid. I read an article about it when I was still with ECO. Humans are at the same level as pigs and anchovies."

I glanced at him with my eyebrows raised. "Pigs? Really?"

"Put a human and a tiger in an enclosed space. No tools. No armor or weapons. Just two animals. You'll see pretty quick where we belong."

I sat up a little straighter, struck by this idea.

"The food chain is falling apart," Tucker said. "That's my point. From protozoa to bees to songbirds to lions—it's all in danger. And whose fault is that?"

"Humans," I said automatically.

"Who razes the rain forest and pollutes the land?"

"Humans."

"Who hunts animals for sport and keeps them as pets?"

"Humans."

A bead of sweat rolled down my forehead. I glanced at the saguaro outside my window again—surely it was a little closer now.

Then Tucker laughed, a wide-open, ecstatic chortle.

"Hot damn!" he cried. "Watch this."

He was staring into the rearview mirror. He had parked facing away from our target to conceal his intentions, even though there was nobody on the street to notice what we were doing. Now he swiveled in his seat to look through the back windshield. I did the same, frowning in confusion. I saw the familiar row of small stores.

A parkway composed of caked earth. A fire hydrant. A slate-colored saguaro with three gaunt arms.

The sun had moved, and the sign in the shop window was now visible, handwritten on cardboard, the print large but uneven. The words on the right side of the sign were more tightly compressed than the ones at the start of each line. Someone had not traced the message beforehand.

BIG TOM'S TAXIDERMY & TANNING

LIFE SIZE & WALL MOUNTS

FURS, HIDES, PELTS, & SKINS

BEST IN EAST TEXAS

"Taxidermy," I read aloud. "That's . . ."

"Dead animals. On display." Tucker spat the words. "Glass eyes and sawdust bodies."

He pointed at the hound dog. It lay in front of the shop, its paws scrabbling in the dirt. On closer inspection, I realized that the animal was trying to stand up. This was a laborious process, requiring several attempts. Once the dog was upright, everything about it sagged—jowls, ears, belly. It shuffled to the door and pushed its way inside, apparently vanishing through a slab of solid wood.

For an instant, I thought the heat had gotten to me. Then I realized there was a doggy door, the flap still swinging, catching the light.

"Now we're in business," Tucker said.

He put the car in gear and pulled away.

IN THE EVENING, WE STOOD together on the sidewalk. There were no lights inside Big Tom's Taxidermy; closing time had come and gone. The wind was strong, the world dipped in shadow. A streetlamp glimmered vaguely at the end of the block. The heat was draining from the air at last, replaced by a delicious chill. Up close, the three-armed saguaro was impressively tall and broader around the waist than I was. From my perspective, the cactus appeared to be holding the moon on its shoulder.

At my side, Tucker held the portable gas canister from the back of the pickup truck.

"This place is evil," he said. "You know that, right?"

"Yeah."

"It's death without purpose. Death for decoration."

"Uh-huh."

"Go on, Corey."

He motioned toward the doggy door. I knelt down and pushed the rubber flap with my fingers. The hinges gave a high-pitched squeak as I peered into the darkness inside the little store. I glanced up hopefully at my brother.

"Are we going to free the dog?" I asked. "Like we did with the horses?"

"Better," Tucker said.

The doggy door smacked my hindquarters as I crawled through. The interior smelled unpleasant—too much air freshener layered in a sickening cloud over something else. In the gloom, I could see only shapes: a rectangle that might have been a desk and a towering, uneven smear in the corner. Its contours were organic—a suggestion of shoulders and stomach.

A brown bear. Standing upright. Eight feet tall. Paws lifted as though about to strike.

I gaped as the creature came into focus against the murky wall. Its pose was aggressive but artificial, the lips curled back in a stilted grimace. I could see its claws, inky hatch marks scored into the darkness. I held still on my hands and knees, waiting to see if the bear would move. My eyes played tricks. The creature's outline was indeterminate, a swarthy, shaggy silhouette against a lightless surface. My breath was so loud that I could not tell whether the bear was breathing too.

Tucker's voice rang through my mind: *Put a human and a tiger in an enclosed space. Just two animals. You'll see pretty quick where we belong.*

There was something on the bear's paw. A taupe object. A cowboy hat. I looked closer, and then I let out a quick puff of relief.

The bear was dead. Somebody was using the poor beast as furniture—its arm a makeshift hatstand. This gave me the courage I needed to stand up. The door was a stain without edges or definition. I groped for the knob, tracing upward with my fingertips until I felt the metal curve of the lock.

Something bumped my knee. An urgent nudge. Warm and damp.

I froze, facing the wall. I did not dare to turn around. The pressure came again, a furred, bristly snout prodding against my leg. There was a living thing in the room with me. A snuffle, maybe a growl.

I screamed, kicking out. My foot made contact with a soft, solid object, and I heard a whimper, followed by claws clicking on linoleum. I fumbled for the lock. Panting with fear, I flew outside into Tucker's arms.

"Good boy," he said, patting my back.

"There's something—something—" I could not get the words out, gesturing desperately over my shoulder.

It was the dog. Wheezing and shuffling, it followed me outside. I clung to Tucker for comfort, though in the glow from the streetlamp I could see that the animal posed no threat. It was ancient, its belly slack, ears nearly dragging on the ground, eyes milky. It might have been blind.

I could not seem to calm down, cradling my head in my hands. I felt a stab of guilt at having kicked the dog, though its torso appeared sturdy and well padded. The animal sniffed my brother's leg, then mine.

"Level Four," Tucker murmured. "Domesticated."

He set down the gas can with a slosh. Crouching low, he stroked the dog's nape, whispering something in its ear that I did not catch. Then, without ceremony, he lifted the animal up in both arms and hurried off down the block. I watched him turn the corner, splashed in amber light from the streetlamp.

He returned empty-handed.

"I left it in a playground," he said. "There's a fence and a gate. It'll be safe there."

Tucker bowed his head. A change came over him, a kind of terrible stillness. To my eyes, he seemed to grow taller. With a swift gesture, he picked up the gas can again and took a lighter from his pocket. His expression was oddly familiar: lips drawn back, brow taut, eyes wide enough to show the whites. I had seen this look before, but never on a human face. In that moment, my brother resembled the brown bear inside the shop—legs braced, teeth bared, eager for the violence to come.

TEN MINUTES LATER, TUCKER PELTED up to the pickup truck. I was curled in the passenger's seat, waiting for him.

We pulled away with a crunch of tires. A fetor of gasoline and smoke emanated from Tucker's clothes, strong enough to make me cough. Without comment, he rolled down the windows, letting in a gush of clean air.

We drove away between the slumbering houses. A massive saguaro lurched into view on the side of the road, spreading its enormous arms like a crossing guard telling us to stop. I turned around in my seat, looking back the way we had come. Smoke was rising against the sky, a pallid river flowing upward. There was an isolated pocket of glow above the inky buildings—a small, artificial sunrise. As I watched, the illumination increased in intensity, charring the sky.

A siren sounded in the distance. Tucker picked up speed.

26

We reached Amarillo on a Saturday. I knew the day of the week because we came upon an intersection that was barricaded off with a sign hanging from the stop-light: SATURDAY STREET FAIR. I could hear live music—a guitarist, a tambourine. Shops had set out tables on the sidewalk to display their wares. Though it was still early in the day, a large crowd was milling around. Mothers pushed strollers. Couples strode hand in hand. There were booths for kids: face-painting, balloon animals, and a caricaturist. There were vendors selling food and drink, the air spiced with cinnamon.

I glanced hopefully at Tucker. I would have loved to spend the morning here, to simulate an ordinary life. I saw a group of boys toss-ing a football back and forth. I imagined joining their game. Perhaps

Corey would be able to throw a football in a perfect spiral, something Cora had never managed. Corey would not mind getting muddy. He was not afraid of a few bruises.

But Tucker's face was set in grim lines. He threw the car into reverse and pivoted away with a shudder of tires. Soon we were heading down a side lane, the sound of music fading away.

"Why did we come to Amarillo?" I said.

I waited, watching him. Instead of answering, he pointed out the window.

"A cemetery," he said. "That'll do."

He turned down a wide driveway between wrought iron gates. The lot was dappled by oak trees, empty except for our pickup truck. Tucker parked in the shade and climbed out on his side. After a moment, I followed suit.

"Why did we come to Amarillo?" I repeated.

He reached into his pants pocket and removed a folded note, handing it to me. The paper blazed in the sunlight, covered in long, complicated words. My reading, I knew, was subpar. *Below grade level*, my last report card claimed, to Darlene's dismay. This seemed to be a roster of corporations and people's names. Proper nouns.

"It's our agenda," Tucker said.

The letters swam and swirled in the fiery light.

"I took it from ECO," he said. "I took a few things from ECO, actually."

"Yeah?"

"Hey, the gun was just *lying* there." Tucker winked. "That roll of cash, too. I took a dime bag and some bullets."

I handed the sheet of paper back to him. He ran his finger down the roster and tapped a particular name.

"We're going to start with this guy," he said.

"Who is he?"

"Come on, let's walk."

We seemed to be in the wealthier part of the cemetery, the headstones tall and immaculate, many of them decorated with wreaths or plastic flowers. There was a marble mausoleum with ivory columns and gargoyles leering at me from the roof. In the distance, I could see where the poorer families' headstones lay—plain markers embedded in the grass, many overcome by weeds. Tucker and I strolled in rhythm, though I took two strides for every one of his. I was wearing overalls with nothing underneath, not even underwear, since all of mine were dirty. It seemed faintly sacrilegious to be dressed this way in a grave-yard, but I decided that boys did not care about that sort of thing.

"Why did we come to Amarillo?" I asked for the third time.

Tucker's answer was swift and expressionless. "We're going to take care of a bad man."

"Bad? What do you mean?"

"Like Big Tom," he said.

There was a lump in my throat. We had not talked about the fire once over the past few days. I stopped walking. The trees surged in the breeze, and my brother slipped away between the gravestones.

Since the encounter at Big Tom's Taxidermy, I'd been having trou-ble sleeping, jerking awake in the night, my throat filled with the smell of smoke, hearing the echo of a nonexistent siren. I was frightened, though it was hard to pinpoint exactly what I was frightened of. Some-times I thought it was the bear. Dead, stuffed, and posed to be eternally vigilant—it haunted me. Other times it was Tucker himself that un-nerved me: his height, his awful stillness, the lips drawn back in a snarl.

My brother had committed a crime, and I had helped him—but I had not known what I was helping him do until afterward—and I had only unlocked a door—but I had known even that was wrong—and Tucker would not have been able to set the fire without me—but he had never asked for my consent—but I would probably have said yes if he had asked. The full measure of my wrongdoing was a tangle I could not unravel.

When Tucker realized I wasn't with him, he came back and stood over me. He was tanner now than he had been a month ago. We both were.

"You and me, right?" he said.

There was a sierra of fat white mountains floating in the distance above the horizon. I kept my gaze there.

"What's your name?" Tucker said.

"Corey," I said without looking at him.

Once more, I heard the snip of rusted scissors. I remembered the tickle of my long locks falling around me. Tucker had done something profound that night in the tornado shelter. He began a process that was still in motion.

"Once upon a time," he said, then paused. He knelt down, lining his eyes up with mine. I could see imperfections in the brown of his irises, flecks of green.

"Once upon a time, there was a tyrant. Let's call him Chicken Man."

I leaned closer, smiling a little. As Tucker slid into his narrative cadence, my worry eased. There was nothing to fear inside a story, especially one crafted and controlled by my brother.

"Chicken Man ruled over dozens of farms," he said. "Except that's not really what they were. You hear the word *farm* and you think pastures and cows, but these were huge buildings filled with thousands of chickens in the most horrible conditions you could ever imagine."

"Oh no," I breathed.

"Chicken Man didn't care about animals. His birds were genetically engineered to have a lot of meat on them, so their chests were swollen and their legs were so skinny that they couldn't even stand up." Tucker frowned. "Chicken Man put them in tiny wire boxes. They never got a chance to fly. The females just laid and laid and laid some more. They got their food and water through a hole. Never set foot outside. Went their whole lives without seeing the sun."

I gasped in dismay. The story held me in its thrall. I was getting used to the sensation: the known world transfigured and brightened by an overlay of pixie dust and words. My brother was both the creator of this realm and one of his own creations. He and I moved together through the story he made; I never knew what would happen next, but I felt safe in his hands.

"Chicken Man didn't care about the roosters either," Tucker said. "They were just food on legs. He murdered them by the thousands, and it wasn't the surprise of an easy death. They saw it coming. It hurt. And the babies . . . No, I'm not going to tell you what happened to the chicks."

In the distance, I saw a figure drifting across the graveyard. A mourner, probably. It looked like a woman's frame, though she was too far away for me to make out any details. A slim, sad silhouette.

"Chicken Man was a monster," Tucker said. "Do you see?"

"Yes," I said.

"Everyone tried to shut him down, but Chicken Man was just too damn rich. I bet he wore a brand-new suit every day. I bet he wiped his ass with monogrammed towels. That kind of money." Tucker made a grasping gesture. "He had the whole state of Texas in his pocket. He was guilty of more crimes against animals than anybody else in the whole corn belt."

My brother's jaw was clenched. The wind swept around me, gushing through the straps of my overalls and tickling my skin.

"It all came down to Corey and Tucker," he said. "Nobody else could stop Chicken Man. Nobody else was brave enough to try."

I felt a swell of pride. "That's right."

"You have to understand, Corey and Tucker valued life in all its forms."

"Yeah," I said. "They did."

"They were heroes," my brother said. "You know that, don't you?"

I shrugged, momentarily unsure, remembering the fire.

As he so often did, Tucker seemed to respond to my unvoiced thought.

"Heroes," he repeated. "They fought for the animals because the animals couldn't fight for themselves."

"Oh," I whispered.

"Corey and Tucker were on a mission. They were trying to save the world."

My brother reached for me, stroking my cheek with his knuckles.

"You're with me, right?" he asked.

At that moment, there was a crackle from the bushes beside us. In a burst of color, a fox dashed away between the headstones. I saw lithe limbs and a bulbous tail. Its clever face was all tufts and points. The creature's appearance felt like an omen, and the message could not have been clearer.

"Level One," Tucker said. "A wild animal."

The fox darted past a mausoleum, its delicate paws landing in the grass without sound. Its sleek fur and sharp ears flickered against the greenery. Then it vanished into a clump of bushes. Tucker chuckled, and I began to laugh too, great wrenching breaths that were almost sobs. Perhaps the fox had taken up residence in the graveyard, found a mate, and had a litter of pups. I wondered if it had dug a den between the coffins, dreaming among the bones.

"The animals sent a sign," Tucker said. "A sly fox. A trickster. He showed Tucker and Corey that they were on the right path. That the animals were grateful."

I reached for my brother's hand, lacing my fingers through his.

"This is all true, you know," he said. "This really happened."

27

We spent the next day at the Amarillo Zoo. We wore baseball caps and sunglasses to obscure our faces. We synchronized the cheap digital watches we had bought at a dollar store, not for any particular reason except that spies often did this in the movies. In our denim shorts and tank tops, we were boys—scuffing our feet, spitting into the grass. Tucker told me to speak as little as possible. If other children came up to me, I was supposed to shrug and wander off. If an adult talked to me, I was supposed to act calm and say nothing. If we got separated, we would meet at the carved wooden sign by the front gate.

I had never been to a zoo before. Mercy was too small to offer one. There had occasionally been talk of mounting a family expedition to the Pacific Zoo in Southern California. Darlene would bring up the idea every so often. *Maybe someday. Maybe when y'all are a little more grown. Maybe if our luck changes.* She would talk about the Pacific Zoo with a faraway gaze and a lilt in her voice. It was one of the few subjects that could make my practical sister wistful. Daddy had been there as a child, it seemed, and he talked about it as a wonderland, stories that lingered in Darlene's imagination. My sister passed our father's dream on to me: tigers and rhinos and waterfalls and giraffes and cotton candy and panda bears and trolley rides and a petting zoo and monkeys of all sizes. But we never had the money to go. Our luck never did change.

Now I smelled manure and fur. I heard the roar of a cheetah, the screech of some exotic bird. I bounced with each step until Tucker laid a hand on my shoulder to remind me that I was supposed to seem like an Amarillo kid—someone who had been here so many times it was old hat. The first hour passed in a glaze of elation. My brother shepherded me from exhibit to exhibit, his hair curling in the late July heat. We shared sips from a water bottle. The place was sprawling and circuitous. There were signposts studded with dozens of arrows, each painted with an image of a different animal—emu, zebra, rhino. We turned a corner and saw three giraffes grouped together on a grassy hill. I climbed up on the bottom bar of the fence to get a better view.

Tucker leaned close and murmured, "When a giraffe dies in the zoo, they have to cut up the corpse with a chainsaw. Otherwise they'd never be able to shove it into the furnace."

I ignored him. The giraffes twisted their long necks to mouth the upper branches of the trees. Purple tongues. Bristly lips. Pronged heads. They wore bemused expressions, as though they were not quite sure how they had ended up in Texas. The runt of the group lingered off to the side. His stance was rather odd, all four legs braced, his knees locked and hooves planted in the dirt. He kept arching his neck awkwardly to one side. It looked as though he was trying to eavesdrop on what the crowd was saying about him.

"That's called *zoochosis*," Tucker said. "That kind of repetitive, weird behavior."

"Zoochosis," I repeated, trying out the word.

"It's a combination of *zoo* and *psychosis*. Some wild animals—Level

One—go off the deep end in captivity. They start pacing or pulling out their fur or acting like that." He indicated the giraffe again. "Vomiting. Eating feces. Licking walls. Sometimes they'll even hurt themselves on purpose."

All around the paddock, people were holding up their phones, snapping photos and taking videos.

"Captivity does funny things to the mind," Tucker said. "In the wild, boredom is an unknown concept, but it's pretty common in zoos. And among humans, of course."

"Huh," I said, considering this.

"The smartest animals have the worst time," he went on. "Elephants, for instance. They're probably sentient, nearly on par with humans. They've got no illusions about what it means to be in a cage. They're prone to zoochosis, sometimes even catatonia. In the wild, elephants can live fifty or sixty years. In captivity, they never last more than twenty." Tucker paused, his jaw tightening. "Octopuses are smart too. They're famous escape artists. And they use their skin to send messages. Every octopus in an aquarium is always bright red, because red is the color of rage."

I glanced around nervously. Tucker was gesturing as he spoke, and a few people had begun to glance in our direction.

"Let's find the reptile house," I said.

My brother did not appear to have heard me. He swept a hand over the scene, a violent movement, his fingers slicing through the air.

"This is everything that's wrong with humanity," he said. "Humans believe that they aren't a part of nature. And zoos reinforce that idea. The animals are on that side of the bars and we're over here. Of *course* we're not the same thing."

I waited for him to come back to himself. Every so often this would happen: Tucker would slip into speechifying, so caught up in the cause that his eyes would glaze over. Sometimes he would lecture for just a few minutes. Sometimes it was hours. My job was to agree and wait for the fit to pass through him like a seizure shaking loose from his brain.

"Zoos aren't just bad for animals," he said. "They're bad for people too. They bring the wilderness into civilization instead of people into the wilderness. They're a fast-food version of the great outdoors." Tucker slammed a fist into his palm. "Zoos give us an illusion of nature, not the truth. They treat animals like paintings in a museum or images on a screen. Like symbols. Not independent creatures with instincts of their own."

"You're right," I said quietly.

I took his hand and pulled him after me. Still frowning, he let himself be led.

"Zoochosis in apes is especially bad," he said. "They show all the same symptoms as people in an asylum. Sitting in a corner rocking and holding their knees."

"Let's go this way," I said, pointing down the hill.

We saw a hippo in a pool, its skin the same muddy hue as the water, its back and bottom as rounded as weathered granite. We observed the seals from an underground viewing area, a cool, gloomy tunnel where the pavement was damp, the air rank with the tang of seawater. The pathways were filled with people—an elderly man shuffling along with a cane, disaffected teenagers, everyone eating ice cream or soft pretzels or cotton candy.

"Let's talk about the plan," Tucker said at last.

"Okay."

He sank onto a bench in the shade and patted the wooden slats beside him. I sat too, grateful to rest.

"Today we're doing recon," he said. "Look across the street."

He pointed through the bars of the fence that separated the cityscape from the animals. I noticed that the top of each spar was armed with a spike. Tucker gestured to a gray, forbidding building across the road. The place appeared to be closed on Sundays, all the windows shuttered and dark.

"That's Chicken Man's office," Tucker said.

I took a deep breath. The air had a unique odor—tilled earth, urine, and something murky and piquant that I assumed was the stench of the animals themselves. A corpulent man strolled in front of us, sweating and drinking soda from a straw. He was fat enough that each step cost him something. I watched him lumber down the hill, pink all over, wiping his brow.

"What about our farm?" I said.

"Excuse me?"

To my surprise, I realized I had an argument to make. The idea came into my brain fully formed, as though some part of me had been working on it for a while.

"You don't like zoos," I said. "But you loved the farm we had at the old house. I remember that."

"Uh-huh," Tucker said slowly.

"We kept animals there. Behind fences, in the barn. Did you ever try to set our animals free?"

Boldly, I met his gaze. Cora would never have been courageous enough to challenge Tucker. My brother was older, stronger, and a thousand times more articulate than she was. His words defeated hers every time, no matter how intense her underlying instincts might be.

Corey, however, wanted this matter resolved. He needed to verify that there was logical consistency in the new world order.

"That's a good question," Tucker said. "An excellent question."

His expression was not what I expected. He seemed to like my audacity.

"I used to open the gates," he said. "I did it every few months. I would unlatch the cow paddock. Leave the chicken coop open. Show the horses the way out of the barn."

"Seriously?" I said.

"Hell yeah. I loved those animals, but I didn't want to keep them there if they didn't want to be kept. And sometimes they would go exploring a bit. Sweetie especially. He wasn't all that attached to us, and he liked climbing around in the neighbor's yard. But by nightfall, he always came back."

"I never knew," I said.

"Nobody did," he said. "Mojo—our old stallion, remember?—he liked wandering too. He'd go down the lane every now and then, poking around, eating people's flowers, but he usually came back after a couple hours. And the cows never even left their paddock. It was their home. They didn't want anything different." Tucker sighed. "They were Level Four. Totally domesticated."

The crowd was growing denser by the minute. Some people appeared to have come right from church, still dressed in their fine clothes and uncomfortable shoes.

"Level Five," Tucker said. "Human beings are in a class by ourselves. You know what sets us apart from the other animals?"

"What?"

"We're incapable of living sustainably. Everything we touch, we change. A wild animal lives in balance with its environment. That's what *wild* means. Humans do the opposite."

I rested my temple against his shoulder. The wind was steamy, the trees whispering, the sky peppered with tiny white clouds.

"Where did you learn about the Classification of Wildness?" I asked.

"I made it up," Tucker said.

I gazed at him in awe. The afternoon light came dreamily through the branches of the tree overhead, dappling his brow.

"One day I'll write a paper," he said. "Get famous like Darwin. It's good, isn't it? People like to organize things in fives. The Trophic Scale and the Fujita Scale have five levels. Hurricanes and tornadoes too."

He held up his intact hand, palm spread, bending each finger in turn.

"Five is always the worst," he said. "The strongest, the most destructive. The opposable thumb."

28

At 9 a.m., I was in position. My shoes were laced with triple knots so they would not come undone when I ran. The street hummed with the Amarillo version of rush hour. Revolving doors cast rainbows on the sidewalk. Somewhere behind me, the zoo was in the process of opening for business. A taxi honked. I heard an ice cream truck. A row of children turned the corner, dressed in green T-shirts with the logo of a summer camp emblazoned on their chests.

A church bell began to toll. I counted the tones. The flock of children pushed past me, surrounding me. They were all the same age, a little older than I was—twelve or thirteen, maybe—and big enough that I was concealed for a moment in a forest of green T-shirts. Somewhere far off, the church bell stopped ringing, and the silence that fell in its wake was profound.

There was a screech of tires. A car pulled up in front of the stark, featureless office across the street. This was my cue. I took a moment to verify the details Tucker drummed into me: right address, black vehicle, a driver in a cap climbing out from behind the wheel. The other children left me behind, shuffling down the block toward the zoo entrance. On the opposite sidewalk, the driver went around to open the car door. I knew what to do next.

A figure appeared, facing away from me—thinning hair, a broad neck, sloping shoulders. Chicken Man. A normal businessman in a blue suit.

Then I saw Tucker. Everything else shifted and blurred. For an instant, my brother was the only thing in focus. He paced toward Chicken Man with deliberate indifference, his face shadowed by a baseball cap, his damaged fingers swinging loose at his side.

I screamed with all my strength, scraping my throat raw. This was my job: I was the distraction. I flung my arms outward and dropped them down, deflating my lungs like a bellows. All along the sidewalk, adults turned to stare at me. A woman with a messy gray braid moved toward me, her arms outstretched, her expression maternal. Across the street, the driver frowned, squinting at me beneath his cap. I kept hollering, though I was running out of breath. Chicken Man glanced upward, as though he could not tell where the shouting was coming from. Perhaps he thought I was above him, falling to the ground.

Afterward, I was glad that he made this mistake. The sky was the last thing he saw.

A gun in Tucker's hand. A wink of bright metal.

My brother lifted his arm. There was a crack.

For a moment, I did not understand. I had the sensation of doubling, as though each eye saw something different and the image would not cohere. I heard Cora's voice in my mind, louder than ever, shouting instructions I could not parse, something about home, something about Darlene. Corey, on the other hand, was ready to do as he was told. Tucker had said there would be a signal. He said that I would know it when I saw it. He said that I should run.

Everything slowed down. Cars drifted along the road as lazily as autumn leaves on a river. Tucker was still standing with his arm raised, point-blank range. His face was contorted, flushed red with anger or triumph. I could not seem to gather my wits—two entities in a single space, disparate personalities overlapping. There was a chaotic moment in which every idea and impression was twinned.

Chicken Man fell. He did not make a sound. There was no blood. It was nothing like TV. His head did not explode like a ripe watermelon; he merely sagged to one side and slumped down behind the car, disappearing from my view.

With a deft motion, Tucker slipped the gun into the pocket of his cargo shorts. No one appeared to have witnessed the shot—except me. No one was sure yet what was happening—except me. A few people were still staring my way. Some were just now recognizing that the report had been a gunshot. One man ducked behind a mailbox. Tucker pivoted on his heel and walked away, moving languidly, as though he had nothing to hide and nowhere to be.

So I ran.

I dashed downhill, the cycling of my knees and the pounding of my shoes mere afterthoughts to the weightlessness of my being. Behind me someone cried out, but I did not look back. Maybe the crowd had noticed Chicken Man. Maybe the woman with the gray braid was chasing me. Maybe Tucker was being hauled off to jail by a furious mob. I kept going. Following my brother's instructions was the only thing I could think of. My head reverberated with Cora's wails, but Corey was the one in charge now, enacting Tucker's plan.

I darted through the zoo gates, avoiding the ticket booth, which was clogged by a massive summer camp group. I jogged into the big-cat house. There was a stitch in my side as I leapt down a set of concrete steps. The lavatories were hidden in damp shadows, stinking of urine and garbage. This was the end point of the first leg of my route. I ducked into the girls' bathroom—a clever smoke screen for Corey—and glanced at my watch. Only six minutes had elapsed since the church bell struck nine.

I waited. My heart was clanging so hard in my ears that I could hear the nuances of my own pulse—systole, diastole, repeat. If I was being chased, I would continue running along the next leg of Tucker's escape route until I eluded my pursuers (Plan A). If no one was following me, I would adopt camouflage and blend into the crowd (Plan B). I fidgeted. The toilet seat was speckled with droplets. A swath of bathroom tissue wound across the floor, patterned with mud and shoe prints. I checked my watch again. A lion roared. Children were giggling nearby. I did not hear footsteps, no shouts of policemen, no sirens.

At last, I pushed the stall door open. In the mirror above the sink, my eyes looked haunted. I tugged the baseball cap off my head and shoved it into the garbage can. Then I pulled a pink handkerchief from my pocket. It was my favorite one; I had brought it from home, though it had lain unused at the bottom of my bag until now. I folded the fabric the way Darlene taught me and tied it over my head. At once, my reflection became female. A tomboy with a short, sassy haircut. A bird-boned child dressed in nondescript clothing: tennis shoes, jean shorts, a gray T-shirt, nothing memorable. Cora disguised as Corey disguised as Cora again.

For a moment, gazing at my own face, I dissolved into disarray once more. Cora and Corey clashed against one another, both hollering so loudly that I could not pick out one voice to follow.

The bathroom door banged open. A woman eased inside, holding an infant in the crook of her arm. She was large breasted, large all over, and plainly suffering from the heat, her shirt stained with sweat. The baby lolled in her arms, its eyes smeary and unfocused, its hands opening and closing like anemones.

"Would you fill this for me, hon?" she said.

She unhooked a water bottle from a metal ring on her fanny pack. As she passed it to me, I stood frozen for a moment, unable to shift gears.

"Hon?" she said. "You all right?"

"Yes, ma'am," I said. I turned to the sink and grappled with the faucet. My hands were shaking so badly that the neck of the container rattled against the spigot. Behind me, the baby gave a querulous cry. I handed the water bottle to the woman, and she took a long pull.

"You have a blessed day now," she said.

I stepped into the sunlight, wiping my sweaty palms on my shorts.

Over the next hour, I changed my identity as often as I could, back and forth between Cora and Corey. I wore my pink kerchief for twenty minutes before removing it and balling it up in my pocket again. I put on my sunglasses instead. My heart kept revving like a car engine, sending surges of adrenaline through my veins. I forced myself to walk casually, taking up the smallest possible space on the wide, sun-soaked pathways of the zoo. Tucker had told me to alter my appearance regularly—he explained that camouflage would keep me safe—but I quickly grew confused about who I was supposed to be. I took off Corey's sunglasses and reached in Cora's pocket, where there was a cheap purple bracelet studded with fake rhinestones. A moment later, I realized that I was still strutting like a boy while dressed as a girl. I stopped in terror, sure that everyone had noticed. Trembling, I flung the bracelet into the grass. I glanced in the reflective surface of a window and realized I was not sure who I was supposed to be just then. The child looking back at me had no definitive markers of either personality.

Sometime later, a group of boys in green summer camp T-shirts headed into the bathroom together without their counselor. I was standing nearby in the shade, pretending to watch a warthog sleeping. Striding blithely in Corey's loping gait, I followed the boys down the concrete steps. I tried not to stare at a man standing at the row of urinals, humming while he peed. The overhead light was on the fritz here too, dimming at intervals.

I tapped one of the boys on the shoulder. He was sandy haired and freckled, a husky child in a cowboy hat.

"Hey," I said. "Switch shirts with me."

"Huh?" he said.

I groped in my pocket and held out a crumpled bill. I smoothed it out and waved it under the boy's nose.

"Twenty bucks," I said.

He had one of those faces that showed every thought in his head. I watched him look at my shirt, touch his own, examine the twenty dollars to verify it was real, then consider all the things he could buy with that money.

"All right," he said.

Five minutes later, I was in the small-mammals house, following a group of children in identical green T-shirts, standing near but not exactly with them. I had been a nomad for a while, but the fragility of this rootless state had not struck me until now. There was no home for me to return to, no door to close. I was as vulnerable as a rabbit in a field, unable to retreat to a safe burrow.

As the minutes ticked past, I moved into the reptile house, dark and cool, the lights kept low for the comfort of the animals. I cowered in corners, in shadows. Over the past weeks, I had learned to never loiter in one spot long enough to be remembered. The goal was to be unexceptional. I wiled away the time at the least interesting exhibits, the ones with the smallest crowds. People flocked in droves to the giraffes and the elephants, but nobody cared about the deer or the foxes—animals you could find in the wild right here in Texas.

Around noon, I managed to switch shirts again, this time with a girl my age. She was not a camp member, just a child on summer break. The two of us were washing our hands side by side in the insufficient flow of the bathroom faucets when I blurted out my request and she complied. She wore a blue shirt with a picture of a robot on the front and a ketchup stain on the sleeve. She was tall, black, and svelte, her hair plaited into tiny coils that glittered with jewels and beads. I did not offer her any money, and she did not ask for any. She seemed pleased just to have a clean shirt. She did not inquire why I wanted to switch, either. She merely gave me a nod and strolled outside to meet her mother by the hot dog cart.

Watching her go, I was overcome by a sensation I had never

before experienced. I missed Darlene so much that it felt like a fever. I wanted to know where she was. I wanted to call her again. I wanted to throw myself into her arms and let her carry me home.

Tucker and I planned to meet at four. There was a side entrance to the zoo that led through a little gate into a garden. I checked my watch once more. Behind my eyes, Chicken Man kept falling. The scene would not stop playing inside my head. My memory was operating like a malfunctioning film projector, the same fragmented sequence of events shown over and over. I saw Chicken Man crumple, transitioning before my eyes from a living creature into an inanimate object, no longer powered by his own muscles and mind.

Maybe that was what death looked like. Maybe he was dead.

I bought a soft pretzel, though I could not imagine eating anything. My throat was silted and grainy; I could barely manage to swallow the occasional sip of water from a drinking fountain. The pretzel was a symbol, a prop to show that I belonged at the zoo.

By the time four o'clock rolled around, my stress had reached such a level that I had become clumsy, tripping over my own feet. I approached the meeting point as the church bell clanged in the distance. The side entrance was small, tucked beside a maintenance building. A copse of evergreens bristled fiercely overhead, their branches interlocked in an inky canopy. There was no one else nearby. The crowds had thinned out as people headed home for their supper. Somewhere inside the zoo, a baby wailed, or possibly a monkey. I leaned against the bars of the gate, cheek to iron, relishing the cold metal.

A shadow moved on the other side of the fence. There was a figure among the trunks, a flash of teeth.

"I see you," Tucker whispered.

Then I was in his arms. I was not sure how it happened—whether I ran to him or he ran to me.

"Are you all right?" he said.

"I think so."

"Nice shirt," he said, setting me down.

I touched the robot on my chest, the ketchup stain on my sleeve.

"Did anybody bother you?" Tucker said.

"No."

"You stayed away from the staff? You hid in the bathroom?"

"Yeah."

He straightened his shoulders. "I'm proud of you. You did good, Corey."

As he spoke that name aloud, I felt the hot pressure inside my chest release a little. I inhaled my first real breath in hours. My brother did not have a scratch on him. He wore jeans, a brand-new cowboy hat, and a tank top that showed off the jagged planes of his shoulders. I wondered what he had done all day. I wondered where he had hidden the gun.

"Is he dead?" I said.

Tucker made his fingers into a pistol and shot himself in the temple. I stared up at him.

"It went like clockwork," he said. "You drew everybody's focus at exactly the right moment. I couldn't have done it without you."

"I didn't know," I said faintly.

"Hm?"

"I didn't know what the plan was."

"I think you did," Tucker said. "On some level, you probably did."

I swung to the side just in time. My stomach emptied itself onto the grass in a single heave. Creamy bile splattered my shoe and a tree. My brother watched but did not touch me. I straightened up, wiping my mouth with the back of my wrist. My throat burned.

"That's just shock," Tucker said. "It'll wear off."

"I didn't know the plan," I repeated.

The smell of the pines was tangy and cloying. Crickets chimed around us, and a robin warbled somewhere. Tucker rocked back and forth on his heels.

"I've been in a sports bar all day," he said. "Just watching the news. A random shooting, they're calling it. The cops don't know what to look for. They don't have a goddamn clue. There were twenty people on the street, and nobody saw a thing."

A tremor ran through me, tingling up my spine.

"I'm cold," I said.

"Just shock," Tucker said.

I might never have been as tired in my life as I was then—a child who had been far away from home for too long. Tucker led me down the path between the trees. I gripped his fingers for all I was worth, even though our heights did not line up and it was awkward for us both to walk while holding hands.

Then he smiled down at me, the smile I loved most, showing no teeth, his eyes crinkled and gleaming. He swung me into his arms as though I weighed nothing at all.

29

At midnight, Tucker and I lay side by side in the back of a newly stolen pickup truck. The moon was high, nearly full, a pearly orb like a spider's egg sac dangling from the sticky web of stars. We were both awake, staring up at the night sky. In school, I was taught to identify the Big Dipper, follow it to the Little Dipper, and locate the North Star. But I could not pick out any constellations now. There was no man-made glow to wash out the Milky Way. There were no trees or buildings to block my view. The darkness was a cloth thrown over the world, glittering with stars like sand on a beach towel, too many pinpricks of light to discern patterns.

Tucker and I had fled Amarillo and vanished into Texas, off the map, off the grid. The air was so dry that my lungs ached. The night was filled with the robotic whirring of desert insects. Beneath my skin, the truck bed was pleasantly warm, retaining the heat of the day. The metal smelled of muddy dog and stale beer. Tucker shifted his weight, readjusting his legs on the plating.

Neither of us could sleep. I was not sure where we were. Somewhere flat. Near the New Mexico border, maybe. I did not know how far a person could travel in six or seven hours. I did not know where we were going, and I did not particularly care. The farther we traveled from Chicken Man's death, the lighter and cleaner I felt. Eventually the whole thing might just be a speck in the rearview mirror.

"I want to call Darlene again," I said.

"Sure," Tucker said. "It might be a little while, though. You'll have to wait until we're back in range of a cell tower."

"Okay."

"Darlene's not like us," he said. "Remember that, Corey."

I did not answer. The burring of the insects ticked up a notch.

"I left the gate open for you," Tucker said. "Just like I did for the horses and Sweetie. I opened the door at Shady Acres, and out you came." He exhaled a slow breath. "Darlene would never have done that. Jane either."

I had napped in the car earlier—dropping into a dreamless void as soon as the adrenaline left my system—and I was off my usual schedule now, staring up at the moon like a nocturnal animal. I was not exactly sleepy, somewhere between alertness and a kind of delirium. A shadow darted across the stars above, maybe a bird, maybe a bat. A wind blew around me, circling the truck bed.

On some level, I understood that something irrevocable had happened. I had crossed a threshold I could not come back from. I did not know yet what it meant for me, but I could feel the transformation; I was changing deep inside, at a level beneath flesh, beneath words.

I rolled on my side to look at Tucker.

"Tell me about Corey," I said. "What was he like?"

My brother made a soft noise, as though he had been waiting a long while for me to ask this question.

"Once upon a time," he said.

I closed my eyes.

"Actually, I have to tell you about Tucker first," he said, interrupting himself.

"Okay."

"Once upon a time, there was a boy who loved animals. I don't know why he did. Tucker lived in a nice house with a nice family and a nice farm out back."

Somewhere in the distance, a bird cried out. It was a broken, breathless screech, echoing across the open fields. I knew that owls often sounded like this—distressed, distraught—when in fact they were nothing of the kind.

"There was an owl on the farm too," Tucker said. "I guess."

It was the first time I smiled all day.

"For a while, life was good," he said. "But nothing lasts forever, and somehow . . ." He trailed off. For a long moment, he lay silent.

"What happened?" I said.

"A dark wizard took notice of the boy's family. He didn't like how happy they were. How loving and carefree. He decided to put a curse on them." Tucker clucked his tongue. "This wizard had power. Mama was the first to fall victim to it. She died in childbirth. It was hard for Tucker, as you can imagine." A sigh. "He didn't blame the new baby, you understand. He loved his little sister from the start. She was a golden girl, a sweet little star. But he had loved his mother too—"

My cheeks were wet. The tears had started without my noticing. I was not sure what I was crying for: my lost mother, our lost farm, or the lost girl I had once been. Maybe I was crying for Big Tom or Chicken Man. For the murder I had accidentally facilitated. For the day I had just survived.

"The wizard made a tornado," my brother said. "He worked a vicious spell that took away Tucker's home, his animals, his father. The wizard had a dark heart and no mercy."

I rolled onto my back again, staring up at the sky, tears dampening my short hair. On a night this clear, I could discern that the stars were not uniform. A few had color, a suggestion of blue or red mixed into their luminescence. Some were larger—as distinct as holes punched in a sheet of paper—while others were so faint that I could only glimpse them in my peripheral vision. If I looked straight at them, they melted into black.

"After the tornado, things were rough," my brother said. "The tragedy opened Tucker's eyes. Maybe he could learn something from it, discover some meaning in it. He still had his sisters, after all. For a little while."

I could no longer see him—the darkness was too complete—but I knew his eyes were fixed on me.

"Tucker had a hero's heart," he said. "He boldly left home. Soon he found a friend. But the guy was two-faced. Not to be trusted. A coward. After that, Tucker was alone a long while. Sometimes he felt he couldn't go on."

The wind dried my cheeks. The tears were no longer coming; the story had begun to soothe me at last. I was not following everything my brother was saying, but I was storing it away, tucking his words into a safe, secret space to keep for some other season.

"Then Tucker found Corey." He smiled at these words. I couldn't see his expression change in the darkness, but I could hear the parting of his lips, and his voice grew sweet.

"And?" I said.

"And the wizard had no power over Tucker anymore. Corey was the bravest, truest boy he had ever known. Together they changed the world."

"They did?" I said.

For a moment, I almost believed again in the purpose of our journey, the certainty of my brother's dream. Almost.

"This is all true, you know," Tucker said. "This really happened."

AUGUST

30

On a rain-swept afternoon, Darlene found herself outside her childhood home for the first time in years. She was not entirely sure how she came to be there. After leaving the grocery store, she had intended to drive back to No. 43, but somehow she ended up inside the path of devastation left by the finger of God.

Seated behind the wheel of her father's pickup truck, still dressed in her work uniform, Darlene stared up and down the street. The sky was heavy, the clouds hanging low. Her old house was gone, of course. The concrete crater of the basement swam with shadows. In the distance, a few isolated, sagging walls—still vaguely reddish after all this time—stood where the barn once was. Darlene climbed out of the car, and the drizzle enveloped her in a gauzy embrace.

What instinct had carried her to this spot? She felt that she was searching for something, waiting for something. As she approached the absence of her former home, droplets of rain kissed her skin. The basement was shallower than she remembered. There was her father's workbench. The cement floor was smudged with mud. The stairs were warped and treacherous now, the wood rotten. Darlene heard the skitter of mice.

More than a month had passed since Cora's last phone call. No contact since, no word. Cora was somewhere in America, on the road, on the run.

Darlene lifted a hand and mimed the surface of the wall that once stood there. The living room window would have been a few inches above her. She reached up and pretended to knock on a nonexistent pane of glass.

Then she pulled her phone from her pocket and texted Roy: *Can I come over? Might be losing my mind.*

Sure thing, he replied.

But she could not leave. Not yet. Some compulsion kept her poised on the edge of the basement. There was an empty water bottle tossed in a corner. A rusty pair of scissors lay in the mud, the blades yawning wide. Darlene stared down at the door of the tornado shelter. It looked small from this height, sealed shut, partially obscured by a fallen beam. She wanted to go inside. She did not know why she wanted to go inside.

With a sigh, she closed her eyes, slipping backward through time. Back to the afternoon of the tornado. The wail of the wind. The musty odor inside the shelter. She remembered shutting the door and bracing her back against it. Keeping her brother inside against his will. *No*, she told him. *No.*

That moment—the discord between her and Tucker—led to everything that followed. Him pleading, her refusing. It was a point of friction like a chip in a pane of glass, tiny but unfixable, fissures spreading outward from that initial chink, weakening the structure, leading to the quarrel in No. 43, the black eye, cracks and fractures snaking inexorably onward, worse ruptures, Tucker's return to

Mercy, the bombing of Jolly Cosmetics, Cora stolen away, a sheet of glass dissolving into splinters.

Darlene inhaled the raw scent of the rain. The drizzle touched her hair gently, smoothing down her bangs. She felt her mind flooded with strange ideas. The tornado was not an act of God, but an act of nature. The wild had come to Mercy that day. As she and her siblings cowered in the bunker, the full force of the wild had roared above them, erasing everything it touched.

Tucker blamed her for their father's death. He believed that he would have been able to rescue Daddy from the tornado if she had not interfered. But Darlene knew better. If she had not taken action, her brother would have vanished into the storm too. She was not responsible for Daddy's death; she was only responsible for saving Tucker's life.

Now she wrapped her arms around her body, swaying back and forth in the rain. For the first time, she wondered if she should have just stepped aside back then. Maybe she should have opened the door to the shelter, the final barrier between the human and the wild, and let Tucker go.

HOURS LATER, DARLENE LAY ACROSS Roy's bed, watching the rain bejewel the window. It was August. Mercy was experiencing a heat wave that singed the sky and turned the grass into matchsticks. The downpour dampened but failed to cool the charbroiled terrain.

Beside her, Roy sprawled motionless and prone, so deeply asleep that he scarcely breathed. Their lovemaking always sent him into a fervent state of rest. The uneven light of evening dappled his skin like leopard fur. Darlene took a moment to relish the muscular definition of his torso.

Then her phone rang. She climbed out of bed—a plush, generous mattress, nothing like the stiff cushions of the couch at home. Roy grunted but did not wake. In the shadows, Darlene knelt down and searched through the objects on the floor, trying to locate her purse.

Roy's house did not have air-conditioning. There were three fans humming in the little bedroom, one in each window and another on the ceiling, creaking with every revolution. The air was a tepid bath.

At last, Darlene found her phone. The number was withheld. There was a clatter of static, and her nervous system jump-started like a car engine.

"Who is this?" she said.

A voice rang out in the distance, all but lost in a flurry of mechanical rustling. The phone went abruptly silent. Disconnected.

Darlene swore aloud, then glanced back at Roy, who was still sleeping. She pressed a hand to her heart, trying to quiet its clamor. It might have been a wrong number. It might have been anyone. She stared at the blank screen and sank back onto the bed, trying not to feel disappointed.

Cora had been gone an eternity and no time at all. A single phone call, over a month ago. Nothing since. Darlene remembered her sister's voice that day, sweetly and cheerfully parroting Tucker's dreadful rhetoric. Their conversation had emptied Darlene out, carving her hollow.

She reached for her glasses and polished the lenses before putting them on. The rain was a silver glimmer against a smoky sky. The bedroom felt cozy and overstuffed, every wall crammed with furniture, the bookshelves and bureaus standing elbow to elbow. The various fans competed to brush away her sweat. Roy rolled onto his side, his eyelids fluttering in dreams. Darlene was still sore from their sex. She could feel the echo of lovemaking in her body in the same way she could feel the rock and shift of waves after a day of swimming, long after she left the water.

Her phone rang again. The screen came to life in her hands, startling her so badly that she nearly dropped it. Once more, the number was withheld. She brought the phone to her ear, fumbling in her eagerness.

"Hello?"

There was a gush of staticky breath. Darlene stuck her finger in her free ear. She heard electronic tones and ghostly whispering.

"Is that you?" she cried. "Are you there?"

"I'm here."

Cora's voice was higher than Darlene remembered. She sounded so small, so young, her words coming across the airwaves like a kitten's mewl.

"Are you all right?" Darlene asked.

"I don't know."

There was a pause. After a moment, Darlene realized that it wasn't a pause: the line had gone dead again. She moaned aloud. The signal was strong at Roy's house, so the fault must be on Cora's end. Wherever she was—wherever Tucker had brought her now—must be far from cell towers.

Roy shifted position, his face buried in his forearms. Darlene could not decide whether she wanted him to wake up and comfort her or let her ponder the situation on her own. They had been dating for only a few weeks. Everything between them was still new, at once heightened and uncertain.

Surely Cora would call back. Surely she would not leave their conversation severed in the middle. Before this summer, Darlene had not understood that waiting was the worst form of torture, more unbearable than physical pain or profound loss. Sometimes she was amazed that she was still surviving it, waiting for Cora with each tick of the clock.

Her phone rang again. She brought it to her ear before the first chime had finished. There was a crackle of breath.

"Sorry!" Cora said. "I have to stand in exactly the right place or the phone cuts out."

"Where are you?"

"Someplace with trees."

"What kind of trees?"

"Big."

"Are you coming home now?" Darlene said. "Please say you're coming home."

"What? I can't hear you."

"Are you coming back to Mercy?" Darlene cried.

A burst of furious rustling. For a moment, Cora vanished into crinkly static. Then she murmured, "Tucker said no."

Darlene's temper surged, but she restrained herself, exhaling through her nose and counting to ten. She was determined not to repeat the mistakes of their last conversation. No shouting this time. No commands, only questions. She reminded herself that Cora was different now—different in ways that were impossible to parse fully from a distance. Her sister was a changeling. Darlene would treat her accordingly.

Then Cora coughed. Darlene did not like the sound—a wet rattle.

"Are you sick?" she said sharply.

"Just a little."

"Did Tucker get you some medicine?"

"Yeah," Cora said absently.

Darlene readjusted her pose on the mattress. She felt an odd tingle of modesty, as though somehow her baby sister might divine that she was dressed only in an old T-shirt of Roy's, the fabric soft from years of use.

"I'm glad you called," Darlene said. "I didn't like the way things went last time we talked."

Cora grunted, a noncommittal response.

"Tell me about . . ." Darlene paused, choosing her words with care. "Tell me what you did today."

"Just stuff. I don't know."

Darlene gritted her teeth. She was trying to divine as much as possible from her sister's tone. During their last conversation, Cora manifested a kind of giddy elation, but now her voice was flat, quiet, almost lifeless. Perhaps this was meaningful. Perhaps she regretted leaving Mercy. Perhaps it was merely the effect of a sore throat.

"Tell me anything," Darlene said at last. "You've been gone so long, and I have no idea what things are like for you."

Cora let out a long, humming note. "Well, Tucker taught me how to handle a rattlesnake."

"He did what?"

"Did you know that the babies are more dangerous than the adults? The little ones have the same amount of poison as the big ones, but they don't know how to control it yet. When a grown-up bites you, it squirts out just a little venom and saves the rest. But the babies dump everything into your blood at once."

She began to cough again, her dulcet tones transitioning into phlegmy barks. Darlene waited for her to get her breath back. When Cora spoke again, her voice had dropped an octave, the gravely growl of a pack-a-day smoker.

"Snakes are good citizens," she said. "They do important work for the planet."

"How long have you been coughing like that?"

"Tucker says I'm getting better."

Darlene felt a hand touch her back. Roy was sitting up, stroking her shoulder blades, his face full of concern. Then he reached for his cell phone and began tapping away with his thumbs. She knew that he was texting someone at the police station or the FBI, alerting them to what was happening. The glow from the screen illuminated his face from beneath. He had recently shaved his head, a bald dome of freckled mahogany.

"Is Tucker with you?" Darlene said. "Is he there now?"

"He's always with me," Cora said.

"Can I talk to him? Please."

There was a pause. Darlene knotted her fingers anxiously in her hair.

"I have to go," Cora said.

"Wait."

"Happy birthday. It's this week, right? That's why Tucker let me . . ." Her voice grew faint. "I kept asking, and Tucker finally said I could . . ."

Darlene waited for her sister to finish the sentence, then realized that the screen had gone dark.

"Are you there?" she shouted. "Cora?"

234 / ABBY GENI

Silence. Darlene flung out a hand in wild anger, connecting with the night table. An old-fashioned alarm clock, a tiny ceramic cat, and a science fiction novel tumbled to the floor. The cat shattered. Darlene stared down with a kind of perverse pleasure at the pieces on the rug.

"I texted George," Roy said. "He's at the station today. I'll get a buzz if they have any luck tracing the call."

He leaned past her, examining the mess on the floor.

"I'll get the vacuum in a minute," he said mildly. "Come here."

He opened his arms. Darlene folded herself into his embrace, and together they slumped against the headboard, Roy cradling her against his chest. She moved to wipe her eyes, then realized that she was not crying. Perhaps she did not have any tears left.

31

In the second week of August, Darlene turned twenty-three. Roy threw her a birthday party at the trailer. It was a Saturday afternoon, the sky cloudless and desiccated, a scorched, flinty shade of blue. As Roy bustled around No. 43 with candles and paper plates, Darlene stared out the window, refusing to help. She had told Roy that she did not want a party, but he disregarded her wishes, deciding with his tone-deaf optimism that she could use some cheering up. Cora's call, three days earlier, had left her "down in the dumps," he said. A celebration was just what she needed now.

Hovering by the window, Darlene felt numb. The next-door neighbors were barbecuing; she could not see them, but she smelled the meat and heard the familiar cadence of a mild marital spat. Other people's children ran between the trailers, their voices shrill, mingling with the cicada song. Roy set the punch bowl on the kitchen table. Jane was adjusting her headband in the mirror. She had borrowed a swipe of Darlene's lipstick without asking and painted her fingernails orange. Roy was light on his feet, beaming around at the decorations, and Jane mimicked him, planting her fists on her hips and grinning. Darlene marveled at her sister's good mood. Jane was full of sass and sarcasm these days—just that morning she pitched a fit about Darlene's method of scrambling eggs—but with Roy she became a different child. Something about his presence brought out her easygoing side.

"No one's going to come to this thing," Darlene said.

"My buddies from the station will be here," Roy said.

"Some girls from the team are coming," Jane piped up.

"I asked a few family friends too," Roy added. "Folks my mom used to play bridge with. My godfather said he'd drop by. I want them all to get to know you."

Darlene gazed blankly at their hopeful faces. Neither of them seemed to realize what they were saying: that her birthday party would be populated entirely by strangers. She turned back to the window.

An hour later, the trailer was packed. Roy put on a playlist of dance music, a tinny beat in the background. He guided Darlene around by the elbow, welcoming his coworkers and poker buddies to No. 43 as though the place were his too. Jane's friends from the soccer team arrived en masse, six or seven girls climbing out of a single minivan like clowns from a circus car. Everyone wished Darlene a happy birthday in a perfunctory way, then turned to talk to someone else. Noise filled No. 43, and Roy was the center of attention, shaking hands and offering beers.

Darlene wondered if temperament was merely a matter of luck. Roy had endured his share of hardship—an absent father, a mother who succumbed to cancer, not to mention growing up black in Oklahoma—but none of it weighed him down. He chose to be a cop because he wanted to help people, to "give something back," and he never complained about the inherent difficulty of the work. He was in a pleasant mood almost all the time, rising out of sadness like a kite on the wind, pulled skyward by his nature.

As the afternoon passed, Darlene left the front door open, letting the guests wander in and out, fanning themselves with their hands and chatting with the people they already knew, no one mingling beyond their original cliques. Darlene felt exposed and invisible in equal measure. Everyone was aware of her, Roy's new girlfriend, but nobody invited her into their conversations.

Then Roy's cell phone rang. He hurried off to take the call, disappearing through the front door into a curl of sunlight. Darlene followed, unwilling to stand alone in the middle of her own party. The sun was dazzling, the streamers on the mailbox wilting in the heat. Jane and her friends lounged in the shady grass on the side of the trailer that faced the ravine, bare legs akimbo, all staring at their phones, evidently texting each other from two inches away. As Darlene watched, the girls burst into laughter that was almost but not quite simultaneous, like cicadas calling and replying within a fraction of a second. A TV blared in the distance. A baby was wailing somewhere. In the summer, everyone in the trailer park opened their windows, and the individual, interior ether of their private lives seeped into the open.

Roy stood by the ravine with his back to No. 43, talking on the phone. He saw Darlene coming and held up a finger. Ever since he shaved his head—something he did every summer, apparently—Darlene had become intimately acquainted with his scalp. His brow was knotted with concern, and the wrinkles rose beyond where his hairline would have been, his head creased all the way up to its crown.

He hung up, slipping his phone in his pocket.

"What happened?" she said.

"Nothing," he said. "It can wait."

"What is it?"

"Let's go enjoy your party. I seem to recall something about chocolate cake."

"No," she said. "Tell me now."

He glanced around, checking to see who might be nearby, then led her farther along the edge of the ravine. The sound of voices quieted and the trilling of the insects increased. Grasshoppers leapt around Darlene's feet, glittering and airy. Their bodies were as long as her palm.

"That was my contact at the FBI," Roy said.

"Did they trace the call?" she asked eagerly.

"No, they didn't trace it. I'm sorry."

Darlene crossed her arms over her belly with an aggressive movement.

"The FBI took the wiretaps off your phone," Roy said.

"What?"

"This happened a few weeks ago, apparently."

"*Weeks?*" she gasped.

"They didn't tell me either. I'm as pissed as you are."

Darlene sat down without really meaning to—the ground rose up and caught her. Roy settled opposite, his brow speckled with sweat. In the ravine, the creosote bushes were withering and skeletal, their branches ashy.

"Are you saying . . ." Darlene trailed off, then tried again. "Are you saying no one else was listening when Cora called me? Nobody is trying to locate her?"

"My contact told me that the FBI's resources are needed elsewhere."

"*I* need their resources." Darlene thumped a fist against her breastbone. "I don't understand how they can do something like this."

"I'm sorry."

She realized that she was now gripping the ground, her fingers digging into the warm soil.

DARLENE DID NOT REMEMBER MUCH from the rest of the day. Faces and bodies swirled around her. No. 43 ebbed in and out of focus.

People touched her arm, leaning close, their voices muted as though underwater. Jane danced in the background among her girlfriends. Sunlight poured through the windows, turning the trailer into a hotbox.

At one point, Roy loomed into view. Darlene blinked up at him. He handed her a small, wrapped package.

"Happy birthday," he said.

"No gifts," she said. "You promised."

He shrugged. "Couldn't help myself."

Inside was a gold locket on a delicate chain. Darlene slipped the catch and opened the pendant to reveal a photograph. She expected to see Roy there—a picture of him to carry close to her heart, maybe—but instead there was a snapshot of Cora. Darlene recognized the image immediately, since she was the one who took it: the same photo used in the Amber Alert back in June.

For a moment, she stood dumbstruck.

"Put it on," Roy said.

A semicircle of people gathered around them, observing this exchange. Somebody whispered, "It's her sister. The one that's missing."

Darlene tried to smile but could not manage it. She did not need a physical reminder of Cora. She already felt as though she were carrying Cora with her all the time, as a weight on her chest that never lifted.

"I'll help you with the clasp," Roy said.

"I can't do this," she said.

Darlene threw the necklace into his hands, turned to flee, and collided hard with an elderly man. Roy's godfather—she could not remember his name. He staggered backward, grunting in shock. Darlene did not stop to see if he was hurt. She bolted toward Jane's bedroom, the nearest refuge.

A commotion behind her. Scuffling and voices. Roy was saying something—maybe comforting his godfather, maybe asking Darlene to come back. She slammed the door, leaned against it, and breathed.

No one had traced Cora's call. There were no more wiretaps on her phone. Darlene could not quite believe it. Throughout the long, terrible summer, she found solace in the fact that no matter how bad things got, at least she was not alone. The federal government—the experts—were aware of and involved in her plight. She imagined men in suits like guardian angels, aiding and protecting her from a distance, unseen but all-seeing.

Now they were gone. In fact, they had been gone for some time. There was a breathtaking cruelty in their logic: somebody did the math and decided Cora was a lost cause. There was another kind of cruelty in their silence. Darlene wondered how long she had believed they were watching over her when she was actually on her own. Again.

On the other side of the door, the music ticked up a notch. Darlene heard footsteps landing in unison as a line dance broke out. Roy had obviously papered over her bad behavior, distracting his friends. It was unlike Darlene to make a scene, but she felt no remorse, only righteous fury.

The whole situation was absurd. It was ridiculous to throw a party here, in the place where Tucker once hurled insults at her and blacked her eye, where Cora was last seen before being kidnapped, where Darlene had spent all summer suffering and waiting. She wanted to usher everyone out—to throw things and sob—but she knew better. She would not draw additional attention to herself. Instead, she would hide in silence until this crowd, too, was gone.

Just for a moment, though, she wished that she could scream the house down. *There was blood all over this trailer*, she wanted to yell at the whole careless lot of them. *There was blood right there, where y'all are dancing.*

32

Hours later, Darlene sat alone in the living room of No. 43. Jane was asleep in her bedroom, Roy shooed back to his own house, the partygoers long gone. Darlene had scrubbed away all evidence of the festivities, stripping the streamers from the mailbox and mopping the footprints from her kitchen floor. Now she lay on the couch, buzzing with anger and energy, listening to the cicadas shriek.

She was thinking about the Sooners, her ancestors in this place. She remembered the stories from history classes long ago. Before Oklahoma was a state, it had been known as the Unassigned Lands. It was a barren, treeless desert then, considered unfit for agriculture and livestock, and unsuitable to house the Indian tribes who had been forced from their homes elsewhere. (They were marched to the

Osage Reservation in the northeast instead.) Only after extensive irrigation and a great leap forward in agricultural techniques did the territory become habitable. Human intervention transfigured it over decades into fertile ground.

Darlene rose to her feet and went to the window, looking out over the dark trailer park. Eventually the government had decided to open the Unassigned Lands to white settlers heading west, folks who were dreaming of adventure and a new home. There was a fever of anticipation. The plan was simple: a cannon would sound and everyone would rush in at the same time. Whoever staked a claim—and could hold it—would own it. First come, first served. It was supposed to be an equitable arrangement. Thousands of hopeful settlers gathered at the border of the Unassigned Lands to wait.

But the Sooners snuck in ahead of the deadline. They were the clever ones—the rule-breakers and rebels. When the cannon fired and a clamor of hooves filled the air, the Sooners emerged from their hiding places and pretended to have arrived with the rest of the crowd. Families in covered wagons came upon new, verdant fields only to discover other people already there, digging wells, planting seeds, and waving their guns to dissuade trespassers. Darlene remembered a story about a man who was found hours after the cannon blast on a patch of ground that had been tilled and plowed, his crops already sprouting, a log cabin half-finished behind him. He had clearly been there for days, but he claimed that the rich Oklahoma soil allowed him to start his farm in no time.

Darlene was proud of this heritage. The Sooners flouted the rules with brio, resourcefulness, and, ultimately, success. Perhaps there was a lesson here. She touched the chilly glass of the window. Shady Acres was a moonlit ocean tonight, the trailers bobbing in the pale gray sea like ice floes.

The FBI had let her down. It was a faceless bureaucracy, and it followed a set of arbitrary regulations. But Darlene did not have to blindly accept her fate. The Sooners, too, had come up against the rigidity and impassivity of the government. Maybe Darlene could do what they had done. When the chips were down, the Sooners did not fight fair; they did not fight at all, sidestepping the law and forging their own paths with gusto and guile.

Darlene fished her phone from her pocket and began scrolling through her call history. It did not take long to find what she was looking for. She dialed and hung up immediately, chewing on her thumbnail.

Then she dialed again and let it ring. A man's voice answered, speaking so fast that Darlene did not catch any words. A staccato blast. Something about a newsroom. The man was Tobias Morgan, a reporter from Chicago.

"This is Darlene McCloud," she said.

"Who?"

"Darlene. The McCloud family. You know, the . . . the orphans."

"Oh," he said. "The saddest family in Mercy, right?"

His voice was sharp and nasal, absent of any Southern softness.

"That's right," Darlene said. "You called me a few weeks ago when my sister . . ."

"Of course," he said. "I remember. Big story. What's shaking?"

"I'm ready to talk now," she said.

"About what?"

Her nerve almost failed her. She had vowed never to speak to any of these people again. But there was no other way forward. She took a deep breath and spoke in loud, determined tones.

"My little sister was kidnapped by my brother," she said. "Tucker blew up Jolly Cosmetics and took Cora with him."

"I know all that," Tobias said impatiently. "What's happened since then?"

Darlene touched the familiar, homey objects on the kitchen counter—the toaster, the spatula, a wooden spoon.

"I don't understand," she said. "You called me six times after the Amber Alert. You said you wanted to interview me. I'm ready now to be interviewed. Cora has been missing all summer, and the FBI are getting nowhere."

Tobias did not answer. There was a rustling on the other end of the line, as though he was rifling through a stack of papers. Darlene pressed on, saying, "I want to bring some attention back to what's happening. I don't want everyone to forget about us."

"It's August," Tobias said. "You're calling me about something that happened back in June."

"It's still happening," Darlene said, her voice rising. "Nothing has changed. I can go on the record. With photos. Whatever you need."

Another pause. More shuffling of papers.

"Nothing has changed," Tobias repeated back to her, each word distinct. "That's the problem. I'm sorry. There's no longer a story here. Not now."

Darlene closed her eyes.

"Fine," she said. "I'll just call a different reporter."

Her voice came out fainter than she meant it to be. On the other end of the line, Tobias snorted—almost a laugh.

"Good luck," he said. "Nobody's going to be interested."

DARLENE CALLED THREE MORE. ONE did not remember her. Another told her to call back as soon as something interesting happened. The third answered in a bleary mumble, as though his phone woke him. He informed Darlene curtly that after layoffs at the paper he was currently between jobs.

At last, she turned her phone off. Then she lay down on the linoleum, flat on her back. She felt as though she had just run a marathon— heart pounding, legs weak, breath chaotic. Her hair fanned around her face as she stared at the ceiling. Perhaps this was rock bottom. But then, she had thought that before, and there was always a little farther to fall.

33

At dawn, Darlene stood outside No. 43, waiting for the sun. The eastern sky was freighted with clouds, blocking and diffusing the raw light. Her feet were bare and she was still in her pajamas. She had not slept at all.

Her thoughts were on the Sooners again. Thieves and renegades. Scrappers and outlaws. Darlene imagined the ghosts of her predecessors moving around her, shadowy figures with shotguns and farm implements, guarding and cultivating their patches of earth.

Yet there was a contradiction here. This land, once so coveted and prized, was now used carelessly, even wantonly. Mercy was small in population but vast in acreage. Houses straggled down winding lanes that led nowhere. Huge swaths of prairie stood empty. Even the trailer park was twice the size it needed to be for the amount of units it contained. The same tendency toward sprawl extended across the state. Oklahoma City was the largest town in America in terms of square footage, though its population was dwarfed by many of the Northern metropolises.

The sun's corona mounted above the scrim of clouds—a fiery sliver, as thin as thread but bright enough to blind. Darlene stepped cautiously across the dirt in her bare feet, avoiding pebbles and the occasional piece of glass. Something scuttled away from her inside the ravine. An animal, maybe a snake.

Oklahoma was supposed to be a desert, a dustbowl, a landscape of thirsty, broken ground. You could still feel the wildness of it under everything. The Sooners had been avaricious, but they were not fools. The lush farms around Mercy were nothing more than an illusion. All the hallmarks of industry and agriculture—the granaries and barns, the restaurants and trailer parks—were as ephemeral as a dream. To the untrained eye, they might appear permanent, but Darlene knew they were on borrowed time. She knew this all too well. If the irrigation systems failed, if a bad drought settled in, if the cattle sickened, if the crops withered, Oklahoma could revert to its inherent condition. Human civilization was tethered insecurely here, as though a strong storm—say, a tornado—could blow it all away, leaving nothing but heat and dust.

The sun detached from the bank of clouds. Darlene watched it float and burn. She understood her mistake now. Reaching out to the media, calling reporter after reporter—she had absorbed the wrong lesson from her ancestors.

More than anything, the Sooners were self-reliant. They did not obey the government's rules because they knew those rules were arbitrary. Last night, Darlene had imagined that she was rebelling against the system when she called Tobias Morgan, but in truth she was just putting her faith in a different system. The FBI and the media were both bureaucracies: impassive, unyielding, autocratic, and capricious. They were different in character, not kind.

Her mistake had been to trust in human systems at all. That was what the Sooners understood. They relied only on their own strength, their own vigor and industriousness. Darlene felt the hint of a smile touch her lips. She stood still, letting the new sunlight warm her skin.

ON HER LUNCH HOUR, DARLENE drove to the police station at a breakneck pace. She found Roy at his desk on the phone, leaning back in his chair with his feet propped up. Darlene stood over him, drumming her fingers impatiently on her hips until he finished the call.

"We have to take action," she burst out as soon as he hung up. "If nobody else is going to do anything, then it's up to us."

He ran a hand over the bald crown of his head. Then he looked up at her with an expression she wasn't expecting—a gratified, eager grin.

"Come for a walk with me," he said.

As they stepped outside, Darlene saw her reflection in the glass door—gaunt, waxen, and restless, her ponytail a shambles. She looked both unwell and vibrantly alive.

"I've been thinking the exact same thing," Roy said.

"Really?"

"Damn straight. The Lord helps those who help themselves."

Darlene felt a wrench in her chest. He was saying just what she wanted to hear, and the relief was almost too much after everything—the party, the humiliating phone call to Tobias Morgan, and her sleepless night.

Roy threw an arm around her shoulders, pulled her close, and kissed her forehead.

"I had an idea about Tucker," he said.

They turned down a side street. There was a car parked on a nearby lawn, all four tires replaced with cinderblocks.

"I've been trying to think outside the box," Roy said. "Like

Tucker. I didn't sleep much. I was at the station all night, actually. After the party, I—"

He broke off, shaking his head.

"I messed that up," he said. "Right?"

She shrugged. "It's over now."

A silence fell, awkward yet companionable. It occurred to Darlene that this was her first real disagreement with Roy. She wanted to make it through to the other side.

"Anyway," he said. "After I left your place, I was thinking about the FBI, and what the guy said to me on the phone . . ." He grimaced. "I couldn't believe they just went and gave up on us."

Darlene reached for his hand, interlacing her fingers through his. There was such compassion in his voice. For a minute, she considered admitting what she had done last night. On balance, though, she decided against it. No one ever needed to know about her moment of weakness.

"I looked through Tucker's file again," Roy said. "He's not careful. He's not the kind of guy to lay low. But he's smart, isn't he?"

"Too smart for his own good."

He nodded. "I started looking into unsolved crimes. Anything recent. Anything that falls inside Tucker's range of interests but outside his previous pattern of behavior." Roy cleared his throat. "I even put out a few feelers to other jurisdictions. Called in some favors. My phone's been ringing all morning, actually."

They passed a house with loud checked curtains glaring in every window. The laundromat on the corner perfumed the air with starch. Roy stopped walking and took a deep, steadying breath.

"There was a shooting in Amarillo," he said. "Somebody went right up to a chicken farmer on the street and shot him dead."

Darlene felt her stomach twist.

"This happened in July," he said. "A couple weeks back."

"Why are you telling me this?" she said.

"They never caught the perpetrator. At the time, they figured it was a random thing. An accident, or some teenager with a grudge and a gun. Last night, I reached out to a contact of mine out that way. He just got back to me. That's who I was talking to when you came by the station."

"Was it . . ." she whispered. "Are you saying . . ."

Roy leaned close. "Are you sure you want to hear this?"

"Yes."

"A few witnesses to the shooting mentioned seeing a child nearby," he said.

"Oh my God."

There was a taste of bile in her throat. She pressed her fingers over her mouth.

"There's more," Roy said.

"More than murder?"

He was staring at her with ferocious intensity. She could almost feel the brush of his gaze against her skin.

"A case of arson," he said. "This happened a week or so before the shooting. Somebody burned down a taxidermy shop in Argon, Texas. A little tiny town. Smaller than Mercy, even."

"Jesus."

"Nobody was hurt. Just your average property crime. I heard about it at the station when it happened, but I didn't think anything of it. But now . . ."

"Now?"

"The thing is . . ." Roy said, and paused. "There was a dog at Big Tom's Taxidermy. Somebody let the animal out before the fire and took it to a playground across the street. Latched the gate and everything. Kept the dog safe. There was a special mention in the paperwork. That's what caught my eye."

Darlene began to speak and failed. She heard a scuffle, and they both turned to see a woman moving along the other side of the street. Darlene recognized Mrs. Watson—Cora's third-grade teacher. She was staring at her phone as she strolled down the sidewalk and did not notice them there. They waited until she ambled out of earshot.

"I'm starting to see a pattern," Roy said. "I believe Tucker's interests are constant, even if his behavior isn't. The chicken farmer in the Amarillo shooting was in violation of any number of health department statutes. And a taxidermist, well . . ."

"Are you saying that Tucker and Cora—that they're—"

Darlene could not finish the sentence. Roy did it for her.

"They're on some kind of spree," he said.

34

That evening, Darlene drove home with a cork-lined bulletin board rocking in the bed of the pickup truck. In the rearview mirror, her own expression intrigued her—obstinate and fierce.

The trailer was empty. Jane was spending the night at a friend's house, and Roy's shift would keep him at the police station for another hour. First, Darlene removed the print above the couch. (It was a faded drawing of a zoo, done by an artist with a poor sense of scale; the animals all seemed too large as they came bursting out of their cages, teeth bared. Tucker had scavenged it from an alley somewhere.) She hung the bulletin board in its stead, then barged into Jane's closet. Among the soccer gear and friendship bracelets and clothes she found what she was looking for: a cardboard tube as tall as her waist. A year ago, Jane won a map of the United States in a spelling contest.

Darlene took pushpins and markers from a drawer. She could feel the physical effects of fatigue—her fingers occasionally trembled—but her mind was as sharp as ever, almost painfully clear. She understood what the FBI and the reporters did not. Her situation was as dire now as it had been when Cora first vanished, when the claxons sounded and the media and the law descended on Mercy. Nothing had changed since that fatal moment except the passage of time. Time, it seemed, was Darlene's enemy. With each day that passed, the collective sense of urgency diminished, even though Cora's plight was no less perilous. The FBI had made its indifference plain. *There's no story*, Tobias Morgan said. All of them were lulled into nonchalance by the months of quiet and inaction.

Darlene drew herself up to her full height. She would be fine without the government or the media's help. Bureaucratic organizations, arbitrary rules—she did not need them. She was clever, scrappy, a survivor. *Sooner born, Sooner bred.* And Roy was on her side.

She unspooled the map of America and pinned it to the bulletin board. She arranged the pushpins and markers by color on the kitchen table. The map had a story to tell. Darlene was sure of it.

By the time Roy arrived, the scene was set. For the next few hours, the two of them worked in a kind of fever. He had been accumulating data for months without fully realizing its importance. He used a yellow marker to circle the area where Cora's burner phone pinged off a cell tower back in June. A swath of the Oklahoma panhandle. A stretch of desert near the Texas border.

With green thumbtacks, Roy marked every account of grand theft auto inside the circled zone. After thirty minutes, the bulletin board bristled like a porcupine. Too many. Darlene wiped the sweat from her brow.

Then Roy took a handful of red pushpins and approached the map again. The states were outlined in black, the highways orange, the rivers purple. One by one, Roy marked a series of towns. Point by point, he made an erratic, jagged line out of crimson thumbtacks. There was, after all, a pattern. Here was the story that no one else could see.

"Tucker's moving west," Roy said.

Darlene met his gaze, nodding.

"Here," he said, tapping the first point. "The fire at Big Tom's Taxidermy."

"Yeah."

"The shooting in Amarillo," he said, indicating another thumbtack.

"Right," Darlene said.

"There," he said, touching a red pushpin in North Texas. "This one was ten days ago. A high-kill animal shelter. The employees locked up for the night and came back in the morning to find the power off and all the cages empty."

"Oh," Darlene said, struck by the image.

"Somebody cut the electrical wires in a few different places. That's expensive to fix, as you can imagine. And they spray-painted the front door with—well—"

He strode over to the table and picked up his satchel. Fumbling inside, he removed a photograph and handed it to Darlene. She saw beige brick, a metal door, and a barred window. The wall was defaced by a stick figure of an animal that blurred into a scribbly blob. Darlene could not tell what it was supposed to represent; the mass of lines could have been the animal's blood pouring out, or maybe a tornado touching down and ripping the creature apart. The sketch was so crude that it could only have been made by a child.

"I'm beginning to get a sense of Tucker's agenda," Roy said.

He pointed to the last pushpin in the row, a tiny town in the middle of Texas. Then he reached into his bag again.

"Have you ever heard of a rattlesnake roundup?" he said.

She shook her head.

"It's a local tradition in a town called Stillwater," he said. "It goes back decades. Thousands of snakes are killed in a single day. They do it to thin the population. That's the theory, anyway. I think it's mostly just for sport."

He retrieved a stack of photos and began laying them out on the kitchen table like playing cards. Darlene saw a pool of red soaking into desert earth. She saw a rattlesnake coiled as though preparing to strike. She saw a man holding a machete. There was a picture of a ditch filled with mutilated carcasses—bare skulls, scraps of jeweled skin and viscera.

Darlene leaned over the table, staring down in dismay. There was a snake being milked. Its jaw was clamped in the fleshy vise of a human hand, its maw wide in a kind of silent scream. A second person's arm was holding a cup beneath the fangs. Darlene saw a few droplets of venom glimmering at the bottom of the glass. In another photo, a group of men in cowboy hats grinned at the camera while holding dead serpents the length of their bodies. There were snapshots of various souvenirs: snakeskin belts, snake heads preserved in amber, baby rattles made of snake tails. There was a petting area fenced with chicken wire and filled with children. Small figures ran to and fro, chasing the reptiles across the pen. A close-up revealed that all the rattlesnakes had their mouths sewn shut with thick black thread.

Darlene picked up the picture at the bottom of the pile. It showed a snake-skinning contest. The participants stood at a table strewn with chunks of flesh and knobs of bone. Several were smiling. There was more blood than seemed possible—splattered on every surface, dripping down the tablecloth, pooling in the grass, painted in smears across hands and faces.

"Those photos are from last year's roundup," Roy said. "It always takes place on a weekend in August. People come from all over the country."

His fingers twitched toward the pocket where he kept his cigarettes, but he refrained from taking one out and lighting it. He never smoked in No. 43. Darlene flipped the photograph over on the table, turning it into an innocuous rectangle of white. One by one, she did the same to all the others.

"The roundup was scheduled for last weekend," Roy said. "A local ranger was going to lead a guided hunt at dawn on the first day. People bought tickets specially—they're pricey—and showed up with all their gear. But when they got to the ranger station, the building was on fire."

"Was it . . ." Darlene began, then let her voice dwindle away.

"The fire had penetrated every room," Roy said. "The windows exploded. A witness said it was . . ." He searched through some papers and read aloud: " 'It was the kind of fire that spoke and sang.' "

"Was it Tucker?" she asked, keeping her tone expressionless.

"I've got no proof," Roy said. "But it fits."

She nodded.

"It was arson," he said. "We know that much for sure. Someone doused the place before lighting it up. The fire burned hot enough to warp the stone and melt the plumbing. Consistent with a hydrocarbon-based accelerant. I'd say kerosene, but it could have been gasoline."

"My lord," Darlene murmured.

"No snakes were harmed," Roy said with a wry smile. "The heat of the fire would have scared them off."

"Safe. Like the dog in the playground."

"Exactly."

He took a handkerchief from his pocket and dabbed the sweat from his forehead and the broad swath of his nose.

"There's something else," he said. "Something odd."

Darlene laughed, a strangled little bark. Roy began gathering up the photographs and tucking them back in his bag. Without looking at her, he said, "A woman at the scene told the officers that during the blaze she saw a kid all alone in the desert. A young boy."

"You mean Tucker?"

"No. I reckon it was Cora."

"She thought Cora was a boy?" Darlene asked, her voice high.

"The woman couldn't give a clear description," Roy said. "She just thought it was strange. A child all alone like that. Standing way out in the scrub, so calm, she said. Watching the place burn to the ground."

THEY ENDED THE NIGHT IN speculation, looking toward the future. They were making a pattern, and patterns could be predictive. Perhaps they could now guess where Tucker was heading. A line of red pushpins in a sea of green pushpins. A narrative cobbled together from photographs and secondhand information. Roy felt certain that Tucker would continue moving west. He had done a little reading, he said. Studies showed that 80 percent of people on the lam traveled west. Nobody knew why—some deep instinct, a desire beneath conscious thought. It was helpful to the police, anyway.

Around ten o'clock, they collected five blue thumbtacks—a whole new color—and marked the towns that might be next on Tucker's list. Darlene felt a surge of powerful momentum. The simple act of shoving pushpins into corkboard was immensely satisfying. Finally, a chance to be proactive. No more waiting. Once again, she felt the spirits of her ancestors moving near, her fellow Sooners watching her with pride and recognition.

Darlene noted that midsized towns seemed to be Tucker's preference. Roy agreed. He hypothesized that Tucker was looking for places too small to have a lot of witnesses, security cameras, or a large police presence—but not so small that the appearance of a strange man and child would spark interest among the locals.

At last, Roy got on the phone, alerting the police department in every town marked with a blue pushpin. He reminded them about the Amber Alert. He talked about Big Tom's Taxidermy, the shooting in Amarillo, and the fire at the rattlesnake roundup. He told them to stay vigilant.

Then there was nothing left to do. On the couch, Darlene lounged with her feet on Roy's thighs, both of them staring up at their map.

"I've been thinking about serial killers lately," she said.

"Hm?"

"Those guys always start out torturing animals, don't they? It's pretty universal."

"Sure," Roy said. "They taught us that at the academy. Harming our dumb friends is a big red flag."

"Well, Tucker was . . ." She paused. "He did the opposite."

"What do you mean?"

"He would save any animal he could find. He became a vegetarian when he was five years old. He took in possums and rats if they looked hungry. He would hide them in our basement and nurse them back to health. He would pick up the bugs drowning in the swimming hole and carry them to land. If a baby bird fell out of a nest in our backyard, Tucker would wrap it in a paper towel and climb the tree to put it back." She nudged Roy with her heel. "I don't know what kind of crazy that is. Do you?"

"I reckon it's something new," he said.

AT MIDNIGHT, DARLENE WAS BACK at Roy's house, too tired to sleep. She had been awake so long that her muscles would not uncoil. Roy snored against her shoulder as she stared at the ceiling. As usual, she wore one of his T-shirts, while he was nude. Three electric fans churned the air into froth. A slim blade of moon glinted in the window. After their long hours of work, Roy had made a few noises about maybe crashing at the trailer for once. But ever since Cora's disappearance, it was Darlene's policy never to make use of her sister's bed; she refused to occupy any space still waiting for Cora to return and fill it.

She rolled onto her side, staring at Roy. His face was divided into stark contours of moonlight and shadow. He was not her first boyfriend, but he was her first since the tornado—the first man she had known, perhaps, as her true self. Darlene dated in high school, lost her virginity in high school, but the girl she had been back then was a stranger to her now. A teenager with a stable home and a loving father. A young woman planning for college, excited to leave Mercy. A girl so far away now that she was barely recognizable.

In his sleep, Roy reached for her, pulling her spine against his belly. At first his embrace was soothing, but soon the warmth of his skin became more than Darlene could bear. The air was stifling, his breath sticky, his arms as heavy as lumber. She extricated herself and stood up. She watched as he reached for her again, groping vaguely across the bedsheets before growing still.

She slipped out of the bedroom. The house was cramped—poky staircase, low ceilings, every room overly furnished. The place had been left to Roy by his mother. When she fell ill, he moved back home to care for her. He tended her until she died, at which point the house passed into his care.

All this had happened a long time before Darlene entered his life. Though she would never have said as much, she was glad for the timing. These days, he never cried for his mother anymore. There was nothing for Darlene to do but listen to his stories about the woman and find ways to compliment her on everything she could think of—her taste in interior decorating, her obvious beauty in old photographs, and, of course, her excellent work in raising her boy.

Darlene stepped into the dark living room. She ran her fingers along the mantelpiece. Every surface in the house was strewn with ornaments—fussy lamps, glass figurines, and carved wooden boxes. All these fragile knickknacks had survived the tornado. The storm had come and gone without leaving a trace here. Darlene wondered what knickknacks her family once possessed; such things had disappeared from her memory over time. Roy's house was a physical representation of an elderly woman's mind—her color scheme, her dislike of empty space, her addiction to ornate lamps—rather than the personality of the man who actually lived there. Darlene wondered if this was indolence on Roy's part, a masculine imperviousness to ambiance, or whether there was a deeper nostalgia at work, an inability to remove his mother's things and claim the house as his own.

She smelled Roy before she saw him. She liked to imagine that it was the perfume of his good heart. He wrapped his arms around her from behind, resting his chin on her shoulder.

"I can't sleep," she said.

"I gathered. You're the most wandering woman I ever met."

"Then why do I feel so stuck?"

His jaw was rough with stubble. He was naked, his skin fiery to the touch. They were similar in height, though Roy was much stockier, his torso twice as wide as hers.

"Come to bed," he said.

He drew her up the stairs. The ceiling fan creaked, rocking a little with each revolution. Roy picked up his pack of cigarettes, lighting one with a deft motion, and exhaled a cloud of smoke against the moonlight, twirled into ripples by the fan. Darlene firmly intended to cure him of this habit. She planned to nag him gently over time until he gave up smoking. In the meantime, however, she had begun to associate the odor with Roy. Against her better judgment, she was starting to enjoy the smell.

Three electric fans hummed in harmony. He put out his cigarette, and Darlene slid into his embrace. With her fingers, she traced the groove that ran down his sternum, a notched canyon between the high slopes of his ribs, blooming with wiry fur. She felt a flare of desire in her gut. There was no accounting for attraction. There was no predicting it. She and Roy were made of volatile elements, each inert on its own but explosive in combination, requiring only the smallest spark—a kiss, a breath—to ignite.

They made love briskly, in the manner of tired people: no foreplay, no acrobatics, only those positions that allowed them both to lie down, one orgasm each, no cuddling afterward. Roy was asleep again almost before their bodies tumbled apart, the smile on his face fading into blankness. Darlene let out a yawn. She felt a ripple of exhaustion pass through her like the aftershock of an earthquake.

Against all odds, this seemed to be the real thing. She had never been in love before, and she was not sure what to do with it, especially now. The timing was all wrong. She was as wretched and bereft as she had ever been, and as happy and satiated as she had ever been.

35

A week later, Darlene was driving Jane home from soccer practice when her phone rang. It was raining, a light patter on the windshield. The day had been a long one. Darlene was pleased to be heading at last toward home, where a hot shower and a change of clothes awaited her. Jane was in the middle of a diatribe about the latest drama in the social hierarchy of the soccer team. It was next to impossible for an outsider to comprehend the minutiae of which halfback had offered a cutting remark to one of the forwards and which sweeper kept making backhanded comments about the goalie.

At first, Darlene did not even hear her ringer. By the time she fumbled in her purse, located her cell phone, and pulled to the side of the road, the rain had picked up, hammering on the roof.

"I've got news," Roy said. His voice was slightly muffled. "They've been spotted."

"Repeat that," Darlene said sharply.

"Tucker and Cora. A definite sighting."

"Where? When?"

"It was one of the towns we marked. Black Rock, New Mexico. About two hours ago."

Darlene put the car in park and removed the key from the ignition. Jane was staring at her, twirling the tip of her braid in agitation. The street was wide and lined with skinny saplings. A mailbox on the corner was in the process of changing color beneath the rain, darkening and glistening.

"How—" Darlene began. "And did they . . . What exactly—"

"Cora stole a candy bar," Roy said.

"A candy bar?"

"They were in a convenience store . . ." A papery rustling, as though he were checking his notes. "Tucker bought a few things. A water bottle, some gum. The guy behind the counter noticed that there was a kid by the door. She put a candy bar in her pocket as she was leaving. He ran out to stop her, but they were already gone. So he called the police."

Rain smashed against the windshield, mottling and distorting the landscape. The canopy of the tree overhead swirled like a cubist painting, chopped into shards of fragmented pigment. Darlene passed a hand over her eyes.

Roy was still talking. "Normally the cops wouldn't bother much with something so small. They'd make a report and stick it in a file someplace. But when they heard it was a man and a child—"

"Right."

"There was a security camera over the door. A squad car went around right away. They got the footage, and they called me as soon as they were certain. They sent me a still frame. It's Tucker. It's definitely Tucker."

"Oh my God." Darlene sagged forward, resting her temple against the steering wheel. Jane's breathing seemed abnormally loud, grating like sandpaper on wood.

"The FBI has been informed," Roy said. "This is a concrete lead, so they'll help us. They'll drop a net around Black Rock. The word has gone out all over New Mexico. This could be it. Tucker's close to the Arizona border, but I don't think he'll get there."

The rain dwindled and stopped. The car windows were speckled with moisture, already evaporating in the heat. Soon enough, the sidewalks would be scorched clean, the sky clear, the clouds burned away into wisps.

"We were right," Roy said, his voice vibrating with pride.

"We were."

"Goddamn."

"I should get on a plane," Darlene said. "The closest airport would be Albuquerque, right? I can be there in a couple of hours."

"Do nothing," he said firmly. "Remember the girl in the Red River? Let's be sure this time."

"I should get on a plane," she repeated.

"Go home. Wait for my word. I'll be in touch as soon as I can."

AN HOUR LATER, DARLENE LAY on the couch with Jane. The TV was on, but both of them were glazed and distracted. Darlene was not even wearing her glasses; at the moment she preferred the world out of focus.

Then her phone buzzed on the coffee table. There was no message, just an image. Roy had texted her what appeared to be a still frame from the security video. Jane leaned in to see the screen too.

It was Tucker. Unmistakably, unquestionably. Darlene felt a moan rise from her belly. The shot was grainy, taken from above. Tucker did not seem to be aware of the camera. His hair was close-cropped and dark, no more ponytail. His brow seemed beaky from this angle, his eyes lost in a pool of shadows. He was holding out a few bills, but something appeared to be wrong with his hand.

Darlene couldn't tell if the distortion was in the image or his flesh. Not enough digits.

After a moment, she realized someone else had been captured in the picture too. An unfamiliar child was framed in the background, a young boy with skinny calves, a pigeon-toed stance, and untied shoes.

Jane turned away, wiping her eyes and sniffling. Darlene looked at the image again. She stared. She brought the phone closer.

The boy was Cora. Darlene gasped as this fact became clear. She recognized her sister's torso, her hunched shoulders, her knobby knees. The harsh light of the convenience store had turned Cora's cheekbones into triangles; Darlene had seen that effect before when her sister was photographed in too much glare. It was definitely Cora. But she was dressed in cargo shorts and a boy's T-shirt. And her hair—her hair! The long brown ringlets were gone, shorn into a sad buzz cut. The contours of her legs suggested that she had lost a few pounds. She did not have a few pounds to lose.

"What has he done to you?" Darlene whispered.

Jane glanced at her. Darlene laid her phone facedown and leaned back into the pillows, her mind aglow with painful ideas.

She tried to conjure up an image of where Tucker and Cora might be at this moment. She could not visualize what the day-to-day experience of their life on the run was like. For a while, she had worried that her sister would die in Tucker's company—not out of any active malevolence on his part, merely neglect and bad judgment. But Cora had been on the road with Tucker long enough now that it seemed she might survive his influence. Physically, at least. What was happening to her mind was another matter entirely.

There was no question that Cora had been a participant in dreadful things. Arson, vandalism, and murder—and those were just the incidents Darlene knew about. The extent of her sister's compliance was something Darlene could not fathom. She pictured Tucker working on Cora's essence like rust on metal, corroding and weakening her. Bringing her into his state of being. Putting his words in her mouth. Hacking off her hair. Dressing her in different clothes. Making her like him—an activist, an outsider to their species.

Darlene heard Roy's voice again, reverberating in her mind. *A young boy, the witness said. So calm. Watching the place burn to the ground.*

All this time, Darlene had been worried about the wrong things. Now she knew: she had not been worried enough.

36

She waited. She waited for hours. She fell asleep waiting and woke on the couch with a crick in her neck and Jane piled against her. Darlene checked her phone and saw that Roy had sent three messages. *Nothing yet.* Then: *No word.* Finally: *Hang in there, babe.* She closed her eyes again.

The rest of the weekend dragged. Jane asked to skip soccer practice for the first time in memory. She wanted to be around family, she said; nobody else would understand. Darlene went to work and came home without recalling anything from her shift. On Sunday, she gave the trailer a thorough cleaning. Sometimes she still imagined that she could smell Tucker's blood in the bathroom grout. She washed the windows and attacked the musty void beneath the kitchen sink. She tried not to text Roy too often. She tried not to stare at her phone. She kept it in her pocket and experienced half a dozen phantom messages while scrubbing the shower stall, feeling it buzz against her thigh and peeling off her rubber gloves in a frenzy, only to find the screen blank.

In the evening, she and Jane stayed up late once more, watching a reality show. Darlene took the couch while her sister lay on the floor, phone in hand, legs balanced against the wall. The air sparkled with the tang of cleaning solvents. The moon poured through the kitchen window like a searchlight.

"They're doing everything they can, aren't they?" Jane said.

"Yes," Darlene said. "The FBI are on it. Finally."

"Roy will let us know if there's any news, won't he?"

"Of course."

It was the tenth time they'd had the same conversation in the past hour, word for word.

"I miss Cora," Jane said.

"I know. I keep buying her favorite cookies. Those weird oatmeal things. They're just piling up in the cabinet. I can't seem to take them off the list."

Jane sighed. "I woke up the other day and wanted to take Cora bowling. I don't know why. I made a whole plan in my head. It was a while before I remembered."

Darlene scraped her fingers through a bowl of popcorn, gathering up the last few kernels.

"I used to think our life was pretty shitty," Jane said. "No more Daddy. No more house or farm. No more college for you."

Darlene nodded. The map of the United States, marred by pushpins, lurked on the wall, a silent presence.

"I want to go back to the shitty life we had before," Jane said.

IN THE MORNING, ROY STOPPED by before work. Darlene was standing at the window, washing the breakfast dishes, gazing at the dewy sky, the air hung with curtains of flaxen heat. Jane was in the shower when Roy parked outside. As Darlene watched, he climbed out of the car and headed toward the house. His shoulders were bowed, his expression defeated. Even the burnished umber of his skin seemed somehow diminished.

In that moment, Darlene knew exactly what he was going to tell her. Something about the leads going cold. Something about the FBI's caseload. Something about hope. For a moment, she was almost too weary to breathe. The greater mechanism of the law was giving up on them again. All their efforts had come to nothing.

Roy knocked, and she let him in. When he began to speak, she preempted him, touching his lips with a forefinger. She marched over to the map of America, still bristling with pushpins. Barefoot, dripping suds on the floor, Darlene removed it from the wall. Roy stood aside, watching her with one hand tucked nervously in his pocket. She wrestled the bulletin board through the front door. She strode out into the sunlit morning, marched over to the ravine, and flung the map away with all her strength, casting its shadow over the creosote and landing with a satisfying crunch of broken branches.

37

A buzzing noise. Darlene turned over, swaddled in sleep. The vibration went on and on as she pulled her mind upward out of dreams, like a swimmer breaking into the open air. She thought it was a cicada—a dozen cicadas in Roy's bedroom. Eventually she remembered that she had silenced her ringer but left her phone on vibrate.

The call was coming from an unknown number. Darlene blinked, trying to collect her wits. Morning light curled in the curtains. It was just before dawn.

"Hello?" she muttered.

"Why didn't you come?" a voice said, in lieu of a greeting. A reedy, falsetto complaint. A child's plea.

Darlene was standing up before she realized she had moved. She glanced around and saw that she was now in the middle of the room, one arm extended toward the wall. Her spine was rigid, her breath tight.

"Is that you?" she said. "Where are you?"

"I thought you would come," Cora said. There was a sound that might have been a sob or a cough: a sputtering exhalation ripe with phlegm.

"What do you mean?" Darlene said.

"I made sure there was a security camera. I took the candy."

"You . . ." Her voice tapered away, her mouth opening and closing without sound. "You did that on purpose?"

"I thought you would come," Cora repeated plaintively.

"I tried," Darlene said desperately. "We all did. We tried so hard. Oh, Cora."

There was a shift in the light, the sun topping some exterior threshold, and the room brightened suddenly, the dingy shapes of flowers in the wallpaper blooming into vivid color. Darlene saw her shadow in the garden, illusory and gray.

"He's acting so strange," Cora said. Each vowel was moist. "He's planning something new."

"Tucker?"

"He says something big is going to happen. I don't know what."

"Cora, please, you need to get away from him. Can you find someone, anyone, who can help you?"

"I don't feel good. I don't know where I am."

Then a squeal of static blared. Darlene jerked the phone away from her head. There was a clatter, a cacophony of indecipherable squawks—maybe Tucker's angry voice, maybe some mechanical dysfunction—and the line went dead.

Darlene tried to scream, but the sound caught in her throat. The air in her lungs felt as solid as clay. In that instant, she pictured all the gateways and apertures she had encountered over the past few months: every TV and computer and phone, even the radio in the car, a hundred interstices through which she had glimpsed her brother, heard about her sister. Gazing at the screen in her hand, Darlene imagined that it was not a blank rectangle, but a closed door. For an instant, the illusion was almost complete, as though somehow she could step through to the other side.

AS THE SUN CLIMBED THE sky, Darlene and Roy sat in the backyard, curled together in a single lounge chair. August was on its way out. Flickers of red and gold were visible among the branches overhead. The morning air was cooler than it had been in weeks. The row of houses blocked the rising sun, the backyard filled with dreary shadows. The sky was a stretch of alabaster.

"She did it on purpose," Darlene said. "She was hoping to get caught. She said so."

"I know, babe."

She was limp in his lap, too heavy with sorrow to even hold up her head. Roy reached in his pocket for a cigarette.

"I let her down," Darlene said. "I failed her."

"No, no," he said, lighting up.

"What's going to happen? Tucker's planning something big. That's what Cora said. Bigger than arson. Bigger than shooting somebody."

Roy exhaled a stream of smoke out of the corner of his mouth.

"Cora's sick," Darlene said. "You should have heard her coughing. She needs me, and I'm not there."

"You are," he said. "You were right on the other end of the line."

"Tucker cut her hair. He dressed her up like a boy. I barely recognized her in that picture. Why would he do that?"

"Crazy as a bedbug," Roy muttered.

"I hardly recognized her."

Darlene knew she was repeating herself. The backyard was a dingy box, the grass unkempt and yellow. A wooden fence stood tall, keeping out any glimpse of the neighbors' houses, creating the illusion of solitude. Roy's mother had been a gardener, and her terracotta pots remained where she had left them, now filled with pebbles and weeds. Darlene was still dressed in her pajamas, Roy in a ratty old cotton robe.

"What's Tucker planning?" she said, more to herself than anything. She was a little surprised when Roy answered:

"He's going to do whatever he's going to do."

"And then something else will happen," Darlene said.

She heard the ring of her own voice—stronger, brighter. Roy seemed to notice the change in tone too; he shot her a questioning look.

"It's something my dad used to say," she said. "I'd forgotten."

She closed her eyes. A memory was rising up from the gray depths, no longer consigned to the void, clearer and clearer. For the first time in a long while she heard her father's hoarse, smoky baritone in her mind. *And then something else will happen.* He said this many times throughout her childhood, offering it like a gift whenever she was worried about a bad grade or fighting with Tucker. He always spoke the words in the same way—as though they brought him immense solace. Darlene never quite understood his meaning, but she was calmed by the simple fact that he was trying to comfort her.

"And then something else will happen," she whispered.

She buried her face in the hollow of Roy's collarbone and stayed there even as the sun mounted the row of houses, flooding the backyard with light. There was nothing as irrepressible as dawn—the wind infused with sudden heat, the birds waking up, the promise and threat of yet another day.

THE WILDLANDS

38

We came at last to California, a place where summer never ended.

Our new home was a mausoleum on a hilltop, an imposing marble structure with flagstone steps and angel figurines on the roof. There was a row of iron portals with corpses inside. The floor was chilly and rough to the touch, and the air smelled of mud and something else, something sour. The darkness had a musty, eternal quality—a cold cavern where the sun never penetrated.

The graveyard spanned a vast stretch of land on the outskirts of a strange new city. The sunlit headstones were ringed by a forest of deciduous trees. Unlike the oaks and elms back home in Mercy, these were unaffected by the seasons, their leaves perpetually green. A few incongruous palms stood here and there among the graves. There was something festive, even silly, about their long stubbled necks and tufted heads in this somber, quiet place.

At the far edge of my view was the ocean. I had never seen it before, and I could not make sense of its size and grandeur. It was not a pond, not a lake, but a second sky, bluer and more chaotic than the one above it. I spent hours each day staring at the distant heave and flux of waves, the rumpled patterns of light.

In California, I was often on my own. Tucker had found a job of some kind, but he would not say much about it. He left every morning at dawn wearing a green jumpsuit, strolling away between the gravestones with a wave. He would fetch our new vehicle from a side street—a silver sedan a few years past its heyday, an old person's car—and he would not return until evening. (Once upon a time, I might have named the vehicle, but there had been so many over the course of the summer—too many to keep track of. I had stopped that game several states earlier, back before Chicken Man.) Tucker came home smelling of hard labor. He often had stains on his clothes: dirt or manure, I thought. I was unaccustomed to being apart from him. For months, my brother had been at my side, sharing every meal, filling every space with his voice, sleeping stretched out next to me, always close enough to touch.

But things had changed. Tucker was acting secretive. He would not explain why we had come to California or where he went each morning. He would not reveal the significance of the green jumpsuit. He told me to wait. Something good was coming, he said.

This was my punishment: his reticence, the distance between us. I had called Darlene against his wishes. Now Tucker was watchful and aloof with me. The bag of disposable cell phones was gone; he threw them away to "remove all temptation." More than once, he had repeated the story of Mike and the betrayal that ended their friendship. *Dead to me*, he said over and over, like a mantra. Then he would stare at me and sigh meaningfully.

I accepted the change in our dynamic with the same bleak weariness that I accepted everything now. No part of me was fighting

Tucker anymore. Cora had been crushed beneath fever and hope-lessness, her voice silenced. The call to Darlene had been her final rebellion. Only Corey remained.

There was nothing left for me but to follow Tucker like a duck-ling behind a fox, imprinted on the wrong species, aware on some level that this was not a safe guardian but lacking any other options. I never questioned his choices anymore, even privately, in my own mind. His will had become my own. His ideas flooded my head, and when he was away I did not think about anything at all.

Every evening, Tucker came home bearing gifts of food and bot-tled water. The two of us would sit on the stoop of the mausoleum and share a veggie burger and a greasy sack of fries. We would stare at the ocean laid out before us, the setting sun freckling the water with thousands of shifting reflections. Behind us, the cityscape would change too, glittery and bustling. I had never seen a town so huge, so loud. There were always sirens wailing. The skyscrapers were painted on the clouds, ethereal and silky. The light from so many windows stained the night with an artificial glow. I could never see any stars.

After a while, Tucker and I would move inside the tomb and close the door. We would lie down on the unclean, leaf-strewn marble, no bedrolls, no pillows. I would sleep uneasily. The corpses in the crypt were sealed behind a row of metal doors along the back wall, but their presence made itself felt. They often insinuated themselves into my dreams, climbing into the open air, tapping my shoulder with their rotting fingers and breathing on my neck with their hollow, papery lungs. There were seven dead people. I had examined the row of iron portals many times. The oldest corpse had been interred nearly a cen-tury earlier, the most recent only a decade ago.

I did not like sleeping in that place, but I was too sick to remain awake for long. My illness had not broken since our arrival in Cal-ifornia. Every night, my feverish brain would drag me down into dreams whether I wanted to go or not. Every so often Tucker would place his hand on my forehead, his palm oddly cold, pleasantly so. Then he would wince and withdraw his arm.

"You're fine," he would say. "You'll be fine soon."

My illness added an interesting note to our situation. In the day-time, I would lounge on the stoop and stare at things, my attention drifting on the wind, changing direction with each gust. I gazed at seagulls and clouds. My watch had stopped a while ago, so I had no way to keep track of time. I would wait in a stupor for Tucker to return, staring down the path where he had vanished, glancing up hopefully at any figure in the distance, watching the shadows scud along, feel-ing the first pangs of hunger, unsure how many hours had passed since he left. I did not know the day, the week, or the month, and I did not care; these were arbitrary designations. I understood now that the forward march of time was an illusion—a human construct. Time was circular rather than linear, composed of the solar orbit and the swing of shadows, rhythms of light and darkness. Everything moved, but nothing changed. Dawn broke, Tucker went away, the city blared, the tide surged, my fever smoldered, clouds floated, evening fell, Tucker returned, always different, always the same.

The mausoleum was a bizarre residence. Even during the day, it had its own peculiar brand of silence. The smell was something I could never quite identify—acidic and dank. What the place lacked in charm, however, it made up for in isolation. No one had set eyes on me or spoken to me in days. The only people there were dead. Tucker told me to watch out for the caretaker—the old man who tended the graveyard, apparently all on his own. I had seen him a few times in the distance, shuffling along behind his broom, his back stooped with age. Once he spent the whole morning roaring around on a riding mower, relegating me to the mildewy interior of the tomb for several unpleasant hours. (Usually I did not go in there alone. I would wait on the stoop until Tucker could join me, and we would brave the corpses together.) As the days passed, I served as faraway witness to a few funerals. One morning I watched a ceremony near the western wall, a little knot of people, the pallbearers striding down the path in lockstep. A preacher of unknown denomination delivered a sonorous prayer.

Sometimes I saw other children. The cemetery was ringed by a barred iron gate that offered a glimpse of the street outside. In the mornings, I liked to observe the bustle of activity as people got ready for work. Grown-ups in crisp clothes strode along, staring at their cell phones and clutching to-go cups of coffee. The children were back in school. I could tell by their knapsacks, their shiny outfits, their resigned demeanor. I kept seeing the same blond girl, her cloud of curls not quite contained by the baseball cap she always wore. Every afternoon, a slender boy with skin like obsidian would lope past the gates on his way home and bang a stick on each bar.

I dreamed sometimes that I walked among them, backpack on my shoulders, eager to begin the fourth grade. But these dreams always dissolved into chaos—I was dressed like Corey, nobody remembered me, the teacher could not find my name on the roll call, and when Darlene came to pick me up from school, she drove right past me as though she did not recognize me.

In my feverish state, I sometimes wondered if I was already dead. It was an otherworldly experience to sit among the gravestones and watch ordinary people living their ordinary lives. Maybe Tucker knew something I didn't; maybe he chose this eerie hilltop as my final resting place. Maybe he had carried my lifeless body to the mausoleum. Maybe my death was the reason he was acting so strange— why he'd taken a job, why he seemed so solemn now, why he kept leaving me alone. Maybe this was the afterlife: you perished without knowing it and became a ghost that only your brother could see. Maybe I was haunting him, bonded to him, unable to leave his side even now. Maybe I would spend the rest of eternity on this sunlit hill, keeping an eye on those distant animals, the living.

39

Tucker took me to the ocean. It was his day off, he said, as he put on shorts and a tank top instead of the green jump-suit. He brought me a bagel with cream cheese for breakfast, something I had never before tried. While I ate, he washed me tenderly with bottled water, scrubbing beneath my arms and shampooing my scalp right there in the cemetery grass. I kept my underwear on in case any strangers were watching—and out of respect for the dead. The day was warm and golden. Every day in California so far was warm and golden. Drying me off, Tucker again laid a hand on my forehead and looked away. He removed a bottle from his pocket and poured a few pills into his palm.

"Take them all," he said. "It's no cure, but it'll help."

I slept through most of the drive to the sea. There was an ache in my jaw and another in my temple. To add insult to injury, I had lost a tooth somewhere in Arizona—a molar—and the raw pulp that remained was now sore as well. I had lost many teeth in my young life, but I had never experienced this kind of pain afterward. My head felt like a piñata midway through a birthday party: bruised, beaten, nearly broken open. The car dipped down a hill, and my eyes slid closed. There was sunlight on my cheek, movement in my bones. For a moment, I thought I was back home, sitting in the passenger's seat of Daddy's old pickup truck with Darlene at the wheel. Maybe she was driving me to school—Cora, not Corey—the fourth grade, I was supposed to be starting the fourth grade. Maybe she was taking me to the emergency room.

"We're here," Tucker said.

I sat up, blinking. The sea was an abstract painting: a band of azure sky above a swatch of indigo water above a ribbon of wet brown sand above a smear of hazel beach. I had never been to the ocean before. It seemed like the kind of place you might encounter in dreams: too raw and wild to be real, yet somehow familiar at the same time, an ancient impression belonging to my species, imprinted in my genetic code, a knowledge deeper than memory. I heard a chaos of distant voices, seagulls crying, the boom of waves, the bark of a dog—no, I thought, a sea lion.

My brother climbed onto the curb in his bare feet. I followed suit. Before I knew it, we were running toward the surf, whooping with glee. The ocean worked a kind of magic on me, and for a while I was filled with energy, able to chase Tucker right into the first, astonishing kiss of a wave. The water glistened and pooled around my feet, ice cold and clouded with sand. Tucker threw his head back and laughed. We kicked splashes at one another. We pelted in tandem toward the seagulls, who launched into flight with indignant cries.

Eventually, though, my head began to throb once more. My limbs grew weak. I sat, and then I lay down, the beach as warm as Darlene's embrace. The gradations between land and water and air were no longer distinct. The horizon was blurry, the brim of the shallows always in motion, the wind laden with spray. All the states of matter were shifting, stone into sky into sand into ocean into sunlight.

Tucker settled behind me, and we arranged our bodies so I lay with my head in his lap. He stroked my hair, which had started to grow out, reaching a shaggy, in-between state that made me look even younger than my age. To a casual observer, my gender was indeterminate. I did not know myself whether I was supposed to be a boy or a girl now. I did not care. My exterior matched the nebulous quality of my mind—a blank slate, empty of identity.

"Once upon a time, there was a place called the Wildlands," Tucker said.

This was not how his stories usually began. I gazed up at him, his face dark against the dazzling sky. He circled my temples with his fingers.

"Imagine a world out of balance," he said. "The sixth mass extinction on the planet. A war between human beings and animals. That's the world Corey and Tucker were born into."

I did not reply. I was captivated by the hypnotic movement of his hands. He traced crosses on my brow, casting shadows along my cheek.

"Corey and Tucker were heroes," he said. "They didn't just sit back and let it happen. They fought against their own species on behalf of the animals."

I nodded. I had heard this from him so many times that it had lost all meaning. It had the same hollow feel as the Lord's Prayer.

"But war has casualties," he went on. "Tucker worried about them. It kept him up at night. He didn't care so much about the ones who died. They were fine. It was over for them. He worried the most about the ones who didn't . . . fit."

My brother was leaning over me, boring into me with eyes as black as tar. The bridge of his nose was sunburned.

"What do you mean?" I said.

He did not break the flow of his storytelling, answering me as part of the tale. "Tucker knew that his actions had consequences.

You can't chase some domesticated horses out of a field and expect them to figure out how to be wild again. You can't free a bunch of lab rats from a cosmetics factory and hope they just shake off years of being tortured and caged. A fire in the desert might scare the rattle-snakes so badly that they leave everything familiar, but then where do they go? Do you see what I mean? There are always going to be outliers."

"Outliers," I repeated. I did not know the word then.

Tucker swung an arm, indicating the ocean, the palm trees lining the road, and the flat, featureless sky beyond, unblemished by even a single cloud.

"Those were the real casualties of the war," he said. "The ones that didn't belong anywhere. A horse on the other side of the fence for the first time. A chimpanzee on the run from a lab. A grizzly bear looking for food in a mountain town. A tiger with zoochosis after years in captivity. Animals that were outside the Classification of Wildness. Outside the ecosystem itself."

His voice grew husky, subsiding for a moment. As he shifted position, he jostled my skull in the cocoon of his legs. His shins bristled against my neck.

"Corey and Tucker," he said. "They were the ultimate outliers."

"They were?"

He smiled sadly. "They would never be able to rejoin civilization. Tucker knew that. They'd been battling against their own kind for too long. It had opened their eyes, transformed their brains. They weren't like other humans anymore." He shook his head. "They didn't fit anywhere. There was no place for them."

I swallowed hard. Usually my brother's stories had a calming effect on me. Not this one.

"So where do we go?" I asked. "Where did Corey and Tucker go?"

"The Wildlands," he said, and his voice was louder now, charged with emotion. I shifted position, gazing up at him curiously. His entire manner had changed, his spine erect, his gaze fixed on the middle distance.

"Those were Mama's words," I said.

"Yeah. I finally understand what she was trying to tell me. Remember what the dictionary said? 'Land that is uncultivated or unfit for cultivation.'"

The roar of the sea increased in my ears. The waves began to roll in with a little more urgency, breaking and casting up a fine mesh of spray.

"The Wildlands were a special place," Tucker said, resuming his story. "A home for strays and runaways. All the refugees of this war."

I can still remember every word he said that day. I can still hear the murmur of his voice in my ear, tangled up with the keening of the seagulls and the boom of the sea. I can still feel his fingertips on my skin, his touch as gentle as the breeze. I can still feel the revelation of my new status—a castaway from the human world, a creature lost and in need of sanctuary.

"The old ecosystem was gone," Tucker said. "Humans had destroyed it. The Wildlands were something new. 'Unfit for cultivation.' That means no people, no civilization. Wild and Tame and Domesticated and Feral—any living thing without a place on the food chain—all the outliers found their way there. All the lost and lonely animals went to the Wildlands."

His face was filled with hope. His fists were clenched on either side of my head, an involuntary gesture, gripping my skull like a vise.

"Green fields, blue skies," he said. "And Corey and Tucker lived right alongside them. The only humans. A brand-new Eden." He thumped his palm against his chest, a triumphant gesture. "This is all true, you know. This really happened."

I yawned. I could not help it. The sunlight and my fever flowed through my bloodstream like a sedative. The medicine Tucker had given me back at the mausoleum was wearing off. I felt my brother's hands sliding beneath my shoulder blades, lifting me up, hoisting me into a sitting position. My temples began to throb, the sun blazing on my nape.

"And in the end . . ." Tucker said, and paused.

The silence stretched on. I blinked at him sleepily.

"What happened to Corey and Tucker?" I said. "Did they live happily ever after?"

"No," he said. "But the Wildlands were the next best thing."

40

We often awoke at the same moment. Our bodies had fallen into rhythm after so long in close company. I opened my eyes in the darkness of the tomb and felt Tucker stirring beside me. We yawned in unison.

"The corpses," he said. His voice sounded different in the black: muffled and tinny. "Do you have nightmares about them too?"

"All the time," I said.

"Last night I dreamed that one of them was trying to smother me. It turned out I was just lying with my own arm over my face. Awful. I don't think we should stay here anymore."

"Really?" I said hopefully.

He got to his feet, slow and cautious in the gloom. I could not see much of anything—a sooty gleam beneath the door, the faint outline of the bench. Tucker's figure was a hole in the world. When he pushed the door open, we reacted simultaneously, ducking away from the flood of morning light. The warble of birds and the murmur of the wind poured into the musty crypt. The palm trees were banded by the rising sun. The ocean was a creamy gray blur, the horizon obscured by tufts of mist.

For breakfast, Tucker and I shared bites of a crushed, three-day-old veggie sandwich. We sat on the stoop, passing a water bottle back and forth. He laid a hand on my forehead and looked away. He gave me pills, which were dusty on my tongue.

"Promise me something," he said.

"Hm?"

"When you die, don't do what those guys did." He pointed back into the mausoleum. "Don't embalm your body and lock it in a box."

I said nothing, watching him.

"I'm serious," he said. "I want you to decompose and feed the trees. I want you to be consumed by scavengers and beetles until there's nothing left of you at all. That's what we're supposed to do. But this tomb . . ." He shook his head. "Those dummies filled their flesh with chemicals so nothing would eat their carcasses and sealed themselves away from the whole cycle of life. Can you imagine anything worse? That's where ghosts come from. That's why they've been haunting us."

I took another bite of my sandwich. I had the feeling that I was moving in slow motion, while my brother seemed sped up, like a video on the wrong setting.

"Am I dying?" I asked.

Tucker did not seem to hear me. He was following his own thoughts. After a minute, he turned to me and said, "It's Sunday."

A flicker of motion caught my eye. A caramel-colored moth flitted past us and landed on a nearby trunk, seamlessly camouflaged against the bark. The bushes around the mausoleum rustled in a placid breeze.

"Are you still with me?" Tucker said. "I need to know."

"What do you mean?"

He tapped my forehead with his fingertip. It was a sharp blow, and it sent painful ricochets throughout the network of my sinuses.

"People let me down," he said. "They always let me down. But you . . ." He scooted closer. "I've got to know. Are we still Corey and Tucker?"

"Yes."

"Do you trust me?"

"Yes," I said.

He reached for his backpack and withdrew his pocketknife. His face was pink with concentration, his mouth taut. He flipped open a long, sleek blade, then tested the point on the bulb of his thumb.

"Do you want to see the Wildlands?" he asked.

The knife glinted in the sunlight. I kept my gaze fixed on it.

"I think so," I whispered. Sudden tears stung my eyes, hot and filmy. I blinked them away; I did not want Tucker to see this evidence of weakness.

"Are you with me?" he said, turning the blade in his fingers.

I met his gaze at last. He leaned forward keenly, staring into my face, though he did not appear to notice that I was crying.

"Do you want to see the Wildlands?" he repeated earnestly.

"I do," I said.

His hand snaked out, grabbing mine. I flinched as he unfolded my fingers, smoothing my palm flat.

"Blood oath," he said. "Blood brothers."

I saw the flow of red before I felt the bite of the incision. Tucker sliced a line across my palm. The gash bisected the creases in my flesh like a highway on a road map. I watched in disbelief as the blood bloomed in beads.

Then Tucker handed the knife to me. There was red smeared along the blade—the juice of my body, as dark as paint. I felt my breath catch in my throat, and I swayed for a moment in the wind, light-headed.

This was a test.

I took hold of Tucker's hand and dove the blade into skin. I carved a bright line from his thumb to his pinkie. Blood puddled in his palm. Coils of crimson trickled down his wrist, outlining the structure of his tendons.

"You and me," he said.

He pressed our palms together, slick and painful, commingling our blood.

AS THE DAY PASSED, TUCKER did not put on his green jumpsuit and leave me. Instead, he lingered while the sun climbed the sky. I spent the hours lying down, my hand wrapped in gauze, my head pounding. Tucker packed up our gear—there wasn't much to collect—and told me we'd be heading out once it got dark. He was restless, bobbing in and out through the door of the tomb. His hand was bandaged like mine; we bore matching wounds. He muttered to himself. He got out pen and paper and sat for a while drawing diagrams. I did not know why he had not left me alone as usual. I pondered this question as I napped. Eventually it dawned on me that most people did not work on Sundays. I had been outside the rhythms of human civilization for long enough that I had forgotten about weekends.

After a while, Tucker began to lecture me. His voice rang through the air as I drowsed and gazed at the ocean. The mist had burned away, the horizon as sharp as the blade of Tucker's pocketknife. He talked and talked. *Forest fires. Invasive species. Algae fields.* Maybe he didn't realize that I wasn't listening. Maybe he hoped that some of his insights might filter into my mind regardless. Maybe he wasn't aware of me at all, speaking his thoughts aloud simply because he could no longer keep them contained inside his person. *The destruction of the rain forest. The food chain. Earth Overshoot Day.* The wind touched my cheek. The sun wrapped itself in clouds. I dozed and woke, dozed and woke, my brother's voice interspersed with daydream and sensation.

Then there was darkness around me. I was inside the tomb again. I wondered if Tucker had carried me—or maybe I had floated inside on the breeze. The cool pressure of the flagstone floor was soothing. The open door was a rectangle of muted light and greenery. I ran a hand through my hair—the hand Tucker had not cut. My locks were short enough to stay out of my face but long enough to catch in tangles around my fingers. I wondered what I looked like now. I had not seen a mirror in weeks.

I blinked. There was a chill in the air. The light had changed once more, the marble floor splattered with helixes of ochre and purple. Time kept passing without my consent. Whenever I shut my eyes, another hour would drift away from me.

"Remember when I told you about apex predators?" Tucker said.

I realized he was sitting next to me, his leg touching mine. I wondered how long he had been there—how long he had been talking to me while I slept. He was rocking back and forth, his knee jostling mine with each revolution.

"In the wild, polar bears walk for miles every day," he said. "Their territory ranges over entire arctic plateaus. Tigers are the same. They live alone. They travel constantly. Wolf packs cross whole mountain ranges on the hunt."

I flexed my fingers, feeling the gauze tighten across my sore palm.

"Most of them live in zoos now," Tucker said. "You take an apex predator and you put it behind bars. Do you know what happens?"

"No," I mumbled.

"Polar bears have been known to wear deep grooves in the floor of their cages from walking the same path over and over. Tigers sometimes pace until they faint from heatstroke." His hands closed into fists, one on each knee. "They can't accept that they're trapped. They can't stop. They can't rest. The idea of captivity is outside their comprehension."

A breeze orbited the tomb, bearing the smell of the ocean. Gulls cried in the distance. I must have slept again, my brother's voice whirling around me. *Add up all the people on earth and the animals we've domesticated.* The seagulls were closer now, singing in a shrill, violent chorus. *Add up all the mammals in the wild.* Tucker's voice grew deeper, more guttural. *Ten thousand years ago, human beings and the beasts of the field made up just .01 percent of all mammalian life.* I sat up, thought better of it, and lay down again. My head was as leaden and unwieldy as a bowling ball. *Now people and domestic animals are twenty times more numerous than all the other mammals on the planet combined.*

Then another voice spoke, hesitant and breathy. *Humans are re-making the world in our own image.* A sweet soprano chimed in. *Certain species are everywhere: apple trees, cows, chickens, rice, dogs. But the plants we don't eat, the animals we don't like—they're vanishing right before our eyes.* A gruff tenor spoke next, echoing as though calling out from far away. *Some people say that man is the animal who laughs. I disagree. Man is the animal who tells stories.* A fading, wraithlike wail finished the monologue. *We have to remember them. We have to tell the story.*

It was the corpses. I was sure of this now. Perhaps Tucker had not said a word in hours; perhaps he was rocking in silence as the voices of the dead rang around us both. The din became unbearable, too many disparate tones overlapping, louder and louder, each one crying to be heard over the others.

Then Tucker was poking me with his forefinger.

"It's time," he said.

41

The pavement was frosty pale, a moonlit river that flowed around the dark shapes of the animal houses. The rhino, a truck-sized silhouette, shuffled moodily around its cage. A wolf howled from the other side of the grounds, its call hanging in the air like woodsmoke. From the gloom behind me came the grumble of a bear. The koala exhibit was illuminated from within by the faint glow of an exit sign, a blood-red eye shimmering in the empty rooms.

It was midnight, and we stood on the grounds of the Pacific Zoo. "Here we go," Tucker said.

This was the secret of the green jumpsuit. My brother had taken a job with the maintenance crew at one of the most famous zoos in the Southwest. He had mopped the paths, swept the animal houses, scoured the urinals, taken possession of a swipe card and a bundle of keys, and received his pay under the table in cash. I was amazed by his cunning. To me, the Pacific Zoo was nothing short of a magical realm. I had heard about the place all my life. My father had been there as a child, and his stories had percolated down to me second-hand through Darlene and Jane.

As a janitor, Tucker was able to familiarize himself with the grounds. He learned where the cameras were, how each paddock was protected, when the security guards went about their rounds. He mapped the layout until he could walk it in the dark. He knew the location of every back door. He had even discovered a few glitches in the system—a loose latch here, a broken surveillance camera there—loopholes that only a maintenance man would ever come upon.

"It wasn't hard to get hired," he whispered. "There's quite a bit of turnover in the janitorial staff. New faces every month or so."

When I looked confused, he explained, "We handle a *lot* of manure. The kangaroos are the worst. That stuff is toxic."

All the symptoms of my illness were gone. My head was not aching, my sore tooth and the palm of my hand no longer reflecting the rhythm of my pulse in jabs of pain. The adrenaline had short-circuited my fever. I felt more alert than I had ever been.

"Are we really doing this?" I said.

"Hell yeah. Tucker and Corey."

He handed me a balaclava. I tugged it on, though I needed my brother's help to get the eye and mouth holes lined up correctly. The fabric was scratchy around my ears. Tucker donned one too, smiling at me, his face distorted by the arrangement of black cloth, a flash of teeth, a glint of eyes, not quite human anymore.

"There are three night watchmen on the grounds," he said.

He explained that there would be two young guys and Abe. The old man would almost certainly be sleeping in his plush chair in the administrative building now. After midnight, Abe ceased to take his guard duty seriously, assuming that any potential vandals would, like himself, be too sleepy for activity. The two youngsters, on the other hand, would be keeping a sharp eye out.

Tucker and I headed toward the panda exhibit. A streak of silver by the southern wall might have been the neck of a giraffe or the trail of an airplane dusted against the sky. The trees were alive with sound, surging in the wind. Entry into the panda habitat—an open area behind a high fence, a sprawling void filled with snuffling—required a swipe card and a key. Tucker had both. I stood cloistered beneath the arch of the back door, scratching at my ski mask and watching him work. It took him a while to find the right key, fumbling through a clattering ring in the darkness. I was vibrating with excitement. I had never been more of a boy than I was then.

The gate opened with a brassy clunk. The shape of the pandas was impossible to parse at this distance. Their black fur melted into the background, while the white stood out in mysterious configurations—two, perhaps three, animals slumbering in a heap, now stirring, beginning to roll to their feet. I had the impression of disembodied movement, a patchwork of pallid fabric like clothes hanging from a line, suddenly imbued with agency, rippling and floating toward me.

"Come on," Tucker said.

We made tracks toward the primates, where our job would be both easier and more complex. The monkeys had been trying to escape all their lives and would be quick to grasp an opportunity, but even the little tamarins and lemurs could be dangerous if surprised—let alone the gorillas and chimps, faster and stronger than my brother and me, capable of crushing our skulls with their bare hands.

Tucker used the janitor's entrance and jogged down a narrow corridor. The exhibits for the monkeys were lovely and large, hung with netting, rope swings, and all manner of toys—an approximation of the rain forest, designed to charm the visitors but unable to fool the animals. The back doors, hidden from the public, were far less scenic. A row of steel squares with plastic handles. For a moment, I was reminded of the portals in the mausoleum.

Tucker fiddled with his bunch of keys. As he undid each lock, I opened the door and we darted to the next enclosure. In our wake, hairy figures flung themselves into the open air as though launched on springs, screaming with joy and alarm. The smallest monkeys moved with the illusion of flight, their tiny limbs splayed. The capuchins were larger and calmer, hooting genially, licking the pavement, and pausing to sniff the air. A few territorial squabbles broke out, resolved in seconds by a baring of teeth.

The primates were not all grouped in one cage but spread over a series of exhibits, some outdoors, some enclosed, some spacious, some cramped, some reeking of urine and rotting fruit, some carpeted by a plush layer of straw. Tucker and I released the gibbons, who leapt clumsily toward the trees. Their arms were long enough to drag on the ground, so they bounced sideways while holding their hands aloft like waders unwilling to commit their upper bodies to contact with icy water. They mounted into the branches, and at once their figures made sense: stubby torsos swinging away beneath deft, slender arms. One gibbon—a youngster with ivory fur—paused high in a nearby pine to gaze down at us. It gripped a branch with one hand and looped its tail around another. With its free arm it made an indeterminate gesture, probably scratching its maw, though I imagined that it might be waving goodbye.

Nobody but Tucker and Corey could have managed this. It was all true—it was really happening.

We did not move systematically down the pathways, since that would have made our progress easier to track and exposed us to too many security cameras. Instead, we crisscrossed the zoo through side routes and back alleys, following a pattern discernible only to Tucker. The crocodile. The moose. The tarantula. The anteater. The capybara. We walked for what felt like miles, mounting hills, ducking through buildings, sliding down corridors as narrow as burrows. I was disoriented, bewildered, and ecstatic. I no longer felt the oppressive grip of the balaclava on my head; I was used to it now, remembering it only when I looked at my brother and saw his face similarly obscured.

We liberated the kangaroos, who grasped the concept of escape at once but took some time to finish the business of fleeing; a dozen of them bounded through the gate and back again like relay runners with no apparent leader. Tucker and I released the lonely orangutan: an inky haystack, a shy posture, a boiled walnut for a face. There were more kinds of deer and antelope than I knew existed—one timid and trembling, another as hefty as a boulder, a third half drowned inside a waterfall of unkempt fur. Some wore spiraling corkscrews on their heads, while others sported short, brutal shivs for antlers. There was a buck crowned by a lattice the size of a shrub, carrying stars in the lacunae between the prongs. We freed them all.

Next on the list were the zebras. Tucker led me behind a maintenance building, sliding along the wall to avoid the glow of a streetlamp and a camera perched on a nearby eave. The zebras were more skittish than the deer. Their instincts went back to the African savannah, after all, where darkness was a time for being hunted, when lions and hyenas were on the prowl. The zebras pranced and pirouetted. Their bodies were a cacophony of white strips and negative space, many animals blurred into a single, chaotic mass. I could not begin to count them. They clattered onto the path in a unified herd and bolted toward the trees, giving vent to their upside-down fire alarm of a call.

After this, things grew more intense and intricate. Tucker whispered that we did not have much time left. We would have to move faster and faster as we went. We opened the gate for the tiger, undoing the bolt and pushing the door ajar. The big cat was sleeping on a faraway rock, a spill of tufted belly, its tail lashing in dreams. Tucker drew me away, whispering that the animal would awaken soon enough, roused by the unaccustomed flurry of sounds, the musk of frightened deer, the whinny of the zebras, the suggestion of prey on the move. The tiger would check the door to its cage—it always checked the door—and one swipe of its paw would set it loose.

On our way toward the polar bear exhibit, I glanced down a slope and saw a lamp shining in the administrative building. Tucker pushed his ski mask up to his hairline for a better look, then ran a hand fretfully around his chin.

"Damn," he muttered.

A gazelle cantered down the pathway, snorting and tossing its head. A pack of shadows slid between the trees—either hyenas or kangaroos, I could not be certain. Tucker turned away, motioning for me to follow him.

The polar bears were asleep on a slab of stone, milky fur shimmering in the darkness. There were three animals—a brother and sister, Tucker informed me, along with an orphaned female who had joined their makeshift family as a young adult. Their cage contained a deep pool, the water pervaded by a soft blue glow that seemed to emanate from the concrete flooring. Tucker unsealed the electronic door, which opened with a ripe, metallic clunk. All three bears woke at once. This sound, according to Tucker, was usually associated with breakfast. I watched them lumbering to their feet, sniffing the air. One was substantially larger than the other two, as massive and pale as a cumulous cloud, his fur marbled with dirt and damp. He took the lead, stalking curiously toward us while the females fell into step behind him.

"You know what a group of polar bears is called in the wild?" Tucker hissed in my ear.

I shook my head.

"Every species has its own name," he said. "A herd of cows. A colony of bats. A murder of crows. For polar bears, it's a celebration." Tucker smiled behind his ski mask. "They meet up so rarely. They live such lonely lives. When there's more than one together, you've got a celebration."

We cut through an alley and climbed over a wooden fence, my brother giving me a boost. Together we approached the gorilla exhibit. We would have to work like lightning here. The animals had a vast outdoor arena in which to luxuriate. There were fake trees and fake rocks, as well as a man-made waterfall. I noted that the gorillas were at rest, lounging on branches, in corners. The big silverback examined his feet. One of the females held a baby in her arms, while another buried herself systematically in straw. I stepped closer to the viewing window.

At once, the silverback was galvanized into motion. His monstrous arm shot out and slammed against a boulder to launch his bulk upward to a higher perch. He rocketed around the cage, booming a territorial shout, flinging himself from branch to branch. The other gorillas seemed unfazed. One of the females gummed a stalk of grass. The baby made an attempt to escape its mother's arms, receiving a slap for its trouble. The silverback landed noisily in the straw and began whacking at the tire swing.

I was roused from my reverie by a clatter behind me. Whirling around, I expected to find a security guard there, maybe brandishing a gun. But Tucker and I were alone on the dark path. After a moment, I realized that the sound had come from above. There was an animal on the roof of a nearby building. I saw it framed in the moonlight—a mountain goat with a curlicue of antlers, its cloven hooves echoing as it moved away.

"Stand by the door," Tucker said. "Get ready to run."

The bolt dropped—the silverback glared—and we were gone.

Down the hill, the reptile exhibit was aglow. A human figure flashed past one of the windows. The guards must have discovered the alligator and the anaconda wandering loose. The lamps were burning in the petting zoo as well. Tucker and I finished the next few enclosures in record time. He unhooked the elephant's cage, pausing just long enough to observe a gray trunk twining through the gap in the door and fishing for the handle. I liberated the rhinos and watched them lumbering into the open, their heads lowered truculently. The ostriches fled into an alley on stiff, wiry legs, kicking up a wake of dust. I unfastened the latch of the aviary, and a vulture landed with a thump a few feet away. Its wings jerked spasmodically, its bald head gleaming. Shrieking raucously, it hobbled through the open gate and glanced around. One by one, the eagles descended too. Their telescopic vision had no doubt captured every aspect of my approach, complete with the flash of the key and the tumble of sawdust carried through the doorway on the breeze.

The hippo. The donkey. The fennec fox. Human voices were yelling now all over the grounds. On top of the hill, a building shone like a bonfire. The zebras were dealing with their fright by running continually. A wolf howled somewhere, answered by a chorus on the other side of the zoo. The pack had evidently been separated in the chaos and were trying to locate one another.

Despite our best efforts, there were a few animals who did not want to leave their pens. Tucker had warned me this might happen—just like the animals back on our farm, before the tornado took them away. It was not our fault, he said. We could only do so much. We tried to free the penguins, but they refused to vacate their pool; they merely squawked and splashed, preening their feathers. The camels, too, seemed uninterested in what Tucker and I had to offer. They only eyed us balefully and spat. Eventually we let them be. If they felt like making a break for it, they would do it on their own schedule.

Other animals were just too slow. The tortoises stood like ice sculptures, their glassy shells glinting in the moonlight. Tucker tried to usher them toward the open air, but they would move only in response to his touch, stepping mechanically forward with each nudge and stopping when he stopped. I was half convinced they were not alive at all. The sloth was similarly afflicted by a largo tempo. We unlocked its cage, and I watched it turn its head millimeter by millimeter and blink like an automaton in a museum display. It would never make it out in time.

The giraffes surprised me. When Tucker and I approached them, they appeared to be asleep on their feet, three adults and two juveniles, their pronged heads in shadow, their necks overlapping like a thicket of tree trunks growing haphazardly toward the moon. Their enclosure contained a few feeders as tall as the animals—baskets on poles covered by thatched umbrellas. Tucker let me open the gate. The hinges squealed painfully as I dragged the massive thing ajar.

Someone had forgotten to oil it. At the groan of metal on metal, the giraffes awoke.

All five of them began to run. They jogged a few laps around their pen, perhaps stretching their legs, perhaps surveilling the scene. There was something of the marionette in their movements, rocking and dipping as though tugged by unseen wires. They were as fast as horses, but their cantering was much more alarming. Each footfall shook the ground. The juveniles were the first to pass through the gate, the adults right behind. As soon as they stepped outside their cage, they seemed to undergo a transformation. They became real before my very eyes. They were the same size and shape as they had been a second ago, but they had density now—odor, breath, heat. I backed away, thudding against Tucker, my mouth agape.

Finally we found the lions. The pride lay in the grass, the females sprawled in a pile, the male visible only as a beige cushion of mane behind a boulder. Tucker unbarred the gate and we ran for our lives. We did the same for the bobcat, the cheetah, and the little serval. Tucker had told me beforehand that we should *never* bolt away from predators like this. The sight of prey dashing into the distance could, in and of itself, trigger the hunting instinct. But in the extremity of this moment, we were not capable of reasoned thought anymore. Our own fundamental instincts took over, and we ran frantically, desperately, holding hands, his bandaged palm pressed against mine.

An alarm sounded overhead. The remaining buildings blazed into life. Someone had evidently decided to turn on all the lights. A sun bear froze in the process of crossing the patio as though electrocuted with shock. A golden eagle soared above our heads, circling the café. We dashed through an alley, heading for the exit. My balaclava was askew, one eye blocked by fabric, but I did not stop to fix it. I followed my brother's lithe figure as he turned a corner and plunged down a hill. The only thing between us and a clean getaway was the flamingo pond.

Tucker paused, clearly tempted. The birds were unperturbed by the tumult around them. Most stood on one leg in the water with their heads beneath their wings. In sleep, they were not recognizably avian—not recognizably anything. They looked like the stems and tufts of some aquatic alien forest.

My brother charged. In an explosion of spray, he ran among their pearlescent forms. Reeds collected around his calves, slowing him, nearly sending him face-first into the pool, but he regained his balance and whooped, flinging his arms over his head. The flamingoes took flight. They collided with one another, flaring their webbed feet and rising in a cloud, blotting out the moon with their feathers.

Tucker clambered out of the pool, damp and shuddering. He led me to a side door, and then we were in the street, surrounded by the thunder of wings.

42

Tucker had parked on a side lane hours earlier. He chose the place for its solitude and easy access to the highway. As we hurried down the sidewalk, my brother's wet pant legs slapped with each step.

In the glow of a streetlamp, I saw a dark orb marring the sleek frame of our silver sedan. It took me a moment to figure out what I was looking at. Then the cat lifted its head. Its eyes were luminescent pinpricks, emerald bright. Its tail swung, stroking the license plate. At my side, Tucker grunted in shock.

There was a leopard on the hood of our car.

The animal released a guttural snarl. I saw the flare of its pointed teeth. The message was clear: it had claimed the vehicle as its own. Ours was the only car on the street to have been recently driven—the only one whose engine would provide heat. My brother maneuvered me behind him, his body shielding mine from view as we backed away. The leopard nestled down again, though its tail kept twitching. It tracked every movement of our retreat with its eerie, reflective eyes.

"Shit," Tucker whispered.

We slid together into an alley. A hollow between two dumpsters provided some cover. In the distance, a siren sounded—then another. A whole choir began to sing. It would not be long before the place was swarming with police.

"Fuck," Tucker said, smiting himself on the forehead. "Everything we need is in that glove compartment. All our cash. The gun. Everything."

"What should we do?" I asked.

A squad car raced down an adjacent street, its lights splashing the alley with intermittent flares of red and white. Tucker pushed me deeper behind the dumpster. The vehicle sped toward the zoo, its siren now sounding a minor key.

"A rock and a hard place," Tucker said.

"What?"

"We'll have to keep moving," he said. "Stay out of sight. Got it?"

We put our balaclavas back on. We crept along the wall, sticking to the shadows. Tucker stumbled over a pothole and cursed. A burro brayed plaintively on the other side of a building. Another police car went haring by, a storm of alarm bells and lights, gone in seconds. I thought I heard the faraway clatter of giraffe hooves.

At the time, I did not fully understand how much danger we were in. I was halfway in the realm of stories—Tucker and Corey on one of their adventures—and halfway in a dream of illness and thrill. Nothing seemed entirely real to me. Any minute now, Tucker might shake my arm to wake me up. I might find myself back in the mausoleum, or even at home in No. 43, roused by Darlene's voice.

Tucker, however, had no illusions about our circumstances. His state of mind was obvious—shoulders rigid, breath quick. He had

planned for us to be miles away by this point. Gone before the police descended and the animals traveled too far from their cages. We
might as well have set off a bomb, releasing not radiation but kangaroos and mountain goats and polar bears. More than a hundred
animals were loose in the city with us, spreading steadily outward
from the epicenter of the zoo.

"Keep moving," Tucker muttered. "It's the only way."

I followed him unquestioningly, just as Corey had always done.
We hurried down a block lined with restaurants and shops. An aw-
ning fluttered overhead, and Tucker froze, glancing up in alarm. I
could not get my bearings. The night sky was at once dark and bright,
a haze of cloud coated with an iridescent sheen, catching and holding
the leftover light from the city. Streetlamps shone in cheerful rows, offering no guidance. Sirens sounded all around us, some climbing the
scale as they moved in our direction, some descending note by note
as they traveled away. A coyote yipped—a familiar voice from quiet
nights in Mercy. It was a strange thing to hear in this urban landscape.

A car turned the corner, its headlights sweeping toward us.
Tucker shoved me behind a row of newspaper stands and crouched
down beside me. As the vehicle passed—a taxi, not a cop car—I
glimpsed something moving on the roof across the street. I thought
it was a squirrel, but when I looked closer I realized it was a monkey
scrambling along beneath a ribbon of tail.

Tucker got to his feet and beckoned for me to follow him. We ran.

An eagle screamed overhead. It was a chilly, windswept sound,
the sort of fierce battle cry that was meant to echo off mountainsides.
I saw a khaki-colored shape wheeling thirty feet above us. The eagle's
wingspan was longer than I was tall. Its talons were spread. Tucker
grabbed my bandaged hand and yanked me onward. We jogged past
a row of garbage cans, an apartment building, and a gas station. We
cut through a playground into another alley.

"Look," I said, pointing.

A crocodile was strolling toward us at a genial waddle. The pavement in the alley was slanted on both sides toward a runnel in the

center, marked every so often by grated metal drains. The animal seemed to be following the gutter in the concrete as though hoping the path would lead to water. Beefy legs. Little eyes. Ten feet long. I heard the gush of its breath, the scrape of its claws. It stank of rotten meat. Tucker squeezed my hand so tightly that I felt my bones pull against their sockets.

The crocodile lumbered past us without appearing to register our presence. Apparently its night vision was not acute. I watched it shuffle into the pool of light beneath a streetlamp. The glow caught each tooth in turn, dozens of blades lodged in a hacksaw of jawbone. The animal's tail swung as a counterpoint to the sway of its belly. It dragged its bulk over the curb and into the road. I half expected it to look both ways, but of course it did not recognize the limits and thresholds of the human world. It crossed the street without haste or concern and slipped into the shadows on the other side.

"Jesus," Tucker said.

Up a hill. Through a parking lot. Past a convenience store. My head began to ache again. My hands trembled with adrenaline aftershocks, and my injured palm prickled. New sounds rang through the air: a parrot squawking, the yowl of a fox, the unsettling laughter of a pack of hyenas. I was not sure why the animals were vocalizing—maybe keeping in touch with their own kind, maybe communicating a warning to other species, maybe trying to overpower the chorus of police sirens. I had never experienced a night so wild and full of perilous music. My nerves jangled in concert. My brother led me down a quiet lane studded with palm trees, but before we had taken more than a few steps, there was a blast of breath—a rhino snorting at the sight of us—and a massive shadow shifted in the gloom. We hurried back the other way.

Tucker was lost. I realized this after a while. There was no method to his madness; he was not leading me back to the car, not leading me anywhere. We passed a mailbox with a dent in the side, and a few minutes later we passed it again. My brother tugged off his ski mask and wiped the sweat from his forehead. His nostrils flared, a sure sign of tension. He mumbled to himself, staring up at the street signs in consternation.

My head was thudding dully. Tucker darted into an alley, then backtracked, drumming his fingers on his chin. He threw his balaclava on the ground and stomped on it. He made a frame with his hands and pivoted in a circle as though attempting to locate true north.

Finally, he tipped his head back and laughed.

"Screw it," he said.

I hovered numbly beside him. The ache in my temple was overpowering.

"Man plans," Tucker said. "God laughs."

He picked me up and swung me onto his back. I gripped his neck in relief, laying my cheek against the muscular plane of his shoulders. He set off at a brisk trot. I closed my eyes, bouncing against his ribs, and when I opened them again we were in a wide, murky park. A canopy of trees crisscrossed the sky, black and whispering, the leaves surging apart every now and then to offer a glimpse of cloud.

"Higher ground," Tucker said.

He hoisted me up onto a knobby branch. I leaned gratefully back against the trunk, my legs slung on either side of the limb, the wind circling my bare shins. Tucker perched beside me. We could see the street—a restaurant, a gas station, and a movie theater with its marquee darkened for the night—but nobody on the sidewalk would have been able to see us.

I don't know how long we sat there. I was so tired that my arms hung limp; I could not even find the wherewithal to lift my hands into a more comfortable pose in my lap. But I did not sleep. First a trio of chimpanzees came into view. The streetlamps bronzed their bodies, turning their fur into straw. Hay bales on the move. A fire hydrant seemed to unnerve them. All three apes shrieked at the sight of it, and they spun away from one another, giving the unknown object a wide berth, pivoting on their knuckles. Their long arms were stiff, their hind legs two-stepping.

Then came the zebras. I heard their hoofbeats before I saw them. They burst into being beneath the fluorescent glare of the gas station parking lot, perhaps fifteen animals in all. One of them was bleeding, a splash of crimson against a lattice of interlocking black and white. Their haunches surged, their manes sticking up like the bristles of a broom. They all wore the same expression—ears erect, eyes rolling, teeth bared. One of them gave vent to a ululation, and the cry was answered by the rest. They were not running flat out; they seemed to have settled into a steady jog, as though they had come to understand that this was a marathon, not a sprint.

A cop car appeared, whizzing down the middle of the street, ignoring the double yellow line completely. Its lights blazed like a firework display, but the siren was off. I wondered if a command had gone out over the police frequency. Maybe sirens had proved coun- terproductive, scaring and stimulating the animals.

The zebras checked at the sight of the squad car, and it checked at the sight of them, skidding to a halt. I wondered what the officer intended to do. He could hardly arrest the animals. The herd huddled defensively beneath the traffic light. There was a momentary stale- mate. The zebras stamped their hooves and tossed their heads. The car gunned its engine but did not budge.

Then, to my surprise, the vehicle reversed. It swerved a little as the driver attempted to steer backward, tires whining against the pavement.

The zebras gave chase. With a drumroll of hoofbeats, they charged. From what I could tell, the inclination struck them all simul- taneously. They hurtled after the police car, skinny legs flying, tails whipping. I wondered if they were chasing away a threat—the way they might gang up on a lone cheetah in the savannah, overwhelm- ing a superior predator by sheer force of numbers—or whether they had decided to follow a perceived ally through an unknown, bewil- dering situation. The police car led the herd down the hill, reversing frantically out of view.

For a moment, everything was quiet. The clamor of sirens had stilled. The animals were no longer calling out with the same frequency as before. Perhaps they had buckled down to the complicated business of escaping. At my side, Tucker was staring across the city with an expression of almost indecent pride. He had shaken off any signs of fear, now basking in the glow of his achievement. I had never seen a human face so suffused with satisfaction.

In the silence, there was motion. Animals everywhere. An enormous bird of prey flitted across the amber wash of clouds. A skyscraper obstructed my view to the west, gilded by the matrix of a fire escape. Something was there—too bulky to be human, its belly rotund, its arms plush with curtains of fur. An orangutan. It was climbing up the outer scaffold, swinging from hand to hand.

A sound caught my ear. A chuckle. Malicious. Nearly human. I glanced up and down the block. There was an elementary school on the far corner. Several ragged black shapes were moving through the playground, gliding beneath the slide and nosing at the swings. Even after the darkness had swallowed them up, I could still hear their voices—the mad merriment of hyenas on the hunt.

The sky began to brighten. Each time I blinked, the clouds along the eastern horizon took on a greater intensity, no longer merely reflecting the city lights but marinating in the fiery glow of incipient sunrise. Tucker checked his watch. He ran a hand down his throat and fidgeted with his collar.

Above the rooftops, I saw a giraffe's head bobbing along. Its body was hidden behind the buildings. The rock and sway of its gawky gait made no sense when only its face was visible—horns dipping, chin rising, ears swiveling. The giraffe stopped to gather a mouthful of maple leaves, then loped behind an apartment complex.

I waited for it to reappear on the other side of the building, but it did not. Instead, I saw a lamp come on in an upper window. The sky was growing lighter by the second. The city was waking up.

There was a scuffle on the sidewalk below. A bighorn sheep emerged from an alley, its coat disheveled. Its hooves made a delicate patter. The animal was the size of a motorcycle, burdened by an arabesque of giant horns.

Then a door opened farther along the street. Twenty feet from the bighorn sheep, a man stepped outside, blurry in the gloom. He strode to one of the parked cars and set his briefcase on top, fumbling with his keys.

The animal reacted swiftly, leaping away. Its whole aspect changed as it gathered momentum, no longer an earthbound boulder of flesh but an airy thing, catching against the wind like a kite. As I watched, it executed a flawless sequence of gymnastic maneuvers. It sprang onto a mailbox, ricocheted off the top of a parked van, and soared onto the roof of a nearby building. The animal mounted thirty feet into the sky in less than a second. Then it paused, listening, framed against the clouds, its coil of antlers pivoting.

The man had not noticed a thing. He opened the car door and flung his briefcase inside. I heard his radio begin to play, and he drove off.

"Stay here," Tucker said.

"What?"

I turned and saw him climbing down from the tree. He landed in the grass and dusted off his thighs. Looking up at me, he put a finger to his lips.

"I think I've figured out where we are," he said. "I'll go get the car."

"No," I said. "You can't leave me alone."

"You'll be safer here," he said.

I twisted off the branch and began to descend too. I scraped my injured palm on the bark as I slid awkwardly to the ground. The cut reopened, blood seeping into the gauze.

"We stay together," I said firmly. "Tucker and Corey."

He gazed down at me for a long moment, taking in my determined expression and the stain spreading over my bandaged hand.

"My blood, your blood," he said.

The landscape was temporarily deserted. No animals. No police cars. No early-morning commuters. Tucker and I crossed the road.

The air smelled of baked goods, mixed with the heady suggestion of the ocean, a salty tang that pervaded everything here. The eastern sky was almost too bright to look at. The row of streetlamps all along the block flickered once, twice, and went out for the day.

"This way," Tucker said.

We turned down an alley. Somewhere far off, an elephant called out, a throbbing note like the blast of a tuba. The walls were a meshwork of shadows. We picked our way through stray garbage and potholes. I realized that my palm was bleeding heavily enough to drip. I paused, investigating the soaked gauze and wiping the trickle onto my shirt, as Tucker walked on ahead.

That was the instant it happened. I could not imagine how something that size had been concealed from our view. For a moment, I did not believe what I was seeing.

A polar bear stepped out from behind a dumpster. The animal gazed at Tucker and me without expression. Its presence seemed like an optical illusion, a refraction of the darkness, a pale stain on a film negative.

People say that in moments of great stress, time seems to slow down. For me, each second became crystalline and exquisite, as hard and complex as gemstone. I had time to watch the animal consider the fact of our presence, tilting its head ever so slightly. I had time to notice that its fur stank of fish and clay. I had time to realize that the lid of the dumpster was askew. Perhaps the creature had been looking for scraps. I had time to remember that polar bears could smell blood, like the cut on my hand and the smear on my clothes, from a mile away.

Tucker took half a step backward, then seemed to think better of it. Retreat was not an option here. The animal was nearly as fast as a car. Its body was topographical, the shoulders an alpine peak, the torso a snowy slope, the hindquarters a rugged cliff face. I was having trouble gauging how far away it was. Maybe twenty feet. Maybe thirty. The polar bear was massive enough to throw off my sense of spatial orientation.

A growl perfumed the dark alley. I saw a flash of tongue. The beast stood with a slightly pigeon-toed stance. Its fur was matted in texture but pristine in hue. It did not move. There was something almost holy in the polar bear's stillness. No need to hurry. The world would wait until it was ready. I had never before been in the presence of any living thing that was absolutely without fear.

Tucker acted first, lunging toward me. I felt his hands tighten beneath my armpits as he hefted me into the air. He threw me with all his strength—the ground lurched away—something struck my temple. A rough metallic surface slammed against my side. Everything was dark. I thought I had been knocked unconscious, but then I saw a scrap of sky overhead. Tucker had flung me into the dumpster.

Panting, I took stock of my surroundings. The interior was half-filled with garbage bags that pooled and pressed around my limbs, gripping me like quicksand. My ribs ached each time I inhaled. There was a chink in the seam of the dumpster. I leaned toward it, unable to extricate myself from the slippery morass of the garbage bags, but able to peer through the hole into the alley.

A gleam of white. A flicker of motion. Tucker's shoulders. I saw my brother framed in the middle of the alley, facing the bear.

The attack happened so fast that I almost couldn't follow it. There was no preliminary crouch, no baring of teeth, no warning signal of any kind, no communion between animals, no celebration. The bear transformed from an immovable object into an irresistible force. It bore down on my brother, its paws landing without sound. There was something effortless, even graceful, in its stride. You could perceive the perfect architecture of its muscles beneath the sway and bounce of its bulk and the flutter of its untidy coat.

I waited for Tucker to run. Surely he would try to save himself. I opened my mouth to yell, but no sound came out; I seemed to be paralyzed the way I sometimes was in nightmares. There was a tearing noise, a damp sigh, something sluicing, another growl from the bear. Tucker did not say a word. My view was blocked by white. The beast was facing away from me now, its fur smudged with blood.

Then I saw Tucker again. I could tell from his stance that he was badly wounded, clutching his side, his lips drawn back in pain. He and the bear began to circle one another, my brother staggering, the animal prowling contentedly. Tucker slid along the wall of the alley, both hands pressed against his gut. Blood fountained over his fingers. There was a ripe gash in his thigh, too, the denim shredded. The polar bear ambled in silence, taking its time. An apex predator in its element.

My brother looked at me. I swear he saw me—my little face pressed to the gap in the side of the dumpster.

The polar bear reared up on its hind legs. If possible, it became even larger than before, its head scraping the clouds. Claws spread. Back arched. A cairn of marble and ice.

This is my last memory of Tucker. This night, this alley. There was no worry or sorrow in his face. His eyes were wide in a kind of rapturous wonder. The bear let out a roar that was loud enough to bruise my eardrums. Tucker threw his arms open, maybe mimicking the animal's posture, maybe asking for an embrace. The bear obligingly folded its body around him, swaddling him in a blanket of snow.

I heard the wet grind of bones breaking. Tucker's hand was still visible—his bandaged hand—the fingers splayed. A shudder ran through his flesh as the bear compressed his spine into fragments. His arm went limp.

My vision blurred, and I wiped my eyes. The polar bear nuzzled its mouth into my brother's clavicle. Its jaws clamped down with an audible crunch. It stayed like that for a moment, head low. Then, with a snarl, it shook Tucker's inert body side to side like a dog with a chew toy. Lashes of crimson spattered the brick wall. My brother seemed weightless in the animal's jaws. All his wonderful breadth—wide back, long torso, strong hands—was nothing compared to the mass of the bear. His limbs flopped strangely, smearing the white fur with blood. The beast lifted one paw high, its claws bejeweled by clots of flesh. I saw the curve of its shoulder and the glittering expanse of teeth. There was no longer any suggestion of softness in its face. Its belly was a patchwork of red, its eyes as pitiless as lumps of coal, its forehead marked with war paint.

The animal reared up onto its hind legs again, dropping Tucker to the ground with a damp thud. My brother did not fall like a living thing. He was no longer the right shape, the right consistency. His bones were pliant, his leg torn, his throat worried open, brimming like a geyser. He was a tumble of flesh, an afterthought. He was prey. The polar bear opened its bloodstained maw and bellowed in triumph.

And just like that, Tucker was gone.

SEPTEMBER

43

Darlene stood outside the morgue with her arms folded across her chest. Despite gathering her courage to open the door for the past twenty minutes, she could not make herself go in. The air was a noxious stew of formaldehyde and bleach. A man hovered at her side—horn-rimmed glasses, a solemn mien, calm eyes. If he was impatient with her, he did not let it show. He stared down at the clipboard in his hands as though it contained all the riddles of the universe, as though he had nowhere better to be than this cramped, poorly lit hallway.

"All right," Darlene said.

The coroner pushed the door open.

There were four metal tables in the morgue. Each gleamed silver beneath its own private spotlight. The floor was tiled, sloping toward a grate in the middle of the room. Darlene averted her eyes, willing herself not to consider the purpose and contents of that drain. Medical instruments lay beside a pristine steel sink. The morgue was located in the basement and had only one window, stuck high on the wall, showing a tousle of evergreen bushes.

There was a fifth table in the corner. Darlene had not noticed it at first, perhaps because it was the only one draped with a sheet. The coroner walked over and patted the white cloth. The air was cold; there was a draft pouring in from a vent overhead. Darlene tucked her hands in the pockets of her denim jacket. She wished Roy were with her. She closed her eyes, imagining him—his honest face, the generous cushion of his lower lip, the starburst wrinkles around his eyes.

"This way," the coroner said.

She moved across the tile as though she were on wheels, gliding rather than walking. The shape beneath the sheet was odd. It did not seem to have the right arrangement of peaks and valleys. With some distant part of her brain, Darlene wondered whether Tucker was playing an elaborate prank on her. Perhaps the coroner would throw off the cloth to reveal a manikin or a crash test dummy. Perhaps Tucker would leap out of the closet, laughing at the expression on her face. He always loved pranks when they were kids.

"Are you ready?" the coroner said.

"Yes. No."

Slowly he lifted the sheet. There: a thatch of brown hair. A smooth slope of forehead. Her brother's nose and chin.

"Oh," she breathed.

Half of his face was gone. She could see exactly where the animal's claws had landed—brutal gouges scored across one cheek. Tucker's left eye was missing, the ragged orifice caky with dried blood. A chunk of his upper lip had been torn away, leaving a gap in the flesh that showed a few teeth. His ear had been gnawed off as well. Darlene saw a shimmer of skull beneath the mottled overlay of tissue.

The coroner was discreet, doing his best to reveal only Tucker's face. But Darlene caught a glimpse of what lay farther down. Her brother's chest was a trench of marbled crimson, his left shoulder chewed down to the bone. She realized that one of his legs was gone, too. That was why the sheet did not sit evenly across his lower body; there was an intact limb on only one side of the table.

"Is this Tucker McCloud?" the coroner asked.

"Yes. That's my brother."

Swiftly, he covered the corpse with fabric again. He made a note on his clipboard and signed the bottom of the page. He murmured that he would give her some time alone. Then, after a moment's thought, he took her elbow and guided her to a chair. Once she was safely seated, he slipped outside.

Darlene breathed amid a cloud of formaldehyde. She tried to remember the facts she had been told. It seemed vital that she stick to the facts. Tucker had been dead approximately thirty-six hours. His body was found in an alley by a woman on her way to work. He had been mauled by an animal—some large predator, species currently unknown. Dead by the time the paramedics arrived. Already gone for a couple hours by then, slipping into rigor mortis.

Roy had warned her that she might experience some aftereffects of trauma. He printed out a list of PTSD symptoms, told her about support groups for people like herself, but Darlene did not believe there were other people like herself. Her circumstances were too specific, her brother unique. She was not experiencing any of the emotions she was supposed to.

Mostly she was furious. The rage that burned in her chest all summer had not yet abated. Tucker was dead, but Darlene was still mad at him. She was mad at him now for removing himself from the world, slipping beyond her reach. She would never have the chance to say what she needed to say, to win the argument once and for all, to list the thousands of injuries her brother had inflicted on her—and Cora—and the whole of human civilization.

Darlene rose to her feet, hands jammed in her coat pockets. These would be her last moments with Tucker. She stepped closer to the shape on the table.

She had seen dead bodies before. She remembered her mother at the wake, so many years ago: the sunken look of Mama's skin and the peculiar, artificial odor of her hair. Then there was Daddy, vanished into the blue. Darlene had been cheated of the chance to see his body, and that was a lasting, painful thing. Perhaps it would have helped her understand that he was gone.

She laid one hand over her brother's heart, the other on his brow. Even through the cloth, she could feel the unnatural coolness of his flesh. The fabric was rough beneath her fingers. She did not remove the sheet; she did not need to see it all again. Tucker's injuries were scored permanently into her psyche. He no longer looked like the person she remembered. The grotesque state of his body made his death a little easier to accept, offering a visual representation of his mental state. His exterior finally matched his mind: normal in places (sleek forehead, sharp chin, splash of freckles), and distorted in others (missing eye, ravaged cheek, torso reduced to a bloody canyon). The boy she loved for most of her life was gone. The man on the table was somebody else.

At last, Darlene wiped her eyes and turned away.

44

Darlene took a cab from the hospital that contained Tucker to a second hospital, across town, that contained Cora. Her siblings were on opposite ends of this unfamiliar, sprawling city. It was evening, the sun hanging low in the sky. Tall buildings lined the streets, coating the pavement in shadows. The wind was ripe with the smell of saltwater. She had never felt a breeze so freighted with moisture; the air in Oklahoma was always bone-dry.

Traffic was bad. The taxi driver made frequent use of his horn, shouting in a language Darlene did not recognize and gesturing with one hand out the window. Bicycles whizzed through the gridlock, as fragile and fleet as dragonflies. Now and then the matrix of streets would line up just so, and the setting sun would poke its fingers down a long avenue into the car. In the rush to get to her sister, Darlene had left her sunglasses back in Mercy.

There was a commotion on the sidewalk. The pedestrians on the corner began shoving one another. A woman stumbled off the curb and into the street with a yell. A horn sounded. The cab driver slammed on his brakes, and Darlene cried out indignantly as the seat belt choked her.

Then she saw it: a warthog charging through the crowd. It ran with its head lowered, a wrecking ball of hooves and tusks. Darlene glimpsed the black spray of its mohawk as people dived out of its path. Its eyes were wild, and there was froth around its mouth.

She gasped in amazement. The warthog was bigger than she would have expected. Longer and broader than a human being. It barged against the knees of an elderly man, who toppled to the side. The beast did not appear to notice. It plunged into the intersection, giving vent to an unearthly squeal. Traffic came to a standstill as the animal darted this way and that. It threaded through the morass of cars, snorting, trying in vain to find a path to safety.

Darlene leaned forward, staring through the window. The warthog's jowls quivered with each footfall. Its belly was a gray hammock. There was something prehistoric about its appearance—the snout elongated, the neck as wide as a telephone pole, the tusks doubled and tarnished and curled. Strange knobs of flesh bulged beneath its eyes. Darlene heard a tinkle of glass breaking as the animal collided with a station wagon, knocking the side mirror clean off. The warthog let out one last screech, then swung to the east and picked up speed.

The cab driver turned around in his seat, pointing a finger in Darlene's face. His cheeks were red with fury. For an instant, she thought he was accusing her of something, but he was merely ranting, spittle flying with each word.

"You see?" he cried in a heavy accent. "You heard about this business at the zoo? You see what we have come to?"

"I heard," she said.

"It's madness. Who would do such a thing? What kind of person?"

"A lone wolf," Darlene said faintly.

This was the expression the newscasters kept using. The police had released a carefully worded statement earlier that day, confirming that the perpetrator responsible for this heinous act of eco-terror had died in the assault. No names or specifics given. No mention of Cora. All that would come later.

The driver grunted and pivoted back to face the street. The taxi accelerated. Darlene leaned her cheek against the cool glass of the window. California unspooled before her, a jewelry store, a movie theater, a pet shop. The warthog was gone. She saw an impatient woman pushing a stroller. She saw a man staring so intently at his cell phone that he nearly walked into a fire hydrant. She saw a child holding a balloon.

For the first time, Darlene felt a stab of sympathy for Tucker. She had the luxury of sympathy, now that he was a body beneath a sheet. He could not harm anyone anymore. Soon he would be cremated, reduced to particles. Tucker was free of the addled, unregulated state he had endured for so long.

Maybe it all came back to the tornado. Maybe everything, in the end, came back to the tornado. Darlene wondered whether the storm transfigured her brother—shattering his temperament and reforming the shards into a new structure—or whether it had merely been a catalyst for a tendency already inside him. She would never be certain. Maybe the seeds of instability were present in his brain since birth, lying dormant, awaiting the right trigger to flourish. If it had not been the tornado, it would have been something else. Perhaps Tucker was always destined to chase wildness.

But it was also possible that he would have grown up normal and sane if the finger of God had skipped over Mercy that day. Perhaps the tornado had infused him with something of its own essence—its relentless motion, its unpredictability, its capacity for destruction. Darlene pictured the funnel cloud roaring through Tucker's mind, scattering the elements of his personality across the landscape, leaving only chaos in its wake.

45

Cora and Jane were asleep in the hospital bed. Darlene paused in the doorway, struck by the loveliness of the image—her sisters sharing a pillow. The lack of expression in their faces made them look more alike; Darlene could see the similarity in the shape of their mouths, the dead-straight brow line and small oyster-shell ears. They did not stir as she set down her purse.

Roy was watching the TV on mute, lounging in an armchair. Darlene noticed a few empty coffee cups on the table beside him. He motioned her over with a wave, and she sank gratefully into his lap. As usual, his body radiated heat. A human furnace. He stroked her hair.

"It was Tucker," she murmured.

"I'm sorry," he said. "Was it awful?"

"Yeah."

"You should have let me come with you."

Darlene shrugged. "It's over."

The hospital room was as blank as a blown egg. The walls were white, the door white, the blinds white and always a little askew, regardless of how much Darlene fiddled with the cords. The window gave onto a brick wall coated with ivy. Darlene readjusted her position in Roy's lap. She gazed across the room at Cora's still figure.

It was blind luck that her sister had been found. Yesterday morning, a passerby came across Tucker lying in an alley—a puddle of blood and flesh—and called an ambulance. The EMTs arrived quickly, but several hours too late to help him.

Then they noticed a dumpster on its side, one corner dented in, claw marks scored into the metal. They decided to investigate. This simple, offhand choice saved Cora's life. Darlene shivered, imagining her sister hidden among the garbage bags. How easy it would have been for the paramedics to overlook her little body.

At first the EMTs thought she was dead too.

Cora was unconscious when she was admitted to the emergency room. A contusion on her forehead. Three cracked ribs. A fever of 106.3. Pulse erratic and thready. She was diagnosed with pneumonia and a double ear infection. The latter had caused a rupture in her right eardrum. In addition, the bloody gum from a lost baby tooth had not been properly cleaned or tended, which led to a severe infection in her jaw. Eventually, when Cora was stronger, this would require surgery. She was badly malnourished and dehydrated. All in all, she was fortunate to have survived.

Darlene took a steadying breath. She reminded herself that Cora was in stable condition now, though her appearance was still a shock. She was hooked up to an IV and a refrigerator-sized apparatus that monitored her vital signs. Heavily medicated. Warm beneath a blanket. Painfully skinny. There was a knot on her temple, a flowering bruise. Her hair had been chopped away in uneven shards that were just beginning to curl at the tips. Her upper arms were thinner than her elbows. Her skin was tattooed all over by fresh welts and scratches.

Darlene closed her eyes, leaning against Roy's chest. He began to massage her shoulders, kneading a little too hard. She winced but said nothing; it seemed petty to critique a generous impulse.

"Hey," he said. "Look at that."

She glanced up at the TV, bolted to the wall at a height that did not suit anyone. She reached for the remote control to turn up the volume, then threw a glance back at her sisters. Jane's arm was visible above the blanket, the golden snake of her braid twining past her elbow. Cora's body was so slight that she scarcely made a bulge beneath the white coverlet. Darlene could hear her pneumonia in each raspy, bubbling snore.

She set the remote control aside. On TV, a newscaster mouthed something. Then an image of an elephant appeared, its ears flared and trunk raised. The animal seemed to be trundling between lanes of traffic toward an intersection.

Darlene sat up straighter. The elephant's haunches towered over the cars on either side. Its ears were ragged around the edges, as though they had been hemmed inexpertly. Something in its posture suggested youth and energy, though its age was obscured by ill-fitting folds of charcoal skin, etched with lattices of wrinkles. To Darlene, all elephants looked ancient. The animal seemed to be in a footrace with a city bus, moving at a quick clip, its tail swinging and trunk erect.

"Damn," Roy said.

A series of pictures flashed across the screen. Animal after animal, all of them in places they had no reason to be. An arctic fox sat onboard a trolley, a whorl of milky fur, hackles raised and teeth bared. A python lurked beneath a mailbox, its curves folded into a puddle of flesh. A group of kangaroos forded the highway, bringing the traffic to a halt. Most of the animals were out of focus, photographed in midleap, but one large male reared up on his hind legs and boldly turned to face the camera. It was disconcerting to see how anthropomorphic his figure appeared in that pose. He might have been a trickster god—a sinister, playful amalgamation of traits both

human and animal: a man's shoulders, a woman's hips, lush chocolate fur, a long equine nose, his ears cupped forward, his eyes dusted
with heavy lashes. His hands were perhaps the most startling part of
him. Leathery monkey paws adorned by cruel, curved talons. Each
claw was as long as its finger.

"I saw a warthog earlier," Darlene said. "Big as life in the middle
of the road."

"Jesus," Roy said.

Then a cell phone video began to play on TV. The quality was
poor, the image pixelated. Darlene rubbed her eyes behind her glasses
and squinted up at the screen. The background seemed to be a public
library. A group of children sat in a circle as a woman read aloud
from a picture book. There were rows of metal shelves and a cart
laden with plastic-wrapped tomes. The video joggled, then refocused
on one of the small upturned faces, a nut-brown girl with a plump
rosebud mouth. She was chewing on the end of her braid, captivated
by the book. Story time at the library. A loving parent filming from
the sidelines.

Then a shape flitted across the screen—a man running. The camera swung. For a moment, the motion and blur were too chaotic for
Darlene to follow what was happening. Roy grabbed her knee, digging in his fingernails.

A lion inside the library. The camera framed the animal, and
whoever was filming it froze. A faint shudder suggested a hand quak-
ing with fear. The beige wall offered surprisingly good camouflage.
The image slid mechanically in and out of focus. No mane. A female.
Golden eyes. The cat's shoulders were hunched in a predatory stance,
her tail swiveling. She was stalking the children on the rug.

"No no no," Darlene whispered.

A woman's silhouette appeared, too far away to show up as
more than a bulky figure in a long skirt. A quick-witted librarian.
She darted toward a red box on the wall and did something with her
hand. The TV was still muted, but Darlene assumed that the woman
had pulled the fire alarm.

The reaction was immediate. The cat checked in midstride, one paw floating above the carpet. She flattened her ears in obvious concern. Her control over her own musculature was immaculate; she became rigid from snout to tail. By contrast, the children leapt up from their places around the circle. They started to holler and dance, reacting to the excitement of the alarm. None of them noticed the predator among the stacks twenty feet away.

The lion turned and slunk off. Shielded behind a metal cart, she paused just long enough to shake the tension out of her flesh. Her stride changed, no longer taut and determined, becoming brisk and businesslike. She padded across the carpet with the lightness and insouciance of a house cat heading off to find a favorite napping spot. The video shuddered to a halt on a single frame: an image of the lion's narrow haunches and tufted tail gliding away between the stacks.

The newscaster reappeared on the screen. Seated behind a desk, he mouthed sternly at the camera again. Darlene scanned the man's face and deduced that the lion had not harmed anyone.

Roy seemed to come to the same conclusion.

"Close call," he said.

"Too close," she said.

All at once, she could not bear to take in any more information. She fumbled for the remote control and switched the TV off.

Cora rolled beneath her blanket, coughing damply. Darlene watched her until she grew still again. A tube curled out of the hollow of her sister's arm, attached to a bag hanging from a rack above her. The fluid seeped constantly into her body, rehydrating her. The nurses used the IV port to inject additional drugs—the antibiotics and painkillers that left Cora too sleepy to move. It would be a while before she could have solid foods. Right now, she was eating and drinking through her blood and peeing into a tube, another translucent bag that the nurses kept examining and changing out. Cora's ribs were bandaged. The knot on her brow was multicolored, melding from green to orange to purple like a kindergartener's attempt at finger painting. There was a deep gash on her cheek, another on her palm. Her eyes were sunken.

Darlene looked away. It broke her heart to consider how little she knew about what had happened to Cora—how little she might ever know. Gone for months. A wide-open landscape. A summer wind heavy with the smell of rain.

Darlene imagined her brother and sister on a dirt road, strolling unhurriedly, both carrying bindles like hobos on TV. She pictured them hopping aboard a freight train, waiting until the engine hit a curve and slowed down, the wheels shuddering, the brakes screeching in protest, Tucker flinging Cora's little body onto the bed of a boxcar and clambering up after her, both of them tumbling onto their backs, breathless. Darlene imagined them sleeping in fields and lonely barns, cushioned on bales of hay. Stealing food for their supper. Breaking into other people's kitchens to swipe a loaf of bread or a jug of milk. She was aware that her imagination was somewhat muddled—a mixture of old movies and childhood chapter books—but the picture was so clear in her mind that it felt true.

Yet it wasn't true, because of the violence. Two counts of arson, some petty vandalism, one murder, and the assault on the Pacific Zoo—and those were just the things Darlene knew about. For the hundredth time, she wondered about her sister's level of involvement. Multiple witnesses had mentioned seeing a child at the various crime scenes. Had Cora been Tucker's righthand girl, helping him of her own volition? Had she converted to the cause, a true believer in his two-person cult, a child soldier in his war? Or had she merely been there in the background? Watching against her will, refusing to participate, present only because she had no other choice?

Cora no longer looked like a boy. The doppelgänger who stole a candy bar and appeared in stark black and white on that long-ago security footage was slipping away, replaced by a child who was neither here nor there. In her slow, terrible healing, Cora inhabited a liminal state that affected every aspect of her poor little body: neither sick nor well, neither awake nor sleeping, neither male nor female.

Eventually Cora would be well enough to answer questions, but Darlene knew better than to expect anything comprehensive from a traumatized nine-year-old. Her sister might be able to address the basics (who, what, where), but the more intricate concepts (how, why) would elude her. She might never be able to fully articulate what happened during her time away. She might not want to.

More than anything, Darlene wondered how her brother ended up dead in an alley, her sister unconscious in a dumpster. But this, above all, would have to remain a mystery. When Tucker died, Cora was already feverish and delirious, perhaps even unconscious. Surely she had not seen what happened to him. Surely.

Maybe Tucker tried to play dead. Maybe he flapped his arms, making himself seem bigger. The coroner had listed the cause of death as blood loss. Hemorrhagic shock. Some animal tore Tucker apart; the attack was so violent that half his leg ended up severed in the gutter. Darlene could not imagine a worse way to die.

She did not know what kind of creature killed her brother. An apex predator—Tucker taught her this term. Once, long ago, he had explained the Trophic Scale. Eventually the coroner would be able to match the bite marks and offer a definitive answer. A tiger, perhaps, or a grizzly bear. All teeth and claws and instinct.

Darlene didn't blame the animal. At least it did not eat Tucker's flesh. At least it left Cora alone afterward. Darlene suspected that the beast was neither hungry nor hunting. It was probably lost and scared, under tremendous strain, out of its element, loose in a brand-new realm of unfamiliar smells and sounds. It perceived her brother as a threat—which, of course, he was—and in the manner of its kind, the animal dispatched him, brutally and efficiently, without conscience or compunction.

46

Over the next few days, Darlene did not sleep much. Roy found an inexpensive hotel a few blocks away from the hospital and took two rooms, one for Jane and one for him and Darlene to share. He scoped out the local restaurants. He urged Darlene to take breaks, to go for a walk or visit the beach. He reminded her that Cora was in the best possible hands. They should see something of California, he said. Her presence would not make her sister heal any faster, he said.

Still, Darlene remained at Cora's side. She shooed Roy and Jane off to the hotel each evening, then slept upright in an armchair. The hospital was always busy. Nurses bustled in and out of Cora's room at all hours, checking her temperature, listening to her lung function, and making illegible marks on her chart. There was little natural light in the room; the only window faced the wall of another wing of the hospital. Darlene could never see the sun. At night, the fluorescent lights in the corridor dimmed, but the flurry of activity was unabated. Mechanical noises floated down the hall. The nurses would examine Cora's IV and cluck their tongues. After a week, it became necessary to move the needle to her other arm. The caustic medication had eaten away at her vein, leaving a messy green bruise.

All the while, beneath the TV, the buzz of the overhead lights, and the footsteps in the hall, Cora breathed. The wet, hoarse rhythm filled the room like a tide. Darlene felt herself drifting back and forth on the current. She watched her sister shift in her sleep. Cora often brushed at her own face, flicking away her straggling, uneven locks. Now and then she muttered, "Where's Tucker?" She never stayed awake long enough to get an answer.

Gradually Darlene learned the layout of the hospital. She knew which staircase led to the roof and which alley the nurses used for their smoke breaks. She visited the tiny office where a witchy woman—her kindly disposition belied by her ferocious eyebrows—explained the complexities of Medicaid.

More than once, it occurred to Darlene that this could have been her life. Long ago, in another phase of her existence, she planned on becoming a nurse too. She had imagined herself far from Mercy, working in a hospital like this one, shiny and sterile, filled with state-of-the-art equipment. She had pictured herself caring for people in need, people in danger, people like Cora.

Yet it was impossible to feel regret just now. Indeed, with Tucker gone and her baby sister within arm's reach, Darlene was almost at peace.

Most mornings Roy turned up just after dawn, bearing coffee and breakfast. Sometimes he brought Jane with him, sometimes not; she was apparently reveling in the glamour of being in California, staying in her own room at a hotel where the outdoor pool had a view of the ocean.

On the tenth day of their visit, Roy strode through the door and handed Darlene a newspaper without comment. Cora slept in a thicket of shadows. Roy took a seat and pulled out his phone. Darlene could smell the musk of his skin, untempered now by the stench of cigarettes.

She unfolded the newspaper and spread it open across her lap. Every article was about the zoo, of course. On the front page, a vulture rode atop a city bus, perched above the windshield like a hood ornament, its bald head gleaming in the sunshine as it commuted downtown. In another snapshot, a pack of wolves prowled in black and white across a tennis court, their haggard forms blurred against the netting.

As Darlene read, she tallied up the numbers. In all, one hundred and eleven animals had been released. Forty-two cages opened. Three security guards fired. Hundreds of thousands of dollars would have to be spent to repair the damage, collect the animals, and make the public feel safe again. The assault on the Pacific Zoo would go down in history as the worst account of environmental activism on American soil.

So far, there was only one human casualty.

Tucker's name had not yet been mentioned. Roy was instrumental in this, acting as the family's liaison with the police, and by proxy, the media. He spent hours on his phone most afternoons, gesturing and holding forth. Darlene was vaguely aware that he had taken more than a few meetings around the city, speaking on her behalf, protecting her. Every few days, the police would release another official statement, doling the story out in careful increments. Piece by piece, they offered enough information to sate the media while withholding the perpetrator's identity. For now.

Ideally, Roy would be able to hold them off until Cora was well enough to leave California. Darlene wanted the storm to break when her family was across state lines. For the moment, Tucker was only named as "the suspect," "the offender," and sometimes "a lone wolf." (According to Roy, the latter was a common euphemism for a criminal who was white. Otherwise the police would have called him a terrorist.) Darlene found the phrase particularly odd in this context, since actual wolves were involved.

Now she flipped to another page of the newspaper, running her finger down the headlines. Several animals had perished over the past week, some struck by cars, others trampled by panicked crowds. A few were shot by local gun owners. There was an article about a fawn who did not make it across the highway with its parents; they were forced to leave its broken body on the median. There was a photograph of a sun bear executed point-blank outside a restaurant by a passerby with a revolver. A mountain of fur on the pavement. Dead before it hit the ground.

Worst of all, a giraffe had been struck by a fire engine. Both the animal and the vehicle were destroyed. The photograph was both spectacular and gut-wrenching. The truck looked like a child's toy that had been stepped on, the dead giraffe sprawled across an intersection. Darlene had never seen one of these animals prone, with the full extent of its height—eighteen feet, in this case—measured out alongside parked cars and sidewalk panels. The black-and-white image did little to diminish the horror. The animal's carcass was torn and bloodied, the rib cage dented inward, one long leg bent the wrong way.

As Darlene leafed through the newspaper, she discovered that a surprising number of animals were already back in custody. One elephant was rounded up within hours of the event. While drinking from a fountain, she was approached by her trainer, who rubbed her forehead, fed her a treat, and led her peacefully home to the roar of applause from onlookers. Four zebras were cornered in an alley and herded into a van. The surviving giraffes returned to the zoo of their own accord, exhausted, shaky, and visibly grieving the death of their fallen friend.

Darlene turned a page, pursing her lips as she read. The warthog, it seemed, was located outside a boutique, lunging at shoppers in a rage and trying to knock the bags of clothes from people's arms. It was promptly tranquilized. A hyena turned up inside a garden shed. The mountain goats proved to be both deft and wily, clambering on top of a UPS truck, then a Honda. Eventually, though, they were lured down with the promise of food. Goats were always hungry.

A gorilla appeared on the beach, picking through the litter strewn across the sand, its fur clotted with dirt, one foot badly injured. A serval was discovered stalking pigeons in an alley. An intrepid cyclist tackled the cat himself, wrapping it in a leather jacket and transporting it back to its cage, sustaining a few scratches and an angry bite in the process.

The squirrel monkeys never left the zoo at all. They made their way into the basement of their indoor exhibit, where they passed the time by breaking into the vending machine, learning how to work the drinking fountain, and generally making the place their own, a replica of the enclosure they had fled.

Darlene wondered if Tucker ever understood what the final consequences of his actions could be. Did he consider that he might end up cold on a morgue table? Did he realize how many animals would suffer and die with him? Did he imagine leaving Cora to be found in a garbage can by strangers?

With trembling fingers, Darlene closed the newspaper and pushed it away. The wildness was suddenly too much for her. The situation was surreal enough to make her doubt her own sanity. She removed her glasses and massaged her temples.

There was a mystery here. Her brother's previous felonies had been straightforward: blowing up a cosmetics factory to stop animal testing or burning down a ranger station to prevent a rattlesnake hunt. In each case, Darlene could draw a bright line from Tucker's actions to the goal he hoped to achieve. Increased public awareness. A change in policy. An end to animal cruelty. Punishment for the guilty.

But the attack on the Pacific Zoo was different. Tucker's ultimate goal in this case was unclear. In captivity, the animals had been safe, warm, fed, cared for, and given access to medicine. Freeing them from their cages was more dangerous to them than leaving them where they were. As an act of protest, it was incomprehensible. Even Darlene, who knew her brother as well as anyone, could not guess what final lesson he meant to teach the world.

Then a new thought occurred to her. Elephants on city streets, gorillas on the beach, injured lions, frightened people—all these things came from Tucker's mind. Perhaps his intent was only this: to make his visions and desires manifest. Rather than releasing the animals from the zoo, her brother might as well have turned his brain inside out, letting the figments of his imagination loose on the landscape.

47

After two weeks in the hospital, Cora was able to sit up, eat, and drink. The orderlies brought her trays on which everything was individually wrapped—miniature cartons of pudding and cups of juice with sealed tinfoil tops. Once a day, the nurses injected her with something to prevent blood clots from forming due to her prolonged inactivity. Based on Cora's expression, the drug burned as it entered her body, but she never protested. Darlene was impressed and unnerved by her sister's new level of stoicism.

The best medicine for Cora seemed to be Jane. The two of them napped together and watched TV. Darlene didn't realize how cautiously everyone was treating Cora (speaking in low voices, refraining from touching her, ignoring her unworldly appearance, asking no questions) until Jane started rattling on about soccer and school as though nothing had changed. Their old dynamic was still there: siblings who shared a bed unwillingly for years, were friendly most of the time, and could get on each other's nerves at the drop of a hat. It never occurred to Jane to treat her sister with kid gloves. She teased Cora about her new haircut. She promised that their room at home was exactly the same as before. She hadn't even cleaned it, she said.

Darlene did not try to join in. She only eavesdropped, pretending to be absorbed in her phone. Jane's customary bluntness was a godsend now. She barged fearlessly into conversational arenas where Darlene would not have ventured for the world. She asked Cora how it felt to almost die, whether her whole life flashed before her eyes. She told Cora she looked like a boy now—or a tomboy, maybe. She looked weird, for sure. Jane even asked whether Tucker was really as crazy as everybody said.

By and large, Cora replied in grunts and monosyllables. If she had been quiet before, she was even quieter now. Darlene monitored her constantly but covertly. Cora had acquired a way of staring intently at things that were not inherently interesting—a pattern of light on the wall, the flow of water from the bathroom faucet—as though she were seeing something other people could not. She ate and drank mechanically. The nurses told her to practice walking, which she did, as weak and off-balance as a newborn colt. When she watched TV, her attention often flagged; her gaze would drift to the window. Cora's hair was a mess, her delicate ringlets shorn into wood shavings, but she did not seem to mind her own appearance. She looked at herself in the mirror now with something oddly like indifference.

She did not cry. The stress manifested itself in other ways. She chewed her fingernails bloody. She startled at ordinary noises: a dog growling on TV or a car backfiring like a gunshot. Sometimes she would pause in the middle of a sentence as though searching for a word and the silence would stretch out until Darlene realized the conversation was over; her sister was never going to finish her thought. On the surface Cora's health was improving, but Darlene still felt uneasy. It was hard to figure out what, exactly, had changed.

Once, long ago, she had been able to read her sister's thoughts through her expressions and gestures. These days, however, Cora possessed a kind of self-control that hid her like a mask. It was an adult quality, a caution and precision that did not suit her little frame. Darlene did not know how to help her. She was scared to touch her sister at all, even to brush her hair from her face or take her hand.

All the while, Darlene continued to follow the story of the zoo. She did her best to shield Cora from it, watching the news on mute as her sister slept and reading articles on her phone in private. She and Roy discussed it in whispers while Cora was distracted. Darlene would have been fascinated by the incident even if it had not been a family matter, a Greek tragedy starring her brother and sister.

She knew about the many animals that lost their lives, most recently a gibbon and a chameleon, both run over by cars. More had probably perished without anyone knowing it yet, reduced to undistinguished roadkill and swept into the gutters. No humans had been killed—except for Tucker, of course—although a few were injured, some quite badly. One woman tried to hand-feed a capuchin and was bitten so severely that three of her fingers needed to be amputated. A leopard in the street frightened a young boy into hysterics. An elderly man got into an altercation with a brown bear in an alley, ending up with a broken arm. Darlene catalogued all these incidents, carrying them around like stones in her pockets.

Some of the animals were still out there. A few would probably adapt to urban living, merging into the bustle of the city. The fennec fox might dig a burrow in a cemetery. The macaw might take its place as the leader of a murder of crows. A portion of the zoo's primates remained on the lam, to no one's surprise. Apes were clever, versatile. The gorillas and chimpanzees would learn from homeless people and raccoons, ransacking the garbage bins for sustenance and sleeping in alleys. They would learn to be shy. They would learn to be silent. They would come down to street level only at night, discovering how to look both ways and hide whenever headlights appeared.

And then there were the apex predators. The lions, the anaconda, the arctic wolves—Darlene knew they would not stay in California. They would journey afield. The eagles would find new roosting places by tracing the earth's magnetic trails. The coyotes would head east, loping down back roads, hiding in garages and gardens until they reached untenanted hills. The bobcats were native to the mountain ranges, experts at remaining concealed. They would climb trees, sleeping above the heads of passing pedestrians, following the currents of their deepest instincts, seeking the life they were built for. The tiger would melt into the redwood forests to the north, camouflaged among the massive trunks, a shimmer in the shadows, a dream.

IN THE MORNING, ROY SAT Cora down for an official interview. He had been in her presence from the beginning, a figure in the background, and she seemed to accept him as part of the busy, overwhelming whirl of the hospital, one of many strangers in attendance around her. Jane was back at the hotel, watching TV in her room. Darlene got Cora breakfast on a tray, plumped her pillows, and led Roy over to the bed. She explained that he was not just a friend of the family—not just her boyfriend—but a police officer, too. She found herself wishing that there was some other term of endearment to describe what Roy was to her, what their summer together had meant.

Cora looked him over as he took a seat beside the bed.

"What kind of cop are you?" she said. Her voice was still phlegmy, and she had to stop every few words to inhale.

"The regular kind," Roy said.

"Do you have a gun?"

"At work. Not here. I didn't bring it on the plane."

A silence fell between them. Roy touched his pocket, an unconscious gesture. Darlene knew there were no cigarettes there—only nicotine gum.

"Were you looking for me?" Cora asked shyly. "When I was gone?"

"Yes," Roy said. "So many of us were trying to find you. We were worried sick. And we couldn't be happier to have you back."

Cora muttered something indecipherable. She sucked in a rheumy breath, then doubled over, coughing into the crook of her elbow. When she leaned back against the pillows again, she looked exhausted.

"What did you say?" Roy said, his voice gentle.

"I was gone a long time," she murmured. "I traveled such a long way."

A breeze gusted through the window, stirring the white blinds. Then Cora held out her fists. Darlene recognized the gesture: her sister was asking to be handcuffed, offering her wrists so Roy could shackle them.

"No, no," he said. "Oh God, no. I'm not here to arrest you."

Cora lowered her hands into her lap again, her expression quizzical.

"I just want to help you," Roy said.

"Help?" she repeated, as though trying out the word.

"You've been through a terrible ordeal," he said. "None of it was your fault."

Darlene looked on. Before her eyes, Cora appeared to grow younger. Her lips were pursed, her brow furrowed as she considered Roy's words, struggling to understand. The hospital pillows dwarfed her. She seemed so little, so weak and weary.

"I was somebody else then," she said at last.

Roy leaned forward, his elbows on his knees. "What do you mean?"

"I wasn't me." Cora spoke slowly, figuring it out as she went. "I don't want that anymore. I don't want to do those things."

A sob rose through Darlene's chest. She turned away, hurrying out into the hall, stifling the sound of her weeping in her palms.

THAT EVENING, JANE WAS GETTING on everybody's nerves, shuffling around aimlessly, knocking things off tables, and whining that she was bored. Finally Roy offered to take her to a restaurant near the beach. Darlene stood at the window, listening to their footsteps recede. From this vantage point, she could see a tiny swatch of sky. The clouds were stretched into ribbons of flimsy gossamer. Cora sipped juice through a straw, now wearing the purple sweatpants and rainbow shirt Darlene brought from home. Overhead, the long strands of cloud were being leached of sunlight. It was as though someone were twisting wet cloth, wringing out each last droplet of glow.

"Come here," Cora said, patting the mattress.

Darlene approached her and sat on the edge of the bed.

"Closer," Cora said.

After a minute, Darlene lay down, pinned between her sister's body and the railing. The pillows were too thin to be of much use, so she folded one in half, doubling it beneath her head. Cora pulled the blanket over them both. A breeze poured in through the window, making the blinds shimmy and buzz.

"Hi," Darlene said.

"Hi." Cora rolled to face her, their noses inches apart. Darlene could see the constellations of freckles on her sister's cheeks. Her eyebrows were thin and feathery, her mouth chapped. Her breath smelled sour from all her medications.

"Tucker's dead, isn't he?" Cora whispered.

Darlene had not been expecting this. Not yet. She started to reply, but her voice caught in her throat. It took her a moment to collect herself.

"Yes," she said, as kindly as she could.

Cora stopped breathing, and a rigidity overtook her flesh, every muscle taut. She squeezed her eyes tight as though trying to block out all sensation.

"I'm sorry," Darlene said. "I really am."

She began hesitantly to stroke her sister's hair. Cora did not move. Darlene tried to think of something to add. Something pleasant. A white lie. Everything about Tucker's demise had been horrific, but Cora did not have to know that.

"He died quick," she said finally. "The coroner told me so. Tucker didn't feel any pain. He probably didn't know what was happening."

The coroner said nothing of the kind, of course. In fact, Tucker's death was prolonged and violent. Cora raised her eyebrows. There was a flicker of something in her face—an adult emotion, maybe sorrow or skepticism.

"Oh, he knew," she said. "He knew everything."

Darlene waited for more—for questions or tears—but Cora did not speak again. The overhead light was off, the door shut, the TV blank, the air thick with shadows. As the evening deepened beyond the window, the room darkened by degrees. Darlene continued to stroke her sister's hair. Long ago, Cora loved to be petted this way, though now she seemed merely to tolerate it, or perhaps not to notice it at all.

"Why did you do it?" Darlene asked, using her gentlest voice. "Why did you run off with Tucker?"

Cora blinked at her with glassy eyes.

"I loved him," she said.

"More than me?"

As soon as Darlene spoke these words, she sucked in a breath, trying to snatch them back into her throat. She never meant to voice this secret fear.

"No," Cora said. "Not anymore."

The darkness was almost complete. A slender current of milky light ran down the wall opposite, the glow cast through the gap between the door and the jamb. Cora hummed a little—her thinking sound.

"I missed you so much I almost died," she said.

Darlene's eyes brimmed and burned. She did not bother to wipe the tears away, letting them soak into the pillowcase.

"What happened to you out there?" she said. "What did you see?"

"So much," Cora said. "Rattlesnakes. A dead bear. Horses."

"A dead bear?"

"Yeah. Weird stuff."

Cora nestled closer, scooting across the gap between them until there was no space left. She folded her body against Darlene's chest. Sudden, astonishing intimacy. Warmth and fragrance. Her little fingers tangled in Darlene's shirt.

"Tucker cut my hair," Cora said. "He cut my hand."

"I know. But you're safe now."

Their breath rose and fell in tandem. Even their heartbeats seemed to be sliding into a shared rhythm.

"I'm safe with you," Cora said.

HOURS LATER, DARLENE WOKE TO a sound in the hall. There was darkness, sweat on her cheek, heat against her belly. She was still in bed beside Cora, crushed against the iron railing. Her sister was limp in her arms, breathing more easily than she had before. Her fever seemed to be gone.

Darlene realized that Tucker would never have a moment like this. There were so many things her brother would never experience—first love, marriage, fatherhood—but Darlene cared less about the benchmarks and more about the incremental beats of human existence, the thousands of moments that made up a life. She did not mind that Tucker would never buy a house or turn thirty; she minded that he would never again feel the pleasure of hearing his favorite song on the radio, never eat ice cream on a hot summer day, never watch his little sister sleeping serenely in his arms.

The milestones were less marvelous than the minutiae. Darlene knew this better than anyone. For a long while, she had endured an extraordinary existence. She was tired of events and turning points.

Now she craved the fine print between the headlines, the empty space between the pillars. More than anything, she wished for undifferentiated and undistinguished time—an ordinary life.

There was a cry, and Cora kicked out beneath the covers. She sat up in bed, panting for breath, and gazed around the room as though she had never seen it before.

"I'm right here," Darlene said. "You're okay."

Her sister mumbled something she did not catch. Something about a celebration.

"It was just a dream," Darlene said. "You're safe, Cora. Remember?"

"That's not my . . ." She trailed off, her mouth pooling open. She stayed like that, gaping at nothing, until Darlene touched her cheek.

"That's me," Cora said, in a tone of wonder. "That's my name."

Then she smiled. It was the first time Darlene had seen her smile since she arrived at the hospital.

The sun was rising outside. Azure light traced each slat in the blinds. A bird fluted in the distance. Cora shuffled her hands urgently through her hair, stirring it into tussocks. She lay back down and met Darlene's gaze.

"Tell me a story," she said.

"Hm?"

"Please. I want to hear a story."

"I don't remember any of those fairy tales we used to read," Darlene said.

"No. Don't make anything up. Tell me the story of us."

Cora's expression was earnest and pleading. It seemed important to her. Darlene bit her lip, trying to decide how to begin.

"Once upon a time," her sister prompted.

"Okay. Once upon a time, there was a family."

Cora closed her eyes and shivered. Darlene felt that she was engaging in a ceremony she did not wholly understand—something Tucker began, maybe. Cora was obviously in the grip of intense emotion. It might have been pleasure at the ritual or grief for their brother, or some combination of the two.

"There were four orphans," Darlene said. "They were Okies. Tough and scrappy. They lost their parents young, but they carried on as best they could."

She paused, unsure how to proceed.

"Darlene was the oldest," Cora said softly.

"Right. Darlene took care of them all. Jane was the middle sister. She played soccer. And Cora was the youngest. They lived together in a trailer in a small town."

A breeze swirled through the window, as crisp and sweet as an apple. Cora was starry-eyed now, waiting to hear what came next.

"Then there was Tucker," Darlene said, choosing her words with care. "He ran away and did some bad things. He came home and took Cora away." She sighed. "It was a tough time for everyone. But they got through it. They survived. Cora made it home safe and sound. Darlene was glad."

There was a clatter in the hallway, muffled voices, the squeak of rubber-soled shoes. The hospital was waking up around them.

"Did they live happily ever after?" Cora asked.

"I don't know," Darlene said. "The story isn't over yet."

Her sister nodded solemnly. The window was brighter now, each slat in the blinds glowing like a bar of neon.

"This is all true, you know," Cora said. "This really happened."

48

On her last day in California, Darlene went to the beach alone. She had never seen the ocean, and this might be her only chance. Roy went to the hotel to check out and pack up their belongings. Their flight was scheduled for the evening. Jane and Cora lay in bed together in the hospital room, arguing without malice. Cora was acting more like her old self, whining that it was her turn for the remote control or swiping Jane's phone so she could watch videos and play games. Darlene bent down to kiss her temple as she left.

An hour later, she was ankle-deep in the ocean. This part of the California coast was composed of craggy cliffs, thirty or forty feet high, with tiny ribbons of beach tucked beneath. Darlene let the surf surge around her bare toes. The silken sprawl of the sea was broken up by distant boats, bright triangles that looked too flimsy to hold their own against the whitecaps. The shallows were cold, pungent, and clouded with seaweed. Her beach was barely a beach at all—a scrim of sand so narrow that each new wave crossed its midline. Darlene bent down and lifted a handful of seawater, watching it gleam and trickle away between her cupped palms.

Apart from the boats in the distance, there were no signs of human life. The cliff blotted out the view of the city completely. Darlene had passed a dozen beachgoers earlier, but she left them far behind, climbing over algae-slick boulders and soaking her jeans to reach this place: a promontory that looked like the end of the world, jutting out from the coast, shielded by a wall of amber stone, pocked with gnarled plant life and bronzed by the wind.

As she stepped deeper into the sea, Darlene thought of Roy, and of her sisters. The weight of Cora in her arms. Falling asleep in unison. Awakening to find that they were still entwined. Darlene felt the bloom of an emotion she did not recognize. An airy lightness, an interior glow. Maybe it was hope.

She did not believe in happy endings—not after the loss of her parents or the tornado—not after the past summer—not anymore. There were no endings in life except death. There was only the present moment, the passage of breath into breath, action and reaction, word after word, a story that was still being told.

At that moment, she heard a scuffle beyond the curve of the cliff face. It seemed that someone else was making their way to her private sanctum. Feeling shy, Darlene walked farther up the sand, carrying her purse and shoes. She settled on a boulder in the cold shade of the plateau and waited.

Something came into view, silhouetted against the ocean. For a minute, Darlene could not make sense of what she was seeing: a tree branch, a flutter of feathers, a bizarre concoction of shapes that did not seem to add up to a human figure. It walked on two legs, but its body was all wrong—incredibly tall, plump in the middle, bulbous and distended.

Nine feet tall. Garbed in black and white. An ostrich.

Darlene's hands closed together in an ecstatic, frightened convulsion. She had only ever seen these creatures in documentaries. The bird's torso was an inky cushion trimmed with frilled lace. Its neck was a lithe gray column. By contrast, its legs seemed to be naked—a blushing, indecent pink.

Darlene held still. She hoped that she was sufficiently camouflaged against the cliff; perhaps the bird would not notice her if she did not move. It took a step along the beach. A wave washed up, submerging its feet, and it paused, tilting its head this way and that, plainly considering the situation. Its beak seemed to be sculpted in a permanent frown. Its eyes were too large for its tiny head. The surf receded again, revealing the sheen of wet sand, which the ostrich examined minutely. It took another cautious step, its claws etching prehistoric footprints on the beach.

Darlene wanted to laugh, or maybe cry, but she was frozen in amazement. The ostrich moved with intense precision, each stride as perfect as a ballerina's plié. It dipped its toes into an oncoming wave. One leg was planted, the other scraping delicate ripples across the surface of the sea. Its head swiveled low on that long, muscular neck, taking a closer look, captivated by the design of the light on the water. Probably it had never seen waves before. Like Darlene, it was a traveler in an unfamiliar realm.

She did not believe in the afterlife. But if there was one, and her brother had found his way there, then perhaps the ostrich was a sign. But she did not believe in signs either. She shook herself; there was no need to reach for the supernatural here. The ostrich on the beach was a direct result of Tucker's actions. Darlene, too, had been summoned to this place by his choices. This encounter felt like a gift from her brother—his final one, perhaps. His gifts had always come with a measure of danger.

Without warning, the ostrich ran. It crashed away through the shallows, splintering the sea into sparkles. An onrushing wave crested against its knees, and it spread its rumpled, stubby wings for balance, the waxen feathers along the edges illuminated by the sun. The creature gave vent to an otherworldly shout, inflating its throat and booming like a foghorn. Almost a laugh.

Then it began to twirl. The ostrich pivoted in a circle, its legs ringed by a tsunami of spray. Around and around again. Darlene had never imagined that a bird could move like that. With each spiral, it wrapped its ankles in a whirlpool, disrupting the orderly flow of waves. It bellowed again, an octave higher this time. Its neck seemed nearly boneless, the head swinging perilously with each revolution. It spun like a child overcome on the playground by a surge of excited energy. There was unmistakable joy in each noisy orbit. It stumbled dizzily but did not stop.

Darlene rose to her feet without meaning to, drawn upright like an audience member in a standing ovation. The ostrich kept on whirling, slamming its broad feet down, splashing along a path parallel to the beach, a mélange of clumsiness and grace. It churned a frothy track through the shallows. As it rotated, the bird held one wing at its side while the other flared open to its fullest extent, a billowing swath of black, the white feathers at the brim as stiff and bright as icicles.

The animal was not performing for anyone. There was no purpose in its madcap twirling, no fight-or-flight response, no biological need. Darlene understood intuitively that something more primal was at work. This was a wild bird, a living thing without language, incapable of laughter or self-reflection, poised at the nexus of land, sea, and sky. This was a creature out of place, out of sync, its life spent in a cage, its instincts drawn from the stark, landlocked plains of Africa, on its own for the first time, miles from everything it had ever experienced, surrounded by an inconceivable wealth of strangeness and beauty. There was no possible response but to dance.

And then the ostrich whirled beyond the cliff wall, following the line of the beach, removing itself from view. Darlene heard it caroming chaotically away. Gradually the sea reclaimed its rhythm. A gull cried somewhere. She could no longer discern the clamor of the surf from the ostrich's splashing.

Darlene hurried barefoot across the sand, rounding the curve of the promontory. As she emerged from the shadow of the cliff, the sun struck her cheek like a slap. She could see the rest of the world now. A broad scythe of beach swung away from her, dotted with sunbathers and rainbow umbrellas.

She shaded her eyes with a hand. The ostrich had traveled farther than she believed possible. It had left the water and taken to the shore, pelting toward the horizon. The bird was moving as fast as a car—maybe faster. Darlene saw people backing away as it approached. She could not hear their cries over the thunder of the surf, but she watched them clutch each other and point. One man lifted his hand to his ear. Probably calling 911, Darlene thought. With a surge of vicarious pride, she realized that the cops didn't stand a chance; the ostrich was already twenty yards past the man. It showed no signs of stopping, dipping into shadows, racing out of sight.

Bells began to ring. All at once, the air was filled with a raucous, metallic clanging, far off but clearly audible over the boom of the sea. For a moment Darlene imagined it had something to do with the ostrich. But no—these were church bells tolling out the hour. It was nearly time to head back.

With a sigh, she felt the reality of her circumstances flood over her once more. She thought of Cora, as confused and innocent as an ostrich spinning in the sea. Darlene could not conceive of what the future might hold for her sister. She did not know what had happened under Tucker's care, how much Cora endured, and how much of the girl Darlene remembered—the girl she had helped to raise—was left inside that strange, boyish figure in the hospital bed. She did not know yet how to help her sister move forward, reintegrate back into the human world. Some of the changes were sure to be permanent. In her flesh, in her spirit, in her dreams and her waking life, in her bones, in her very essence, Cora was going to be left with scars.

And then something else will happen.

Darlene heard her father's voice echoing through her head—or perhaps it was Roy, repeating the phrase to console her—or maybe it was her mother, so many years ago. Tucker's voice was there too, and Jane's, and all the people Darlene had loved in her life, some missing, some dead, and some, like Cora, finally reclaimed.

And then something else will happen.

Like an ostrich on a beach.

Maybe this was what her father had been trying to tell her. In his plainspoken way, he was reminding her that change was both inevitable and unstoppable. That little ripples could cause greater waves, unfurl into unexpected patterns. He was telling her not to dwell on the past or fret about the future, since every moment was followed by another, some wonderful, some terrible, all unpredictable and unknowable beforehand, all essential components of the complexity of a vast and marvelous world.

EPILOGUE

The lions are hungry. As I walk through the long grass with a bag of raw meat slung over my shoulder, I can hear their hoarse, indignant yowls. There are nearly twenty of them in the paddock. When they see me coming—my lean, upright figure wading through a lake of shimmering prairie—they nuzzle against the fence in greeting, marking the wire with their scent. Years of this behavior have bowed the lattice outward at the bottom, creating a permanent bulge in the chain-link.

All my lions are rescues. Most of them are of advanced age, dumped here by circuses or zoos that no longer wanted them. A few came from private owners who were interested in an exotic pet and had no clue what they were taking on. The cats have a good life now. They luxuriate in the grass, sleeping twenty hours a day. They wrestle like cubs when the mood strikes them. At night, they prowl the fence, driven by instinct, though there is nothing to hunt and they are well-fed. Sometimes their battle song wakes me.

Now I toss the meat through the aperture in the gate. Charlie, a shaggy male, lingers by the fence, hoping to be petted. He is ancient in leonine terms, almost twenty, blind in one eye, and his mane has taken on the character of a dandelion gone to seed. I thread my fingers through the chain-link and scratch behind his ears. He purrs louder than an engine.

This is the Wildlands.

I founded the Wildlands Animal Sanctuary—its official name—over twenty-five years ago. Back then, I had two horses, three dogs, and an acre of land. Now I oversee a dozen employees and my grounds sprawl over several hundred acres. I am the caretaker of eighteen lions, thirty-six cows, two tigers, a snow leopard, five cheetahs, seventeen bears, six pigs, twelve horses, fifty-two dogs, three donkeys, countless feral cats who come and go, and a goat named Sweetie. The Wildlands are a haven for forsaken animals. They come to me from farms, zoos, pet shops, shelters, poachers, the pound, and dogfighting rings. All strays and runaways. All, as I learned so long ago, outliers.

Throughout the morning, I circle the grounds, following my usual route. A spurt of motion in the corner of my eye turns out to be a cheetah chasing its favorite ball. In the distance, I hear an agitated whinny. One of the horses is in a snit about something. Not an emergency. Like an experienced parent, I listen and can grade the intensity of faraway vocalizations, determining which may require my attention. The cows are on the move, ambling down a hillside, lowing contentedly, chewing continually. Most of the herd is related by blood. If given the choice, cows will spend their whole lives in family groupings. When calves are removed from their mothers—a common practice on farms—it causes heartache. I stroll through their paddock, checking the size of the salt lick and the water level in the trough.

I look in on each of my animals on a daily basis. I am in charge of their food, their medical care, their emotional health, their living and dying. I know all their names, though the animals themselves don't. Names are a human concept.

I tend to them with the help of my employees, who are also in charge of fundraising and ticket sales. They help with the animals, but the bulk of their work is grant-writing and tourist-wrangling. They manage our social media, since both "social" and "media" are somewhat outside my purview, and they handle all the interactions with the press, which I will not do, for obvious reasons. The sanctuary is sustained by donations and paying customers. People come for miles to see my animals. A network of metal walkways wends through the park, twenty feet off the ground, supported by intricate scaffolding. I am used to going about my work while hearing voices high above me, the click of camera shutters, and the clang of footsteps. This innovation was my idea. Animals rarely look up. In zoos, the constant presence of humans at eye level causes immense distress, triggering the hunting instinct in predators and fight-or-flight in the rest. Animals in zoos are overstimulated and flustered, always aware that they're being watched. At the Wildlands, however, my charges pay no attention to the throngs who ramble through every afternoon. The walkways lift the visitors out of the animals' field of vision.

I am the only human who lives on the grounds. I can almost see the whole park from my bedroom window. The Wildlands are a sanctuary for me as much as they are for my lions and dogs. We are the creatures who don't belong anywhere else, the ones who have ended up outside the Classification of Wildness, neither one thing nor the other, without a place in the world. We are the true casualties of the Age of Humans.

I am older now than Tucker ever got to be. I think about that nearly every day.

Decades have passed since the summer I disappeared, but I was never quite the same after. I have been a vegan since childhood. I buy local produce, compost my trash, and dry my clothes in the sun. My arms and legs are mottled with scars, the bite of a lion etched into my forearm and the kick of a horse gouged through my thigh, healed and shiny and pink. (Other scars can be traced back to Tucker. The stroke of his knife blade still crisscrosses my palm.) I wear my hair in a boy's cut, now embroidered with gray. I misplaced my vanity during that summer on the run. I have made my will and sent a copy to Darlene, my executor, with instructions that all my assets should be given to the Wildlands. My organs will be donated, my body returned to the earth without embalming, and a tree planted over my remains. In every way, I try to move through the world without damage, leaving behind no carbon footprint, casting no shadow, and creating no ripples, as light and immediate as an animal.

This is Tucker's fault, of course. I have become his legacy.

In the afternoon, the heat picks up, burnishing the landscape of the Wildlands. The lions sprawl in slumbering heaps. One of the tigers takes a dip in her pond, drawing a crowd. Above my head, people jog along the walkways to take pictures of her swimming. I continue my work. I have been making bloodsicles for my predators and saving them in the big freezer for a sweltering day like this. Now I haul a few loads of frozen, basketball-sized chunks of blood and viscera back and forth on a dolly, distributing them among the bears and big cats. The grizzly is thrilled, rearing up on her hind legs so she can use her front paws to carry her treat into the shade. The lions spar with swats over who will get the first bite. The snow leopard dyes his paws and throat crimson, licking away in a daze.

Tucker would have loved this. There are moments when I would give anything to talk to him again. I would tell him about the Wildlands. About the family he never really got to know. About Jane, now a soccer coach living in Oklahoma City. About Darlene and Roy and their children, different in size but identical in coloring, their skin like honey, their wishbone bodies lighter than air. I would tell my brother that I am still discovering what it is to be human. I would tell him that I learned about love not from him, but in spite of him. Without parents, my models of affection and adulthood were Tucker and Darlene. My mother gave her life for mine—the most dreadful and wonderful epitome of love. I don't remember my father, but he taught Darlene how to love me, how to find me, and that tells me all I need to know. My brother, on the other hand, showed his devotion to me through an ardent kind of make-believe, the creation of a private universe. He adored me fiercely and remade me completely. During our summer together, I was his work of art, his brother, his changeling.

I don't know if he loved Cora. I don't know if he ever knew Cora.

I have told the story, written down everything that happened to us that summer, and in this way Tucker lives on in me. The strangest things remind me of him: the jingle of car keys, the smell of woodsmoke, the tang of root beer on my tongue. Many years ago, I took possession of Tucker's ashes, removing the urn from Darlene's mantel. He now rests on my kitchen windowsill, overlooking the lions' paddock. We both made it to the Wildlands in the end.

This is all true, you know. This really happened.

Even now, so long after my brother's death, there are times when I still find him in my dreams. I will feel the vibration of wheels on pavement. Oklahoma rolls out before me, the grass baked yellow from the heat, the sky as taut and dry as parchment. In that moment, I feel the freedom I felt on the road, something I have never experienced since—disconnected from all the bonds that circumscribe a life, unhooked from family and society, apart from morality and the possibility of consequence, beyond even the flow of entropy and time.

Behind the steering wheel, Tucker guns the engine and laughs, a bark of unfettered joy.

And just like that, we are gone.

ACKNOWLEDGMENTS

Thanks to Scott, the love of my life. Thanks to Milo, my someone and my sunshine. Thanks to my mother, who taught me to love words and live with passion. Thanks to my father, who taught me that science is beautiful, learning is lifelong, and that something else will always happen. Thanks to Patsy, who makes magic wherever she goes. Thanks to Joe, who shares part of my brain and who always texts me back. Thanks to Laura Langlie, the best agent in the universe, my champion and my friend. Thanks to my editor, Dan Smetanka, who knows everything. Thanks to Megan Fishmann—I was told before I met her that she walks on water, and it's true. Thanks to all the splendid people at Catapult and Counterpoint Press. Thanks to my beloved Oklahoma family, who welcomed me into their remarkable homeland. Thanks especially to Christie, Brooke, and Andrea. Thanks to dear Bendix, the inimitable Rebecca Makkai, and Laurie, my guide. Thanks to my amazing, nearly centenarian grandfather. Thanks to Steve, who shares my poetic sensibilities, and Keven, who understands my feelings about dogs. Thanks to StoryStudio Chicago, my literary home away from home.

ABBY GENI is the author of *The Light-keepers*, winner of the 2016 Barnes & Noble Discover Great New Writers Award for Fiction and the inaugural *Chicago Review of Books* Awards for Best Fiction, as well as *The Last Animal*, an Indies Introduce Debut Authors selection and a finalist for the Orion Book Award. Geni is a graduate of the Iowa Writers' Workshop and a recipient of the Iowa Fellowship.